Forei
Italian Nights

JULIA JAMES

JENNIE LUCAS

THERESE BEHARRIE

MILLS & BOON

First Published in Great Britain 2023
By Mills & Boon, an imprint of HarperCollins*Publishers*
1 London Bridge Street, London, SE1 9GF

www.harpercollins.co.uk

HarperCollins*Publishers*
Macken House, 39/40 Mayor Street Upper,
Dublin 1, D01 C9W8, Ireland

FOREIGN AFFAIRS: ITALIAN NIGHTS © 2023 Harlequin Enterprises ULC.

Claiming His Scandalous Love-Child © 2017 Julia James
The Secret the Italian Claims © 2018 Jennie Lucas
Marrying His Runaway Heiress © 2020 Therese Beharrie

ISBN: 978-0-263-31851-7

MIX
Paper | Supporting
responsible forestry
FSC™ C007454

This book is produced from independently certified FSC™ paper
to ensure responsible forest management.

For more information visit: www.harpercollins.co.uk/green

Printed and Bound in Spain using 100% Renewable electricity at
CPI Black Print, Barcelona

CLAIMING HIS
SCANDALOUS
LOVE-CHILD

JULIA JAMES

For Pippa – thank you for all your hard work!!

CHAPTER ONE

THE SONOROUS MUSIC SWELLED, lifting upwards to one last crescendo before falling silent. The hushed murmurings of the congregation stilled as the priest raised his hands and began to speak the words of the ancient sacrament in the age-old ceremony.

Inside his breast Vito could feel his heart beating strongly. Emotion filled him, and he turned his head towards the woman now standing at his side.

Gowned in white, her face veiled, his bride waited for him. Waited for him to say the words that would unite them in marriage...

Eloise sipped her champagne, her eyes drifting around the gilded *salon privée* of the hotel, one of the most famous on the Promenade des Anglais in Nice on the Cote D'Azur in the South of France.

The *salon* was crowded with women in jewels and evening gowns, men sleek in tuxedos. But Eloise knew with absolute conviction that no other man present could possibly compare with the man she was with. For he was, quite simply, the most devastatingly handsome male she had ever seen in her life, and her pulse quickened every time she looked at him. As she did now.

Her eyes returned to his tall, distinctive form, so superbly sheathed in a hand-tailored tux, his sculpted Roman profile and the sable hair that moulded his well-shaped head. Her gaze caressed the smooth, tanned skin, taut over high cheekbones and chiselled jawline, the ready smile of his mobile mouth as he chatted in French—which he spoke as well as he did English and his native Italian— to the others in their little group. She felt her stomach give its familiar little skip.

Is this really me, being here like this? Or am I dreaming it?

Sometimes she thought it must be the latter, for the past weeks had been a headlong, heady whirl in the arms of the man at her side now, at whose feet she had, quite literally, fallen.

Memory, warm and vivid, leapt in her consciousness...

She had been hurrying along the airport concourse towards her departure gate, where her flight was already closing. It was her first holiday for ages, snatched before she knuckled down to look for a new placement as a nanny. Her most recent post had come to an end when the twins she'd been looking after had started school.

They would miss her for a bit, but they would soon adjust to her absence, Eloise thought—just as she herself had coped with a succession of nannies and au pairs in her own childhood. Her mother had not just been a mother with a busy job, but one supremely lacking in maternal feelings, and Eloise had long had to acknowledge this— just as she'd had to acknowledge that, because she'd been born a girl, her father—faced with her mother's adamant refusal to have any more children—had abandoned them both to seek a new wife who would give him the sons he craved.

Eloise's mouth tightened in a familiar fashion at the thought of her father rejecting her for his new family, playing no further part in her childhood.

Is that why I became a nanny? Eloise sometimes wondered. *To give warmth and affection to children who don't see much of their parents? Like me?*

She certainly loved her job—even though her mother had never been able to understand it. Just as she couldn't understand why her daughter would have preferred her father to stay in her life. Her mother's views were simple—and stark.

'Fathers aren't in the least necessary, Eloise. Women are perfectly capable of single motherhood! And it's just as well. Men let you down—far better never to depend on them. Far better to raise a child on your own!'

Eloise had refrained from pointing out that actually she had been raised by nannies, not by her mother...

But I'm not going to be like that—and I won't pick a man who'll desert me, either!

No, her life would be very different from her mother's—she was determined on it. She would prove her mother completely wrong. She would fall deeply in love with a wonderful man who would never leave her, never let her down, never abandon her for another woman, and never reject their children, whom they would raise together in loving devotion.

Just who that man would be, she had no idea. Oh, at twenty-six she'd had her share of boyfriends—she knew without vanity that her blonde good-looks had always drawn male attention—but none had touched her emotionally. Not yet...

But I'll find him, I know I will! The man I'm dreaming of! The man I'm going to fall in love with! It will happen one day.

But as she'd raced onward to the closing gate that day, she had been fine with being footloose and fancy-free, ready for a good holiday, travelling as lightly and comfortably as she could, wearing jeans, a T-shirt and casual jacket, and well-worn pumps.

The shoes must have been a tad *too* well worn, for suddenly, without warning, she'd skidded, her foot shooting sideways. She had gone careering down in a heap on the hard floor, her pull-along cabin bag slewing in the other direction, slamming into the legs of another passenger. She'd heard a short, sharp expletive in a foreign language, but had paid it no attention. Pain had been shooting up her sprawled legs, and she'd given a cry.

'Are you all right?'

The accented voice had had a low, attractive husk to it. But as Eloise had lifted her head, still feeling the sting of pain from her fall, her line of sight had impacted with a crouched pair of very male trouser legs, the fine light grey material straining over hard-muscled thighs.

She'd lifted her gaze further up. And the breath had just stopped in her throat. She'd stared. She'd been able to do nothing else.

A pair of dark, deep eyes fringed with inky lashes had looked at her with an expression of concern. 'Are you hurt?'

She'd tried to speak, but her mouth had suddenly been completely dry.

'I…' she croaked. 'I'm…fine.'

She started to get up, but a pair of strong hands was lifting her to her feet with a strength that made her seem completely weightless. But then, gravity seemed to have disappeared already. She had the strangest feeling that she was floating two inches off the ground.

People were walking and hurrying and talking all around them, but it was as though they didn't exist. She just went on staring helplessly at the man she had knocked into.

'Are you sure you are all right? Would you like me to summon medical assistance?'

There was still the same warm concern in his voice,

but it had a hint of humour in it, too, as though he were well aware of how she was staring.

And why...

A slanting smile sifted across his face. Eloise felt her insides go hollow. The thickly lashed dark eyes washed over her, and the hollowness increased a thousandfold.

'I believe this is your bag,' he said, and stooped to rescue her carry-on.

'Thank you...' Eloise answered faintly.

'My pleasure.'

He smiled again. He didn't seem to mind that she was still gazing at him, drinking in his dark, expressive eyes, his sable hair, the sculpted mouth with its slanting smile, the cheekbones that seemed to be cut from the finest marble.

She swallowed. Something was happening and she was reeling from it. And it had nothing whatsoever to do with having just tumbled down at his feet, or her luggage slamming into his legs.

Realisation hit. 'Are *you* all right?' she exclaimed, contrition filling her voice. 'My bag thumped right into you!'

He waved a hand dismissively. '*Niente*—it was nothing,' he assured her.

With the fragment of her brain that was still functioning Eloise registered that he spoke in Italian—then simultaneously registered that his gaze was as focused on her as hers was on him. She saw his eyes narrow minutely, as though studying her in great detail. Studying her and finding that she was entirely to his liking...

She felt colour run up into her cheeks, and as it did so she saw a glint spark in his gorgeous dark eyes. It was a subtle message between them that only heightened her colour and made her suddenly, piercingly, aware of her body and its reaction to being looked at with such intensity.

Oh, my God, what is happening?

Because never, *never* had she felt such an immediate overpowering response to a man. She gave a silent gulp of awareness. He was speaking again, and she dragged her fragmenting mind to order.

'Tell me, which gate are you heading for?'

Belatedly Eloise recalled what had been uppermost in her head until a few moments ago. Her eyes shot to the display by the gate further down the concourse, which now read, 'Flight Closed'.

'Oh, no!' she said with a wail. 'I've missed my flight!'

'Where were you travelling to?' he asked her.

'Paris…' she answered distractedly.

Something flickered in the man's eyes. Then, in a smooth voice, he said, 'What an extraordinary coincidence. I'm on my way to Paris myself.'

Was there the slightest hesitation in his voice as he named his destination? She had no time to think as he continued to speak.

'Since it was my fault you missed your flight, you must allow me to take you there myself.'

She stared, her mouth opening and then closing like a fish. A fish that was being scooped up, effortlessly, by someone who was—and the fact came to her belatedly— a very, very accomplished fisherman.

'I couldn't possibly—' she began.

The dark, beautifully arched eyebrows above the dark, deep eyes rose. 'Why not?' he said.

'Because—' She stopped.

'Because we don't know each other?' he challenged, again with that querying lift of his brows. Then his slanting smile slashed across his features. 'But that is easily remedied.'

His mouth quirked, making her stomach give a little flip.

'My name is Vito Viscari, and I am entirely at your service, *signorina*—having caused you to miss your flight.'

'But you didn't,' Eloise protested. '*I* did. I skidded. Crashed my bag into you.'

He lifted his free hand dismissively. 'We have already agreed that that is of no account,' he said airily. 'But what *is* of account is finding a medic to check your foot. There's plenty of time before our Paris flight leaves.'

Eloise looked at him dazedly. 'But I can't just swap flights—my ticket won't let me.'

The amused look came again. 'But mine will. Do not worry.' He paused a moment, then said, 'I have frequent flyer miles to use up. If I don't use them they'll be wasted.'

Eloise looked at him. Whatever else there was about him, he was not someone who looked as if he gave the slightest consideration to something as money-saving as air miles. Everything about him, she registered, from the tailored suit that fitted his lean body like a handmade glove, to the gleaming black hand-stitched shoes and the monogrammed leather briefcase he was carrying told her that.

But he was talking again as he helped her forward. Looking down at her with that warm, admiring look in his eyes that made her forget everything except the quickening of her pulse, the heady airiness in her head.

'So,' he was saying, and his Italian accent was doing wonderful things to her, as well as the effect his warm, admiring eyes was having on her, 'am I to call you only *bella signorina*? Though if I do,' he murmured, his lashes sweeping over his eyes as his gaze dipped to meet hers, 'it would be nothing but the truth. *Bellissima signorina…*'

She took a breath. The air seemed to have too much oxygen in it suddenly. 'It's Eloise,' she said. 'Eloise Dean.'

He smiled again, warm and intimate, and she felt breathless.

'Come,' he said again, and there was that low husk in

his voice again, 'lean on me, Signorina Eloise Dean. I'll take care of you.'

She gazed up at him. He seemed very tall, she realised. And absolutely devastating...

Her breath caught, her lips parting softly, her eyes wide as she just stared up at him, drinking him in. The sculpted mouth quirked again. Long lashes swept down over deep dark eyes.

'Oh, yes,' he said softly, 'I'll take care of you...'

And Vito Viscari had done just that ever since. It had only been much later that Eloise had learnt that Vito hadn't been travelling to Paris at all. He'd been heading for Brussels. He'd swapped his destination to Paris for one reason and one reason only, he'd openly admitted to her, with a caressing, bone-melting smile. To woo her. And win her.

And he had succeeded. Succeeded quite effortlessly.

She hadn't put up even a token reluctance at being wooed and won by Vito Viscari. In fact, Eloise thought with rueful admission, she had participated in the process with every sign that being whisked away to Paris and romanced in the most romantic city in the world by the most gorgeous, devastating man she had ever met was in the nature of a dream come true!

And it still felt that way all these weeks later. Weeks that had passed in a complete haze, her feet hardly touching the ground, as Vito had whisked her across Europe from one luxurious hotel to another—each and every one a Viscari Hotel, one of the world's great hotel chains, owned by his family.

He had told her he was making an inspection of all his European hotels, of which it seemed there were a great many, situated in Europe's most beautiful, vibrant and historic cities from Lisbon to St Petersburg. And as Eloise had travelled with him, cocooned in a haze of romantic bliss, all thoughts of returning to the UK to start work again had begun to fade. How could she think of giving up Vito? Being with him was as intoxicating as champagne.

Yes, but even champagne runs out in the end—and in the end we always wake from our dreams...

That was what she had to make herself remember.

Now, as she stood beside him in this glittering environment of luxury hotels and high society, she could hear that voice inside her head. For, however intoxicatingly romantic it had been to waft across Europe in Vito's arms, feeling herself headily on the brink of something she had never before felt for a man, there were still questions she could not blind herself to.

Can I trust my own feelings? How real are they? And what does he feel for me?

Oh, he desired her—there was no doubt about that, no doubt at all! But was that *all* he felt? Certainly now, as he glanced down at her, she saw the warm glint in his eyes and knew that desire was real, burningly real—in her, as well as in him. Desire such as she'd never felt before for a man.

'Eloise?'

Vito's voice, his soft, oh-so-sexy Italian accent that always made her breath catch, set aside her thoughts.

'They're serving supper—let's go through.'

Together they walked into the adjoining *salon*, where a lavish buffet supper had been laid out. A woman glided up to Vito—a few years older than Eloise, more Vito's age, immaculately gowned in a clinging designer number in blonde satin that matched the pale blonde of her hair. It was their hostess, holding this evening party at the Viscari Nice to which, of course, Vito had been invited.

It had not taken Eloise long to realise that Vito moved in high society circles—not just in Rome, but in all the sophisticated, cosmopolitan places where rich people gathered. His looks, his wealth, his background all made him a favourite—as did his bachelor status. That last, she was only too aware, drew women to him like moths to a flame. Including, so it seemed, their hostess tonight.

'Vito—*cherie*! How lovely that you're here for my little party! I must drag you away some time to talk over old times together!'

The woman's wide smile passed from Vito to flicker over Eloise. The pale blue eyes glittered with a hint of frost.

'So, you are our gorgeous Vito's latest, are you? *How* he loves beautiful blondes!'

She gave a tinkling laugh, and glided off.

Vito looked down at Eloise, a rueful expression in his eyes. *'Mi dispiace,'* he said. 'Stephanie was quite some time ago—long gone, I promise you!'

Eloise smiled forgivingly. It didn't bother her, and nor did any of the attention that other women lavished on Vito. Oh, he was charming and polite to all of them, but Eloise knew that the sensual glint of desire in his eyes was for her and her alone.

But will it last? Being the woman in Vito's life?

An invisible tremor went through her. One day would she be the next Stephanie? The next beautiful blonde ex?

Or was something else growing between them? Something that would mean much more to both of them? *Could* there be?

Again, the questions hovered in her mind. Seeking answers that it was too soon for her to give. Reminding her of the need for caution where her heart was concerned.

Hadn't her mother fallen head over heels in love, committed herself in marriage on a whirlwind of romance, only to find out too late how deeply incompatible she and her husband were on matters that were of profound importance to them both? A discovery that had torn them apart and lost their daughter her father.

I mustn't make the same mistake. It would be so easy to tell myself I'm in love with Vito! Especially when I'm living this kind of dream existence...one gorgeous hotel after another!

But his European tour would be completed soon, for it was all part of Vito making his mark in his new role as head of Viscari Hotels. It was a role he'd been jettisoned into at the young age of only thirty-one, after the unexpected death of his father.

'I've had to step into large shoes,' he'd told Eloise, his face shadowed. 'I'm the only Viscari left—the only one to carry on the legacy. It all rests on me now. I can't let my father down.'

Had there been a tension in his voice that was more than grief for his lost father? But all he had gone on to say was how Viscari Hotels had been founded by his great-grandfather, the redoubtable Ettore Viscari, at the end of the nineteenth century, during the heyday of luxury hotels. He had then passed it on to his son, and thence to his two grandsons—Vito's father, Enrico, and Vito's childless uncle Guido.

It had been Guido who'd overseen a major expansion of the chain across the globe, as more and more international locations had become fashionable destinations for the rich clientele the hotels catered to.

Now, as the fourth generation of the Viscari family, it was clear to Eloise, that Vito was pressingly conscious of the legacy he had been left to run, and of the demands it made on him—including much of his social life, as it was this evening and all the evenings since she'd been with him.

'All this socialising with people who are or who will be guests at the hotels is unavoidable,' he said now. 'But, however wearing it gets, I can never let it show.' The shadows had left Vito's face. 'Your being with me makes it so much less onerous!'

It lifted her heart to hear him say such things, and she felt a familiar little thrill go through her—a thrill that was accentuated when, as he helped her to a plate of delicious food, she saw a telltale glint in Vito's dark, lustrous eyes.

Soon—oh, very soon—he would murmur his farewells to their hostess for the evening, take his leave of the other guests smoothly, courteously, and then whisk Eloise away to his suite to have her entirely to himself! To indulge in a night of exquisite, sensual bliss...

A tremor of anticipation went through her. Making love with Vito was like nothing she had ever known! His skilled, sensitive touch could bring her to an ecstasy that left her breathless, took her soaring into a stratosphere she had never known existed—and that seemed to sweep away all her questions and wariness about her headlong romance with him.

As she lay in his arms later, her heart beating like a wild bird, she felt emotion pour through her. Felt full of longing...

Oh, Vito—be the one for me! Be the one man for me!

It was so easy—so dangerously easy—to believe that he was that one man she could love.

But dare I believe it? Dare I?

She could not answer—only knew in those moments that above all else she longed to dare. Longed to believe he was the man for her. Longed to let herself love him.

CHAPTER TWO

VITO EASED THE throttle and settled down into a cruising speed along the *autostrada*. They'd just passed the Franco-Italian border at Mentone and were heading to his next stop, the Viscari San Remo, along the Riviera dei Fiori.

It had been a crowded morning, meeting with his managers at the Monte Carlo Viscari, outlining his strategy, addressing their specific issues, taking in their input and feedback. That had been followed by a working lunch, and only now, in mid-afternoon, were they travelling on. Heading back into Italy.

He was filled with mixed emotions. It was good to be back in his homeland after weeks out of the country, that was for certain, and yet he was all too aware that his extensive European tour—necessary though it had been—had been something he'd welcomed for quite different reasons than simply to make his mark as the new head of the company with his management teams.

It had got him out of Rome. Given him a lengthy break away from the city and the complications that it contained. Complications he could well do without.

Automatically, his mouth tightened. Those complications still awaited him, and in a couple of days they would be in the forefront of his life again. Somehow he would have to deal with them.

But not yet.

Deliberately, he shook them from his thoughts. No need to spoil these last few carefree days—not when he had Eloise at his side.

Eloise! He turned to glance at her, and as his eyes lit briefly on her beautiful profile he felt his spirits lighten. How totally and absolutely glad he was to have followed through on that first overpowering instinct that had speared him as he'd raised her to her feet from the concourse at Heathrow airport.

Of course it had been her glowing blonde beauty that had first captivated him—how could he possibly have resisted such a gift! He'd always had a passion for blondes, ever since he'd been a teenager, first discovering the enticements of the opposite sex, and as he'd looked down at the gorgeous, long-legged, golden-haired beauty who'd been gazing up at him with celestial blue eyes out of a face that was as gorgeous as the rest of her, he'd been instantly smitten.

The immediate desire he'd felt for her then had been richly fulfilled in Paris, and it had seemed the most natural thing in the world to continue his European tour with her at his side. With every new destination he'd reaffirmed how right he'd been. For it was clear to him that it was not merely Eloise's stunning looks that were so captivating. Unlike so many of his previous *inamoratas*—the elegant Stephanie in Nice, for example—Eloise was possessed of a sweetness of nature he had not encountered before. She was never capricious, never demanding, never out of temper. Her sunny mood seemed constant, and she was always willing and complaisant, easy-going and smiling, happy to do whatever he wanted to do.

He had never known another woman like her.

His eyes went back to the road ahead. There was a slight question in his expression now. In a couple of days they'd be in Rome.

Will we still be together?

Or would it be time to end their affair? In his many previous love affairs it had always been he who'd moved on, bidding his lover a graceful farewell before waiting for the next beautiful blonde to cross his path and catch his interest. He'd enjoyed every affair, had been faithful and attentive during the course of each one, but when he'd ended them he'd had no regrets about knowing it had run its course.

A frown shadowed his eyes. Would it always be like that? One easy affair after another? Until—

Until what? What is it that I want?

It wasn't a question he'd ever posed to himself so insistently. Yet he knew the answer to it all the same. Maybe he'd always known it.

I want to find a woman I can love as deeply as my father loved my mother!

That, he knew, was what had always been his goal. But was it attainable?

Maybe that's why I play the field—because I don't want to be disappointed in love. I fear the impossibility of making a marriage that was as happy as my parents' marriage.

A shaft of sadness went through him. Yes, his parents had been supremely happy together, and he, their only child, had had the benefit of it—had been adored by both of them. Now there was a rueful expression in his eyes. Maybe even a little spoilt.

But Vito knew that knowing he was the apple of his parents' eyes had also made him supremely conscious of his sense of responsibility towards them—to be worthy of their devoted love for him. That shaft of sadness came again…and something more. Since his father's untimely death life had not been easy—not for his stricken mother. Her widowing had been cruel indeed, and Vito knew that the haunted look of grief in her eyes would never leave her.

But maybe when I marry—give her a grandchild? Then she might be happy again!

Who would be his bride, though? Again, his eyes flickered to Eloise, his expression questioning.

What is she to me—and what do I want her to be? Could she truly be the woman who will come to mean everything to me?

He did not know and could not tell. Not yet. Not until they reached Rome and there was an end to this constant travelling. For now, he would just continue to enjoy their time together.

'Did you know,' he said smiling, 'that San Remo is renowned for its flower market? And that every year the city sends its finest blooms to Vienna, to adorn the annual New Year's Day concert?'

'How lovely!' Eloise's smile was as warm as ever. 'I've always adored watching that concert on TV. All those Strauss waltzes! And I'll never forget the night we spent in Vienna!' Her smile widened. 'Tell me more about San Remo,' she invited.

With her cerulean blue eyes fixed smilingly upon him, Vito was only too happy to oblige.

Their stay in San Remo was fleeting, and soon they were driving on towards Genoa, before turning south towards Portofino, and then the pretty villages of the Cinque Terre and the Tuscan coastline. Rome was only a day away now.

As they neared the city Eloise could feel her mood changing. These last few days with Vito it seemed her ardency in his passionate embrace had been even more intense than ever. She had clung to him as if she would never let him go.

But I don't want to let him go! I don't want this to end. I want to stay with him.

That was the emotion that was distilling within her as every passing kilometre brought them nearer to Rome. And when they finally entered the city, as she watched Vito tangling with its infamous traffic with long familiarity, she could feel that emotion intensifying.

Will he take me to his apartment? she wondered, as they drove into the Centro Storico, where all Rome's most famous landmarks and sights were.

But she realised they were pulling up outside the Viscari Roma—the original Viscari Hotel. Vito was telling her about its history, and she could hear the pride in his voice as he did so—could see how eagerly he was greeted as they made their way towards an elevator that whisked them up to what had originally been the attics, now redesigned as a penthouse suite.

Eloise let Vito lead her out on to a little roof terrace, gazing out at the city beyond.

'*Roma!*' He sighed, sliding an arm around her waist and pointing out the famous landmarks that could be glimpsed, and the outline of the fabled seven hills—they looked low, to Eloise's eyes, but she marked them fondly all the same, for they were dear to Vito.

And he is dear to me.

The thought was clear in her head, catching at her consciousness. Making her lean into him even more, wrap her arm around his strong, lean waist. He turned to her, gazing down at her, and in his dark, long-lashed eyes Eloise saw desire, felt her own body respond as his mouth swooped to graze her tender lips, parting to his.

It did not take them long to make their way indoors again and take full advantage of the privacy and luxury of the penthouse's master bedroom.

'Welcome to Rome, my sweetest Eloise,' was Vito's soft murmur as he swept her away.

And all thoughts as to why Vito had brought her to yet another hotel instead of his own apartment, even though he was in his home city, fled from her utterly in the heady passion of his lovemaking.

Vito frowned, setting down the phone abruptly and swinging restlessly and with displeasure in the leather chair at his desk in his office. *Accidenti*, this was not what he wanted! Yet his mother had been adamant.

'You absolutely *have* to be there tonight,' she'd said, her tones strained.

But attending the function as his mother was insisting was the last thing he wanted to do—let alone on his first evening back in Rome after so long an absence. What he wanted to do—the way he wanted to spend the evening—was quite different!

To show Eloise Rome by night…

His expression softened. Eloise! Just thinking about her cheered his mood—a mood that had been tightening all day as he'd caught up on corporate affairs here at his head office. He'd wanted the evening off, to spend with Eloise, but now he'd be on show as the head of the Viscari family, no longer only the heir apparent while his uncle and father ran the business between them. Now everything rested only on him—the whole future of Viscari Hotels.

A bleak, painful look showed in Vito's eyes. He leant back in his chair. His father's chair. Four generations had preceded him. And they had created and held on to the legacy that now rested upon his shoulders and his alone.

Except… His eyes darkened now. That legacy was *not* his alone…

Vito's hands gripped the arms of his chair. What had

possessed his uncle Guido to leave his half of the Viscari shares not to his nephew—as had been the long-held understanding in the family, given Guido's lack of children of his own—but to his widow? That disastrous decision had, Vito knew, contributed to his father's heart condition, hastening his premature end fifteen months ago, when he'd been frustrated in his attempts to buy back Guido's shares from his widow Marlene.

Vito knew his parents had always considered her a social-climbing interloper into the Viscari family, hungry for power and influence. And that was why, Vito surmised, Marlene was adamantly refusing to sell her inherited shares, despite the handsome premium offered to her.

His eyes hardened to pinpoints. It was the same reason that lay behind Marlene's most persistent and ludicrous fixation.

When she had married Guido, ten years ago, she had arrived from England with her teenage daughter Carla in tow, and ever since Guido's death one obsession had dominated her. One way for her to cement her position in the Viscari family permanently.

Dream on, thought Vito, his mouth thinning. Marlene could have all the dreams she liked, but she would *never* achieve her ambition—her ludicrous, fantasy-driven ambition.

Vito was adamant. She was *never*, however much she wanted it, going to get him to marry her daughter.

As Vito walked into their suite at the Viscari Roma Eloise's eyes lit up. She got off the sofa and hurried to him to kiss him.

'Miss me?' asked Vito, smiling, throwing himself down on the sofa, loosening his tie and slipping open his top button with relief.

Dio, it was good to see Eloise again, even after the space of only a few hours, and he felt his spirits lift, shifting the pressure that had settled over him after his mother's phone call.

'Beer?' Eloise asked, crossing to the built-in bar.

'Definitely,' Vito said gratefully. 'What would I do without you?' he asked appreciatively, taking a first cold, reviving mouthful.

'Fetch your own beer!' She laughed, nestling into him as he lifted his free arm to draw her against him more closely.

He laughed in return, a carefree sound, stretching out his long legs in front of him. At his side Eloise relaxed into him and his arm around her tightened. The soft expression in her beautiful blue eyes was a balm to his troubled thoughts of the evening's ordeal ahead and what lay beyond.

I have to settle the business of Guido's shareholding. I have to get Marlene to agree to a price and get those shares into my ownership.

Into his head came an image, a memory that haunted him—would always haunt him. A voice imploring him, pleading with him. *'Pay whatever it costs you!'*

Emotion clutched at him like a knife thrust into his side. His eyes shadowed painfully.

He took another mouthful of beer, wanting a distraction from his anguished memories.

'Is everything all right?'

Eloise's soft voice had a note of concern in it, and she was gazing at him questioningly.

I wish I could take her with me tonight!

The function was to be at Guido's opulent villa, to mark the presentation of some of the Viscari artworks to a gallery—an occasion that, as Vito knew only too well, would see Marlene queening it over his mother with relish. His mother would be seething silently, and would make waspish comments about her despised sister-in-law.

Having Eloise at his side would make it more endurable. Vito's eyes glinted sharply. And it would also make it obvious to Marlene that there was no chance he would have the slightest romantic interest in her daughter!

Oh, he and Carla got on well enough—despite the friction between their mothers—and she was highly attractive in her own dramatically brunette way, but she had her own romances and his taste was for blondes. Beautiful, long-legged blondes, with golden hair and blue, blue eyes.

His gaze washed over Eloise's face now. He felt a strange emotion go through him. One he had never felt before and could give no name to. For a moment he wished he had not brought her here to the Viscari Roma, but taken her straight to his own apartment. But would that have been wise? Would it have given her a message he was not yet sure about?

Or am I sure—but not yet admitting it?

That was what caused him to hesitate. And there was another reason, too, for not having taken Eloise directly to his own apartment. His mother would leap to conclusions—conclusions he was not yet ready to draw.

We need time, Eloise and I—time to discover what we truly mean to each other.

Besides, tonight's function would be riven with tensions, and the last thing he wanted was to expose Eloise to the discord twisting through the Viscari family over the matter of Guido's shareholding.

Let me get Guido's shares back first, and then I can focus properly on Eloise—find out what I feel for her and she feels for me.

So for now he only made a rasping noise in his throat

as he answered her question. 'There's a family function I've got to go to tonight that I can't get out of,' he said. 'It's a total pain, but there it is. I'd far rather spend the evening with you. I'd planned on showing off Rome to you.' He made himself smile. 'Trevi Fountain, Spanish Steps…' He gave a sigh. 'Well, it will have to wait till tomorrow night, that's all.'

He swallowed down the rest of his beer and set the empty glass down on the coffee table, absently patting her hand before disengaging himself from her and getting to his feet.

'OK, I'm recharged now. Time to shower and get into the old tuxedo.'

He rubbed his jaw absently. He'd need to shave too. He glanced at the slim gold watch around his wrist as he lowered his hand. Hmm…maybe there was just time for something more enjoyable than a shower and a shave right now…

He held down a hand to Eloise, who was looking up at him, a slightly blank expression on her face. It dawned on him that this was the first time since he'd swept her off to Paris that they wouldn't spend the evening together. His blood quickened. Well, all the more reason for making the most of this brief time before he had to tear himself away and go and do his familial duty—try yet again to sort out the problem of his uncle's shares. But he didn't want to think of that—not right now. Not when he had this precious time with Eloise.

She took his hand and he drew her up to him, using his other hand to spear into the lush tresses of her unbound hair, cradle the nape of her neck and draw her sweet, honey-eyed lips to his…

She responded immediately, the way she always did when he kissed her. He felt the fire glow within him… within her. He murmured to her in a low, throaty voice as he let her mouth go, only to guide her towards the bedroom…the waiting bed. Desire kindled, quickened… consumed him.

Eloise! The woman he wanted…

It was the last conscious thought he possessed for quite some time thereafter…

CHAPTER THREE

'WELL, I THINK that all went off exceedingly well!' Marlene Viscari's voice was rich with satisfaction as she bestowed a gracious smile upon Vito and his mother, who was standing beside him as she had been all evening, with a fixed expression on her face.

His mother was not the only one with a fixed expression. Carla Charteris, Marlene's daughter, was wearing one too. Vito hadn't seen her for some time, and the last he'd heard of her was that she was in the throes of a torrid romance with Cesare di Mondave, Conte di Mantegna, no less. Presumably, he thought, Carla was as eager to get back to him as *he* was eager to get back to Eloise.

Marlene was speaking again, graciously inviting him and his mother to stay for coffee now that their guests had departed.

'We have so much to discuss,' she said. 'Now that you are back from your little jaunt, Vito!'

Her attempt at lightness and her referring to his essential business tour as a 'jaunt' grated on him—just as everything about her did.

But a moment later his every brain cell went on high alert.

Marlene sailed on. 'And we really do need to settle all this business about the allocation of the shares, do we not?'

Vito tensed, his eyes like gimlets. What was Marlene

up to? He'd been keeping checks on any movement in the markets, listening to the rumour mills around the hotel industry in case Marlene was making any moves to dispose of her shareholding in any way other than by selling to him, but there'd been no sign of any suspicious activity at all.

Not even from Nic Falcone, who had made no secret of being more than keen to take any bites going from Viscari Hotels to feed his ambitious plans for his own start-up hotel chain. Vito had been keeping very close tabs on *that* particular rival!

But surely even Marlene wouldn't be so disloyal to the family she'd married into as to contemplate such a betrayal of her late husband's trust? Nevertheless, he could not afford to ignore her blatant hint just now.

He turned back to his mother. 'Mamma—I'll see you to your car, then stay for coffee with Marlene.'

He exchanged significant eye contact with her and she nodded, casting a sharp look at her sister-in-law, who had a look about her of a cat about to engage with a bowl of cream.

Her expression had changed when he returned to the salon. Marlene was sitting down, Carla standing behind her, and the fixed look on her face was stonier now, so much so that he wondered at it. Was something wrong with Carla?

But it was her mother he must attend to right now. He would hear her out. Too much depended on her. The whole future of Viscari Hotels—the legacy he was dedicated to protecting—rested on his shoulders. Even though the legacy was now fatefully split between himself and Marlene Viscari—who was entirely free to dispose of it however she wanted.

Unless he could find a way to stop her. And he *had* to—somehow he had to!

Into Vito's head sprang the vision he hated to allow in—the vision that sent anguish spearing through him like the point of a blade. His father, stricken after his heart attack, lying in a hospital bed in the last few minutes of his life, his hand clutching at Vito while Vito's mother collapsed, sobbing, at his side.

'You've got to get those shares back—Vito, you must... you must! Whatever it takes—whatever it takes get them back! Pay whatever price she demands. Whatever it costs you! Promise me—promise me!'

And he had promised. What else could he have done with his dying father begging him so? Binding him with an unbreakable obligation.

Unbreakable.

The word sounded in his head now as he heard Marlene out. She was taking her time in getting to the point, asking him about his tour as they drank their coffee, but eventually she set down her cup and glanced briefly at her stony-faced daughter—who had left her coffee untouched, Vito noticed.

'And now,' began Marlene, setting her gaze upon Vito, 'we must look to the future, must we not? The matter of Guido's shares—'

At last! thought Vito impatiently.

A benign smile was settling across Marlene's well-preserved features...a smile that did not reach her eyes. And at her next words he froze.

'My poor Guido entrusted his shares to me, and of course I must honour that trust. Which is why...' her unsmiling eyes held Vito's blandly '... I can think of no better way to resolve the issue than by a means long dear to my heart.'

She paused, and in that pause Vito felt his brain turn to ice.

'What could be better than uniting the two shareholdings by uniting...' she beamed, glancing from Vito to her daughter and back '...the two halves of our family? You two young people together!'

Disbelief paralysed Vito. What kind of farce was Marlene trying to play out? Urgently he threw a look at Carla, waiting for her to express the same rejection and revulsion that he was feeling. But, like a shockwave going through him, he registered that there was no such reaction from her. Instead she was turning a steely, unblinking gaze on him.

'I think,' she said, 'that's an excellent idea.'

He stared, hearing the words fall from her tightly pressed lips.

Oh, hell! thought Vito.

Eloise tossed restlessly in bed. How long could that family function of Vito's go on? It was way past midnight already. She'd spent a forlorn evening. Calling Room Service for a dinner she had only picked at, staring unseeingly at an English-language TV channel. Missing Vito. Feeling left behind.

Finally she had resorted to bed—but the huge kingsized mattress seemed empty without Vito's lean, muscled form.

She tried to think positively. Maybe Vito was spending some time with his mother—after all, he hadn't seen her for weeks now, while he'd been inspecting his hotels. It was natural for her to want to spend a little time with her son.

A thought struck her. *Maybe Vito's telling her about me!*

But what would there be to tell? That elegant Frenchwoman in Nice—one of his exes as he'd admitted—had acidly called her Vito's latest beautiful blonde.

Implying I'm just one in a long line... None of them meaning anything special to him.

But *was* she something special to Vito? And did she want to be?

I want to find out! I want time with him, a proper relationship with him. I want to find out what he means to me and me to him!

Living in Rome, being settled here, would surely show her that? She could get a daytime job as a nanny—maybe to an ex-pat family—while Vito took up the reins of running his family hotel business. She would learn Italian cooking—how to make fresh pasta, even!

She felt her imagination take over, seeing herself cooking dinner for Vito, being part of his everyday life. Eagerness leapt within her. Bringing with it a realisation of just how attractive to her that image was—and why.

It must mean he's important to me—far more than just a passing romance! Mustn't it?

She tossed and turned, knowing for certain only that she wanted Vito back with her tonight. That she missed his company.

She must have fallen asleep eventually, for the next thing she knew she was awake.

'Vito...?' she said, her voice warm with drowsy pleasure.

He was standing by the window of the bedroom, silhouetted against the pale curtains. He didn't move for a moment, but went on looking down at her.

A thread of uneasy disquiet went through her. 'Is everything all right?' she asked.

Vito felt her anxious gaze on him. Savage emotion seared through him. No, everything was *not* all right! It was the damnable, impossible *opposite* of all right!

His fists clenched in his pockets. In his head he heard Carla say, yet again, those fateful words.

'I think it's an excellent idea.'

Fury and disbelief had exploded within him. 'You can't possibly mean that!'

Carla hadn't answered, had only tightened her mouth, while Marlene, with a little light laugh, had got to her feet.

'My dear Vito,' she'd said, relinquishing her daughter's hand, which had promptly closed like a vice over the back of the chair instead, 'you must know how much I would love to welcome you as my son-in-law! It is my long-held dream!'

The triumphant expression in her eyes had made Vito's fury sharpen.

She'd scarcely left the room before he'd rounded on his step-cousin.

'What the *hell* are you playing at, Carla?' He hadn't minced his words. 'You've always stone-walled your mother in her insane obsession about us marrying— just as I have! And as for Guido's shares... I've told you that I'm more than willing to pay a generous price for them—'

Carla's voice had cut in tautly. 'Well, the price is marriage to *me*, Vito.'

He'd shot right back at her, his voice icy. 'Carla, I will not engage in your mother's demeaning and quite frankly distasteful fantasy about the two of us marrying.'

Two spots of colour had flared in his step-cousin's cheeks. 'So you think it *demeaning* and *distasteful* to marry me?'

There had been an edge in her voice that had made Vito pause.

'That isn't what I said,' he'd retorted.

He'd taken a breath—a heavy one—staring hard at her, his eyes narrowing.

'Carla, what's going on here? The last I heard you were

running around with Cesare di Mondave—the two of you were all over each other!'

His eyes had rested on his step-cousin, taken in the sudden paling of her face, the flash of burning emotion in her violet eyes.

Slowly, words had fallen from him as realisation had dawned. 'So that's it—he's finished with you, hasn't he?'

The two spots of colour in her cheeks had flared again. 'You are not the only one, Vito, who considers it "demeaning and distasteful" to marry me,' she said tightly.

Immediately his expression had changed. 'Oh, Carla, I'm sorry.' His voice had been sympathetic—genuinely so. 'Sorry because…well, to speak frankly, it was always going to end that way. The Conte di Mantegna can trace his bloodline back to the ancient Romans! He's going to marry a woman who can do the same! He might have affairs beforehand, but he'll never marry a woman who—'

Carla's voice had sliced across his. 'A woman, Vito, who is about to announce her engagement to another man!'

There had been viciousness in her tone—clear and knifing.

'And marrying me is the only way you're going to get those shares back!'

She'd stormed off, leaving him to feel the pitiless jaws of Marlene's steel trap biting around his guts. Jaws he still felt now as he stood looking down at Eloise.

Eloise! She could blot out for him the trap that had been sprung.

He lowered himself down upon the bed, sweeping her up into his arms. Her soft, slender body was like swansdown in his embrace, her hair like silk, her skin as soft as velvet. He crushed her to him and she murmured to him. Words that were like balm to his stormy soul.

This was where he wanted to be! Here, with Eloise.

He hugged her again, and as he did so he could feel her breasts peaking against the fine lawn of his dress shirt, feel their crests grazing him...arousing him. His mouth nuzzled into the silken hair, seeking the satin skin beneath, and he glided his lips over her throat, her jaw, soon reaching their goal—the soft, parting lips that sought him, too, clinging to him.

He heard her give the soft little moan that he knew so well was a presage of her growing response to him. He gloried in it...revelled in it. He deepened the kiss, his hands going to his shirt buttons to free him from all this unnecessary clothing. Free him from the jaws of the trap that had been sprung on him. Free him to find what he sought most.

Eloise in his arms and he in hers, her body welcoming his, her mouth clinging to his, her breasts swelling against him, her thighs parting for him, taking him into her, taking him to the only place he wanted to be—the place only she could take him.

The rest of the world melted away like honey on a heated spoon—melted and flowed and became only and entirely what he was feeling now, what he was doing now. Because there was nothing else. Nothing else mattered and nothing else existed—only this, only now...

Only Eloise.

And when the fire had consumed him, consumed them both, and after a long, long burning died away, leaving only the warm, sweet glow that was their tangled limbs, their clinging bodies, only then did the words form in his head.

I'm not losing this!

'Is everything all right?'

Eloise's voice was rich with concern. She'd asked Vito that question last night but he hadn't answered, only swept her away to the sensual paradise he always took her to, blotting everything out except the bliss of his possession. Blotting out the unease and disquiet that had nipped at her when he'd come into their bedroom, gazing almost sightlessly down at her with his tense stance, his closed face…shutting her out.

That same unease came again now, as they breakfasted out on the roof terrace of their suite. There was an air of abstraction about Vito, despite his sunny airy smiles and words.

'Everything's fine,' Vito assured her, making his tone as convincing as he could. He would not trouble Eloise with his troubles.

But even as his gaze lingered on her another woman intruded into his vision. Carla, lashing out in the pain of rejection by her lover, who had spurned her in order to marry a woman from his own aristocratic background, driven to make that outrageous ultimatum to save her own stricken pride.

It was the only way to get Guido's shares back.

Frustration seethed in him—and more than frustration. Grief—tearing, abject grief.

Again he recalled his last memory of his father—begging him with his dying breath to get back the shares that would safeguard Viscari Hotels, protect the legacy that was Vito's duty to pass on to his own son, to the next generation.

And the memory of his own grief-stricken voice, making that promise to his father—the last words his father would hear him say before sinking into unconsciousness and death…

How can I betray that promise? Betray what he begged me to do in the last moments of his life?

Emotion knifed him like a blade in his heart. How

could he betray his father? Break the promise he'd made that nightmare day?

'Vito?'

Eloise's voice invaded his consciousness, made him refocus on her. He put a smile on his face, though it was an effort. But for Eloise he would make that effort.

I don't want her affected by any of this—it's too grim, too damn awful!

No, he wanted her protected—insulated. Until he was free of this hideous nightmare closing in on him.

When it's all over—when I've got those shares back—then...

Then he would be free to do what he wanted—focus on Eloise, on discovering just what she meant to him.

Discovering whether she's the one woman for me.

But there was no chance of that yet—not until he'd found a way to smash his way out of the trap that Marlene had sprung on him to fulfil his deathbed promise to his dying father.

'Sorry,' he said, trying to hide the effort it cost him, 'I'm planning my work day already. Speaking of which—I really have to make a move and head to the office.'

He smiled at Eloise apologetically, scrunching up his napkin and getting to his feet, downing his coffee as he did so. Leaving her was the last thing he wanted to do. But he had to get to his desk. Find a way—somehow!— to extricate himself from Marlene's trap.

As she watched him leave Eloise's eyes were troubled.

Is he finishing with me? Is that why he's being like this? Evasive?

The questions were in her head before she could stop them. Bringing with them a painful clench of her stomach. A painful self-knowledge. A painful truth.

I don't want my time with Vito to end.

* * *

Vito sat at his desk—the desk his father had once sat behind. The pressure in his head tightened. He heard Carla's shrill, vicious voice—*'Marrying me is the only way you'll get those shares back!'*

Forcibly, he fought down his anger. Maybe in the morning light his step-cousin would realise how impossible—how insane—her demand was. Maybe Cesare di Mondave would rush back to her and ask her to marry him.

The brief flare of hope died instantly. He didn't know Cesare well, but he knew enough of him to be sure that *il Conte* would have some aristocratic female lined up somewhere in the background as his eventual bride-to-be, once he'd done playing the field with sultry, voluptuous types like Carla Charteris.

A pang of sympathy for her shot through him, despite the ugliness of the scene last night. If Carla really had fallen hard for Cesare di Mondave, however unwise that had been, he could only pity her. Losing someone you'd fallen in love with would hurt badly…

Not that he'd ever been in love himself.

Without conscious thought, he found Eloise's beautiful image in his head. Eloise, who had literally fallen at his feet and whom he had lifted up into his arms—his life. Emotion surged within him. Whatever it was he felt about Eloise, one thing he knew with absolute, total certainty. He did not want to part with her—not yet! No way was his romance with her played out.

But until he had sorted out the unholy mess of Guido's shares he was not free to think of Eloise. He felt his teeth grinding. Here he was, one day back in Rome, and Marlene thought she could corral him with her ludicrously offensive scheming. His expression sharpened. She had made no such move while he'd been making his tour of the European hotels.

So why don't I just take off again? If I'm not in Rome, she and Carla will be stymied.

So where to go? Somewhere far away… The Caribbean would be ideal! The latest addition to the Viscari Hotels portfolio was taking shape on the exclusive island of Ste Cecile—he could combine a site visit with whisking Eloise away from this impossible situation here in Rome!

Mood lifting, Vito reached for the phone, wanting to tell her immediately. It rang as he touched it and he snatched it up impatiently, eager to get rid of whoever was phoning him.

It was his director of finance.

'What is it?' he asked, trying to hide his impatience.

'I've just had a phone call,' came the reply, and Vito could immediately hear the note of clear alarm in his voice. 'A financial journalist I know—asking for a comment on a rumour that's just hitting the wires that Falcone is in discussion with Guido's widow about her shareholding. What do you want me to say?'

Vito froze. The new hotel in the Caribbean, and his trip there with Eloise, went totally out of the window.

Fifteen minutes later, his face stark with anger, he was confronting his step-cousin in her apartment in the Centro Storico.

'Carla, you can't go on with this! It's madness and you know it!'

Marlene was obviously flirting with Falcone to hasten her nephew's consent to marry her daughter. Surely to God Carla could see how insane the idea was? They'd always got on well enough, and he'd kept an eye out for her when she'd arrived in Rome as an awkward teenager while she found her feet socially. And she was not responsible, after all, for her mother's unpopular marriage to his uncle.

'You haven't the slightest interest in marrying me!' he bit out.

'Actually,' she snapped back, her stony gaze flashing into bitter animation, 'I *do*! I want *everyone* to see me marry Vito Viscari!'

'What you want,' Vito ground out, 'is for *Cesare* to see you marry me—that's all!'

'Yes! And then he can go to hell—for ever!' There was all the venom and all the fury of a woman scorned in her voice.

'And after the wedding?' Vito came back with angry sarcasm, determined to make her see reason. 'When Cesare realises what he's lost—then what? You're stuck married to me!'

But her eyes only glittered manically. 'I shall throw parties! Huge parties! And everyone will see how totally, blissfully happy I am!'

He gave a heavy, defeated sigh. For 'everyone' read 'Cesare' again.

He played his last card. Looked her straight in the eye. Expression totally serious. Spelled it out to her.

'Carla, it's impossible for me to marry you. I'm…involved with someone else—someone I met in England.'

There—he had said it. Stated it openly.

The words hung in his head, portentous. But all he got from his step-cousin was a harsh, derisive laugh.

'What? Another of your endless parade of blondes?' she countered. 'Don't trot that line out, Vito! I know you! Women come and go in your life like butterflies—they never mean anything to you!' Her expression altered suddenly, twisting with pain. 'Just as I never meant anything to Cesare—'

She broke off abruptly, her expression venomous again, but this time with a haunted, manic look in her eyes.

'So—like I said—if you don't want my mother to sell Guido's shares to Falcone you'll announce our engagement! Right away, Vito, *right away*!'

Her voice was rising, and he could hear the note of hysteria plain in it. If he went on any more she'd just threw a full-blown fit of hysterics.

For one long, angrily fulminating moment he went on glaring at her, her words knifing in his head. Then, without another word, he strode from her flat, fury burning in him.

His own words echoed in his head—*I'm involved with someone else...*

Eloise! Her beautiful, trusting face lifted to his.

I can't do this to her.

Resolution speared in him. Whatever it took, there had to be a way—there *had* to be—of stalling Marlene, of extricating himself from her daughter's desperate, drowning clutch that was trying to drag him down with her.

As he climbed into his waiting car his mobile rang and he glanced at it angrily. It was his mother, and he knew he had to answer it—knew, too, that he could not let her know what Marlene was doing now, touting Guido's shares to his rival to force his hand.

But at his mother's first panicked words, Vito knew it was too late for prevarication.

'Vito! *That woman* has just phoned me! She's threatened to sell Guido's shares to Falcone if you don't announce your engagement to Carla—so you've got to! You've just *got* to!'

'Mamma,' he said in a hollow voice, 'you cannot mean that...'

There was a stifled cry down the line. 'Vito, you made a *vow* to your father! He begged you with his dying breath!

Don't betray him, Vito—don't betray your own father. You promised to get Guido's shares back, and you can't break that promise—you *can't*!'

He swallowed. 'Mamma, I cannot do what Marlene demands—'

'You must! Vito, you must!' There was desperation in her voice.

He closed his eyes. He could hear how distraught she was. He had to calm her down somehow, anyhow. 'Mamma—listen. *Listen.* I will put out an announcement. OK?'

It wasn't OK—it was total opposite of OK—but it would buy him something that, right now, was the most vital thing for him to get. Time—time to control this runaway situation. It would give him time to manoeuvre, to come up with a way out of this, time to *think*!

He heard the rush of emotion and relief in his mother's voice. 'Oh, thank goodness! I knew you would never, *never* break your promise to your father, my darling son!'

Automatically, his mind racing, Vito went into soothing mode, seeking to calm her—get her off the line so he could focus on how to neutralise Marlene, think through the implications of what he'd just agreed to.

It's an announcement, that's all—it's not a wedding! That's all Carla really wants—to shove her engagement to me into Cesare's aristocratic face in order to save her own face. And I can go along with that—just for now. Until I can find a way to calm her down, get her onside so that the two of us can persuade Marlene to sell Guido's shares directly to me without this farce of me marrying her daughter!

He sat back, his expression steeled. He was playing for time, that was all. He was staying Marlene's hand, placating Carla, calming his distraught mother—finding a way out, a solution. A means to keep his promise to his dying father.

He headed back to his office. His first priority—after authorising that damn announcement—was to scotch those rumours about Falcone getting hold of any of the Viscari shares. He'd need to speak to his direct reports and his board members, to industry analysts, financial journalists... His mind raced down the list.

And, above all, he had to speak to Eloise.

You can't announce your engagement to Carla and not explain the situation to Eloise!

He swore again. The need to get back to his office, do what had to be done there, was overwhelming. Rapidly, his mind raced. He could make the calls from his hotel suite, then talk to Eloise. Explain—

Explain what? Dio mio! *Explain I'm going to get engaged to another woman!*

Another curse of burning frustration dropped from his lips.

I didn't want any of this! All I wanted was to have Eloise with me in Rome—just her and me, being together, exploring our relationship, finding out what we mean to each other. Time together.

And now Marlene and Carla were smashing that to pieces. Caring nothing at all for the complications of his own life right now. Of what was important to *him.*

But, like icy water washing over him, he knew what was really overriding what he wanted. He *had to* fulfil the promise he'd made at his father's deathbed.

A hard, heavy weight pressed down on him. There was no escape. None. This was happening at the very, very worst time. But he must not let it endanger what he had with Eloise.

But how to keep her safe from it? Away from all the gossip that would inevitably break out once his engage-

ment to Carla was announced? He would never expose
Eloise to that!

A surge of protectiveness went through him as a possibility occurred to him—not perfect, but at least doable.

*I'll take her to Amalfi—she can stay there, waiting
for me. I'll explain why—ask for her patience, her trust,
while I extricate myself from Marlene's trap, give Carla
time to see sanity. To come down from the hysterics she's
throwing all over the place!*

But, even though he knew that getting Eloise out of
Rome was essential, a sense of impending loss assailed
him. He didn't want to park Eloise down on the coast—
he didn't want to part with her *at all*, not even for a short
while! Pressure like a vice crushed his skull. Pressure
from his uncle, who had willed away half the Viscari legacy, from Marlene, hell-bent on forcing his hand, from
Carla, intent on hitting back at the man who'd spurned
her, and from his father, who had bound him with an unbreakable chain of love and loyalty, and his mother, desperate for him to accept that chain around him.

For an instant a vision flared in his mind—a vision
so unbearably tempting he almost reached out his hand
to seize it.

*He and Eloise, walking hand in hand along a tropi-
cal beach in the moonlight. The Caribbean waves kissing their bare feet in the warm surf. Far, far away from
here—far, far away from all that assailed him now! Free,
oh, blissfully free of it all!*

Let Marlene do her worst! Let her! Let his uncle's
damn shares pass out of the family.

*I could do it—I could let it happen. I could grab Eloise
by the hand and fly away with her...leave all this behind
me. Just be with her.*

The vision hung in his head like a jewel, and his longing to seize it was painful inside him. Then, as the vice

around his skull tightened, he let the vision go. Dull, piti-less resignation filled him. He couldn't run—he couldn't abandon his duty, his responsibility.

I have to see this out. It's a battle I have to face—and find a way to win.

Because one thing he was adamant about. Whatever price he was going to pay for Guido's shares, it was *never* going to be marrying his uncle's stepdaughter.

CHAPTER FOUR

ELOISE'S EXPRESSION OF delighted surprise at his arrival at their suite in mid-afternoon was a balm to Vito. As he caught her hands, lowering his mouth to her uplifted lips, he felt his spirits lift—as they always did when he saw her.

'This is wonderful!' she was exclaiming, her voice warm. 'I didn't expect you till this evening. I was about to go down to the pool. I've been out exploring this morning—I found the Spanish Steps and the Trevi Fountain!'

Vito smiled, basking in the expression in her face, the open glow in her cerulean eyes. Oh, she might have to stay discreetly out of sight in Amalfi, but only for as short a time as he could manage.

I'll explain what I've got to do, and why, and she will understand. I know she will!

He could trust her—he knew he could. Trust her to understand just what he was up against. He'd wanted to insulate her from all this mess around Guido's shares, but now that he had no choice but to involve her he knew he could rely on her sympathy, her cooperation. On her patience in waiting for him finally to be free to focus only on her.

He drew back, making some comment about her morning's expedition, then shrugged his jacket from him, loosening his tie and turning up his cuffs. Keeping his voice as deliberately casual as he could, he said, 'I've got some phone calls to make, but while I do throw a few things together.' He smiled, his gaze caressing. 'We're going to spend the weekend in Amalfi!'

He waited for the expression of delight he had expected to cross her face, as it had done whenever he'd announced their next destination in Europe, but instead there was a different expression. One of confusion, uncertainty.

'But we've only just got to Rome,' she replied.

'I know,' he said soothingly, 'but... Well...' His mind raced. 'Something's come up, and that's why I want us to get a weekend away.'

That was what he wanted—one last weekend with Eloise before he endured taking on the appearance of a man engaged to Carla Charteris for however long it took him to extricate himself from it.

'Is it...is it just the weekend we'll be away?' Eloise was asking, and Vito had to focus on what she'd said.

'Well, why not pack everything?' he returned, again seeking to make his tone casual. 'In fact,' he went on, as if the thought had just struck him, 'maybe you'd like to stay on there—it's a particularly beautiful stretch of coastline, as I'm sure you know, and the Viscari Amalfi has a spectacular clifftop location. You'll like it far more than here in Rome, I promise you.'

He bestowed a warm, reassuring smile on her. But once again he saw only doubt and uncertainty in her eyes.

He dropped a kiss on her forehead. 'I'll join you down there again as soon as I can get away from here. Things are a bit...pressured right now.'

Had an edge got into his voice? He didn't know—knew only that there was a faint frown on Eloise's brow and her eyes were searching his. Discomfort filled him—he didn't want to have the conversation he would have to have with her right now. He would explain everything to her tonight, when they were safe at the Viscari Amalfi. Right now his overriding priority was to get on the phone and crush the speculation that Nic Falcone might be getting hold of any Viscari shares.

He glanced at his watch. 'Eloise—I have to make those calls. You get packing, OK?'

He smiled distractedly and went off to the small office that the suite came with, immediately putting a call through to his finance director to assure him that, whatever rumour was circulating about Falcone, it was without any foundation. As to his forthcoming engagement—he would say not a word for the moment. Time enough to deal with that when it hit—and when Eloise was safely in Amalfi.

It was complicated, it was stressful, it was damnable—but he *would* pull this off. And then finally—dear God, *finally*—when all the shares were back in Viscari possession, when Marlene had been seen off, and the spirit of his father was at peace, he could focus on Eloise.

And find out just what she meant to him.

But now was not the time to think about Eloise—about why he had no intention of doing without her yet.

The call to his financial director connected, and immediately Vito focused only on that.

For now…just for now… Eloise would have to wait.

Listlessly, Eloise opened the lid of the suitcase she'd extracted from the closet. It was ungrateful of her, she knew, but she really didn't want to go down to Amalfi. For weeks and weeks now her life had been a non-stop parade of packing and unpacking, one hotel after another.

But Vito wanted to be off—yet again.

Another frown furrowed her brow, anxiety pecking at her eyes as she mechanically started to transfer her clothes from where she'd hung them up only a couple of days ago. What had Vito meant when he'd suggested that she might like to stay on in Amalfi after the weekend?

She felt a stab in her side.

Oh, Vito—don't you want to be with me?

Was that it? The stab came again. Was this his way of finishing with her? Of turning her into one more of his legion of *ex-blondes*, like that woman in France.

She felt her expression tighten, a clawing in her stomach. Whatever uncertainties she had as to how much Vito meant to her, the thought of him finishing with her like this was showing her a mirror to her feelings, throwing them into sharp focus.

I don't want him to finish with me!

That was the cry that came now, silently, as she folded and packed her clothes. That was what dominated her mind as emotion welled in her. She did not know if she was in love with Vito—did not know whether she wanted him to be the one and only man in her life, to make her life with him—but she knew by the stab that came again that she did not want him finishing with her...

I don't want us to be over! I don't! I don't!

She closed her suitcase, heart heavy, and as she did so heard the bell at the door to the suite ring. A long, insistent sound. She frowned—then realised it must be for Vito. Maybe he'd sent to the office for some documents to be delivered.

She walked into the reception room, hearing his voice in rapid Italian coming from the office. He sounded... *different*. Though she could not understand what he was saying, there was a terse, insistent tone to his voice, and it was bereft of his usual laid-back, full-on charm.

The doorbell sounded again—longer this time. Eloise pulled open the door.

A woman sailed in. She was around her own age, with dark, striking looks, chicly dressed in a vivid cerise outfit, her face in immaculate full make-up, dramatic violet eyes, and brunette hair coiled in a serpentine mass at the nape of her neck. She looked, Eloise could not help but register, a total knock-out.

For a moment—just a moment—Eloise thought she could detect a kind of stricken look on the woman's face. Then it vanished. Hardened. The dark violet eyes looked past her, through the open door to the bedroom to the suitcase on the bed.

'Good,' said the woman, 'you're packing.'

Eloise blinked. It seemed an odd thing to say, especially as Eloise had no idea who this woman was. But presumably, she reasoned, the woman was something to do with Vito.

'Er…yes,' she made herself reply. 'Vito and I are going to Amalfi.'

In a flash, the woman's expression changed, emotion ripping across it. 'Oh, no, you're not!'

She strode in, pushing right past Eloise.

Dazed and shocked, Eloise could only stare at her, bewilderment on her face. She was bewildered, too, as she registered that the woman had spoken to her in English—English that was completely unaccented.

'Excuse me,' she said faintly, 'but who *are* you?'

The woman rounded on her. strong emotion in her eyes. 'Vito hasn't told you yet, has he?' she said.

That stricken look flashed again in those violet eyes. She took an intake of breath, hissing like a snake. It was audible to Eloise, who was standing there looking even more bewildered.

'Told me what?' Eloise uttered falteringly.

The woman stared at her, her eyes like points of light. 'I'm Vito's fiancée,' she said.

The world seemed to tilt, as if Eloise were hurtling off a plunging platform. Her mouth gaped open. There seemed to be a vacuum in her lungs. No air could get in. No oxygen. She gasped, but still no oxygen went in. She could feel dizziness in her head and then, out of nowhere, nausea biting like a wolf in her stomach.

She stepped back. Staggered. Clutched the wall for support. *'What?'* she gasped. 'You *can't* be!'

Daggers knifed from the brunette's eyes. 'Well, I *am*,' she said.

There was bleakness in her voice, but Eloise was deaf to it. All she could see was the woman looking at her, with that stricken look on her face that must be an echo of her own expression.

The woman sighed harshly, her face convulsing. 'Look,' she said, with a kind of twisted pity in her voice, 'you need to know—Vito's *always* got a blonde draped over him! You're just one more. So don't think you're anyone special! He'd have finished with you anyway soon enough. It's what all men do. *All* of them!'

The woman's voice seemed to break a fraction, and her eyes flashed with pained bitterness.

'So get out while you can—go back to England. Vito's marrying *me*! You wouldn't understand why—and you don't need to! But there's no way you're staying on here. Just be *glad* you're shot of him! I'm doing you a *favour*.'

Her words were cutting into Eloise, into her flesh. Her face looked bleached. This couldn't be true—it just *couldn't*.

Then suddenly into the nightmare footsteps sounded, rapid and hard, coming down the short corridor from where Vito was working.

As he erupted into the lounge, his expression furious, Eloise threw himself into his arms.

'Vito! Oh, Vito! Tell me it isn't true! This woman says she's your fiancée! Tell me it isn't true!'

She felt Vito's arms tighten around her, muscles jerking, and she twisted her head to stare back at the woman standing there, who had dropped such a bombshell into her life. Above her head she heard Vito snarl something in Italian she could not understand. She could feel his muscles steeled, taut beneath her clutching hands.

Then the brunette was answering, still in English. 'Well, I'm here now!' she threw back, and again her face contorted with strong emotion. 'And it looks like it's just as well! Don't even *think* of sloping off to Amalfi!' She rounded on Eloise, her voice rising dangerously. 'I won't have it—do you understand me? I *won't*!'

Now there was a note of impending hysterics in her voice.

Eloise felt Vito's arm slash upwards, cutting across the mounting hysteria. '*Basta!* Carla—*enough*!' There was fury in his voice—and a whole lot more.

Then Eloise was clutching at him. 'Vito—please... please tell me it's not true! Tell me you're not marrying her!'

Her eyes were huge and pleading. Bewildered and distraught.

He could see Carla's face contorting, that twisting flash in her eyes. 'Tell her, Vito!'

'Vito, please!' Eloise's voice was faint with dread.

His jaw clenched. Two opposing forces were pulling him apart. There was Eloise, desperate for his assurance—and every instinct in his body wanted to send Carla packing, her and her mother both. Tell them to go to hell—to do their worst! And then, overlying that, in his head like a death knell, there was his father's desperate dying plea to him...

Get them back, Vito—my son, my only son! Get Guido's shares back. Don't let her sell them—I beg you. I beg you with my last breath...

He looked at Eloise's stricken face, heard her stricken voice. 'Tell me it's not true! Tell me you're not marrying her!'

What could he say? How could he say it to either of them? It was impossible—just impossible!

Time—that was what he needed. If he could just get rid of Carla now—get rid of her so he could talk, explain, make everything right with Eloise! Get her to understand what was happening and why.

And there was only one way to get rid of Carla, hysterical as she was. Because if he didn't...

If I deny the engagement—if I send Carla packing the way I want to do more than anything else in the universe right now—then she'll be straight on to Marlene and Marlene will be on the phone to Falcone...

And Falcone would snap up the shares and divide Viscari Hotels in half at a stroke. Destroy what it had taken four generations of Viscaris over a century to build up.

I'll have betrayed my father, my family—given up the legacy I was left to guard. My mother will be devastated.

He took a razored breath. He *had* to buy time—*had* to get Carla out of here believing she had accomplished the coup she'd so clearly come to achieve. *Had* to pack her off so that he could get back to Eloise and tell her everything she needed to know.

Words formed in his head. Words he had to say— words that would cost him more than he'd ever dreamt he'd have to pay.

He looked at Eloise, his face working.

'Yes,' he said, and his voice seemed to be someone else's, not his—never his...not saying these words to Eloise. 'It's true.'

A cry broke from her. High and unearthly. It was like a blade in his lungs to hear it. She reared away from him, jumping to her feet. He did likewise, reaching for her hands again.

'No! Don't touch me! Don't *touch* me!' She backed away, her eyes wild.

'Eloise—I'm sorry. I'm *so* sorry!'

Guilt lacerated him at what he had just said. Words he'd had to say, could not deny. Even though he *would* deny them—explain them—the moment he could.

Crimson-tipped nails snaked around his wrist like a steel cuff. 'Time to go, Vito,' said Carla, with that desperate, manic look still in her eyes. 'We've got an engagement ring to choose!'

His head swivelled. Eyes that should have burned her on the spot lasered her. But he could do nothing except look across at Eloise.

'I have to talk to you,' he said. His voice was hoarse, urgent. 'I have to explain…explain everything. Do you understand me? It's essential that I talk to you!'

Into his words, his expression, his eyes, he poured all that he wanted her to understand. All that he so desperately wanted Carla *not* to understand!

'I'm so sorry! I'm so desperately sorry it has happened like this! I wanted to speak to you earlier—to tell you— to *explain*.'

'Vito!' Carla's nails dug into his wrist.

He prised them free, stepping towards Eloise. She flinched away. He could not bear it that he could not speak openly, truthfully. Could not bear to see her looking at him the way she was—with horror and revulsion on her face, rejection of him in every stricken line of her body.

Eloise—who was always so welcoming, so ardent, so eager for him…

But now there was only rejection. Shutting him out. Turning away from him.

He seized her hand, would not let her tear it away— not until he'd said what he could, what he must. Even in front of Carla.

'I want you in my life, Eloise! I want you and I'll find a way. I'll find a way somehow!'

But there was no understanding in Eloise's stricken gaze. Only blank horror and stark shock.

A rasp came from Carla. There was vehemence in her voice, her flashing eyes. 'No, you damn well *won't*! You *won't* keep her as your mistress! You won't make a fool of me—no man will *ever* make a fool of me again! And you won't make a fool of *her* either!'

Vito ignored her—his only focus was Eloise.

He could see that Carla's words had hit home. Her face was as white as a sheet. *Dio*, he needed to talk to her—to explain. But he could do nothing now. Nothing except say again, with all the urgency in his being, 'Eloise—wait for me! So I can explain.'

His words were disjointed, staccato. Eloise heard them as if from very far away—across a divide, the chasm that had opened between them as if an earthquake had shaken her world to its foundations.

She wheeled around, her hands going to her face. A terrifying sob mounted in her chest, filling her whole being. A sudden wave of nausea assailed her and she turned, rushing into the bedroom to reach the en suite bathroom.

She stood, shuddering, by the basin. Emotion ravaging her. Shock pummelling her. Words pounding in her head.

What am I going to do? Dear God, what am I going to do?

She stared at herself blindly in the mirror. She couldn't stay here—it was impossible!

With hideous mockery she heard Vito's voice.

'I have to explain—'

Her face contorted. Explain? What was there to explain? That woman had said it all—in a single, devastating word.

She was his *fiancée*—and Vito had not denied it. Had admitted it to her face.

A choke almost smothered her.

*And I was asking myself if he was the man who would
be my life! The love of my life—my husband!*

Hot, stinging tears burned in her eyes. Fool, *fool* that
she had been!

The words that had been hurled at her forced themselves into her head.

'Don't think you're anyone special!'

She closed her eyes in misery. That was exactly what
she'd been thinking—hoping…

*But all I was to him was one more blonde…filling in
the time until he got married.*

A wave of nausea rose again. No, it was even worse
than that. Not just until he married.

'You won't keep her as your mistress!'

A sob broke from her. Misery and humiliation and
pain. With another sob, she straightened, made herself
open her eyes, made herself look at her stricken, tear-
stained reflection.

I can't stay here.

That was for certain. Vito had said he would return
to 'explain' everything to her, hoping she would 'understand'. Her face hardened, eyes like stone now. Well, his
hopes would be in vain. That woman had been right—
his fiancée—Vito wouldn't make a fool of her. Not any
longer. Not one moment longer.

Stiffly, she turned away, walked back into the bedroom. At least she was already packed. Another sob
threatened to break, but she refused to let it. Refused to
let any more emotion break through, break *her*.

Numbly, she picked up her suitcase, fetched her handbag. Then she turned and went out of the bedroom, out of
the suite, out of the hotel. Out of Vito's life. The life she
could no longer be part of. Could never be part of—whatever she might once so stupidly have thought.

As she climbed into the taxi that the doorman had hailed for her she said only one word to the driver.

'L'aeroporto.'

A wolf was tearing at Vito's throat as, yet again, he punched 'send' on his phone while his car was log-jammed in the infamous Roman traffic. Eloise wasn't taking his calls, wasn't acknowledging his texts. He'd been inundating her with both non-stop since he'd finally despatched Carla back to her harpy of a mother with a massive diamond on her finger, its glitter echoing the manic glitter still in Carla's eyes.

He was beyond caring—Carla could flaunt the dia-mond all she wanted. Flaunt it in front of the man who was refusing to marry her, flaunt it in defiance and bitter fury, until she finally came back to earth and accepted the absurdity of what she was doing, the outrageous way she was behaving, and refused to be a pawn for her moth-er's ambitions.

But all Vito wanted—wanted with all his being—was to get back to Eloise. To explain the trap that he was caught in, and how desperately he needed *time* to force it open and free himself so that he could focus on the one thing in his life he wanted to focus on. Eloise.

On being with her, living with her, having her at his side. Here, in Rome, making a journey together to dis-cover what they meant to each other.

I've got to make it right with her! I can't endanger what we have! She's too important to me!

Even as the words formed in his mind he realised the truth of them. He had realised it from the moment he'd seen Eloise recoil from him and he still felt the stab in his guts that recoil had inflicted.

When I explain everything to her she will understand—I know she will! She always understands...

But he had to get to her first. Had to make sure she was there, waiting for him. Urgently he texted yet again, telling her he was on his way back, that he would be there as soon as he could, telling to wait for him.

But as he drew up at the hotel the doorman stepped forward. And what he told him stopped Vito dead.

The transatlantic flight went on and on. The steady drone of the engines in Eloise's ears was endless. As endless as the bleak bitterness filling her. Over and over again, like a ghastly video loop, the nightmare scene with Vito's fiancée played on in her head, forcing her to see the ugly truth about the man she'd so recklessly, blindly taken on trust. The man who'd swept her off in a whirlwind romantic haze, a wish-fulfilment dream, with a heady intoxication of the senses that had blinded her to his true nature.

All that passion, all that romance, all that devotion— and it had been nothing, nothing at all!

Because all along Vito had known perfectly well that back in Rome was the woman he was going to make his future with, the woman he was going to marry.

No wonder he didn't take me to his apartment! No wonder he didn't take me to that family function that first evening—his fiancée would have been there as well!

He hadn't even intended for her to stay in Rome at all, had he?

I was just going to be stashed away in some little love-nest in Amalfi, to be visited for sordid, secret sex sessions, kept as his convenient mistress.

She felt the nausea rise again from the pit of her stomach, revulsion filling her. And, more than that, pain, a sense of the deepest betrayal. Misery swept over her and she closed her eyes, feeling hot tears seeping beneath her lashes. It hurt—oh, how it hurt!

Memories, a thousand of them, pushed aside that tormenting video loop, crowded it out. Memories right from that very first moment when she'd gazed up from her sprawl on the airport concourse to see Vito looking down at her. She'd been captivated from the start, from that very first glance of his dark, melting eyes.

Memory after memory bombarded her—the sense of heady excitement and wonder, the tremor of desire building up in her, that incredible, unforgettable first night together, when he had taken her with him to a place so wonderful, so beautiful, that she had never known her body could take her there. And, thereafter, day after day, night after night. Vito…always Vito.

Always Vito.

She choked back a sob. All gone—gone, gone, *gone*! Ripped from her by a truth so ugly that she could not bear it.

Yet bear it she must. There was no other option. No other option but to flee, as she was doing, broken and tearful, yet steeling herself with a bitter anger at how he had lied to her—oh, not in words, but in deeds.

He had no right—no right to romance me! No right to have an affair with me! No right to let me think...

Another sob choked in her throat. No right to let her think…hope…that theirs was a passion that might lead to emotions that would bind them together for all their lives…

When all along he had been planning a very different future for himself.

And there it was, back again in her head, that hideous video loop—his fiancée bursting in, denouncing him, throwing savage pity at her, ripping her stupid, stupid illusions from her. Trampling on everything she had been starting to hope.

Trampling on the dreams she had started to long to come true.

Her hands clenched in her lap and she closed her eyes tighter shut.

And still the flight went on, and on.

When—after a lifetime, it seemed to her—the plane finally landed at JFK, she knew there was only one resolution to keep. She had said it all in that single text she had sent to him, after deleting unread the storm of texts that had arrived on her phone, deleting unheard all the voicemails. One single response from her had said all that needed to be said.

You are the most despicable man I know. Stay away from me for ever. Eloise.

CHAPTER FIVE

IT WAS STILL afternoon in New York, despite the hours since she'd fled Rome. But her mind was in some strange, dislocated no-man's-land which let her stare out of the taxi's window at the busy concrete canyons passing her by on her way through Manhattan.

She'd texted ahead from the airport and received a directive to go straight to her mother's apartment. As she whooshed up in the elevator, having collected a key from the concierge, a little ripple of nausea hit again, but she banked it down. A wave of weariness followed—weariness that went much deeper than the physical, was much more than jet lag. She needed to sleep—to claim oblivion from the devastation in her head.

Inside the apartment, she found the spare room she'd used before, and dumped her case. Her eyes felt as if they were being pressed with weights—she could barely take off her shoes before collapsing down on the bed, pulling back the covers to slide beneath the quilt.

Moments later she was asleep.

She must have slept for hours, adjusting overnight to New York time, for it was morning again when she surfaced. She opened her eyes, blinking. A cup of coffee was being placed on the bedside table beside her.

She shuffled up to a sitting position, pushing her long hair out of her eyes, looking at the person who had put it there, who was standing looking down at her with a questioning look on her face.

She took a breath. 'Hello, Mum,' said Eloise.

'Let me get this straight.'

Eloise's mother's voice was clear, and it penetrated right into her head like a drill.

'You let some spoiled, self-indulgent Italian playboy pick you up—literally!—and you went off with him without a thought, without the slightest hesitation or consideration, got tumbled into bed by him within twenty-four hours, and *then* you trotted along at his heels like a little poodle, only to discover—' her expression was scathing '—that, lo and behold, he not only turns out to have a fiancée waiting for him in Rome, but fully intends to keep you as his handy mistress on the side! Eloise, how *could* you waste yourself on a man like that?'

Eloise closed her eyes. 'I don't know...' she whispered. But she did know—knew exactly how it had happened. *Why* it had happened. 'He seemed so wonderful,' she said brokenly.

Her mother snorted. 'Yes, well, women make fools of themselves every day.' She took a breath. 'I should know. I made an idiot of myself over your father.' She gave a heavy sigh and got to her feet. 'Well, you can stay here as long as you want—though don't waste your time moping over the man! You're well rid of him!' Her voice changed, becoming businesslike. 'Best to start working again. I'll ask around my acquaintances for anyone who might need a nanny—that will take your mind off him.'

Eloise's face paled, and a look of anguish came into her eyes.

Her mother's expression changed again. 'You'll get over it, Eloise,' she said bluntly, but there was a resigned thread of sympathy there as well. Her voice softened a fraction. 'And you got out just in time—unlike me, with you already born and your father deserting us for his brood mare! With *you*, however, it's completely different. No repercussions—thank heavens!'

She glanced at her watch.

'I must go,' she said, back to her habitual brisk tones. 'I'm late for work.'

She brushed her cheek briefly against her daughter's, then walked out, leaving Eloise lying back against the pillows, her face bleak as an Arctic waste.

No repercussions, her mother had said. But she was wrong. Totally wrong.

There was a dark, bleak look in Vito's eyes. It had been there for days—ever since he'd opened that curt, damming text from Eloise. The words were incised into his brain as if with a chisel.

You are the most despicable man I know. Stay away from me for ever. Eloise.

For days, he had rejected her order, continuing to bombard her with texts and voicemails with an increasing sense of desperation…longing for her. He had to find her, talk to her, explain—

But he hadn't found her. She had headed to the airport and vanished. Presumably she had gone back to England—but with dismay he realised he had absolutely no idea where she might be. She'd worked as a live-in nanny—she didn't have an address of her own. She could be anywhere…

He'd set investigators on to it, but they'd drawn a blank. All further texts and calls to her mobile had been blocked.

She does not want me to find her. Wants nothing more to do with me.

And with every passing day, and still no way of finding her, that was what he *had* to accept.

Eloise was gone.

Her absence from his life was a vast, desolate hollow opening inside him—a sense of loss that gave him a bitter answer to the question he had asked about her ever since she'd come into his life.

I wanted to know if she was truly special to me—if she was coming to mean more to me than any other woman I've known.

His mouth twisted painfully. Well, now he knew. She had become far, far more than just one of the women in his life. He knew now that she'd been quite, quite different. Knew by his constant longing for her, his need to see her there, in front of him, holding out her arms to him, lying beside him in his embrace, being with him, at his side, all the time...

To know the answer to that question now, with her absence so unbearable to him, was a cruel irony indeed. As cruel as the pain of missing her so much. As cruel as the frustration that bit into him.

I begged her to wait and hear me out—to let me explain why I said what I did in front of Carla! If she had only given me a chance to explain about Marlene and the shares. Explain about Carla and her manic need suddenly to have a fiancé!

But she had not—she had vanished instead. Rejected him totally.

I thought she would be sympathetic, understanding— like she always was! Always there for me.

But only the malign shadow of Carla was there now, her manic bitterness unabating. He could see it in the blindness of her eyes, the gauntness of her face. He did not care.

And as with each passing day he became bleakly resigned to the fact that he could not find Eloise, he felt a kind of slow fatalism numb him. If Eloise was gone— if she could not be found—then what reason was there to balk any longer at this grotesque way of fulfilling his deathbed promise to his father? Saving Viscari Hotels from dismemberment. Protecting the legacy he had been born to guard.

So, with grim decision, he determined to let Carla have her garish wedding, announcing to the world she had not been rejected by her aristocratic lover but that she was making a dynastic match of her own to fulfil her mother's obsession. But, he spelt it out freezingly to his gaunt-faced step-cousin, within six months the marriage must be annulled. Carla could give any face-saving reason she wanted—he would not care. He would keep Guido's shares, handing over their market value to Carla when they parted.

And then it would be done. Over.

The dreary, crushing numbness pressed down on him. The numbness that would never lift now.

'Time to tidy up your toys, Johnny.'

Eloise's voice was bright. As bright as it was brittle.

Her four-year-old charge was a happy lad, and unspoilt despite his parents' wealth. It was Eloise's task to keep him that way. She had been glad—grateful—to find a post so quickly, via her mother's contacts, and had moved out to the Carldons' massive mansion on Long Island.

Johnny's father was based on Wall Street, at the family banking house, where his mother Laura worked as well, though she planned to work part-time from home once she had her second child. Until then young Johnny needed a live-in nanny. His parents usually stayed mid-week at their Manhattan apartment, putting in the punishing hours that top jobs on Wall Street demanded, so they could spend long weekends on Long Island with their son, so Eloise was often in sole charge of Johnny, alone in the Long Island mansion apart from the Carldons' housekeeper Maria and chauffeur Giuseppe.

It had been an uncomfortable jolt to hear the married couple speak Italian to each other, but Eloise had gritted her teeth and endured it.

Just as she was enduring her entire existence.

There was a bleakness inside her…a tearing misery she could not shed. Her mother's bracing admonition *'You're well rid of him!'* seemed only to make the world bleaker still. She knew the truth of her mother's words—but all they did was pain her more. As painful as the tormenting memories of how happy she had thought she'd been with Vito, of the shining hopes she'd been filled with.

She could tell herself all she liked that she'd tried to be cautious about her whirlwind romance, that she'd warned herself that it might be nothing more than a starry-eyed infatuation, an intoxicating dream.

Her expression bleached. It hadn't been that at all, though, had it? Not a dream—nothing but a sordid, clandestine fling with a man promised to another woman.

I wanted to know what I felt about him! Wanted to know if he was going to be the man I'd spend the rest of my life with! I found out the truth too late…

That was the cruelty of it. Her hopes and dreams had already started to weave around him—and now, four thousand miles away from him, they still had the power to haunt her.

A toxic mix of anger and misery filled her, rising up with a familiar sick feeling in her stomach. She fought it back. Oh, what use was there in feeling like this? Her mother was right! She *had* to get over it—*had* to put Vito in the past. Stop her useless anguish over it all! There was no choice for her but to get over him—turn off, smother, kill whatever it was she'd felt for him. No matter what those feelings had been—or might have become—it didn't matter now.

Now, and for her entire future, only one thing was important. There was only one joy to look forward to, only one meaning for her life. Only one way to heal her bruised and battered heart. Only one outlet for the love inside her.

She lifted her chin, fighting the dumb misery inside her. She would *not* let it win. She must not. Her future was changing—changing for ever—and that was *all* she must focus on now!

Emotion welled up in her, fierce and protective. Her time with Vito had been a disaster—but out of it had come a blessing she had not looked for and which now would be the reason for her life.

The only reason.

Another wave of nausea hit her…

Vito stood, stiff and immobile, at the altar rail of the church of Santa Maria della Fiore. Its showy, baroque splendour fitted the tastes of his bride, who was burning with desperation to show the world she was *not* a discarded, spurned creature, too lowly to be *contessa* of an ancient name, but was instead the enviable bride of one of Rome's most eligible and desirable bachelors, her glittering wedding as lavish as Marlene could devise.

All Vito was required to do was go through with it.

Keep his promise to his dying father. Get back his uncle's shares. Make the Viscari legacy safe at last.

Whatever it cost him to do so.

Into his head fleetingly, like a bird soaring high and out of reach, memory flashed.

Eloise—her arms opening to him, drawing him close to her, the scent of her, the fragrance of her hair, the silk of her skin, the warmth in her eyes, the tender curve of her mouth—

He shook the memory from him. She was gone from his life. What she had been to him was over. What she might have become he would never know.

He shifted his stance. What use to think of Eloise now, as he stood on the brink of marrying another woman? A woman he did not want, did not desire. But who brought with her the means to safeguard what his family had built up for over a century.

All around him he heard the organ music swelling, the choir's voices lifting, and knew that his bride was approaching. He heard the congregation rising to its feet, saw the officiating priest start to step forward. In minutes now he would commit himself to marriage.

Words thrust themselves into his head as he stood there, rigid and immobile, as if chained where he stood by forces he could not defy. Making himself endure it with a strength he had to find.

Is this what you want me to do, Papa? Is this how you want me to get back your brother's shares? Is this the price you want me to pay for them?

The choir's soaring voices reached a crescendo before stilling.

Every muscle in Vito's body tensed, as if he were forcing himself to stand stock-still. Carla was beside him, the folds of her couture wedding dress brushing his leg, her lace-veiled figure as rigid as his, the rich fragrance of her heavy perfume cloying.

He did not look at her. Could not. Could only sense the tension racking her as she stood beside him. Driven by her own demons.

And she was taking him with her, and for that he damned her utterly.

The sonorous voice of the priest sounded over his head.

Latin words were murmured and intoned as the words of the wedding service proceeded. Words that would bind them in holy matrimony.

A cold, icy shudder went through him. Clearing the numbing blankness in his mind. The priest was talking again, saying the most potent words of all. Would he take this woman for his wife?

Vito's eyes were on the priest, then on the altar beyond. Then he turned his head slightly, to look at Carla's veiled figure, trembling with tension. He *had* to do this. He had come this far, had done all this, to fulfil his promise to his father. What choice did he have now?

What choice? The question seared in his head. Demanding he answer.

For one long, endless moment he stood silent as that question burned in his head. Then he took a breath and gave his answer…

Everything seemed to have gone into slow motion. Or perhaps it was just his brain that was going slow. He watched the priest incline his head towards him, as if he had not quite caught his response. Behind him, he heard a kind of susurration, like the buzzing of insects. And beside him he could hear Carla give an intake of breath that was like a razor in its sharpness.

And its disbelief.

He turned his head to look at her. She was staring at him. Staring at him through her veil with an expression in her eyes that was something like an alien out of a sci-fi film.

He closed his eyes a moment, then opened them again. 'I won't do this, Carla,' he said.

His voice was quiet, audible only to her. But there was a certainty in it that infused every word.

'I won't do it to me—and I won't do it to you. This is a travesty. An abhorrence. This is not what marriage is about—on any terms, or for any reason. You deserve better. And so do I.'

And so does Eloise—she didn't deserve what I did to her.

A low, scarcely audible sound came from Carla's throat. Her eyes distended and she swayed, her body starting to fold. Instantly Vito's arm came around her. The priest stepped forward to help support her between them, and then Carla's mother rushed forward, consternation on her face as they escorted Carla to the vestry. His own mother hastened after them, anxiety all over her face.

As he helped the stricken Carla to a chair, he turned towards Marlene. His voice, when he spoke, was very calm—but with unbending steel in it.

'I will not go through with this, Marlene,' he said, his eyes boring into hers as fury leapt in her face. 'You may tell everyone that Carla couldn't face marrying me, or that she is ill—whatever you want to say to protect her. But I will no longer be party to your machinations. I will pay you twice what Guido's shares are worth—but I will no longer be blackmailed by you. Do your worst, if you must.'

Behind him came a cry of anguish. It was his mother, rushing forward to clutch his arm. He turned to her, leading her a little way away to give them privacy. This was nothing to do with Marlene or her daughter. This was between his mother and himself.

And his father.

He felt the strength of his resolve to hold dear every value he possessed. Every value that made life worthwhile—that had to guide every life in order for it to be... *honourable.*

'Mamma,' he said now, and his voice was as gentle as his hold on her, though the resolve, the strength, was still in his expression. 'When you stood beside my father at your wedding you promised to love and honour him. And I, too, honour him—which is why I will not bind myself to the promise I made him. To marry Carla would be… dishonourable. Whatever the reasons for such a marriage, they cannot be justified. Neither for her, nor for me.'

He took an unsteady breath.

'I'm sorry that I have not had the courage or the resolution to say this until this moment. I have tried to do my best by my heritage, by my promise to Papa. But not at this price.'

He looked at her stricken face, into her anguished eyes.

'To marry Carla like this would be to dishonour all that I hold dear—all that you and Papa taught me to value. Self-respect, honesty, integrity… I will not strike this devil's bargain—' he cast a punitive look towards Marlene, huddled with Carla '—because it would shame me, it would shame my father, and it would shame you.'

Gently he put his arm around his weeping mother's shoulder. 'Time to go home, Mamma,' he said. 'There is something I must do. Someone I must find.'

Find Eloise.

And find out what she means to me once and for all.

CHAPTER SIX

'WHAT DO YOU say to Nanny Ellie?' Johnny's mother prompted.

'Thank you!' exclaimed the little boy, gazing at the cover of the jigsaw box, which depicted an unfeasibly cute dinosaur.

Eloise had bought it in Manhattan, having taken a day's leave to travel in.

As Johnny lifted off the lid and emptied the wooden pieces on to the table Laura turned to Eloise.

'Well, how did it go?' she asked.

There was both friendliness and concern in her voice.

'Fine,' said Eloise. 'No problems. It's all "steady as she goes".'

'That's great!' Laura said warmly. 'When's your next appointment?'

'Next month—unless something crops up.'

'Let's hope not,' said Laura. 'Keep up the plain sailing!' She smiled. 'Now, why don't you go and put your feet up? Take the evening off. Johnny and I can get stuck into this jigsaw, and John's promised to be home by bathtime.'

'Yay!' contributed her son enthusiastically. 'I like bathtime with Dad. He lets me splash!'

'Does he, now?' said his mother severely, and exchanged a woman-to-woman look with Eloise. Then she turned back to her son. 'OK, so first we need to find the edge bits—especially the corners. Have you got any of those?'

Eloise left them to it, slipping away to her own generous quarters. There was an ache in her that had nothing to do with the day's journey in and out of Manhattan. Johnny was a happy child, and his parents were warm and loving, united in their love for each other and both devoted to their son.

The kind of family Eloise longed to make for herself. The kind of family she'd once thought she might make with Vito—

No! Don't go there! Don't think about those naïve hopes that you once wove into the baseless fabric of your stupid dreams.

She had told myself that maybe their romance was like champagne—warned herself that one morning she might wake to find it flat and stale.

But it hadn't turned flat and stale—it had turned to bitter, bitter gall.

A gall she must swallow. Drink down all her life.

At least she had her mother's support. And there was an irony about that that Eloise found only added to that bitter taste.

'It won't be easy, Eloise, but who said being a woman was ever easy? Certainly not when some selfish male has messed up your life!'

No, it wouldn't be easy. But it had to be done. Her love would have one focus now—one focus alone.

As she closed the nursery door behind her a peal of laughter broke out from Johnny, echoed by his mother. That ache smote her again.

A happy little boy, with a happy, loving family surrounding him, a doting mother and father in a happy marriage together...

That can never be for me. Not now.

Sadness pierced her, haunting the blue of her eyes. She had dreamt all her life of making a happy family…not like her own…and yet now that was beyond her for ever.

Vito threw himself into the chair behind his desk and deep desolation filled him. The board meeting he'd just emerged from had been bruising—slamming into him just what he had done.

What Marlene had done.

She had fulfilled her threat—sold Guido's shares to Nic Falcone. Sold them the very day Vito had walked out of the church. And just now Nic Falcone had sat arrogantly across the boardroom table from him, demanding his pick of the Viscari portfolio—as befitted the new half-owner of Viscari Hotels.

The resulting discussion had been…*difficult*. Grim-faced, along with the rest of his board, Vito had played hardball as much as his position allowed, and finally a memorandum of agreement had been achieved. But the loss of every property that Falcone had taken from him drove a dagger into Vito's heart.

He sat now, a bleak, brooding expression on his face.

Only one prospect could lessen that grievous loss.

Finding Eloise.

I will not give up on her! I cannot!

He had to find her, to discover whether he could salvage anything from the hideous mess he'd made of things, something that was worth fighting for.

The long, grim months without her had only shown him what he had lost when she'd left him. So he'd renewed his efforts to discover where she'd gone, reactivating all his lines of enquiry. But all had drawn a blank. Only one—a wild, maverick attempt—remained. Would it work? *Could* it work? To this point it had not.

His sense of desolation deepened. His expression sombre.

The sound of his phone ringing hardly made him stir. Until the caller started to leave a message. Then, as if an electric current had suddenly galvanised him, Vito snatched up the phone. Heard out the caller.

When the call ended, he promptly summoned his PA. 'I need you to book a flight for me tonight,' he told her.

And then, and only then, did his eyes light with animation. With relief. With an emotion that had not been there for long, deadened weeks.

With hope.

'Wowee! Wowee! Come and *see*!'

Johnny's exuberant call drew Eloise to the nursery window, where her charge was gazing out onto the carriage sweep. The long, low scarlet automobile drawing up with a throaty growl of its powerful engine made her start.

Vito had driven a car just like that...

Instantly memory bit. Her and Vito, cruising along the *autostrada*, her eyes on him. He'd looked so impossibly glamorous and gorgeous, with his designer dark glasses, his hands curved around the wheel, revelling in the power of the steering...

She forced the memory from her head. Vito was an ocean away from her and she had to get on with her life without him—make the future that awaited her now without him. What was the point of thinking about their time together?

She stared bleakly down as the car door opened. As the driver got out.

Faintness drummed at her, and a disbelieving gasp was wrenched from her throat.

It was Vito.

Vito here—now—outside the house. Walking up to

the house, disappearing from view under the porch she could not see from the angle of the nursery window. She felt numb with shock.

Johnny raced to the nursery door. 'I want to go down and see the car!' he exclaimed.

The next moment the house phone was ringing, and Johnny dashed to snatch it up.

He turned excitedly to Eloise. 'The car man wants to see *you*! Come on, come on, come on!' He tugged her towards the door.

His little hand made no impact on her total immobility. Her total inability to think, to pull one shred of rational usage from her brain.

Only one phrase existed in it.

It's Vito—it's Vito—it's Vito...

But it couldn't be. It was impossible. Completely impossible. Vito was in Italy. In Rome. With his wife. It could not be him because he did not know where she was. So how had found her? And why—?

Raggedly, her mind zig-zagged incoherently, her thoughts flying everywhere, borne on emotions that were tumbling about crazily inside her, like rocks in a washing machine. Urgently she sought to get a grip on herself, to fight through the shock smashing through her.

Johnny let go of her, yanking open the door, haring out. With a start, she hurried after him—he was her charge and she must look after him. But at the top of the stairs she froze.

Vito was in the hall below, talking to Giuseppe. She heard Italian, saw Giuseppe shake Vito's hand. Saw Vito turn his head as Johnny tugged urgently on her hand to go downstairs. Saw the expression on Vito's face.

'Eloise!'

He had taken off his dark glasses and he was just star-

ing at her. Staring at her and drinking her in with his eyes
as if she were water in a parched, parched land.

'Eloise...' He said her name again. A faint, exhalation
of breath, like the sighing of the wind.

She met his gaze. Felt herself reel with the force of it.

Then, from the door at the back of the hall, the rotund
figure of Maria erupted, rushing up to Vito, breaking
into voluble Italian. Vito was smiling at her, and Eloise
could hear him replying, his voice warm. Thanking her.

Numb still, Eloise let Johnny tug her downstairs. He
broke free of her at the bottom and rushed to Vito, pulling at his trouser leg.

'I *need* to see your car!' he exclaimed.

Vito looked down at him, hunkered down beside him.
Smiled at the little boy. Against her will, Eloise felt her
heart skip a beat.

He used to smile at me like that.

No—she mustn't think of that...mustn't remember.

'Do you, now?' Vito was saying, obviously amused
by his eagerness.

'Yes!' confirmed Johnny, oblivious, as only a four-
year-old could be, to the tension, the atmosphere blazing
all around him. 'Come on, come on!'

He seized Vito's hand with all the confidence of a
well-loved child and made to drag him to the front door.

Vito straightened, gently disengaging his hand from
Johnny's. 'In a while, OK?'

He ruffled Johnny's hair, in a friendly, easy fashion,
and again Eloise felt emotion scissor through her. But not
memory this time.

No! Don't think of that either—just don't! Don't!

She'd never seen Vito with children before—never
seen this easy, unforced attitude. His obvious amusement.
Enjoyment. As if it came supremely naturally to him.

The scissoring emotion came again.

Then Giuseppe was stepping forward. 'Why don't I show you?' he said to Johnny, glancing at Vito for agreement.

Vito nodded, a grateful look on his face. Giuseppe swept Johnny away, and Maria bustled forward busily to open the door to the library, beckoning to Vito…and then to Eloise.

But Eloise could not move. Vito's eyes went to her, rooting her to the spot. The easy smile that had been there for Johnny had gone. Now his expression was as grave and as stark as the tension visible in every line of his body as he walked towards her at the foot of the stairs.

'Eloise—I have to talk to you.'

His voice was low and vibrant. With the same urgency in it that she had heard the day he'd told her that he was indeed marrying the woman who had stormed into their suite, stormed into her life, destroying everything in her path. Trampling over what they had…what they might have had.

Hideously aware of Maria, still holding the library door open, Eloise stumbled past her into the spacious room. Vito strode after her. Only when Maria had shut the door, giving them privacy, could she speak.

'How did you find me? It's impossible that you have!' Her voice came out high-pitched, half strangulated.

'Yes,' Vito said, his voice stark, like stone scraped bare, 'you *made* it impossible. And I know why, Eloise—I understand why you did.'

Her eyes flashed. However Vito had found her—and for whatever reason!—it was impossible for her to have anything more to do with him. She felt emotion sear in her. But it didn't matter how her eyes were drinking him in, how faintness was drumming inside her just at the very sight of him, because everything was still impossible—totally impossible!

He was speaking again, and she made herself hear as he reached inside his jacket pocket, took out a much-folded piece of paper, colourful and glossy. He opened it out, and it looked to Eloise as if it had been torn from a magazine.

'This is how. Maria saw it and got in touch with me.'

He held the page out to her. She wouldn't approach. Her head went up. Emotions pounded inside her, but there was only one that she could allow. Anger. Only anger.

'However you did it, you've wasted your time! If you're here to tell me you'd like me to come back with you and be your adulterous little bit on the side, your convenient mistress, your *poodle*, you can forget it! Go back to your wife, Vito! Go back to her. Because I didn't want to know then, and I don't want to know now—I'll *never* want to know!'

She could see a tic working in his cheek. 'Please look at this, Eloise.' He pushed the piece of paper towards her, across the table, rotating it so that it was facing her.

She could see the photo on it even from this distance. It was Vito—and her.

She was in evening dress, and Vito was standing beside her—it must have been at one of the endless round of cocktail parties during his hotel tour, when she'd followed him around like a trusting little poodle...

But there was another photo, too, on the facing page—just of Vito by himself. It was his head and torso, face-on, looking at her directly off the page.

And beneath it was a headline that blazed in huge letters—words in Italian. She knew the type of magazine it was—one of those ritzy, glossy weeklies that focused on celebrities and high society.

'It says,' Vito intoned, and there was something strange about his voice, '"*Help me find her, my most beautiful Eloise!*" I had to find you, Eloise. I *had* to. Because I have something to tell you—and something to beg of you.'

He walked towards her, his stride purposeful. His eyes were on her, never moving, not for a second, fixed on hers like a laser beam as he came up to her. There was only a metre between them. His closeness was unbearable. He was out of reach. Barred from her by marriage... by betrayal.

'I don't want to know! I don't know want to hear!' she cried, shaking her head as if to block out his voice. Trying to defend herself by going on the attack.

Emotions warred within her—the blaze of overwhelming reaction at seeing him again burning through her like a forest fire. Doused by the cold, fierce fury at what he had done to her.

She forced words through her narrowed throat. 'I won't go back to you, Vito! I told you that you were despicable—'

'Yes,' he said tightly, 'I behaved despicably to you. But...' He took a scissoring breath. 'I didn't intend to. I was...trapped.'

A bitter laugh broke from Eloise. 'Yes, that's what married men always say! Oh, don't tell me, Vito—your wife doesn't understand you, does she?'

There was vicious mockery in her voice. Fuelling her anger. Anger she had to keep fuelled, filled to the brim, spilling over into the hostile venom she was hurling at him.

Because if she didn't feel anger at Vito, then...

No, I can't allow myself to feel anything else! I can't... I can't!

His face had tightened even more. His cheekbones were exposed like carved marble, his mouth like a whip. She could see the steeled tension in the set of his shoulders, how he was holding his body rigid.

'I have no wife.' The words fell like stones from him. 'The wedding never went ahead.'

The expression in his eyes made her breath stop. There was a starkness in them that was like bleached bone.

'That's why I am here, Eloise. To tell you that.'

Her face convulsed. For a moment—just a moment—emotion flared in her like phosphorus. A longing so intense it burned within her. She felt her hand flutter to her abdomen, felt the longing burn again. Longing to clutch at the dream that hovered, soaring now at what he'd just told her.

No wife—he has no wife! So could we—oh, could we…?

But then the flare was extinguished. What difference did it make? What difference could it make? After what he'd done to her.

'And do you expect me to throw myself into your arms?' she cried. 'Tell you I forgive you for what you did to me? Is that what you expect?'

Vito's mouth tightened. He shook his head. 'I expect nothing, Eloise.' He drew a heavy, leaden breath audibly into his lungs. 'I have come here only to explain to you why I did what I did.'

He paused, not letting his eyes drop from hers.

'I ask only that you listen to me now.' He swallowed. 'I know you refused to let me talk to you, refused to let me try and explain, and I can understand why—but now that…that I have no wife after all, I beg only one favour from you. To hear me out.'

His stark gaze bored into her again.

'Will you grant me that favour?' he asked.

Eloise felt her mouth tighten, her chin lift. She felt as heavy as lead.

'You intend to trot out excuses for why you behaved the way you did? Is that it?' There was a coldness in her voice she did not bother to hide.

He gave an infinitesimal shake of his head. 'Not excuses—reasons. Reasons I had no chance to explain to you in Rome. Reasons I must give you now.'

He took a breath, hoping she would let him explain before she fled from him.

'I agreed to marry my step-cousin, Carla,' Vito said, as if cutting the words from himself, 'because it would allow me to obtain the shares in Viscari Hotels that her mother, Marlene, had inherited from my uncle Guido— her late husband. That was the reason. The *only* reason.'

Eloise reeled back, her face paling as if he had struck her, as his words impacted on her. She stared at him, gall rising in her. 'You traded me for a handful of shares,' she said.

Her voice was hollow, her eyes distending. The bitterness in her throat burned like acid. In her head, thoughts tumbled like falling rocks. Each one smashing into her.

That's all I was to him—all the value I had. Less than a handful of shares in his precious hotel chain! And for that—for nothing more than that—he agreed to marry another woman. Thinking I'd go along with it.

Pain knifed through her.

'You traded me for a handful of shares!' She hurled the words at him again, her face convulsing now. '*That* was why you put me through what you did! You agreed to *marry* someone for *that*?'

That tic came again in his cheek. 'As you say,' he said tightly.

She stared at him. 'How *could* you, Vito? How could you stoop that low? With all your wealth, to want yet more—to be prepared to *marry* for it! Stringing me along while you did so, making a fool of me—bringing me to Rome right under the nose of the woman you were going to marry? And you *really* think that coming here and telling me all that to my face is going to make me change my mind about you?'

There was derision in her voice, open scorn. Raw anger. She had to put it there—because only that could quench that phosphorus flare of hope and longing.

He moved restlessly. There was about him an air of withdrawal, as if he'd shut himself inside himself. His eyes had blanked now—there was nothing in them, no emotion...nothing. He picked up the magazine page, lying abandoned on the tabletop, folded it mechanically, and slipped it into his breast pocket.

Then he looked across at Eloise again. 'I've said what I came to say, Eloise,' he said. 'I've sought you out to say it—to explain to you why I behaved as I did. And,' he went on, and now his voice was weighted down as if with lead, 'for one other reason.'

He looked at her, and there was a bleakness in his eyes now that had not been there till this moment. A draining of hope.

'I sought you out because I needed to know, Eloise, just what we had come to mean to each other. To discover if...if there could have been anything more to us than a summer romance.' His expression twisted. 'When we arrived in Rome all I wanted was to focus on you! But—'

She cut across him, her voice scathing, bitter. 'But the little business of your *marriage* got in the way! So then I just turned into a prospective mistress, didn't I? To be neatly stashed away in a love nest in Amalfi!'

Vito's hand slashed through the air. 'No! It was never that! *Never.* I just wanted—'

'You wanted to get hold of some shares. Yes, you said.'

Eloise's voice was harsh, grating. Her eyes as hard as stones. She couldn't bear this. Couldn't bear to have Vito saying such words to her. Vito who had callously set her aside for the sake of some extra shares...

But you could have him back! You could have him back right now—all you have to say to him is that you want him. Need him in your life. And that it's not just you who needs him.

Temptation, overpowering and overwhelming, hovered in front of her.

I could have the dream! I could have Vito in my life... in my future. Making a family with me.

But then, like cold acidic water, came the knowledge that it was impossible. He was not a man whose values and choices she would ever want to understand. Not a man she would inflict on anyone, let alone—

She took a shuddering breath, her mind shearing away from the future that must be hers, and hers alone, with no one to share it with her. She made her voice indifferent.

'Look, Vito—forget it. You made your choice—those shares were more important to you than I was. Well, they can stay that way.'

She took a step backwards. Claws were ripping into her, shredding her.

For one long moment he looked at her, his face unreadable, closed. Expressionless except for one tic high in his cheek, the pressure of his set jaw.

'I'll go,' he said. His voice was staccato. Terse. Infinitely distant. 'I apologise for disturbing you like this, and you have my assurance that I will make no further attempt to communicate with you. I accept that our time together is...gone. That there is nothing left between us. The fault for that is mine entirely. Goodbye, Eloise.'

He turned away, walked back towards the door of the library, every line of his body rigid as he disappeared from her view.

The claws inside her tore again, and her throat was as tight as drawn wire. For a single agonising second she wanted to hurl herself forward, catch at his shoulder, throw herself into his arms...

Beg him not to go.

But she would not let herself.

Somewhere beyond she was dimly aware of the sound of a car's engine, and the scrunch of gravel beyond the library windows. She heard footsteps cross the hall, heard a murmur of Italian—presumably him speaking to Maria or Giuseppe—and then the sound of the front door opening. Dimly, in part of her consciousness, she was aware of conversation in English, of another male voice, one with an American accent. The other voice, low-pitched, was Vito's, but then it was cut off by the closing of the front door.

And still she could not move.

Then suddenly, abruptly, there was more noise out in the hallway and the chatter of a youthful voice, and a moment later Johnny erupted into the library, rushing up to her.

'Daddy's home! He's come home to play with me! We're going swimming!'

Eloise jerked to life, like a statue animated. 'That's lovely,' she said, but her response was mechanical.

Beyond the window she saw a flash of red, heard a throaty, familiar roar fading into the distance down the driveway.

'Daddy!' Johnny did an about-turn, seeing his father in the doorway. 'Swimming! Swimming!' he shouted excitedly.

'Swimming it is,' said his father with a grin. Then his eyes went to Eloise, their expression changing. 'Well, well, you're a dark horse, Nanny Ellie! Vito Viscari, no less! That's some beau to have!' He grinned down at his son. 'Of course if you were Junior, here, his main attraction would be that very neat Ferrari he's just roared off in—Johnny was trying to persuade Giuseppe to let him get into the driving seat.'

'Vroom-vroom!' chirped Johnny in happy agreement, and ran around the room as if steering a car.

'But I suspect,' John Carldon went on, addressing El-oise once more, with an amused look open in his face, 'that for you it's more likely to be the film star looks that a totally unfair Providence has heaped upon him! Laura will be mad as fire that she missed him!'

The amused look deepened.

'Maybe, now that she knows he's…ah…coming call-ing,' he went on, 'she'll snap him up for a dinner party. Oh, and, of course,' he went on blithely, 'if you need time off to head into Manhattan now that he's Stateside, just let us know. Presumably he stays at the Viscari when he's in New York?'

He frowned suddenly. 'Or maybe not. It's not a Vis-cari Hotel any more, is it? That was one of the ones that went over to Falcone.'

He shook his head, not seeming to notice that his son's nanny had frozen.

'Bad business, that,' he went on, his voice sombre now. 'And pretty tough on the guy—seeing half his inheri-tance wiped out, just like that. It made quite a stir in the financial press—even over here. Half the entire company was sold over Viscari's head by his uncle's widow to his biggest rival. Nic Falcone has scooped up a real treasure pot—taken his pick of the prime locations. A blow that heavy will take some recovering from. But Viscari'll do it, I'm sure. I can't see him not fighting back. Trying to rebuild everything that's been ripped from him.'

His expression changed, and the glint was back in his eye.

'Of course he'll be here for other reasons, too, won't he? Other attractions!' He grinned at her.

But Eloise did not smile back. Could not. Could not move a muscle. Could only hear her employer continue talking as he caught his son's hand to stop his peregri-nations.

'Hotels aren't my usual investment sector, but if Laura gets her dinner party I'll make sure some of the guests are useful to him. After all,' he said teasingly, 'if Vito Viscari's your beau we should keep him sweet. We don't want to lose you before we have to!'

His expression changed again, and he glanced down at his son, who was tugging on his hand.

'OK… OK, Junior—no need to pull my hand off. Swimming it is—see you later, Nanny Ellie.'

He headed off, Johnny still tugging at him excitedly, chattering away.

Slowly, very slowly, Eloise turned away, walking up the stairs back to the nursery quarters on legs that did not seem to be hers any more.

Vito opened the throttle, letting the powerful engine roar. Wanting the noise to drown out everything that was knifing through him. The bitter, bitter taste of total defeat.

I should never have sought her out! Never!

Because to have seen her again, to have his gaze rest on her in the flesh, not just in his memories, had opened the floodgates within him!

He had spent all those precious weeks in Europe with her, wondering if he dared believe she could be the one woman in the world he could fall in love with. He had spent these last brutally grim weeks missing her with an intensity that was like a knife in his guts.

Finally finding her, seeing her, had been like a brand on his flesh. Making everything crystal-clear to him.

Emotion had surged within him. He had been desperate to get her to understand why he had done what he had. Desperate to win her back.

But it had been a disaster—a catastrophe. Smashing his hopes to pieces.

Did I really expect more?

He railed at himself, his grip tightening on the wheel of the car.

Did I really expect her just to fall straight back into my arms as if the past nightmare months had never happened?

He should have known better. Should have realised how impossible that was.

In his head her scathing accusation rang again.

'You traded me for a handful of shares!'

His hands clenched again around the wheel.

Dio, I messed up from beginning to end! And I've lost everything I wanted to keep—everything!

Bleakness seared across his mind as he faced what he'd done, what he'd lost. He'd wanted to keep Eloise in his life—discover exactly what she meant to him—and now he'd lost her for ever. She'd made that clear enough! He'd wanted to keep his promise to his dying father—and he'd broken it. He'd wanted to keep the Viscari legacy intact—and he'd had it smashed it to pieces.

It's all been for nothing—less than nothing... I betrayed Eloise's trust in me and I've betrayed my father's trust in me.

He drove on, filled with bleakness and despair. He would leave New York tonight...fly down to Ste Cecile. That hotel, at least, was still his, for Nic Falcone already had a strong existing presence in the Caribbean, and wasn't interested in the Viscari project there—though he'd helped himself to the pick of the rest of the Viscari North American portfolio. Including the uber-prestigious Viscari Manhattan.

Out of loyalty to his former manager there, Vito was staying in his usual suite—though every sign of the Falcone rebranding was like a whiplash across his shoulders.

But I can't give in—and I will not go under!

His jaw steeled, eyes hardening. If Falcone was mopping up existing Viscari Hotels—well, there would be *new* Viscari Hotels opened. It would take time, but time was something he would have a great deal of now. So much gaping time to fill…

Time to rebuild his legacy. Restore what he had lost.

Pain sliced through him again, severing his flesh. What else could he do now? What else was left for him?

Her name cried through his head like a fleeing ghost.

Eloise! What use was it to find you and lose you all over again…?

Fool! Fool that he had been! To hope for her forgiveness—her understanding.

To hope for reunion…

'Mum, I need your help.' Eloise's voice was urgent as she spoke on the phone from her room at the Carldons'. 'Can I stay at your apartment tonight? I *have* to go and see Vito this evening.'

'Vito?' Her mother's voice sharpened down the line. 'Eloise, do *not* tell me he's the waste-of-space Italian you got so disastrously involved with—'

Eloise's throat tightened. She had never told her mother Vito's identity, and her mother had never asked—had specifically told her that, given Eloise's decision, she had no need to know, and that it was irrelevant anyway.

'Yes,' she admitted grittily. 'Vito Viscari. He found out where I was working and—'

Again her mother interrupted her, in her usual forthright manner. 'Viscari? As in… Viscari Hotels?'

'Yes,' said Eloise.

She did *not* want an inquisition about Vito's identity. All she wanted right now was her mother's help in a very practical way. But her mother's attention had snapped on Vito's name.

'Vito Viscari! Good grief! I had no idea.' There was

open surprise in her voice. Then her tone changed. 'Why are you meeting him?' she asked sharply.

'I… I have to talk to him,' Eloise got out.

'Well, make sure that's all you do! This is *no* time for rushing into anything! You've been quite rash enough as it is—'

She broke off, and Eloise could hear a voice in the background. Then her mother was back on the line, her voice crisp and brisk.

'Eloise, I have to go now. Let yourself into the apartment—I'll be working late.'

She rang off. Slowly, Eloise replaced the handset. Emotion was roiling within her. Phoning her mother had been the *easy* phone call to make…

With slightly shaking fingers she dialled the number for the Viscari Manhattan. He *would* be staying there—wouldn't he?

But it isn't even his hotel any more…

She felt a stab in her stomach. That stab came again as the voice down the line intoned, 'Falcone Manhattan—how may I direct your call?'

She made herself focus on what had to be done, and left the message she had to leave.

'My name is Eloise Dean. Please tell Mr Viscari, when he arrives back at the hotel, that I urgently need to see him. I'm coming into Manhattan tonight and will be at the hotel at eight.'

It was all she could bring herself to say. All she could bring herself to hope.

CHAPTER SEVEN

TENSION WAS RACING through Vito. Was he insane to put himself through this for a second time in one day? He'd been intending to head straight for JFK, ready to take the next flight to the Caribbean as if all the hounds of hell were tearing at his heels.

And now—

Now he was waiting in the elegant bar of the hotel that had once been his but was no longer, with a dry martini in front of him, doing his damnedest to steady his nerves. Watching the entrance like a hawk.

Eight o'clock, the message had said. It was five past now. Would she come at all? And why was she coming?

He felt emotion spike in him, and clamped down on it.

I'd hoped so much, pinned so much on telling her what I wasn't able to tell her in Rome...and it made no difference to her at all.

He remained unforgiven.

A sense of bitter irony assailed him. All his life women had come easily to him. His looks, his charm, his wealth, his social position—all had meant that his love-life had been sunny, plentiful, effortless. Any woman he'd smiled at had responded to him. Including Eloise.

Did I expect Eloise to be like all the other women? So keen on me that she would snap me up again after a simple apology?

He frowned. No, that had not been it. It had been because he'd longed for her to forgive him—to accept him back in her life.

The searing sense of loss he'd felt when she'd fled from Rome came again, with double intensity. A humourless smile thinned his mouth. He'd questioned himself as to what Eloise meant to him. Well, losing her had shown him, hadn't it? Losing her not once, but twice…

And the bitterest truth of all was that it had only taken setting eyes on her again this afternoon for him to know, with blazing clarity, that *she*, of all the women in the world, was the one who meant most to him. The time dividing them had vanished in an instant, and he'd known that everything he'd desired her for was still blazingly true. He wanted her—and she was still lost to him.

Unless her coming here tonight means…

No, he must not hope. He'd hoped before, and had had his hope smashed to pieces. Better—safer—to finish his martini and steel himself for seeing her again.

Maybe for the last time ever…

He lifted his glass, but it froze halfway to his lips.

She was there, in the entrance, and her eyes were fixed on him.

Eloise's eyes went to Vito immediately. He was sitting at the bar. Slowly, she walked towards him. His expression had become masked as he'd seen her, and she felt emotion swirl within her, troubling and troubled. But she tried to set them aside. She was here for one purpose only. To say the words she must say. *Unsay* what she had thrown at him so angrily. So unfairly.

'You traded me for a handful of shares!'

Only it had not been a handful, had it? It had been the severing of his legacy—an entire half of it handed to his rival.

'Hello, Vito,' she said.

Her voice sounded strange…far away. She looked at him, but could not quite meet his eyes. Or perhaps it was his eyes not meeting hers.

She swallowed. 'Thank you for seeing me.'

His expression shifted minutely. 'I was en route to JFK,' he said. He moved his martini glass, gestured to the stool at the bar beside his. 'What is it that you want to say?'

His expression was wary, cutting her off from him. She perched herself on the stool, setting her handbag on the bar, taking a breath.

'I didn't realise,' she said, 'just what those shares meant. Johnny's father told me—he assumed I knew. He told me…told me you'd lost half of the Viscari Hotels.' She took another breath. 'I'm so sorry, Vito.' Her voice was small. She made herself go on. 'So sorry that I made it sound so…trivial. I didn't know. Didn't realise.' She swallowed. 'Didn't understand.'

The barman had glided up to them, hovering attentively, knowing full who Vito was even if he no longer owned the hotel.

Vito went into courtesy mode. 'What would you like to drink?' he asked Eloise.

There was nothing more in his voice than there would have been if she were a minor acquaintance.

She hesitated. A thousand memories pierced like needles under her skin. Once she would have said, *Oh, a Bellini would be lovely!* But now she dared not. And not just because of the memories.

'OJ, please—and water,' she said, and the barman nodded, and glided away again.

Unwillingly, Eloise registered that his uniform was now emblazoned with the Falcone logo—so was the drinks menu, and the bar mats, and anything else that had writing on it. Vito's rival had branded his new possessions as his own. Slamming home to her what had been taken from Vito…

There was an awkward silence, and Eloise knew she must speak again. Made herself do so. 'If…if you'd married your step-cousin, would you have lost the hotels?'

He shook his head. Tersely he answered, 'No. Marlene—my uncle's widow—would have handed me the shares after the wedding. That was her plan. Her way of getting me to marry her daughter, Carla.'

Eloise frowned. 'But why…?' She paused while the barman set up her drinks, then moved away. 'Why did she want you to marry her daughter? Why did Carla want to marry *you*? Was she in love with you?'

Was *that* why Carla had raged? Because of raging, furious jealousy?

But Vito was shaking her head. 'No, she was in love with another man—who'd just dumped her to marry another woman.'

A hiss escaped Eloise and her eyes widened with disbelief. The irony of what Vito had just said…

He was speaking again. 'I was to be her…her face-saver, I guess.' His voice twisted. 'Even if the only way she could make me do it was through her mother's bribe.'

Eloise was silent a moment, absorbing what Vito had said—and the bitter irony of his step-cousin reaching for him to assuage her pride, thereby causing Eloise's own galling humiliation at Vito's deceit. Then she reached for her orange juice, drank it down.

She spoke again—asked the question she had to ask. 'Vito, if you'd already made the decision to accept that… that bribe, to marry Carla and get your uncle's shares, what made you think it was acceptable to start a relationship with *me*?'

There was harshness in her voice, and she heard it—

but it was justified. Above everything, that was the one thing he could not defend.

But he was staring at her. 'Eloise... Marlene dropped her bombshell the first evening we got to Rome!'

Shock ripped through Eloise. 'You agreed to marry Carla *that night*?'

Violently, Vito shook his head. 'No! I told them it was insanity and walked out!'

Coldness pooled in her stomach. 'Yet the very next day you were trying to bundle me out of sight to Amalfi! Obviously you'd changed your mind about Carla by then—and decided to keep me as your convenient mistress!'

'No! Eloise—how can you *think* that? How *can* you?' He took a ragged breath. 'I just wanted you out of Rome—away from all the...the complications.'

He drained the last of his martini. Agitation possessed him—adrenaline was surging, and yet being reigned in simultaneously. Just having Eloise there, so close—so far—was a torment. And to what purpose?

When she's asked me all her questions she'll go. She'll still go. And I'll still be on my way to JFK...never to see her again...

'Out of Rome till *when*, Vito?' she was demanding. 'And what *for*? You were going to *marry* Carla!' There was a lash of anger in her voice now, and derision too. What the hell would the point have been of her staying down in Amalfi?

His eyes were on her. Like lead weights. 'No,' he said. 'I had no intention of marrying her.'

Eloise's face contorted. She had wanted to be calm, yet emotion was jumping inside her, replaying the nightmare of that scene in Rome. 'Vito, you said to my face that you were her fiancé!'

The line of his jaw was taut. 'I said it to get her out of there. To...placate her.' The memory of that hideous moment was like magma in his head. 'I needed her to believe I was going to go through with her mother's scheming.' He reached for his martini glass, but it was empty. 'I just needed *time*.'

'Why?' Eloise demanded in a hollow voice. Whatever Machiavellian games Vito had played, they sickened her. First rejecting Marlene Viscari's bribe, and then appearing to accept it.

And trying to keep me on a string as well...

'Time for Carla to calm down. She was totally strung out—manic!—you could see that for yourself! Given time, I desperately hoped she'd realise that marrying me would not solve her problems—would only make her more miserable. And once she'd seen that her mother would have had to abandon her ludicrous hopes of our ever marrying. It would resign her either to finally agreeing to my offer to buy the shares from her at a handsome profit— as I have been trying to do—or remaining the sleeping partner she's been since Guido's death. Then, finally, I'd have been free to come back to you. Free to—'

He broke off.

How can I tell her here, now, when she is barely being civil to me, that I thought she might be the woman I was falling in love with?

She saw the veiling in his eyes, felt his withdrawal. It hurt like a splash of acid on her skin. There was so much distance between them—so much had parted them.

Including her own impetuous flight, and her refusal to listen to him. She had refused to give him time to explain that ugly scene. Had stormed out instead, denouncing him, judging him unheard. Compunction smote her.

He was speaking again, and she made herself listen.

'But after you'd left—disappeared—and made it totally clear that you wanted nothing more to do with me... He hesitated, then continued heavily, 'It seemed...less important to refuse Carla.' He took a sharp intake of razoring breath. 'So I agreed to marry her after all.'

His eyes flickered away, his jaw tightening.

'It seemed the fastest way to get the shares out of Marlene's clutches. Carla could have her glittering, face-saving wedding, but six months later she'd apply for an annulment on the grounds of non-consummation and we'd go our separate ways. I'd keep Guido's shares—and pay Carla a premium price for them.'

Eloise looked at him. 'You told me there was no wedding.'

'In the end I couldn't go through with it.'

Eloise's eyes were piercing. 'Why not?'

The silence stretched between them. She saw his hand clench on the surface of the bar, then relax forcibly.

'It would have been dishonourable,' he said eventually, in a low, strained voice He did not look at her while he spoke. Could not.

There was silence again. Thick, impenetrable. Eloise could feel a vein throbbing at her temple. She looked at Vito, letting her eyes rest on him, trying to see him clearly—not with the haze of heady romance that had bathed him while she was whisked from one European city to another, and not with the bitter anger she'd felt at his betrayal. A betrayal he had not intended, but had committed all the same.

Her eyes rested on a man prepared to marry a woman solely for financial advantage. Because he'd been bribed to marry her.

A man prepared to sell out, to put profit before people.

That was the taint in his character that would stain him for ever. Impossible to love such a man, to want to make a family with him…

Emotion stabbed at her again, and it made her voice harsh as she spoke again.

'You couldn't resist it, could you?' she said tautly. 'You imagined you could string Carla along, stash me away somewhere secretly for the duration, get hold of the shares, and come up smelling of roses!' Her voice filled with derision, lashing her own stupid hopes as well as him. 'Still, you turned the bribe down in the end, so at least your conscience is clear now!'

A laugh broke from Vito—harsh and brief. 'I hardly think so,' he said.

He caught the barman's eye—beckoned him over, ordered another martini. To hell with it—he was going to hell in a handcart here, and he might as well go there with another martini in him! It might numb him against the ride...

Eloise was frowning. 'What do you mean?' she demanded. 'You did the decent thing in the end, Vito—'

He turned towards her. His expression was savage now. '*Did* I? I'll go and tell that to my father's tombstone, shall I?'

She was staring at him. Staring at him with clear blue eyes—as clear as her conscience.

'What do you mean?' she said again. There was blankness in her voice. Incomprehension.

Vito seized the second martini as it was placed in front of him. It burned as he swallowed. Burned like the memory he did not want to remember. But which had forced itself into his head.

'*Get the shares back, Vito, my son, my son! Any way you can—whatever the cost...pay any price...promise me—promise me!*'

His father's breathless, stricken voice, his dying gasps...imploring him, begging him to promise.

Time sucked him back to the present and he slid his eyes away from the clear blue eyes gazing at him with incomprehension.

'When my father had his fatal heart attack,' he said, his voice dull, his gaze fixed on the way the green olive in his martini was speared—as *he* had been speared, 'I rushed to the hospital. The doctors said he had little time left. My mother was there—'

He broke off.

'It was…very bad. My father wanted to speak to me, say his last words to me. He…he begged me…made me promise that whatever it cost, whatever price I had to pay, I would get back the shares his brother had left to Marlene. He said I must not lose the legacy that four generations of our family had built up from nothing. I must not betray that. I must do whatever it took to get the shares back into Viscari possession. Keep them safe.'

His eyes darkened.

'That day—the day you left me…' he took another razoring breath '… Marlene threatened to sell her shareholding to Nic Falcone if I didn't immediately announce my engagement to her daughter.'

Eloise stared, shock ravaging through her. 'She did *what*?'

That wasn't a bribe—that was blackmail. Blatant, vicious blackmail. *Forcing his hand in the most ruthless way imaginable.*

Vito looked at her. His eyes were blank. 'That's why Carla confronted you—demanded I tell you I was her fiancé. And that,' he said, biting the words out viciously, 'was why I could not deny it. I had to *somehow* keep my promise to my father.'

He reached for his martini again. Took another burning slug.

'A promise I betrayed when I jilted Carla at the altar. Marlene sold the shares to Falcone that evening.' His expression twisted. 'So, no, my conscience is *not* clear—it never can be. *Never!* I can argue with myself all I like, say that I was right not to marry Carla, but it doesn't absolve me of breaking my promise to my dying father! *Nothing* can—'

He fell silent, hunched over his martini glass. Seeing before him only the contorted face of his father, hearing only the broken, stricken sobbing of his mother, feeling only the desperate, frail clutch of his father's failing grip on his arm as death swept over him and took him from his wife, his son, for ever.

And then, faintly, he was aware of another touch on his arm. A gentler one now. And a voice speaking.

'You gave this promise to your father on his deathbed?'

There was questioning in the voice now. But not accusation. Something else.

The voice was speaking again. 'Vito, is *that* why you agreed to Marlene's blackmail?' She would not call it a bribe any longer—it had not been a bribe. 'Because of that deathbed promise?'

His face convulsed. 'Why else?' His voice was as tight as wire pulled to breaking point. 'And now I've betrayed it—betrayed my father. Lost the hotels—broken my promise to him!'

The hand on his sleeve pressed, and he felt a warmth coming through the pressure.

'Vito—listen to me—*listen*.' There was an urgency in Eloise's voice now, as she spoke, but then she paused. She could not bear to see Vito like this—so…so stricken, so self-accusing.

I have to make this right—I got it wrong, yet again! And now I have to make it right. For Vito's sake—

And for more than his sake? No—no time for that now. No time for speculation or thinking about herself. Or thinking about—

She cut her thoughts off, focusing on this moment alone.

'Listen to me,' she said again.

She saw him about to lift the martini glass and stayed him with her other hand, letting it close over his. Letting the touch of his fingers under hers surge like an electric current through her. He turned his head to look at her, and his stricken eyes made her throat tighten.

'You should not have had to make that promise,' she said. She took a breath, ragged in her lungs. 'Because...' she took another breath, her eyes fastening on his '...this situation is not of your making. *Or* your father's! Aren't you forgetting one tiny little detail? It was your *uncle* who chose to leave his shares to his widow! Whatever his reasons for doing so, *he* has to take the responsibility for what has happened now! This hotel—' she gestured around her '—and half of the rest of them now belong to your rival—well, that's *his* doing, not *yours*.' She took a steadying breath. 'Don't you see that, Vito?'

He was staring at her, frowningly. As if what she had said made no sense. She had to *make* him see it. So she plunged on, emotion streaming through her.

'Vito, tell me—tell me right now: if your father hadn't extracted that terrible deathbed promise out of you would you have entertained for one moment Marlene's blackmail?'

He shook his head, his mouth tightening to a grim line. 'No,' he said.

It was as if a garrotte around her throat had loosened, and she felt the blood flow through her veins again, rich and warming. Releasing so much from her. She gave a long, slow exhalation, her eyes never leaving his.

Her expression changed, thoughts crowding into her head. Maybe Vito's father had been dying, but he'd placed a burden on his son that had almost destroyed him. Crippled him with unnecessary guilt.

Her eyes hardened. Hadn't her own father done the

same? Making her think all through her childhood that if only she'd been a boy he would not have abandoned her?

Vito's voice cut across her familiar darkening thoughts.

'Do you…do you really mean what you said about it being my uncle's responsibility, not mine?' He spoke as if he could not bring himself to believe what she had said. Did not dare to believe it.

'*Yes!*' she replied immediately, without the slightest hesitation, and with vehemence in her tone.

He felt her hand squeeze tightly over his, reinforcing the vehemence of her voice.

'Didn't he think his widow might use her ownership of his share of the hotels malignly?'

Vito was silent a moment. 'I think,' he said slowly, 'that he hoped it might make us…my parents, myself…accept Marlene more. Maybe,' he said, and the words were being dragged from him now, 'if we'd been more…welcoming to her, she wouldn't have felt she had to… I don't know… prove she was part of the family in her obsession with me marrying her daughter.'

'Vito—don't think about it any more. It's over—it's gone. Don't let it haunt you any more—please!'

She took a breath, then paused, her face working. Part of her, somewhere inside her head, was thinking how strange it was that she should be here, comforting Vito. Yet it felt right too. *So* right.

There was something else she needed to say. Something she had to acknowledge.

'Vito—' She took a breath, knowing she needed to say what she had to say *now.* 'Now…now that I understand what was actually going on—not just what you did about Carla, but *why*—and what the whole grim, ghastly situation was, and the horrendous pressure you were under to sort out a mess which was *nothing* to do with you, I know…' She swallowed. 'I know I have been…unfair on you. I judged you too harshly. And...and I'm sorry, Vito! I'm truly sorry—'

She broke off, her voice twisting, not able to say more. A heaviness was crushing her. Emotions were roiling. Emotions she did not want to think about—not now. They were too much...

Gently, she felt him squeeze her fingers.

'And I,' said Vito, his voice low, intent, 'am truly sorry too.' His voice changed. 'If I could take back time—do it differently—I would have told you sooner. Explained the situation. '

His expression was changing. If he had done that— if Eloise had said to him in Rome what she had said to him now...

If she had shown me that it was not up to my father, or to me, to sort out what Guido had done! Not at the price I had to pay for it!

And though it haunted him still—not going through with the promise he'd made his father in order to set his mind at rest—he knew that Eloise had set him free from the guilt that had consumed him since he had walked away from Carla. His eyes rested on Eloise. There was gratitude in his face, and wonder, too, that it was the woman he had wronged who had given him this gift now.

Instinctively, without thinking, only knowing it was an imperative he could not halt, he turned her fingers in his, lifted them to his mouth, brushed them with his lips after a dip of his head towards her.

'Thank you,' he said. Softly. Gratefully.

He felt her hand tremble in his, felt her slip her fingers free, saw her clutch at her glass, busy herself with taking a gulp.

'I'm sorry—I should not have—' He broke off, contrite.

Her eyes flared back to his, her head shaking. 'No— *I'm* sorry—' She took a breath. 'Vito—'

She couldn't say any more. The brush of his lips on her hand was quivering in her head, and she could feel her heart-rate quicken. She swallowed, looked away, set down her glass.

Vito was speaking again, saying her name.

'Eloise—' He stopped abruptly. His brow furrowed, uncertainty flickering in his eyes.

She saw him take a breath. Her quickened heart-rate was not slowing down. The room seemed hot suddenly, despite the cooling chill of the air-conditioning.

'Eloise—' He said her name again. 'Tell me—if you want me to go, leave you alone now, for me to go back to Italy, then I'll do so. I'll take the first flight out and I won't trouble you again.' He paused, and it was as if his eyes were pouring into hers now. 'But if…if you think that maybe there's something left…something of what we had…something that can become—'

'Become what, Vito?'

She found her throat dry suddenly—so, so dry. Emotions were scissoring inside her. It had been so easy to hate Vito—so easy to condemn him for what he'd done to her, to write him out of her life, her future.

But now… Seeing him this afternoon, for the first time in so long, she had been in a state of absolute turmoil, shredded inside with conflicting emotions that seemed to contradict each other, override each other, cancel each other out. But she had found no resolution. None.

I've forgiven him for what he did, and yet—

A sense of wariness possessed her. Once, in a different lifetime, she had given herself to Vito, rushed off with him to whirl her way through a haze of carefree weeks, soaring in new-found ecstasy with him. But then she had crashed and burned. And her life now was totally different—changed completely for ever. A new future awaited her—one that she must bend all her powers to in order to get it right, bringing responsibilities she could never abandon. She could no longer afford to be impulsive...

I have to be careful this time—I have to be!

She felt wariness claw at her again, but even as it did she felt her heart beating faster as she gazed at him, drinking in everything about him the way she always had... from the feathered sable of his hair, to his long, ink-dark eyelashes, the beautiful line of his mouth, the elegant length of his hands, the superb cut of the bespoke designer suit sheathing the lean, muscled body that she knew so intimately...

She felt the rush of her blood, felt heat curl in her body. Her heart cried out to him.

Vito—oh, Vito—how much I've missed you!

But she had to fight it down—she *had* to! She couldn't just succumb, as she had at that first fateful moment of falling at his feet.

I can't do that again. I can't. I mustn't. Too much is at stake—far too much.

He was speaking, and she made herself listen, dragged herself out of the swirling confusion in her head.

'I don't know, Eloise,' Vito said. 'I don't know—but I want to find out. That's why I came—why I had to find you.' He swallowed. 'At the very least you had to know *why* I'd done what I had. I owed you the truth, even if it changes nothing.'

She shook her head, negating his fear. 'But the truth— the real truth—*does* change things, Vito. It changes so much—'

His eyes were holding hers, intent, questioning. 'But does it change enough?'

She slid her gaze away. 'I don't know.'

They were his own words, echoed back.

Just for the briefest moment she felt the touch of his fingers on her hand, as it lay inert on the bar-top.

'Perhaps,' he said quietly, 'we might try and find out.'

He shifted position, leant towards her slightly. There was a quickening in his voice as he spoke.

'Eloise, would you have dinner with me? Just dinner. Here—now. Just so we can… I don't know…talk things through, maybe? Or maybe *not* talk them through. Maybe just have a companionable meal together? See how we get on? I won't pressure you—you have my word. And besides…' He looked at her now. 'Pressure is the *last* thing we need now—either of us.' He took a breath. 'So, what do you say?'

There was a diffidence in his voice, an uncertainty. It struck her that never had Vito *ever* sounded uncertain before. Unsure of her response.

But he always knew what my response was going to be, didn't he? He knew I'd just acquiesce instantly, totally! Go along with everything he said, everything he wanted!

A poodle—that was what her plain-speaking mother had called her. Jumping up eagerly every time he said, *Walkies!* He hadn't been arrogant about it, or demanding, but she'd always gone along with him in everything. She'd kept telling herself to be careful, but in the end she hadn't been careful at all, had she?

But now?

What was the truth of it? What was the truth of how she felt about Vito? How could she know?

All she knew was that she had to find out. Because now, with the future she was facing, it was essential for her to make the right decision about Vito—about what she meant to him and he to her.

And what he would feel when he—

No, that was too far, too fast. For now this was about themselves, only that. That was what she must first discover.

So, slowly, she nodded her head. Saw his eyes flare

with relief, with gladness. Felt a little lift inside her in response.

He lifted a hand, had the barman scurrying over to him.

'We'll be dining here,' he said. 'We'd like the menu, please.'

A minute later the maître d' glided out of the restaurant, greeting Vito with respectful familiarity, assuring him that standards were every bit as high now, despite... He grimaced, left it at that. Being tactful about the change in ownership.

Five minutes on and they were seated at their table, their choices for dining made. A strange, powerful sense of familiarity encompassed her as she sat across the table from Vito—as she had sat a hundred times, in a score of Viscari Hotels across Europe. Yet again she felt emotions tumble about inside her head, jumbling the past and the present. So familiar—and yet utterly changed.

But it feels good to be here with him...

Emotion flickered like a candle in her head, casting light and shadows.

It feels...right.

She veered away from the thought again, knowing with a steadying breath that above all she must be careful... cautious. The day had brought so much turmoil to her...

She took another little steadying breath. Vito was right—they needed calm. That was it. Calmness, ordinariness. Ease...

No pressure. No pressure at all.

She felt herself steady and the candle ceased to flicker, burning calmly instead.

When the chosen wine arrived, instinctively Eloise moved to cover her glass. She sensed Vito's eyes, curious on her, and gave an awkward smile.

'Empty calories,' she said, knowing she must give a

reason. Then, with sudden decision, she took her hand away, let the sommelier fill her glass. Half a glass would not hurt her.

She felt Vito's eyes on her, warm now, and was aware that his gaze was sweeping over her figure. It filled her with self-consciousness, and she was glad her top was as loosely cut as it was, despite her gain in weight being only slight.

'You look beautiful,' he said, his voice as warm as his gaze.

Eloise felt colour stain her cheeks. 'Don't—' she said. It was half a whisper, half a plea.

Immediately his expression changed. 'I'm sorry—I have no right—'

She shook her head. 'No—no, it's not that. Please, I'm sorry— I—'

He held up a hand. 'We'll keep this light,' he said. 'No pressure, I said, and I meant it.' His eyes were soft with humour, half-rueful, half-conspiratorial.

Her own gaze softened. 'Thank you,' she said. The flare of colour faded and she took a mouthful of wine. The chilled crisp Chablis tasted so good, and she set the glass down with appreciation and regret. Even without her own compelling reason to avoid alcohol, drinking too quickly like this with Vito was the last thing she needed. She needed to keep her senses set to 'sensible'.

She watched him take a mouthful himself, then look across at her. Saw him take a deliberate breath.

'So,' he said, 'how did you end up with that little bundle of energy, young Johnny, to look after?'

The humour was uppermost in his voice now, and Eloise gratefully followed his lead. Clearly he wanted to talk about things that were not imbued with deep, heavy emotions, with no troubling memories of a past that had gone so wrong. No pressure, he had said, and she was glad of it.

'It was a contact through my mother,' she said. 'She knew the Carldons were looking for a new nanny and put me forward.'

'Your mother lives in New York?'

'Yes, in Manhattan. She works downtown. I'm staying at her apartment tonight.'

Why had she said that? Was it to let him know not to have any expectations? What was she *thinking* of, entertaining such a thought? She focused hurriedly on what he was saying in reply.

His glance flickered towards her. 'I didn't know she was American,' he said.

Eloise shook her head. 'She isn't—she's British. Or at least she was *born* British. Maybe she's taken US citizenship by now—I don't know.' She gave a slight shrug. 'We don't communicate a great deal now—not that we ever did, really.'

She could not hide the sardonic tinge to her voice as she said that.

Vito heard it, and wondered, but did not follow through. *No pressure*, he'd promised, and he would keep his promise. So all he said was, 'If I'd known she lived in New York I guess I'd have tried to find you that way first.' He paused a moment. His eyes on her still, but slightly veiled. 'You never told me—'

She met his gaze head-on. '*You* never told *me* about your aunt having half the Viscari shares and holding them over your head.'

For a moment Vito didn't answer. Then he said slowly, 'We never really talked much about our families, did we?'

She bowed her head. 'No, we didn't.'

There was a silence. Vito took another mouthful of wine. Strange emotions were building in him, but he wanted to disperse them. He didn't want things getting heavy—not again.

Deliberately he lightened his voice as he set down his glass. Reverting to a safer subject. 'Young Johnny's definitely a cute kid,' he said, his voice upbeat now. 'And he definitely likes cars!'

'Especially fast ones,' Eloise answered dryly, following his lead and grateful to do so. She felt as if they were skating on paper-thin ice, and right now she wanted the security of dry land. Easy subjects. 'His father owns quite a few.'

'John Carldon...' Vito mused, recalling the brief introductory exchange with Eloise's employer earlier that day. 'Is that the banking Carldons?'

'Oh, yes,' answered Eloise, even more dryly.

She paused. Should she say this? There were overwhelming reasons not to—but powerful ones to do so.

Conflict swirled in her. Then she spoke. 'He...he mentioned to me that...that maybe you'd like to come over some time. He said he'd see to it that there were people invited who might be...ah..."useful" to you. You know—about the hotels, what's happened to them...'

Vito smiled, slightly in surprise. 'That's good of him,' he said. 'My task for the next few years is going to be raising finance for expansion. It can't be fast, obviously, but I have to show the world that Viscari Hotels may be down, but I'm far from out.'

There was grimness in his voice, a resolution that Eloise could not be deaf to.

'Can you do it?' she asked tentatively.

Vito looked at her. 'Yes,' he said. There was no hesitation in his answer—not the slightest. *'And,'* he went on, and the note of resolution was even more pronounced, 'I will do it with a lot less weight on my shoulders—a lot less self-inflicted guilt, thanks to you.'

His eyes went to her, softened.

'Eloise, thank you—thank you for what you said to

me. You've made it possible for me to look ahead instead of looking back.' He shook his head. 'I can't undo what my uncle did…' He eyed her with mixed emotion. 'And I do still feel conflicted about the promise I made my father and the circumstances of it. But I also know that there is enough of my grandfather and my great-grandfather who founded Viscari Hotels in me to mean that I can, with patience and determination, get things back to what they were. Falcone won't get the better of me! I won't let him!'

His voice changed, lightened.

'And if your boss is happy for me to talk investment with him and his contacts, I'd be delighted to accept any social invitation he names!' His eyes rested on her, wariness in them. 'Would that be all right with you, though, Eloise? I wouldn't want to impose my company on you.' Vito was frowning. 'I don't want to cause any awkwardness,' he said.

'You won't,' she assured him, realising what he meant. 'The Carldons are very easy-going. And I guess Johnny might be allowed to mingle for a short time—just to check out all the guests' cars, you understand!' she said humorously. Then, daringly, in the same humorous voice, she went on. 'While all the female guests check *you* out, Vito!' she said mischievously. 'Laura Carldon is already sighing over you!'

He laughed, but there was a questioning look in his face now. 'And what about *you*, Eloise?'

His eyes, so deep, so dark, searched hers, and she felt their power, felt a wash of weakness go through her—a wash of longing.

She felt the colour flush her cheeks and she tore her eyes away. But she could not tear her ears away.

'You know I have eyes only for you—and all my sighing will be for *you*, Eloise.'

Her gaze flew back to his, met it and mingled. She seemed to feel her heart stop in her chest. 'Vito—please, I—I...'

'I've missed you so much—'

There was a hollowness in his voice now. He moved to reach for her hand. He could not help himself.

Would she have let him take it? He did not find out—waiters were gliding up to them, serving their first course. Maybe it was good that they were—maybe it was good that it meant she did not have to answer him.

Instead, as they were left to themselves again, Vito made himself start another innocuous line of conversation—something anodyne about New York and all its frenetic busyness.

I promised her no pressure—just an easy evening, easy dining. Nothing more than that.

But even as he made himself remember that he could feel emotion coursing through him. Feel hope flaring. Desire kindling.

But was desire enough?

What is she to me? Be careful, Vito, he warned himself. *You came here to discover that, and when she rejected you again you were about to part with her for ever. So just because now she has softened towards you, don't just tumble down into being blinded by her beauty! You can't afford to get this wrong again.*

They were words he had to keep reminding himself of as the meal progressed. With deliberate effort he kept the conversation away from anything that might be heavy. And as the time went by he felt the tension ebbing away from him, little by little. Felt himself relax and slip back into the kind of easy companionship that they had always had.

At one point he even found himself leaning back, lifting his wine glass and saying, 'Do you remember, in Barcelona, when—?'

Whatever the recollection was, it seemed to come naturally, and she answered just as readily, capping it with another from a different city—one of so many they had visited in their weeks together as they'd toured the Viscari Hotels of Europe. He laughed at what she'd said, and felt a kind of gladness washing through him.

She was relaxing before his eyes, her gaze mingling easily with his, her smile ready, her conversation eager, enthusiastic. As if the time separating them had never been…

'Coffee?' Vito's enquiry came with the lazy lift of an eyebrow.

Eloise gave a replete sigh, glancing at her watch. Did she have time for coffee? Her eyes went back to Vito. She didn't want to leave now.

It feels good to be with him—so good!

Emotion caught in her throat but she suppressed it— and the memories that went with it.

'Do you have to go?'

Vito's voice brought her back to the present, and with a little start, a flush in her cheeks, she shook her head. 'Not quite yet,' she said.

They ordered coffee, and Eloise was conscious that she was lingering over it. Conscious, too, of Vito sitting opposite her, his gaze on her. Their conversation was desultory now as, little by little, breath by breath, she felt the atmosphere change between them. Charge and thicken.

He signed the bill, thanked the staff for their meal, then brought his gaze back to Eloise. She was sitting there, poised, two lines of colour running across her cheeks, flushed—and not just with the half-glass of wine she'd drunk. Her beauty overwhelmed her, drowned his senses.

His eyes met hers. He could no longer resist saying what was burning in him. 'I would ask you to stay,' he said, his voice low, husky. 'But I said no pressure. And

you had my word on that. Although for all that...' He
shook his head, as if there was nothing he could do about
it. 'For all that, I cannot deny what I would ask of you had
I not given you that promise.'

She saw him draw breath, felt the force of his eyes
pouring into hers, felt the heat in her cheeks, and she was
unable to tear her gaze from him as he held it with his, so
effortlessly, as he had from the very first...

'I can't...' she breathed. 'I mustn't.'

He looked at her still. 'I know,' he said. The husk was
still in his voice, but there was regret too. 'It would not
be...wise.'

He shut his eyes for a moment, as if to recover his
senses. Then opened them again. A different expression
was in them now.

'Eloise—everything went wrong for us in Rome. When
we arrived all I wanted was time with you, to get to know
you, explore our feelings. But time was what we never had
together there. So...' He took a breath, his eyes intent, focused on her totally. 'Maybe we could have time now—'

Slowly, she nodded.

His expression lightened. 'I'm planning on visiting the
Caribbean. Falcone isn't interested in any Viscari proper-
ties there, and I need to reassure my staff on that score.
And I need to visit the site of the latest Viscari Hotel, on
Ste Cecile.' He made a wry face. 'It was where I wanted
to take you when I was so desperate to escape Rome!'

He shook his head, as if to shake the grim memory
from him.

He looked straight at Eloise. 'Would you come there
with me now?'

He saw rejection in her eyes—but saw conflict, too,
and a flash of longing.

'Oh, Vito... I can't take any time off now—the Carldons need me.'

'Then may I come and visit you out on Long Island?'

Slowly she nodded. 'I... I usually have the weekends off, when the Carldons are home with Johnny.'

He smiled. His familiar warm, sweeping smile. 'This Saturday?'

Again, she nodded slowly. She could feel her heart-rate quicken, and made herself check the time.

'I have to go now,' she said. She looked across at him. 'Vito—it's...it's been good. Tonight—dinner... Just... just being with you. But I... I...well...please, I can't rush things... I...'

She fell silent, let her eyes drop. Emotion was thick in her throat.

This time yesterday I had no idea that tonight I would see him again. That all my feelings for him would be so different! That all my anger would be purged! That I'd be here with him, like this... Like I used to be...

But *was* it like it used to be? It couldn't be, could it? Not any more. Never again could there be just a casual romance between them. Now it could only be all...or nothing. And she did not know which. Not yet.

She felt the touch of his hand on hers, lightly brushing it with his fingers.

'It's whatever you want, Eloise,' he said. His voice was soft, intent. Sincere.

Her eyes lifted to his and for a moment, a long, long moment, their eyes simply met—acknowledging, accepting.

'Thank you,' she whispered, her voice low.

Then she drew back her hand, picked up her bag, got to her feet as he did likewise.

'I'll get the hotel limo to take you to your mother's apartment,' Vito said.

But Eloise shook her head. 'It's OK, I'll take a taxi. I'm used to New York now.' She smiled.

He walked her to the kerb as the doorman summoned one of the waiting cabs, then helped her in.

As she lowered herself into the seat he felt a rush of longing for her. How beautiful she was—how truly beautiful! From her golden hair to her long, long legs. Her slender waist and her full, ripe breasts, straining against the fabric of her top as she fastened her seat belt across her. Fuller and riper, surely, than he remembered...

He dragged his thoughts away. Made himself do nothing more than smile down at her as he closed the door, as she lifted a hand to wave him goodnight. The cab pulled off into the melee of Manhattan traffic. He watched it till it disappeared from sight.

Inside the cab, Eloise closed her eyes. Her head was in a whirl—and not just from the wine she was no longer used to. From something much, much headier.

Vito! Oh, Vito! My desire for you is as strong as ever! But I cannot just yield to it headlong!

Yet for all her self-admonition she felt the blood surge in her body, quickening her hectic pulse, heating her cheeks. Her eyes went to the window, to the traffic beyond, the neon lights and illuminated street signs, and they all blurred into a whirl of colour. Anguish filled her face. This time yesterday things had seemed so simple, the future so straightforward. Rigid, unforgiving—solitary. But now...

Now there was turmoil in her heart—turning her upside down, inside out, round and round and round.

A smothered cry came from her lips.

CHAPTER EIGHT

VITO PACED RESTLESSLY across his bedroom. He could not sleep. His mind was wide awake, replaying every single moment he had spent with Eloise that evening. Emotion jangled within him—one moment soaring, the next crashing, tangling itself into intractable knots within him. He'd tried to make sense of them, but it was hopeless.

He ran his hands through his hair, striding out into the lounge of his suite, stopping by the windows, staring out over the street below, and beyond that to the darkened mass of Central Park. As if he could see across the city to where she was—he did not know where precisely—at her mother's apartment.

Is she sleepless too? Is she thinking of me as I think of her? Unable to think of anything else at all?

It was a hope he kept on feeling, darting through him, keeping his heart-rate high. Longing filled him. For her to be so close—and yet so far!

Was it just desire that made him feel so? He knew desire was there—how could he not? It had leapt, fully formed, the moment he had set eyes on her, both that afternoon and then again that evening, as she walked into the bar.

Will I ever not feel desire for her?

The question hung in his head, and as he gazed unseeing at the cityscape beyond, seeing only the image that blazed like a jewel in his mind, he knew the question was unnecessary. The answer was foregone.

I will desire her all my life...

Even as he acknowledged it he felt another, deeper emotion well up beneath. His longing for her was not mere desire.

It is for her—for her herself! Everything about her—

He hauled himself away, feeling his heart pounding, hectic and strong. He did not know what name to give what he felt—knew only that it was an emotion that was the most powerful he had ever felt.

Resolved into a single word. A single name.

Eloise.

'All set?' Laura Carldon smiled at Eloise.

Eloise nodded, but a hollow feeling was emptying her insides. Her nerves were jangling.

Laura Carldon's smile widened. 'Great—you have a fantastic day with your gorgeous, gorgeous guy today! And, like I said, John and I are going to start looking for a replacement for you, now that—'

Consternation filled Eloise's face, making her cut across urgently. 'No—please—it's not necessary! I mean—it's too soon—I don't know—I just don't know!'

Laura Carldon looked at her straight. 'Ellie, Vito Viscari is giving you time, but you know...' and now her voice became pointed and her gaze penetrating '...there is only one outcome possible. You *know* that, Ellie—you know you do.'

Eloise's face paled. She knew why her employer was saying that—but it wasn't as straightforward as she thought it was. It wasn't straightforward at all! How could it possibly be?

To her relief, Laura backed off. She'd gone into big sister mode when Eloise had got back from Manhattan and blurted out everything about Vito, and her employer had been far more sympathetic to her predicament than her mother had been.

Eloise could still hear her mother's blunt advice ringing in her ears.

'You must do what you want, Eloise—and take the consequences of your decision. Just as I did. But it's your decision, not mine. What is it you want to do?'

But that was just it, wasn't it? she thought now, wretchedly. What *did* she want? And what did Vito want?

And, most importantly of all, what will he want when—? No, don't go there. Not yet. Not yet by a long, long way.

The hollow feeling scoured her insides. No, straightforward was the last thing it was.

'I've got to *know*, Laura!' Her plea was heartfelt. 'I've got to know what *he* feels. I've got to know what *I* feel! What we feel about each other—about…about *everything*!'

'Well, that's exactly why you need to spend time with him,' Laura Carldon said encouragingly. 'To start finding that out! An afternoon with him here on Long Island is ideal! Show him the sights, hit the beach, go shopping in the boutiques—have a nice long, lazy lunch. Have *fun*!'

In the hours that followed, Eloise heard her employer's admonition echoing in her head. Vito had arrived and been welcomed by Laura—she was casually dressed, but looking a carefully composed knock-out.

Laura's aside to Eloise of, 'OMG, he's *gorgeous*!' had been clearly audible.

And then Johnny had rushed out even more enthusiastically to greet the gleaming Ferrari Vito had rented while in the USA.

Eloise had climbed in and Vito had headed down the driveway, waving back at Johnny, hoisted up in his mother's arms, who had waved back mightily, mouthing, *Vroom! Vroom!* ecstatically.

Only as they turned out on to the roadway beyond the Carldons' extensive grounds did Eloise look at Vito in the confines of the car, punishingly aware of his presence so, so close to her. She felt her heart catch.

He was focusing on the road, and it gave her a precious moment to take in his gorgeousness—the feathered dark hair, the dark glasses, the chiselled profile, the way his cotton knit polo shirt moulded his leanly muscled torso, the glint of his gold watch at his wrist, the long length of his tanned bare forearm...

She gulped inwardly. The impact he had on her senses was as powerful—as overpowering!—as it had ever been. And by the same token she knew—had known from that first appreciative glance at her as he'd arrived—that he, too, was finding her just as appealing.

Thanks to her employer's insistence, she was looking just the part for a day out on fashionable Long Island—courtesy of Laura's own wardrobe.

'I'm keeping all this for next time around, but this will fit you perfectly now!' Laura had said, pulling out of her vast closet a pair of navy blue elastic-waisted trousers and a carefully constructed but very smart blue and white boat-necked, loose-fitting striped top, both with an extremely upmarket specialist fashion label. A pair of low-heeled white sandals and a straw shoulder bag completed her outfit.

With her hair pushed back off her forehead with a white headband, snaking down her back in a long plait, she looked, Eloise knew, both stylish and slim. And the appreciative glint in Vito's eyes confirmed it—sweeping her instantly back to a thousand memories of his eyes lighting upon her as she walked up to him in any number of his hotels across Europe. He'd only ever had eyes for her.

As if he'd read her mind, he glanced at her now as he drove, and even with the covering of his dark glasses she felt the force of his gaze.

'So, where shall we go?' he asked. There was a smile in his voice…around his mouth.

'The south coast is the most popular, and has the best beaches, but the north coast is less crowded and more historic,' she said.

'Well, I've never been to Long Island at all,' Vito said, relaxing his shoulders into the car seat that moulded his body, 'so it will all be great.'

He forbore to say that crossing a desert would be 'great' if he could do it with Eloise.

Eloise!

Her name billowed in his head, catching at his throat as his eyes drank her in, and he revelled in her presence at his side after the long, long months of being apart from her.

Did I really once take it for granted that I could spend any amount of time with her that I wanted—that she would always be there for me?

The thought was troubling. Its resolution less so. Never again, he knew with absolute certainty, would he ever take her for granted.

Did I win her too easily? Woo her too effortlessly? Did I assume she would wait to hear me out about the trap that Marlene had sprung on me—assume she would wait until I'd extricated myself from it?

Well, there would be no more assumptions about Eloise. He felt his pulse kick. She had the same impact on him now as she had had the very first time he'd set eyes on her, as she'd gazed up at him with her huge, beautiful blue eyes. He knew only that it was essential that he get this right. That they discover, once and for all, what they might be together. The most important question of all.

'OK,' he said, and deliberately he made his voice light and cheerful, 'tell me everything you know about Long Island!'

Eloise was glad of the lead. Glad that they could just chat, in a friendly, unforced way, about somewhere that—just for a change, she realised—she knew more about than he did. Previously, while they'd been touring Europe, most of the cities they'd gone to she had never been to before. It had been Vito who'd been knowledgeable about them. It was curious to think that this time around it would be *her* telling *him*.

Perhaps it was more than curious—perhaps it was symbolic? Symbolic of the subtle but undeniable change in their relationship. She was no longer the compliant girlfriend, endlessly willing to be anything he wanted. For the first time she felt more... More *what*, precisely?

More equal. More... I don't know... More grown up? Less...reliant?

It was something to ponder. But maybe not right now. When she had time—time to think, to feel, to try and know her own mind. Her own heart.

She gave a little shake of her head. For now, like Vito, she wanted only to keep the day easy. Enjoyable. 'Fun,' Laura had said. Well, that was good advice.

'OK,' she began, 'so, originally Long Island was home to several Native American peoples. Then, as they were moved off by the incoming Europeans, it was settled as farmland, both by the Dutch and the English, and then in the nineteenth century the railroads expanded, bringing yet more settlers, especially at the New York City end—Brooklyn and so on. But by the end of the century the very wealthy New Yorkers were heading up here to build their massive mansions.'

She moved casually into a description of what she'd learnt about Long Island since arriving at the Carldons' to be Johnny's nanny. It seemed to work, and as she chatted, interrupted by questions from Vito, she could feel herself starting to lose the acute self-consciousness she'd had since they'd driven off. Unconsciously, it all became… familiar.

Easy.

Natural.

By the time they stopped for lunch, in one of the attractive and extremely well-heeled resort villages of the east end of the Hamptons, she felt for the first time that maybe—just maybe—Laura Carldon's instruction to 'have fun' might be just what she was doing. It was *good* to be with Vito again! His sense of humour was so attuned to hers, and the smiling glances he threw her way, the observations he made—all just seemed to come naturally.

As if we'd never been apart.

It was a strange, beguiling thought. And yet she knew, with a sobering reminder, that it could never be as it had once been.

But what could it yet be?

That was the question that haunted her. Yet even as she thought it she felt resistance. Sitting here in the late summer's heat, beneath the striped awning of the shoreside restaurant, watching the sun sparkle off the azure sea, the array of expensive yachts bobbing in the harbour, how *could* she be haunted by it? How could she do anything except what she was doing—enjoying being with Vito.

The answer to my question will come, and what will be, will be.

That was all she knew for certain. All she could know for now.

Vito leaned back in his chair, replete after an extremely good lunch of freshly caught fish, washed down with a cold beer. A light breeze lifted the heat, as did the shade of the awning. Across the table, sipping at iced tea, Eloise was regaling him with tales of the Vanderbilts and the Morgans, and all those other mega-rich Americans from the Gilded Age who'd built their huge baronial mansions on the Gold Coast North Shore.

'I believe some of the mansions are open to the public,' she was saying. 'They're really the closest the Americans come to having stately homes! In fact,' she went on, 'I think quite a lot of the mansions were decorated with the contents of French *châteaux* and Scottish castles that were shipped over here in the nineteenth century. Fireplaces, mirrors, panelling—that sort of thing.'

Vito made a face. 'Well, I suppose we Europeans should take that as a compliment! Raiding our history to create theirs!' he said lightly. His expression changed. 'Do you remember our visit to Versailles, that very first time in Paris? You wanted to see the Trianon palaces as well—both the Grand and the Petit—so we did the whole lot in one day!'

Eloise smiled. 'You were very forbearing,' she said.

'I wanted to please you,' he replied.

Her gaze flickered. *Had* Vito wanted to please her? Had he made an effort for her? Not just on that day, but throughout their time together? Did his air of charm and ease camouflage the amount of effort he'd put into their relationship?

Her mother's view was that it had been she who'd done

all the pleasing, who had gone along with whatever Vito had wanted. Maybe, though, that wasn't fair.

Just because I didn't notice it, it doesn't mean he wasn't doing it...

A little glow formed inside her, and her smile at him was warm. 'It was a wonderful day!' she said. 'I shall always treasure it!'

His dark velvet eyes softened. 'We had good times, didn't we?' he said.

She took another sip of her iced tea. 'Yes, we had good times,' she echoed. Her expression changed, becoming troubled. 'Is that what we're trying to do now, Vito? Recapture the past? Make today...and the next time you visit...like the times we had together?'

Eloise's eyes slid away, out over the sparkling blue water of the quayside. From here, Europe seemed so very far away. So very long, long ago.

Her eyes shadowed. 'We can't go back, Vito,' she said, her gaze returning to him.

She saw him give a quick, decisive shake of his head. 'I don't want to go back,' he said.

He paused, and she felt his eyes suddenly reaching deep inside her—felt it like a jolt of electricity passing through her innermost being. She felt emotion flex around it like a strong magnetic field, engendered by him.

He spoke again, his words clear. 'I want to go forward, Eloise. Into the future.'

She heard him speak, felt the slug of her heart, felt his gaze holding hers. She saw him lift his hand, gesture all around him.

'A future for the two of us.'

His eyes were fixed on hers. He could not take them from her. In his head his own words echoed—*'the two of us.'* That was what he wanted. A future with Eloise. Only Eloise. He knew that—felt it all the way through him with a certainty that was flowing through him now as if a sluice gate had opened. It was as ineluctable as the tide flowing in from the depths of the ocean, lapping at the shore.

He felt all his emotions—so turbulent, so torn—finally resolved, after so much confusion. *This* was what he wanted—he knew that now, knew it with a certainty that he could not deny or question. It was all coming together now, in this moment.

Emotion flowed with the tide of certainty in a powerful sweeping through his consciousness. He did not need more time, more wondering, more questioning. It was not necessary. He knew—he *knew*. Knew everything he needed to know about Eloise—about his feelings for her. More than desire, more than passion.

There is nothing she can say or do that will change that. I want my future—my whole future—to be with her. To be with Eloise.

It was a name he had said so often, and it had meant what he had not yet known—but now he did.

Eloise.

The woman he wanted—the *only* woman he wanted. The only woman he would *ever* want in his life.

I wondered if it was her—wondered if she could be for me, if we were destined to be together all our lives. And now I know. She is—she is that one.

The certainty of it seared through him. His hand dropped, seeking hers to turn it over in his, to mesh his fingers with hers—mesh his life with hers.

For a moment—so brief—he felt her hand tremble beneath his. And then she slipped it away, out of his grasp. The expression in her eyes changed.

'Do you mean that?'

Her voice was little more than a whisper, and the expression in her eyes was one he could not read—as if a fine veil had fallen across them, dimming them.

He took a breath. 'Yes—beyond anything. Beyond everything.'

He spoke in a low voice, but there was certainty in it, a clarity she could not misunderstand. He paused, holding that veiled expression in her eyes, feeling in his chest the thump of his heart, as if giving emphasis to every word he said.

'You may say this is too soon—too fast. But for me it is not. For me, Eloise, it has been in the making ever since you left me.' His eyes worked, showing a flash of pain. 'When you left—it hurt, Eloise. But I could not allow myself to give in to the pain—I had to continue with the bitter farce of my engagement to Carla. But the pain was there all the time, deep within me.'

He paused again.

'It was that pain that made me turn away from her on our wedding day—that gave me the determination to show that this was something I could not—*should* not— go through with. And that pain...' He took a breath, ragged now. 'That pain stayed with me all the while I searched for you—and it stabbed me yet again, deeper and more dreadfully, when, after I'd finally found you, you told me—again—to get out of your life.'

He paused once more, his eyes searching hers now, trying to pierce that fine veil that still masked them.

'There is only one time I do not feel that pain, Eloise. It's when I'm with you—'

He reached for her hand again, hardly aware that he was doing so, knowing only that it was a need within him he had to obey. And this time she did not withdraw from him. This time she let his fingers mesh with hers, fasten around hers. Warming his.

'And there is only one reason for that, Eloise—there

can *be* only one. Because you've become my life—the reason for it.' His hand gripped hers, his voice urgent. 'Eloise, make your future with me—make our future together.'

'Do you mean that? Do you truly mean it, Vito?'

It was the same question, the same doubt, the same low, strained tone of voice. The same searching of her eyes.

'With all my heart,' he said. 'We are so good together— we are so *right*! It's always been like that, Eloise—*always*! From the very start.'

Her expression changed. 'I was just one more leggy blonde in your life…' she said.

Vito shook his head, his thumb caressing the surface of her hand. 'Oh, no—so much, much more.' His voice was as caressing as his touch. 'Eloise, I *knew* there was something different about you—everything with you was so…so *natural*. So *right*.'

He took a breath, knowing what he had to say now.

'Eloise, believe me—please, please believe me—if you felt I ever took you for granted it was not so, not in the way you fear! Yes, romance has always come easy to me—I admit it, confess it. But you…you were always different. It was that sense of…of *rightness* between us. How we were together. It was that I took for granted, not you!' His voice changed, becoming darker, with a thread of pain in it. 'Losing you has shown me that all I want…all I crave…is to make my future with you. My precious Eloise.'

His eyes were soft as he said her name, as soft as velvet, and she felt their power over her senses…and her sense.

'It's too soon,' she faltered.

But her blood was surging in her body, quickening her pulse, heating her beyond the external heat of Long Island in the summer.

'But you're not saying no?' Vito's reply was quick, his eyes still holding hers.

Heat fanned out across her cheeks. Emotion was powerful within her. Impelling her onwards. Sweeping her forward on a tide, carrying her out of the safe harbour where she had taken shelter after the storm of Vito's betrayal.

But—whatever answer she might want to give—she had to hold back. She must not let herself be swept away—not again. Not now, when it was not just about herself. Or him.

Her eyes dipped. 'You said no pressure—' She could hardly get the words out.

Instantly she felt him acknowledge what she'd said. His hold on her hand slackened, relinquished her. He nodded, his mouth set, but resolute for all that.

'And I will abide by that. You have my word.' Briefly, he touched her knuckle with his forefinger. 'I have told you what I feel. I will not change, Eloise. I am here for you...for your future...if you will have me. Always. Whatever life brings us, I will be here for you.'

He took another breath and then, as if with a deliberate act of will, he reached for his beer, taking a last mouthful to finish it. She watched him—watched the strong muscles of his neck as he swallowed, watched the curve of his fingers around the glass. Heard the echo of his words inside her.

'Whatever life brings us...'

If that were true...

She felt emotion flare within her. Emotion that she dared not give a name to. Not yet...

He set down the glass, smiled across at her. An open smile, an easy smile. As if the intensity of their discourse had not happened at all.

'So,' he said, 'where shall we go after lunch?'

Relief filled her—and something more. Something that hovered over the rest of the afternoon like an aura around her, a golden haze that she wanted to immerse herself in. But it was a temptation she dared not indulge in.

Not yet… Not yet…

The most important question of all—the one she *had* to discover the answer to—still awaited. And everything would depend on the answer.

CHAPTER NINE

THE RENTED FERRARI crunched slowly along the gravel as Vito swung it up to the front door of the Carldons' house, turning off the engine. Silence lapped around them. He turned to Eloise. He was smiling, but she could see in his eyes a tension, a question.

For the rest of the day, as they'd taken their ease, exploring the far reaches of the island like tourists, they had kept things simple, light-hearted. Fun. Unpressured. But now, at the moment of their imminent parting, she could feel that pressure mount again.

'Will you think of what I've said to you?' Vito asked, his voice low, his eyes expressive.

Eloise's gaze flickered. 'How could I not?' she countered.

He nodded. 'For now, that is all I ask,' he said. Then his expression changed. 'I must fly down to Ste Cecile tomorrow,' he said. 'I can't postpone it any longer.'

'Of course,' Eloise said. Her gaze flickered again. 'Will…will you be coming back to New York afterwards, or going straight back to Rome?'

His answer was another question. 'Would you rather I went straight to Rome?' he asked.

His eyes rested on her, but she could see there was a veil over them. Her hand twisted on the handle of Laura Carldon's straw bag. She could feel her heart beating.

'I… I think you should come back to New York,' she

said. Her voice was low, as if she found speaking difficult. She made herself look at him straight. 'Because you asked me at lunch if…if I…' She swallowed. 'But then, you might change your mind when you're in the Caribbean.'

His voice cut right across her. 'No—I will not be changing my mind, Eloise! I meant what I said—I meant it with all my being! And nothing can change that—nothing!'

There was no veil in his eyes now, no hesitation in his voice. Only certainty.

He took her hand. 'I want no dissension between us ever again. I will never try to hide anything from you again, as I did in Rome. Nor will I hide my feelings for you.'

She felt colour flush along her cheekbones, saw long lashes dip over his dark eyes. She held completely still as his head lowered to hers and his mouth brushed softly on her lips, which quivered beneath his brief, caressing touch—a touch she had not felt for so, so long… As he drew back again his eyes held hers, as they had done so often before.

'Vito, I—'

Her voice was a breath, her eyes aglow—yet in his face was a wariness she knew she must not, dared not ignore. But what she was going to say?

The noise of the front door being tugged open made her start, and a small powerhouse of energy barrelled out on to the wide carriage sweep, closely followed by Laura Carldon.

With a resigned grin Vito opened his door, and a gleeful Johnny clambered in and settled himself on his lap, grabbing the steering wheel with enthusiastic cries of 'Vroom, vroom!'

Laura Carldon leaned on the open door. Eloise saw

that she was still looking a total knock-out, even though she'd simply spent the day at home.

'I couldn't hold him back any longer!' Laura laughed. She held out her hand to her son. 'Come on, Mr Trouble, out you get!'

Her son ignored her. 'Make it go!' he ordered Vito. Then, belatedly, he added, 'Please! Please! *Please!*'

Vito cast a look at Eloise's employer. 'Are you OK if I just drive down to the gate with him and back? I'll be very careful.'

'Yes! Yes! *Yes!*' shouted Johnny, adding another, 'Vroom! Vroom!' for good measure.

Laura smiled. 'You're a very lucky young man,' she informed her son, and she stood back and closed the car door for Vito.

'Sit quietly, Johnny,' Eloise instructed, 'or Vito can't start the engine.'

Good as gold, Johnny settled on Vito's lap, his hands still on the steering wheel. Vito started the engine and pressed the accelerator to let the engine give its characteristic throaty roar, then lessened it to start the car moving very slowly, his hands resting lightly over Johnny's, giving the little boy the sensation that he was steering. Johnny chortled happily to himself, clearly in his element.

Eloise watched them—the little boy sitting on Vito's lap, and Vito quite at ease with him, advising him to steere right as they veered left, and talking to him about the car. Her expression was strange…her gaze intent as she watched him interact with the little boy.

The expedition did not take long. Soon they were circling back to the front door again, and Vito let Johnny sound the horn in a satisfyingly loud manner before lifting him out of the car and handing him to his waiting mother. He climbed out himself, gracefully, opening the passenger door for Eloise to emerge.

Laura cast a grateful glance at Vito. 'Thank you! As you can see, Johnny's just a tad obsessed with cars!'

'Vroom! Vroom!' confirmed Johnny happily, and ran around driving an imaginary car.

Vito grinned indulgently. 'I think the English term is "petrol head",' he said.

Laura caught her perambulating son. 'Now, what do you say to Signor Viscari, young man?'

'Thank you, thank you, *thank you*!' Johnny said in a rush.

Vito ruffled his hair. 'You're welcome,' he said.

He glanced at Eloise. She was standing very still, just watching him. Her expression was very strange. As if she were both a million miles away and simultaneously totally focused on him. Absently, he wondered at it, then turned his attention to her employer.

'He's a great kid,' he said, and grinned, nodding at Johnny.

Laura beamed—both at his praise for her beloved young son and at being the recipient of Vito's mega-voltage smile. 'And you're great with him,' she responded. 'A natural. But then...' She smiled at him, but her eyes, Vito could not fail to see, had darted to Eloise, who still had that strange fixated look on her face. 'Italian men are famed for being great with children.'

There was a minute pause—so brief Vito wondered if he'd actually noticed it.

Then Laura went on, with distinct self-consciousness, 'You'll be a natural when it comes to your own!'

Her voice was light, but once again he was sure she glanced between her lashes at her son's nanny.

Then her gaze went back to him. 'Will you come in for drinks? My husband will be home soon from the golf course.'

He shook his head, made his voice regretful. 'Thank

you, but I'd better not. I'm flying down to the Caribbean tomorrow, to check on my latest build there, on Ste Cecile, and I must spend this evening touching base with my affairs back in Europe.'

Laura's face fell—but not, Vito felt, because he'd refused her offer.

'But you'll be coming back to New York?' she said quickly.

He saw her throw another swift look at Eloise, who was still standing quietly, her expression unreadable.

'Most certainly,' he assured her, his smile warm.

Laura's face relaxed. 'Great,' she said. 'And then you really must come over for dinner—or maybe brunch at the weekend.' She looked down at her son, who was tugging on her hand. 'Just wait a moment, Johnny…' she began.

Eloise was there instantly, galvanised into action. 'I'll take him,' she said, conscious that she *was*, after all, the nanny.

She turned to Vito.

'I hope you have a good trip tomorrow, and that everything is…is OK at the site, and with—well, everything,' she said, feeling awkward. Feeling a whole lot more than awkward.

'Thank you,' he said. 'I'm sure it will be. The build is all on schedule, and we're still on track to open as planned next month. Maybe,' he said, and now it was as if his eyes were speaking, 'you'll be able to take some holiday time round about then.'

'Definitely!' Laura's voice was enthusiastic. 'We'll make sure she's free.'

Vito smiled at her. 'Thank you,' he said.

It was what he needed to hear—he needed to know that Eloise would be free to come with him, to be with him.

If she wanted to.

But does she? Will she? Is what I said to her what she wanted to hear?

His eyes went to her now. She was hunkered down by Johnny, asking him about his day with his mother and Maria. Then her employer took her son's hand, talking straight to Eloise.

'Ellie, I'll take Johnny indoors—you say goodbye to Vito. No need to rush.'

Laura lifted a hand in farewell to Vito, with a final admonition for him to come over next weekend, and wished him a good flight south. Then she swept inside with Johnny.

Vito's eyes went back to Eloise, who'd straightened. She was clutching her straw bag tightly on her shoulder. He went up to her and took her hands, holding them lightly, his eyes only for her.

'Thank you for today,' he said softly. 'It has meant so much to me.' He took a breath. 'Think, I beg you, on what I have said. I mean every word, Eloise. I could not be more sure of them,' he said.

The grip on her hands tightened momentarily, and his voice deepened.

'I want you to be my future, Eloise—to be with me always, to make your life with mine. I have no doubts, no questions, about that. What happened between us—that nightmare in Rome—has only served to make me absolutely sure of that. *Absolutely* sure. You mean everything to me—and you always will.'

He gave a smile—a brief, flickering smile. 'Take all the time you need before giving me your answer. If it is when I return to New York—or even if it's later, or next year, or at any time—I will be ready for it.'

For one last, endless moment his eyes held hers and she felt their force, their power reaching into her, trans-

forming her. She felt again that shimmer of joy she had
felt in the car, before little Johnny had erupted upon them.

Her expression changed. *He'd been so good with him.*
Laura Carldon's description echoed in her head. 'A natural', she'd called him.

She felt her throat tighten suddenly. Then Vito was
lifting her hands to his mouth, one after another, kissing
each softly. She felt joy, deep emotion, felt a golden glow
encircling her—transforming her.

'Oh, Vito!' Her voice caught, and then it was her hands
that were tightening on his before, with a reluctance she
could not hide, she drew them from him, stepped away.

Emotion filled her, overflowed as she watched him get
back into the car, lower the window to crook his elbow
across it as he turned on the ignition. His eyes were on
her—warm, soft, filled with emotion.

'My Eloise,' he said, and in his voice was all the emotion that was in his eyes.

Then, with a wave of his hand, he engaged the engine
and the car moved away, crunching down the drive to
disappear through the open gates on to the road beyond.

She went on watching until she could hear it no more.

But inside her head she heard still the echo of his last
words to her.

'My Eloise.'

To her relief, Laura Carldon did not grill her about Vito.
Eloise needed mental privacy to let the turmoil inside her
find its resolution, and though she went through the motions of looking after her charge she knew her mind was
not really on Johnny.

With the Carldons in their Manhattan apartment mid-
week, there was only Maria, her beaming manner indicat-
ing that she was taking it for granted that Vito had flown
the Atlantic to claim Eloise as his own.

Yet Eloise knew it could not be that simple. She must not rush, nor make assumptions—must not, above all, be carried away with all the emotion swelling in her breast, hearing only that yearning echo of his words to her.

'My Eloise.'

Because it was not just about her—not just about the two of them. It could not be. It was about much, much more. Into her head came the image of her mother—falling so head over heels in love with her father. A love that had proved so disastrous in the end. And not just for her mother.

I can't make the mistake she did.

Far too much was at stake for that.

I have to be sure.

Restlessly, unable to sleep for all the thoughts and emotions circling endlessly in her head, she paced her bedroom, feeling the import of the decision she *had* to make. Not just the one she *wanted* to make...

Over the baby monitor she heard Johnny stir in his sleep. She smiled faintly as she thought she heard a murmured 'Vroom, vroom...' as he dreamt, doubtless of fast cars. She heard, too, in her head, Laura Carldon's voice, praising Vito's manner with her beloved son.

She pressed a hand to her mouth, feeling emotion surging up inside her.

Surely I can be sure of him? Surely I can?

When he was back from the Caribbean—when he came to see her again—she must delay no longer. She would put her future in his hands. Tell him everything. Everything that was in her heart and more—oh, so much more...

And with all my heart I hope he'll feel the joy that I do.

Her employer, having returned to Long Island on Thursday, made it very plain that she had no doubt that Eloise was making the right decision. The *only* decision, to her mind.

'You and Vito can have the run of the place till Sunday,' she said meaningfully.

Eloise's gaze veered away, her colour heightening.

'John and I are away Saturday night with friends, and Maria and Giuseppe will be at their daughter's that evening too. So you can have fun here, you and Vito, with young Johnny.'

Her expression changed. Took on that pointed look it had had when Vito had dropped her off.

'Ellie, you can see from the way he is with Johnny that Vito's going to be a *great* family guy—he is *definitely* marriage material, not just good for a tempestuous romance. He's a *keeper*, honey. So keep him!'

She swept off, not giving Eloise a chance to reply, leaving her words to echo in her head. A little knot formed in her stomach. Tomorrow—whatever came of it—she would know how her life would be. Her whole life.

She felt the knot tighten.

It stayed tight right up until the moment when Vito's Ferrari swept up the drive, shortly before lunchtime on Saturday. Johnny excitedly rushed her downstairs, where Vito was greeting Giuseppe warmly in their native Italian, handing him a bottle of champagne to chill. Her charge was pleading for another ride in the Ferrari.

Vito stooped down, ruffling Johnny's hair with an easy gesture. 'Definitely,' he promised him. 'But not right now, OK?'

Then he straightened and looked up towards the head of the staircase, where Eloise was poised.

His eyes blazed as they lit on her, and she felt their force. Reeled from it. Her hand tightened on the banister as if to steady herself. For steady she must be. This was not the time to rush down the stairs and into his arms...

In her mind's eye she was back as she had been the day Vito had first found her in Long Island, her heart thumping, pulse pounding with disbelief that he was really there, in the flesh, after all those anguished months since she'd fled Rome. How she'd stood paralysed and trembling, emotions knifing her from all directions.

How different it is now from then.

'Eloise…'

Vito's soft utterance of her name summoned her, and he stood gazing up at her as she started to head down towards him. She'd dressed with care that morning, not wearing one of her usual casual outfits she adopted when on nanny duty. Today—consciously—she wore a warm vermilion sun dress, smocked over her bust, with shoestring straps and a floaty calf-length skirt.

It had passed muster with Laura, who'd checked her out before she'd set off with her husband earlier.

'Ideal,' she'd said. 'And wear your hair down—at least until you go swimming.'

Eloise's expression had tautened. 'I can't swim! Not until—'

'Exactly,' Laura had responded, and there had been another meaningful look in her eye. Then she'd nodded. 'I want it all sorted, Ellie, by the time we get home tomorrow—understood?' she'd said, clearly in big sister mode. 'And I expect your engagement ring diamond to be the size of the Ritz, OK? Though maybe that's the wrong hotel, in the circumstances!'

She'd laughed, and swept off.

Now, as she made her graceful descent to the hall below, Eloise could feel the loosely gathered folds of her dress floating around her bare legs, her long hair falling like a waterfall down her back. Her make-up was subtle, but emphasised the blue of her eyes and the golden tan she'd acquired during the summer, and she knew, with absolute certainty, that the glow in Vito's dark, lambent eyes was for her and her alone.

And it always will be.

She felt joy lift inside her and a smile part her lips. She saw his eyes warm, and he stepped forward towards her. He took her hand and kissed it, murmuring to her. Behind him Giuseppe hovered shamelessly—ready, as Eloise was well aware, to report back as required to his wife Maria.

The lover come to claim his beloved—and have their happy-ever-after ending...

She felt that little lift of emotion again—and then behind it a downward drag, as if of deep water pulling at her. In her ears rang Laura's admonition, and she felt a longing inside her...a longing to tell Vito all she yearned to tell him.

But the timing must be right—perfect... Later—when we are alone...

Certainly not right now. Right now it was time to respond to Vito's arrival, and to listen to Giuseppe saying that he would serve lunch out at the pool house in half an hour. This gave Johnny an opening to demand that Vito come up and see all *his* cars—namely the extensive collection of toy vehicles that adorned his day nursery.

So the three of them duly went back upstairs, where Johnny and Vito got stuck into some intensive playtime. Eloise sat back, watching Vito sprawled on the carpet with her charge, entering into the childish spirit of racing toy cars—with appropriate vocal soundtrack. She felt a huge upwelling of emotion ballooning inside her.

'He's going to be a great family guy.'

Again, she could hear Laura's words in her head. And she knew them to be true. So, so true. Which meant...

The house phone went and she picked it up, then turned to Vito and Johnny. 'That's lunch,' she said.

They headed down to the pool, set amongst the spacious lawns of the Carldons' mansion, complete with its own pool house opposite.

Under the shaded terrace Maria and Giuseppe were setting out a lavish *al fresco* lunch. Maria, beaming from ear to ear, fussed over them as they took their places, chattering away to Vito in too-rapid Italian. Her eyes were only for him as his wickedly attractive smile brought the colour to her plump cheeks.

And to Eloise's as well—she could feel her stomach clench with raw, quickening desire.

Then Johnny's needs diverted her, and she had to pay attention to him, helping him to cold roast chicken and salad, letting him pour—carefully—juice from the iced jug at his place.

As she did so Maria and Giuseppe departed, and Vito hefted the opened champagne bottle from its ice bucket, gently pouring out generous measures for them both. He set hers before her, and lifted his glass to her.

'To us,' he said, and let his gaze rest on her.

The simple toast dared her to refute it—but she did not, and he felt his spirits soar.

Yes—she will say yes to me! I know she will. It is in everything about her—her whole attitude towards me, her eyes upon me, her smiling at me... It can mean only one answer for me. Yes—yes and yes!

He looked at her over his glass, watched her take a sip from hers, let his eyes mingle with hers, let the openness in her gaze let him in, welcome him. Warmth filled him—and a joy he had not felt before in all his life. How perfect everything was—how absolutely perfect!

Eloise—my Eloise!

Then a little voice was piping up indignantly. 'To me too!' Johnny said, lifting up his beaker with both hands.

Vito duly tilted his glass to him. '*Saluti!* To you as well, young Gianni! That's Italian for Johnny.'

'That's what Maria calls me!' Johnny exclaimed, pleased, and drank a hefty slug of juice.

Lunch passed convivially, with Johnny clearly in his element having both of them paying him attention. But for all the child-centred conversation Eloise knew that another conversation was taking place too—between her and Vito. A conversation that was leading towards only one answer. An answer that she would give later, when the time was right. Perfect.

But before that, inevitably, came a session of pool play.

Watching Vito strip down to his swim shorts, exposing his lean, sculpted torso, his long, powerful thighs, brought back that flush of colour, the raw rush of desire, of burning memory, to Eloise. Even as he disported himself with a gleeful Johnny in the water, with huge amounts of splashing and chasing, in a game involving a myriad of inflatable pool toys, Eloise could not take her eyes from him.

She'd used the excuse of being too full and too lazy to do anything but relax in a shady lounger, sipping at the last of her allotted glass of champagne, and it afforded her the wondrous opportunity to feast her eyes on Vito.

Vito, Vito, Vito!

Oh, how the memories rushed back—themselves in Europe, day after day, night after night! Yes, it had been a dream of a romance then—but now... Oh, now it was so, *so* much more!

Yet again, Laura Carldon's words sounded in her head.

'He's a keeper, honey, so keep him!'

And she would—she *would* keep him. Keep Vito close by her side, in her heart, all her life...*all* her life...

Surely what she desired so much would be! Surely all her fears were groundless, baseless! Surely Vito would sweep her into his arms with joy.

Emotion welled up in her, filling her, bringing joy and wonder to her whole being.

'I'm thirsty!'

Johnny's piping voice from the pool roused her from her reverie.

Effortlessly hefting the little boy up to the deck, Vito followed suit himself, and both of them came up to her. Eloise handed Johnny a beaker of chilled diluted juice, which he gulped down noisily, while Eloise wrapped him in a towel, sitting him down beside her on the lounger to pat him dry.

He handed back the beaker and gave a huge yawn.

'Time for your afternoon nap,' she announced.

It was Vito who carried him up to his nursery in the main house, then settled him on his bed with a light throw over him. As he fell asleep Maria's head came round the door. She announced that she would sit with him, and ushered Vito and Eloise firmly out of the nursery.

As they headed downstairs Eloise felt Vito's fingers slide between hers, catching her hand. The gesture felt so right, so natural. Her heart gave that little lift again.

Out by the pool house Maria had cleared away the remains of lunch, replacing them with a tray of freshly made fragrant coffee, and Eloise poured them both a cup. Vito sat himself down not on a lounger but on the padded swing seat, patting the place beside him. She took it without hesitation—but with a quickening of her pulse. Her eyes fluttered to his, then back to her coffee cup, and studiedly she sipped at the contents, burningly conscious of Vito at her side. So close—so close now…

As she bent her head slightly to drink she felt the soft brush of his hand down her back, smoothing the long fall of her hair. It sent a million shimmers through her.

She set down the coffee on the low table beside the seat, aware that Vito was doing the same on his side.

'Eloise…' The husk in his voice was audible in the sensual murmur of her name.

She turned to him—and reeled. The blaze in his eyes was open now, filling his dark, dark eyes, turning them to liquid fire. Desire was blatant in them. He did not speak, nor did she, as his other hand lifted to her. The tips of his fingers grazed the delicate outline of her jaw with a feathering lightness that sent those shimmers reverberating through her again. With infinite slowness, infinite gentleness, the tip of his finger shaped her mouth, and at her back she felt his hand press into the hollow of her spine, starting to draw her to him.

She should speak—halt him—should say to him what she must say…what she had been waiting to say, what she had waited so long to say but had dared not until she had known for absolute certain that to speak was right…

But his mouth was lowering to hers, her name was soft on his lips, and then his mouth was on hers, and her eyes were fluttering shut so she could take absolute focus on the bliss of the sensation of his mouth brushing hers—like water on a parched desert. Unconsciously her hand lifted to him, to glide around the strong column of his neck. She let her fingers splay into the silkiness of his hair, to mould the shape of his head to her palm as her other hand flattened against his muscled flank.

His mouth was opening hers, deepening their kiss, and she gave a little moan of pleasure in her throat. It seemed to shake him, so that he jerked her towards him, his hold on her strengthening.

'*Por Dio*, but I've missed you so much!'

His voice was thick as his mouth drew away fom hers momentarily, and she could hear the naked desire in his voice, bringing back a hundred memories—a thousand— of all their nights of passion. She felt faint, her blood rushing in her veins, sending heat to her core, and she could feel her breasts swelling, their peaks cresting. How long since she had felt like this in Vito's heady embrace? Too long—oh, too, *too* long.

Her breathing quickened, and with a hunger that his touch had released in her she pulled his mouth down to hers again wordlessly, knowing only that she wanted him, craved him, needed him now—*right* now.

He answered her need, crushing her mouth with his, sending a million nerve fibres into overdrive, catching at her lips with his, with skilled expertise, with mastery and possession. And she was his—oh, she was his—and he was hers, hers, *hers*.

For ever now—for ever he is mine!

The words soared in her mind, exultant. The world had gone—disappeared—the air and the sun had gone too. There was only Vito and herself. Only her body, quickening to his, aching for his possession as he had possessed it so many times before. She felt the muscles in her legs strain as she yearned towards him, wanting with a primal urgency to feel her swollen breasts crushed against him, to press her body against his.

Her need for him was answered, and he groaned, devouring her mouth yet more deeply. His hand left her face, stroked sensually down the column of her neck, palmed the rich swell of her breast, and she moaned with pleasure. His thumb caught at its crested peak and she moaned again, straining towards him. Then his hand was gliding still lower, down over her flank, cupping her hip.

Her thighs loosened and the heat in her core was melting her now, as she felt the rush of her own arousal. And then his hand was shaping that vee, pressing into it through the flimsy material of her sun dress with exquisite sensation as her hunger for him climbed and climbed. His long fingers splayed upwards, curving around the swell of her abdomen.

And then he froze.

Time stopped. Halted.

In a fraction of a second—less—he had pulled away from her, was staring at her with disbelief in his face. The material of her sundress was pulled taut against the curve of her body, outlining with absolute delineation those revealing contours.

Words in Italian broke from him. Disjointed. Shocked. Disbelieving.

As if pulled out of the drowning tide of physical desire, Eloise realised what he was seeing. What all the carefully chosen outfits she'd worn in his company had been designed to conceal. What now could be concealed no longer.

He jack-knifed to his feet, still staring down at her, horror-struck.

It was that horror-struck expression that penetrated her thoughts like some huge, heavy battering ram, shattering the crystalline delusions of her hopes. And then, even as it did so, his expression changed. Closed.

He took a step back.

'Is it mine?'

The cruelty of the words was like a knife. Slashing through what she had thought was between them. Had hoped, longed so much was between them.

But her fears had been right all along. That was the hideous, unbearable truth of it. The fears that had driven her from that moment in New York when she had discovered that her flight from Rome had *not* been the end of her affair with Vito. Could never be the end—because the consequences of it would be with her all her life.

All her child's life.

The child whose father was now staring at her with a look of horror on his face. Telling her what she had dreaded to know.

Rejection. Rejection just as my father rejected me.

The pain of it made her faint, but she must give an answer.

'I think you had better leave, Vito.' Her voice came from very far away.

'Do you carry my child?'

The vehemence in his voice was searing, and the burning in his gaze was upon her like a laser.

She looked at him, her expression twisting. There was a gaping hole inside her that was getting larger every second, swallowing her.

'Do you *really* think, Vito—' the words were gritted from her, each one heavier than a stone, harder than granite '—that I would have let you come near me again here in the USA if I had been carrying another man's child? Do you really think that?'

His expression changed. She could see it happening, see logic morphing through his eyes to create an entirely different expression. One that chilled her even more than his horror had chilled her.

'So when were you going to tell me?'

The question was tautly spoken, with a distant dispassion that made it sound almost remote. Yet there was nothing remote in the emotion that was surging through him now, leaping in his blood, his heart. Nothing remote in the voice that was crying out in his head.

She carries my child! My child—our child!

He felt faint with it…with the knowledge of it. With the wonder of it. But another emotion was slicing through him, freezing his face as she stumbled into her answer.

'Today. Later— I mean…' She swallowed, stumbling, stammering again, hardly knowing what she was saying so huge was the hole inside her, swallowing her. 'This afternoon. I was going to tell you while Johnny was hav-

ing his nap, but then you kissed me and…' Her voice
trailed off.

He did not reply, only went on looking at her. His face
was shuttered still, and it reminded her with a blow of
how he'd looked when she had come to him in the bar of
the hotel that was no longer his—that her mistrust of him
had caused him to lose, along with half of his inheritance.

Wary. He looked wary. As if she could do him irrepa-
rable damage. As if she already had.

Again.

She reached a hand towards him, but he stood too far
from her. 'Vito, I—'

There was urgency in her voice. Desperation. But he
would not hear it. Refused to hear it. Emotion was storming inside him, but he refused to hear that too. Refused everything except the harsh, harrowing question he wanted
to throw at her now. Even as he prepared to speak it he
knew it was not what he wanted to say. What he wanted
to do.

*Wrap your arms around her—sweep her to you. Hug
her closer than the child she carries so that you are inseparable from her, inseparable from your child.*

But his voice cut across all that.

'How could you not tell me the very moment you
knew? How could you keep it from me? *How?*' he demanded again.

Emotion stormed through him—and horror too.

'Dio mio,' he breathed as realisation hit him. 'I might
be married to Carla! Do you not see that? I could have
married another woman.'

Cold pooled in him. Had he not jilted Carla… The
horror of what he might have done, in total ignorance,
made him harsh.

'I could have married Carla and never known I had a
son, or a daughter! Were you *insane* to do such a thing?

To carry my child without my knowledge? To risk denying our child its father? How *dare* you do such a thing?' Anger lashed from him at the enormity of what she'd done. 'How *dare* you?'

The cold was pooling in him again, arctic in its horror. Had he not found her again—had he not come to America—she would have borne his child—*their* child—without his knowledge. A child who would not know its own father—who would be deprived of his love, his devotion.

Memory thrust into him of his own father, whom he had loved so much, and to whom he had been the apple of his eye, his beloved only child. There was memory and there was grief—always that stab of grief that would always be there—for the loss of his father, taken before his time. And now *he* might have been a father parted from his child—parted by his total ignorance of its existence.

I would not have known I had a child to love!

His mother, so despairingly bereft since his father's untimely death, would never have known she had a grandchild.

Pain convulsed him at the thought of what had so nearly been lost. A child bereft of its father, never to know its doting grandmother, to be raised in an alien land by a woman who thought it acceptable to deny a father his child...to deny her child a father who would love his child with all his heart and being.

'How *dared* you not tell me?' he hurled at her again.

His fury excoriated her, made her gasp with the force of it. She had never felt it before—never known it. She had always been the cherished one, the desired one, the wooed one, the one Vito had sought only to win her back. And now the tide of his fury was drowning her so that she could not breathe, could not speak, could do nothing but stand there, aghast, as it poured over her.

His was face was contorted as a harsh intake of breath ravaged his lungs. His mouth twisted as he spoke.

'We shall be married the moment it can be arranged. Our child will *not* be born out of wedlock. That is all that matters now. Nothing else.'

He saw her try to speak, but he would not let her. What could she say in her defence? *Nothing!* There was nothing she could say to justify her silence! Justify the risk she had run that he might marry another woman, lose his own child...

He plunged on, his voice knifing the air.

'All that matters is that you are pregnant with my child and that had I not found you, here in America, I would not have known about it.'

He looked at her, his eyes bleak.

'How could you do that, Eloise? *How?* Knowing all these months and never telling me! Keeping it from me? What kind of woman *does* that?'

He shook his head. A heaviness was crushing him. Crushing everything he'd hoped for, longed for. How could this be the woman he'd thought her to be? Longed for her to be?

He could not stay here—not now. He had to get away. The storm inside him was impossible to bear—impossible!

Her face was stark, as white as a sheet, and she was reaching towards him, imploring him with her very gesture.

But he held up his hands, backed away. 'I have to go,' he said, his voice staccato. 'I can't speak more now—'

He broke off, throat convulsing. He could not take this in—could not do anything except turn away from her, stride across the lawn, while in his head the blood drummed like a hammer in his skull.

He thought he heard her cry out, call out his name,

that same note of urgency in it, but he would not hear it. Would not—and could not. Could only reach the driveway, throw himself into his car. Gun the engine to hear it roar, deafening the roaring in his head. And accelerate away…away, away.

But in his head only one question echoed—pounded him.

What kind of woman keeps a child from its father?

The answer tolled in his head like a death knell—the death knell of all his hopes, all his longings.

No woman *he* could ever love.

CHAPTER TEN

SOMEHOW ELOISE SANK back onto the swing seat, her whole body shaking, trembling. How long she sat there, she didn't know. Time had stopped. Life had stopped. Everything had stopped.

Unconsciously, she slid her hand across her abdomen, feeling the telltale swell that had revealed the truth to Vito. A choke broke in her throat. Oh, God, this was supposed to have been the moment their future was sealed by the knowledge that their union was indissoluble, that they would be there for each other for ever! For each other— and for their child…

Telling him was going to be the most wonderful moment of all! The moment I declared how absolutely I trusted him, how absolutely I wanted to make my life with him!

Instead…

The choke came again, and then another, and then a sob, and then she was breaking into pieces, with sobs forcing themselves up through her stricken throat, her whole body shaking and trembling, her hands cramming into her mouth, the tears scalding in her eyes as convulsions of weeping overcame her.

They possessed her utterly, allowing nothing else in—no other emotion other than the final devastation of her hopes. It was like that nightmare day in Rome—but worse… Oh, so much worse!

As the wild sobbing finally ebbed, and there were no more tears to shed, her body exhausted, she wrapped her arms around herself as if to hold herself together. Dully, she realised she could not, *must* not, go on sitting there as shadows lengthened over the pool.

With agonising slowness she got to her feet, her eyes lighting on the champagne bottle, mocking her. A smothered cry broke from her.

She made her way indoors, having piled the coffee cups on to the tray, and headed for the kitchens. Maria would still be upstairs with Johnny.

But when she got indoors it was to find Maria and Johnny busy baking. Johnny rushed to her, telling her he was making brownies for them all, but her smile at him was wan, and she was burningly conscious that Maria's eyes were sharp with concern on her.

'Signor Viscari?' Maria ventured.

'He had to get back to New York. An unexpected call—' Eloise just managed to get the words out.

But Maria was not deceived, Eloise knew, and she shook her head in sorrow, with worry and anxiety open in her face.

All Eloise could do was wait until the brownies were in the oven, then take Johnny upstairs.

'But I want to go in the Ferrari!' he wailed.

'Vito's gone, Johnny,' Eloise said, and the words tolled in her heart.

Desolation filled her. Vito had talked of marriage— but what marriage could there be with him now, filled with anger at her? Only hours earlier she had dreamt of her happily-ever-after ending—of Vito declaring himself to her, and she to him, and then her crowning their happiness, their union, with what she had longed so much to tell him: that they were already blessed with the fruit of that union that was to be for all their lives.

Impossible now! Impossible to contemplate marrying him when his reaction to her pregnancy had been horror!

I can't—I won't marry him like that! It would be a disaster—as disastrous as my parents' marriage was! It would be impossible to do the same!

Round and round the words went in her head, round and round as she somehow got through the rituals of looking after a fretful, fractious Johnny, urged a reluctant Maria to go on her customary visit with her husband to their daughter. For she longed only to have the house to herself, to see Johnny to bed and then head to her own quarters, numb with misery.

As she lay in her bed, sleepless, staring sightlessly at the ceiling, her hand rested on her abdomen. Anguish filled her. Filled every cell in her body. After all her hopes and dreams of Vito to have got it so, so wrong…

Just as I got it wrong in Rome.

She stilled, her eyes distending suddenly. The words had come into her head without volition, without realisation. But now they hung like a burning brand in her consciousness.

She felt her heart leap. She *had* got it wrong in Rome—got it totally, completely wrong! She had totally misunderstood Vito's behaviour there.

What if I'm doing it again now? What if I'm making exactly the same mistake? Ruining everything with my own assumptions!

Urgently she tried to replay in her head that hideous scene by the poolside, when all her hopes and dreams of happily-ever-after had come crashing down around her in the bomb blast of Vito's fury at her. Desperately she tried to remember what he'd said—the words beneath the anger.

'What kind of woman keeps a child from its father?'

That was what Vito had hurled at her! His final condemnation of her. Never giving her time to answer. Never giving her a chance to explain before storming off.

Because the answer she had been desperate to give then was the one that had haunted her from the moment she had discovered she was pregnant. An answer whose roots went back all her life, to the festering pain of her own rejection by her father.

A woman who fears the same rejection now of the child she carries.

It was *that* that had silenced her ever since Vito had found her here in America. That had made her so wary, so scared of telling him what their affair had resulted in.

And that's what I have to tell him—I have to!

She felt her pulse surge again, new emotion filling her overriding the despair and desolation that had consumed her till this moment. Resolution flowed into her. She would *not* give up on Vito! She would not! She wouldn't let his anger with her be the final nail in the coffin of her hopes and dreams.

As the sleepless hours passed her resolve and courage strengthened. She had got it wrong with Vito before, misjudging him for his apparent engagement to his stepcousin. And she had got it wrong now...so catastrophically wrong. Bringing down his anger on her head.

But when I went to him before I made it right! So maybe... Oh, maybe...

If she went to him again would he listen to her? She did not know—could not know. Could know only that for the sake of her chance at happiness she had to make the attempt. Far too much was at stake for her not to do so.

Vito stared out of his hotel room window, looking at the tops of the trees in the green oasis that was Central Park visible. Memory assailed him of how he had stood there by night, so short a time ago, when Eloise had come to him at the hotel to tell him how she had misjudged him, misunderstood him. How they had made their peace after such bitter discord and distrust. How hope had flared within him once again.

But all hope was gone now. Dashed and destroyed. She was not the woman he had thought her to be. She had been hiding from him—day after day after day—the most important thing of all.

How could she do it? How could she talk to me, smile at me, laugh with me—let me kiss her!—and all along know she was carrying our child! She knew it and did not tell me!

Cold ran through him like an icy sluice. How close he'd come to marrying Carla! A hair's breadth! Right now, at this very moment, had he not found the strength of mind to refuse to do so, to walk away from his devil's bargain with her and her mother, he might be married to her! In total ignorance that here in America a child had been conceived—a child who would be born while he was still locked in that unholy marriage, waiting for the annulment he had insisted they must seek once Carla's injured pride and wounded heart had been soothed with their sham marriage.

More memory assailed him—how Eloise had refused to listen to him when he'd found her at the Carldons'— how only a chance word from her employer about how disastrous the loss of Guido's shares had been had brought her to him to make her peace. His face contorted. And still she had not told him she was pregnant with their child! Still she had kept it secret from him!

Emotion seared through him—as it had done over and over again since that moment when his hand had shaped the swell of her abdomen, revealing her condition.

What kind of woman keeps a child from its father?

That was his condemnation of her and it lashed him

over and over again. And that condemnation was like a sword stabbing at *him* too. For it destroyed all that he had let himself hope for—all that he had dreamt of recovering, renewing, discovering with Eloise. His Eloise.

But she isn't that woman! She isn't the woman I thought she was.

All that could ever be between them now was the empty formality of a marriage—as sham, surely, as the one he'd contemplated making with Carla.

The bitterness of it mocked him.

The ringing of the phone penetrated his angry, stricken thoughts. In rapid strides he snatched it up. It would be the front desk, telling him that the hotel limousine was here to take him to the airport. He was flying back to Rome to tell his mother, to bring her here not for a joyous wedding, but for a joyless one—one that would legally unite him to Eloise so that their child would be born within wedlock.

His mind sheered away—it was too painful to contemplate so grim an event.

A moment later he had stilled. It *had* been the front desk—but not for the reason he'd assumed. Slowly, he replaced the handset. A sense of *déjà vu* came over him.

Eloise had come to the hotel.

His expression tightened. What could she possibly say to him now?

After what she had done, what could she possibly say?

Eloise could feel her heart thumping like a sledgehammer inside her as the elevator swept her up to the penthouse floor. Instinctively her hand went to her abdomen, splaying over the swell of her body. The period of nausea had long passed now, and she was glad of it. But for all that there was a churning in her stomach. Nerves stretched taut as wire at what she was facing.

I have to try—I have to try!

Yet as Vito opened the door to her, stepping back to let her in, she could feel her heart plummet. His face was closed—as shuttered as a locked door.

'You wanted to see me.'

His voice was unemotional. The statement devoid of anything to give her hope.

She swallowed, nodded. Crossed to the window opposite, then turned. Deliberately—unlike all the other times she'd met with him here in America—she was wearing a tight-fitting stretch top that moulded her body, revealing totally what she had so assiduously sought to keep concealed from him. Now she flaunted it, lifting her chin as she prepared to speak. Seeking the courage she must find.

She saw his eyes go to her body, cling to the rounded contour. Saw a sudden flash in his expressionless eyes. But *what* had flashed there? Anger? Or something else?

She had to find the words she must say, hard and halting though they would be. So much depended on them. *Everything* depended on them.

Before I was so cautious—so scared of him finding out before I was ready to tell him! But now—now caution is my enemy.

'Vito, I have to talk to you—I *have* to!' The words blurted from her.

He looked at her. 'Do you? I see no necessity for that. The only necessity is for us to arrange our immediate marriage. To legitimise the child you carry.'

His voice was cool, with no emotion in it. But when she had walked into his suite emotion had seared within him. Pain like none he had known. A double blow. Not just because his eyes had lit upon her again, seeing her pale hair drawn back, the fine bones of her face needing no make-up to announce her beauty to him, but because now, for the first time, he could see the state of her pregnancy—her thickening figure, the five-month swell of the child she carried.

Our child.

She had paled at his words, a sickly pallor bleaching her skin.

'Vito—*please*!' The words came from her faintly. 'Please! Hear me out! I beg you! Before...' Her voice trembled. 'Before—when it was you coming to me, when you'd found me here in New York—I refused to listen to you! But please don't do to me what I did to you! Give me a chance—a chance to...to explain...'

Her voice trailed off. She felt herself sway, tension racking her, blood draining from her.

'May...may I sit down?'

She did not wait for an answer, only lowered herself to a sofa, feeling her head clear. Her hands were clutching her bag, as if for dear life, and she held it on her knees, against the swell of her body. Her fingers touched the material stretching across her abdomen, beneath which her precious, precious child was cradled. Whose whole future was at stake now, at this very moment.

It gave her renewed courage to speak. She lifted her face to Vito, across the gaping space between them. Still he had that shuttered look on his face, closing her out. Rejecting her...

'What is there to explain?' he said. 'Your actions have said it all. You are not the woman I thought you were—how could you be, to do what you did?'

The faintness drummed at her again, but she forced herself on. So much depended on what she said.

I kept silent too long—now I must speak.

Her mouth was dry, her throat constricted, but she knew she must force the words from her. Inside, she could feel her heart slugging with hard, heavy beats, could feel acid in her stomach. Every muscle in her body felt weary, exhausted.

After her long, sleepless, fretful night, she'd risen early, finding Maria in the kitchen, begging her to look after Johnny until his parents returned. Then she'd travelled in by train to Manhattan. En route, she had phoned her mother's apartment to ask if she might call by later. The call had gone to voicemail, so she had simply said, her voice strained, that she might need a good lawyer soon.

Because to marry Vito with him thinking so ill of her, looking at her as he was doing now, with his closed, shuttered face, unforgiving, unrelenting, would be impossible—just impossible! All that would be left to her would be some kind of painful, agonising sharing of their child…

Unless…

Once again resolution seared within her. She had to try and win him back—she had to try and recover what her secrecy had cost her. Make good the ill she had done. Too much was at stake for her not to. Far too much.

'So, what is it you want to say?' Vito was demanding, as still she did not speak. 'And what can you possibly say that will change anything?'

His voice was terse, inexpressive, condemning her unheard, condemning her for her deed alone. Not for its cause.

'Vito, I… I want to try and make you understand why I did not tell you I was pregnant.'

She took a hectic breath, then went on, trying to keep her voice steady, to quell the emotions bucketing within her.

'At first, when I discovered it, I was simply in shock—unable to believe it. Through my mother's contacts I'd been offered the position at the Carldons', and of course I had to explain to them the change in my circumstances.

They've been wonderful—even offered to let me continue working after the baby is born if I want. My mother too...' Unconsciously her voice became guarded. 'She has been completely supportive, and I am very appreciative of that. But it was *because* of my mother that I...that I never got in touch with you.'

A frown furrowed Vito's face and his dark gaze transfixed her. She wished he would sit down, for he seemed to be towering over her, brooding and overpowering. It hurt to have him like this, so condemning of her, when before he had been so eager for her.

I have lost his favour and I never knew how much I valued it—how much I took his wanting me for granted.

'How so?' Vito's question was grating, his frown deepening.

She swallowed again, nails pressing into her palms. Forced herself to continue.

'I've never told you anything much about my family— my childhood. About my mother, even. But now I have to.'

She took another breath, forcing herself on, despite the stoniness of Vito's expression.

'When...when my mother was young—my age—she fell in love...hopelessly in love...with my father. They had a whirlwind romance, got married only a handful of months after meeting, swept away on a tide of passion. They thought they would be blissfully happy for ever!'

She heard bitterness creep into her voice. It was still there as she continued.

'But there was nothing happy-ever-after about it at all. It was a classic case of "Marry in haste, repent at leisure." They proved entirely unsuited. My mother was a career woman; my father wanted a traditional wife. And...' she swallowed again '...he wanted a large family. With lots of sons.'

Her voice thinned.

'My mother was not maternal. *Is* not maternal. When I was born she told my father outright that she wasn't going to get pregnant again, would have no more children. Would not give him the sons he craved.'

Her troubled gaze slid past Vito, out of the window, across the expanse of Central Park and the cityscape beyond. Out into the fatherless wasteland of her own childhood.

'So he left her. He left the UK, went to Australia, got himself a divorce and married again. This time around to a woman who was prepared to stay at home and cook his dinner and raise a large family. Which she did. All boys.'

Her gaze came back to Vito. Not seeing him. Seeing a man she had never known. Never would know. Who had not wanted her. Who had rejected her from the moment of her birth.

Her mouth was dry as sand as she spoke again. 'I've never seen him—my father—not since I was a baby. If he walked past me in the street I would not know him. He would be—*is*—a complete stranger to me. He refused all contact with me. Wrote me out of his life as though I did not exist. And, for him, I *don't* exist. I was a girl, and he wasn't interested.'

She gave a little shrug.

'My mother let him go—in the end was glad he went, for it freed her to work as she wanted to. With the help of nannies and au pairs and boarding school she raised me in what spare time she had. Which wasn't much.'

She shrugged again.

'She's always ensured I was well looked after—just not by her. And in her own way,' she acknowledged with painful honesty, 'she loves me, and I her, but it's never been a...a close relationship.'

She got to her feet. Restless suddenly. She paced up and down, trying to find the words she needed to say now.

Vito was not moving. Only his eyes traced her steps. She paused suddenly, looked at him, chin lifting, eyes focusing on him.

'Because of my father, Vito—because of his absolute and utter lack of interest in my existence—when I discovered I was pregnant the first thing I thought of was him. I realised that there were terrible echoes in my situation to my parents'.

He started, his expression changing. 'I am *nothing* like your father!'

She threw up her hands, eyes widening. 'Vito, as far as I knew you were *marrying* another woman—even *before* our child was born! *That* was the truth of what I was facing when I realised I was pregnant!'

Her words seemed only to incense him. His dark eyes flashed with anger.

'*Por Dio*, do you really think I would have married Carla—would even have consented to the farce of our engagement—had I known you were pregnant? That—*that* is what appals me so much, Eloise. That because I didn't know I might actually have married Carla! I might now be married to another woman! The thought of it freezes my blood!'

She reeled from his accusation, but she fought back. She had to fight back.

'But I didn't know that, Vito! To my face you told me you were engaged to Carla! How should I have known it for a lie?'

'I tried to tell you.' His voice was harsh. 'You refused to let me.'

She blanched. Closed her eyes for a moment as if to acknowledge the justice of his accusation. Then she opened them again to acknowledge it.

'Yes, I know—and I have had my punishment, have I not? Had I not fled Rome—'

She broke off. What use to go over that again? None. It was gone now. It was the future that counted—that she had to try and save.

'But I *did* flee Rome. And I faced, here, a future without you. A future as a single mother—as my own mother is. Vito—what else could I have done? You were engaged to another woman—would be marrying her, I assumed. To have informed you that I was pregnant would have achieved nothing!'

She saw him move as if to speak again and stumbled on, desperate to make him understand why she had kept silent.

'Vito, even if…even if you had not married Carla because I'd told you I was pregnant, and you'd married me instead—even setting aside all the dreadful complications of the Viscari shares—how could I *possibly* want a husband who'd *had* to marry me? Not married me out of choice! Not because he'd *wanted* to marry me! But simply to legitimise a child he'd never intended to conceive and never wanted in the first place! When all you'd wanted—all I *knew* you wanted, because of that nightmare scene in Rome, when Carla stormed in on us—was to marry *her*, not me! Just what kind of marriage would that have been, Vito? What kind of husband would you have been? What kind of father would you have made, forced into it unwillingly?'

Again she saw him try and interrupt her, but she would not let him. She ploughed on. She had to say this—say it all. Bitter and hard though it was.

'I wrote you off, Vito. I had to. It was all I could do. I had to face the future on my own—just as my mother had to. Only when you tracked me down—and only when I realised just what you had been through with Carla, and the loss of half your heritage—did I know that I must re-evaluate my decision.'

She rubbed a weary hand across her brow.

'And that is what I did, Vito. From the moment you said, "No pressure", that is what I did. Hour by hour, day by day.'

She looked at him with infinite sorrow and sadness in her eyes, in her voice.

'As you wooed me again, courting me again with every glance, every smile, everything started growing again between us. And I started to hope—oh, Vito, I started to *hope*! When you told me it was not the past you were seeking to recapture but our future together—then I knew that everything was changing for ever.'

Her expression changed, her face working.

'But would it be enough, Vito? That is what I wanted to know! My parents were romantically in love—but their utterly opposing views on children severed them completely! What if we were the same? What if the child that I want so much—so rejoice in bearing, that's so absolutely precious to me—what if that was the very, very last thing you wanted? What if, instead of uniting us, our child divided us?'

She shook her head, all the fears that had racked her open in her face. Her voice dropped.

'How would I know that you would not be like my father? That was what haunted me! I *had* to know you would not be like him before I entrusted you with the knowledge of our child—before I entrusted my life to you! *Our* lives to you! I *had* to get it right, Vito! I'd got it wrong about you *twice* before! First I was weaving dreams about you while we were in Europe, wondering if you were The One! Only to crash and burn hideously when Carla appeared! And then—dear God...' She rubbed a weary hand across her forehead. 'I got it wrong again—disastrously—over Carla and your uncle's shares! So I could not, just *could not*, risk making a third mistake over you! Not when our child's happiness would be at stake.'

She paused, her expression changing. Softening.

'It was when I saw you with little Johnny. When I saw how easily you spoke to him, how natural you were with him, how patient, how you so obviously liked him...' She gave a little choking laugh. 'And yesterday—all that time playing with him, paying him attention, enjoying his company...'

She swallowed.

'It confirmed to me everything I'd come to believe about you, made me trust in you. Trust that you would always be a good father to our own child. So then I knew— I finally knew—that the time had come when it was safe to tell you, knowing you would welcome the news, rejoice at it.'

She fell silent. Then lifted her eyes to him, her face contorting.

'Instead—'

Her hand pressed against her mouth. Vito had not moved—not a muscle. He stood as immobile as a statue, his face as closed, as shuttered as it had ever been. Rejecting her. Rejecting what she was telling him. Rejecting her plea for understanding.

'Instead,' she said dully, heaviness weighing her down, crushing her with a sense of hopelessness, 'you reacted in horror. You were appalled to discover I was pregnant. And every fear I possessed was proved right.'

She fell silent. She had said it all.

For an endless moment the silence stretched. Then Vito spoke.

'I was appalled at your *secrecy*, Eloise. Not your pregnancy.'

His voice was remote, as if coming from a long, long way away.

'*That's* what I condemned,' he said.

The silence came again—longer now. Unbearable. Faintness was drumming at her again, but she had to speak, to ask one last question. The only question in the universe.

'And do you still condemn me, Vito, after hearing why I kept it secret from you?'

She saw him take a breath, saw his chest rise, heard the sharpness of its intake.

'I don't know,' he said.

Abruptly he turned away, pacing across the room. A million thoughts were in his head…a million emotions burned through him. Jangled and tangled, jarring and marring. Making no sense.

He halted, looked back at her. 'What do you want, Eloise?'

There was only neutrality in his voice, but it was deceptive. She started as he said it, looking at him warily.

'What do I want?'

She heard her own voice echo his. Heard it again in her heart. What *did* she want?

Her own thoughts answered her.

I want my happy-ever-after. The one I've longed for all my life. My determination from a child has been to find the right man, fall in love, make a family. Live happily ever after.

But were such things even possible? When Vito had first swept her away she'd wondered if it had meant that he was 'The One'. Then she'd crashed and burned in Rome, over Carla and those shares. Then here, in America, it had seemed to be within her reach again. Then, yesterday, she had crashed and burned again.

And now—

New thoughts came.

Maybe what I've longed for all my life is just a dream—

a dream I dreamt because I wanted to recreate my parents' marriage as it should have been, so I could have the childhood I craved. Maybe that's why I clung to that dream.

She let her eyes rest on Vito. She had been through so much on his account—happiness and bliss. Despair and rejection. Hope and fear.

But of all those emotions, clashing and contradictory, what was the one emotion that remained?

She knew its name. Knew it because it was the emotion that leapt in her every time her hand shaped her body, cradled the life growing within.

But if that was not what Vito felt she must not name it.

Coward!

The word stabbed at her, shocking her.

More words came, forced their way in.

You don't dare tell him because you fear his rejection! It was his rejection in Rome that slayed you! His rejection yesterday that did the same! But Vito isn't your father! So tell him—tell him now what it is you want!

She looked at him again, so short a distance away. Their lives would be linked for ever now, because of the child she carried. They were bound indissolubly because of that.

And for one reason more. A reason that would bind her to him all her life.

Slowly she spoke, never taking her eyes from him. Declaring everything.

'I want, Vito, you to love me and our child as I love *you* and our child. That is all I want,' she said. 'All I will ever want.'

Her eyes dipped. What would he say? How would he reply? She could not see his face, with her eyes lowered, but she heard his voice. It was strange…so strange.

'All my life,' he said slowly, in that strange new voice,

'I have wanted to find a woman I would love as dearly as my father loved my mother. Their marriage, to me, seemed all that marriage should ever be! And when I lost my father it was…unbearable. It still is, Eloise. Every day I miss him, grown man though I am. A father is for life—'

He broke off, and her eyes lifted, going instantly to his face, where emotion shadowed his eyes.

Then the shadow lifted. 'Eloise, *that* is why I was so harsh with you! I couldn't bear to think that you might have taken our child from me! That you might have thought a child did not need its father—'

'But I don't! Vito—that's why I feared to tell you! I couldn't have borne it if you'd rejected our child as my father rejected me!'

Her voice was a cry.

'Never! As God is my witness, *never* will I reject our child—and never, Eloise…oh, Eloise…never will I reject *you*!'

He came towards her, caught her hands. Emotion was pouring through him, a tidal wave.

'Do you mean it? What you said? That you want only my love?'

She lifted her face to his. Tears swam in her eyes.

'Yes! Oh, yes! But only…' the shadow was there in her eyes again '…only if you love me…'

Her answer was a kiss. As swift, as swooping as a summer swallow, silencing her doubts.

'If you had told me even a second before I found out I would have embraced you as I do now!'

As he spoke from his overflowing heart his arms came around her, holding her close, so close against him.

'Oh, Eloise, my Eloise, my precious, beloved Eloise— how could you think I would not cherish a child between us? I understand your fears—now that I know them—but you never had need of them! Not for an instant!'

A breath shuddered through him and he held her a little away from him now, so he could speak to her. His gaze poured into her.

'It was *my* fears, Eloise, that made me condemn you. The thought of what might have been… To have had a child growing up here, away from me, unknown to me, kept from me by the very woman I had fallen in love with.'

Her face worked. 'If I'd only spoken earlier…'

He shook his head. 'If I had only let you speak—let you explain your secrecy…'

She swallowed. 'And if I had let you speak in Rome—let you explain about Carla, about everything…'

He gave a shaky laugh. They had come so close to losing each other. To losing what was most precious between them.

'Never again!' he breathed. 'From this day onward, my beloved, we shall always, *always* hear each other out! About everything!'

Her answering smile was wavering, and tears still weighed on her lashes. But inside her huge, sweeping emotions were lifting her high. Joy was lighting within her…happiness was soaring. And then the tears suddenly cascaded down, shedding their burden. Her face convulsed.

'Eloise!'

Alarm was in his voice and he wrapped her to him again, enveloping her as sobs broke from her.

So many emotions—so many hopes, so many fears, so many dreams. And now those dreams had come true. Vito was hers, and she was his, and their child was theirs for ever…

He let her weep, let all the emotions spill out of her, echoing the tumult draining from him too as he cradled her in his arms, murmuring in his own language to her, words and fragments of words that held a lifetime's love in them.

And when at last her tears were shed, and a wondrous peace eased into her, a shining joy filled her to the brim, his hands gently lifted her face away from where it was buried in his shoulder.

His eyes were soft and filled with a tenderness that caught at all her senses. His kiss was as gentle as a summer's breeze, as true as the love between them. Happiness filled her.

As he drew back his eyes held hers, entwining with hers. 'How blessed I am,' he said. 'To have you and our child to be born.'

'As blessed as I am,' she echoed, her face softening with love. 'To have you and...' She paused, then smiled as she spoke on. 'And our son to be born.'

Vito stilled. 'Son? You *know*?'

She nodded, drawing a little back from him, nodding. Smiling. So joyous to be telling him.

'I had early tests done, because I was anxious to know all was well, and they asked if I wanted to know the baby's gender. I said yes, because I'm never one to bear suspense!' She gave half a laugh, then smiled again. 'And because I knew Johnny would ask once he realised I was having a baby, once I'd started to show.'

She paused a moment, her expression changing.

'Vito—what was your father's name?'

The question hung in the air, heavy with portent. He knew why she had asked, and he loved her the more for it.

'Enrico,' he answered. There was the slightest choke in his voice.

'Enrico...' Eloise echoed, with the same musing smile playing around her lips. 'Would Rico be the diminutive form, do you think? Suitable for a baby?'

Vito's long lashes swept down. 'Entirely suitable,' he

said. His hand slid over her abdomen, and there was a look of wonder on his face. 'Little Rico,' he murmured.

'Little Rico,' she echoed tenderly.

He kissed her again—gently, softly—his hand resting where it was. Family already...as they would always be.

The jarring ring of the phone startled them, and with an exclamation Vito relinquished her to answer it.

He listened, then frowned. 'We have a visitor in the lobby,' he announced. 'She wishes to speak to you.'

Eloise frowned, too, then came to the phone.

'Mum?' she said incredulously.

Her mother's crisp tones penetrated even to Vito.

'I came the moment I got your voicemail. Eloise, what on earth is happening? The last I heard was that you'd decided to accept this man after all! So why this talk of custody challenges?'

With difficulty, Eloise cut across her mother. 'Mum—ignore that! It's all right after all—it's all right! In fact...' she gave a laugh of pure emotion '...it's wonderful! Just *wonderful*! Mum—'

But the line had gone dead. Slowly she replaced the receiver. Glanced at Vito.

'That was my mother,' she said unnecessarily. 'And I have a bad feeling that she may be about to make an appearance.'

There was foreboding in her voice, but Vito only smiled reassuringly. 'It is time I made her acquaintance,' he said.

Eloise made a face. 'She can be very...formidable,' she said cautiously.

'I shall be prepared,' Vito said resolutely. 'And I shall take pains to assure her that I will be *nothing* like your father! If you wish to make a glittering career for yourself you are *entirely* free to do so—though of course, as a nanny, I would hope that your first devotion would be to our child. And perhaps,' he added tentatively, 'to our other children, if that is a happy proposition for you? But of course if not—'

She did not hesitate to reassure him. 'Oh, Vito, as many as we want!'

A rap on the door interrupted this exchange, and Vito crossed with long strides to answer it.

The woman who sailed in was severely dressed in a sharply cut navy suit, with immaculate hair and a brisk manner. She stopped short, her eyes raking Vito. Then she went to her daughter.

'Would either of you care to update me?' she said, her English accent accentuating the cut of her question.

'It's all sorted,' Eloise provided. She crossed to Vito, wrapped her arm around his waist. 'It's all wonderful. Fantastic. Blissful!' She gave a sigh of happiness.

Her mother's gimlet eyes surveyed them for a moment longer, as if assessing what she saw. Then, abruptly, she nodded.

'Good,' she said. 'In which case Vito might as well be party to this.'

She sat herself down on the sofa, extracting from her handbag a bulky envelope which she placed on the coffee table. Eloise, a bewildered expression on her face, slid onto the sofa opposite and looked at the envelope. Vito came and sat down beside her, a slight frown of curiosity on his face as Eloise pushed the envelope at him.

'Well, don't just stare at it—open it!' Eloise's mother instructed impatiently.

Her tone of voice changed, and she looked at Vito.

'Eloise will be the first to tell you that I am unlikely to make a doting grandmother—I leave that office to your own mother!—but nevertheless please believe me that I will take my responsibilities to my grandson very seriously. As I trust this demonstrates.'

She nodded at the envelope, which Vito was beginning to open. It yielded a bulky document, which he unfolded and looked down at. Stared at.

Then his eyes flashed upwards. 'I don't understand...'

There was no expression in his voice. Nothing except incomprehension. And shock. Total shock.

Eloise looked up at him, consternation in her eyes. 'Vito, what is it?'

Nervelessly he handed the document to her, but his gaze was still on her mother. He said something in Italian that Eloise did not understand. She stared at the document. It was in legalese, formal and convoluted, but as she gazed, and made herself read it, she felt herself go completely still.

Her eyes, too, flashed up to her mother. 'What *is* this?' she asked. Her voice was like a ghost.

Her mother stood up and looked at them with an expression of complete satisfaction on her face.

'It is, Eloise, exactly what it says it is.' Her voice was as brisk as ever, with a snap of impatience in it directed at her daughter. 'It's a certificate for the shares originally owned by Vito's uncle! Now owned by your son.'

The satisfaction was even more marked now.

'What?' The question exploded like a bullet from Eloise. 'Mum, what have you *done*?'

'Oh, for heaven's sake, Eloise, don't be so obtuse!' The snap was even more marked. 'It's perfectly obvious. I've acquired Marlene Viscari's shareholding.'

Eloise stared—she could do nothing else. But above her she could hear Vito's voice. Sounding hollow. Disbelieving.

'But they were bought by Nic Falcone,' he said.

He swallowed, still staring. Incapable of anything other than disbelief and paralysing shock. What the *hell* was going on here?

'No,' Eloise's mother contradicted him, 'they were bought on his behalf by the hedge fund Nic Falcone had to enlist in order to fund the acquisition. I have now bought them from the hedge fund at a price they did not wish to refuse. Falcone had no say in the matter—though I believe he is not best pleased!'

She snapped her handbag shut with a decisive click.

'However, his displeasure is of no account. The shares are now the property of your son—although,' she said kindly, her gaze sweeping Eloise and Vito, 'the two of you are his proxies until he reaches majority.'

Shock was still detonating through Vito. Shock and incomprehension.

'Mrs Dean,' he said, his voice still hollow, 'I don't understand…'

Eloise's mother held up her hand in an imperious fashion. 'I don't use my married name—when I set up in New York I reverted to my maiden name. Forrester,' she said, with something of a snap. 'I saw no reason to credit my faithless ex with any part of what I had achieved without him!'

Vito's mouth opened. Then closed. Then, from somewhere very, very deep in the recesses of his brain, a synapse fired.

He stared at Eloise's mother. 'Forrester…' he said.

He paused. Another synapse fired, giving him a possible explanation of what he'd just heard.

'Good God,' he said tonelessly, 'Forrester Travis…'

Disbelief was the only emotion in his voice.

'Oh, for heaven's sake, Eloise!' came her mother's snap. 'Don't tell me you've never explained to him what I do!'

Eloise looked at Vito. 'Mum runs some kind of investment firm,' she said belatedly. 'With a guy called Travis. Somewhere downtown.'

A noise escaped from Vito's throat. 'Your mother is

Susan Forrester?' he said blankly, as if he could not credit his own words. 'Susan Forrester of Forrester Travis.'

He took a breath, his gaze going back to Eloise.

'*Cara mia*, Forrester Travis is one of the world's foremost hedge funds! It has something like thirty billion dollars under investment—'

'Thirty-four point five,' corrected Susan Forrester, one of the most outstandingly influential women on Wall Street. She drew breath. 'Well,' she said dryly, 'if my daughter really never told you about me at least I can be satisfied you haven't made up to her for her prospects!'

Vito got to his feet. Looked at Eloise's mother. His mind was still reeling with who she was and what she had done.

'Thank you,' he said quietly. 'Thank you from the bottom of my heart.'

'It was the least I could do,' said Eloise's mother. Her expression changed again, and she sighed. 'I told you I won't make a doting grandmother, but whatever Eloise says about me I want only her happiness.'

There was the slightest catch in her voice, and then she squared her shoulders.

'Well, now that everything is sorted I must go. I'm lunching with the president of Banco Brasilão, and clearly...' her voice became dry '... I am quite unnecessary here.'

Her voice became even more dry.

'Vito will need time to assimilate the situation, and doubtless to phone Italy and apprise his own mother of her forthcoming welcome transformation into a grandmother! I look forward to making her acquaintance in due course, and to reaching some degree of mutual agreement as to the style of wedding you two are to have.'

Eloise leant forward to catch her mother's hand. 'Mum,' she said, and her voice was charged with emotion, 'thank you.' She swallowed. '*Thank* you,' she said again. 'For everything.'

She couldn't say any more—her throat was suddenly tight again. She could only press her mother's hand, hoping by that feeble gesture to express her gratitude for what her mother had done—waved her Wall Street wand and restored to Vito the Viscari legacy that Marlene had so ruthlessly disposed of. The legacy that Vito had sacrificed to win her back…the price he had paid for her love.

He gave it up for me! Put aside the vow he made his father for my sake.

And now he had been rewarded for his sacrifice, and she was glad with all her heart and so, *so* grateful to her mother! She felt her eyes mist and knew, with a deep sense of familiar irony, just how much her mother would hate such emotionality.

'Silly girl,' her mother said, but Eloise could hear a difference in her voice from her usual briskness. She patted Eloise's hand and then drew her own back, glancing at her slim gold watch. 'I must go,' she said. 'My car will be waiting.'

The briskness was back in her voice, and in her manner. She held up a hand in farewell and was gone.

Vito turned to Eloise. 'Did I just dream that?' he asked.

Then his eyes went to the documentation on the coffee table. The papers that had restored to him at a stroke what Marlene's machinations had wrenched from his family. He shook his head slowly in wonder. Then another thought occurred to him.

'Your mother talked about a wedding—but…' there was hesitancy in his voice '…is that something you want, *cara mia*?'

She wrapped her arms around his neck. 'Only if you do,' she replied.

His face lit. 'It is my dearest wish!'

His mouth swooped to hers, kissing her tenderly. Then less tenderly. More sensually. At once within Eloise desire quickened, answering his.

Vito paused, though his arms were tight around her. 'If your mother and mine insist on a fancy wedding, it could take a while to organise. So I was thinking…in the meantime perhaps we might pre-empt our honeymoon.'

He smiled wickedly.

'How about testing out the new Viscari Hotel on Ste Cecile?' He grazed her lips with his persuasively. 'Do you think the Carldons would let you disappear for a long weekend?'

Eloise laughed. 'Considering Laura Carldon has been desperate to get us together, I'm sure they will! And if she balks—well, her mother and mine are good friends. That's how I got the job as Johnny's nanny and it might help.'

'Great.' Vito grinned. 'And, speaking of the Carldons, what about if I offer Maria and Giuseppe the pick of the Viscari Hotels collection for an extended holiday? I need to say thank you to them—after all, had it not been for them I would never have found you.'

Eloise's grip on him tightened. The very thought of Vito never finding her….

'Tell me,' Vito was continuing, 'how long do you think the Carldons will need to replace you? That will set the timing of our wedding.'

'A few weeks, I should think. Laura has already mentioned it to me as a possibility. Vito, they must come to the wedding—and Johnny too! Maybe,' she mused, 'he'd like to be our page boy?'

'More likely our chauffeur!' Vito laughed. He swooped another kiss on her mouth. 'Any more wedding details to be finalised right now? Or can we get on with what I've been longing to do for so long?'

She lifted limpid eyes to him. 'What might that be, Vito?'

A wicked smile quivered at her lips. And was answered by his.

'This,' he said.

With a single scoop she was in his arms and he was striding with her into the bedroom, lowering her gently down upon the bed's surface.

'This,' he repeated, and came down beside her. 'This,' he confirmed, and started to make love to her.

Eloise was the woman he loved, the woman who carried the son he already loved, who melded them into the family they would always be.

Always.

CHAPTER ELEVEN

CARIBBEAN MOONLIGHT SHAFTED through the slats of the
louvred windows of their room, and the slow beating of
the ceiling fan high in the vaulted roof echoed the beating
of her heart. Vito led her towards the bed, his fingers entwined with hers, his naked body outlined in all its masculine perfection by the silver light of the slanting moon.

With a little sigh Eloise folded herself down onto the
cool surface of the sheets, letting her thighs splay loosely,
her moon-silvered hair flow out across the pillows. Displaying herself to Vito.

For a long, timeless moment he gazed down on her.

'How beautiful you are—how entirely beautiful to
me...' His voice was a soft, heartfelt murmur.

She trailed a hand softly across her ripening figure.

'Make the most of it,' she said, and smiled. 'Soon I'll
be like a barrage balloon!'

'Impossible!'

He shook his head and came down beside her, his hand
resting on hers, his mouth lowering to graze the rounded
surface below which their precious son was growing, paying homage to his unborn child whose mother he loved
so, so much.

Then his mouth lifted from her only to dip again, grazing the valley between the ripened breasts that were cresting for him alone. Desire quickened in him and his thigh

moved across hers, his palms cupping her sweet, full breasts.

She gave a little moan in her throat at the sensations he was arousing with his thumbs teasing over the hardened coral peaks. He felt her spine arch, felt her thighs part to let his fall between them, felt her revelling in the sensual pressure it created in her body's core, in the warmth beginning to heat there.

Her hands folded around his back, pressing her to him as her mouth reached for his, wanting more, so much more...

Their kiss was deep, arousing, and he felt his body surge with need, heard her breath quicken and knew his own was quickening too. His kisses deepened, opening her mouth to him even as her body was opening to him as he moved across her fully, one hand sliding to the nape of her neck to lift her head, to arch her body as he slid within.

A gasp of pleasure broke from her as he did so, and one from him as well, as he felt her fullness all around him, felt the delicate tissues of her body engorge, felt the absolute fusion of their two physical beings echoing the absolute fusion of their hearts.

He started to move upon her in the ancient rhythm of the union of male and female, as old as time and as powerful. He felt the passion build within him, within her, between them both, felt her thighs straining against his, her spine arching more. His mouth devoured her urgently, driven by a need so overpowering he could not resist it, could not delay it.

Words broke from him and she heard them through the drumming in her senses, felt the mounting urgency in her own body, flooded now with a supreme need for the fulfilment that she craved. His pace quickened, sending her into vortex after vortex of climbing arousal.

Her hands clutched at his shoulders, nails digging into him, and her body strained against his, moving with hypnotic whorls against him, feeling his possession of her deepen further yet as she lifted to him, took him in more deeply, closed tight around him, clasping him with her whole body, melding their tissues, becoming one single sensual being. One single beating heart.

And then one single tide of ecstasy was flooding across them, making them cry out in unison with a pleasure so intense it was a conflagration of their limbs, their bodies, that went on and on and on…

An eternity later, when time had resumed, and the slow beat of the ceiling fan was marking the seconds yet again, Eloise lay in the cradle of his arms, feeling a peace fill her that was so profound it was as if there had never been anything else in all the world.

Vito smoothed her hair, glorying in the tangled locks spun from finest silk. He smiled at her, his eyes warm with love for her. One arm was around her; the other rested protectively across the swell of their child.

Suddenly his expression in the dim moonlight changed. Became one of wonder.

'Eloise…' His voice was a breath.

Her eyes widened. She knew suddenly what he had felt. What she too had felt. A tiny fluttering within.

'He moved!' Vito's voice was husky. 'I felt him move!'

Her eyes clung to Vito. 'It's the first time—the first time I've felt him move!'

Her own hand moved to her abdomen, beside Vito's.

'Oh, Vito, he's real! He's real—he's real!' Her voice caught. 'I knew from the scans that he was there, but this… Oh, this is him making himself known to us!'

She felt tears of joy prickle in her eyes, heard the catch in Vito's echoing voice.

'Little Rico—our son. Our child.'

He kissed her, tender and fierce at the same time. How blessed he was! Eloise, his child, and all the other blessings rich upon them. The relief of knowing that his family legacy was safe again, that it was already in the possession of his precious son…

Eloise's arms wrapped about him, holding him close against her. Happiness enveloped her. Soon now they would be married. United for ever. Vito's mother would be flying over to start the preparations as soon as she and Vito returned from Ste Cecile.

'She's ecstatic!' Vito had told her. 'She cannot wait to meet you!'

His expression had softened.

'All this has brought joy back into her life, and I know that she will make the most welcoming mother-in-law you could ever wish for.'

He'd given a laugh.

'As well as styling our wedding in New York—with your approval, of course!—she's already planning Rico's christening in Rome!' He'd looked at her. 'Do you think your mother could find time in her schedule to fly to Italy for it?'

'Of course she will!' Eloise had assured him. 'We may be Rico's proxies for the shares, but she'll want to ensure he grows up knowing it was his non-doting grandmother who got them for him!'

'Well, my mother will do double doting, I promise you that!' Vito had laughed again. 'We'll have to make sure she doesn't spoil him.'

Eloise's eyes had softened. 'She can spoil him all she likes,' she'd said. Her eyes had shadowed. 'My only regret is that Rico will have no grandfathers to do likewise.'

'Yes,' he'd said, sadness in his voice. 'In my father he would have had the best grandfather a boy could dream of!' His expression had changed. 'Is there no chance your father might—?'

Eloise had shaken her head, her mouth tight. 'No. If in years to come Rico wants to make contact with his half-cousins, then I will support him in that. But for me...' She'd looked away. 'I won't risk it, Vito. And I don't want it either. He made his choice. He didn't choose me. Not even to stay in touch and send birthday cards. So I won't choose him either.'

She had touched his cheek, her eyes searching. 'Not everything in life is perfect, Vito. You and I both know that—we each have our own deep sorrows. But—' she'd taken a reviving breath '—we also have more than our share of joys!'

He'd kissed her then, in agreement, in reassurance, in love, and now she lay within the cradle of his arms, here on this beautiful tropical island where they would later come back for their real honeymoon, their bodies sated after their desire for each other—a desire that would endure for ever...even through her barrage balloon phase.

Eloise grinned to herself. She knew, without any doubt at all that the greatest joy of all was their love for each other, and for the child waiting to be born into that love.

The sonorous music swelled, lifting upwards to one last crescendo before falling silent. The hushed murmurings of the congregation stilled as the priest raised his hands and began to speak the words of the ancient sacrament in the age-old ceremony.

Inside his breast Vito could feel his heart beating strongly. Emotion filled him—and he turned his head towards the woman now standing at his side.

Gowned in ivory, her face veiled, his bride waited for

him. Waited for him to say the words that would unite them in marriage...join him in marriage to the woman he loved more than life itself.

To Eloise, his beloved bride...

* * * * *

THE SECRET THE
ITALIAN CLAIMS

JENNIE LUCAS

CHAPTER ONE

FAMILY MEANT EVERYTHING to Hallie Hatfield.

Family meant home. It meant being safe and protected even when times were bad. Even when the money ran out at the end of the month. Even when the kitchen cupboards were bare. Family meant always having someone to watch your back, as you watched theirs.

As Hallie had grown up, in an old wooden house built by her great-grandfather, playing in the woods with her brother, learning songs from her mother, tinkering in the garage with her father, she'd known, even as a child, exactly how she wanted her life to be.

Someday she'd get married. She'd raise children, just as her own parents had, without much money but with lots of love. She and her future husband would grow old together, living close to her family, in a cottage with a view of the soft, green Appalachian hills where she'd been born. Their lives would be full of music and comfort. Because family meant everything.

Then, at nineteen, without warning, Hallie lost everything. Her family. Her home. All the meaning and security in her world.

Now, at twenty-four, the only family she had was the tiny newborn baby in her arms. Living in New York City, she had no job, no money and, as of today, nowhere to go.

But *this* as a solution?

No.

Hallie took a deep, furious breath. "No. Absolutely not."

"But Hallie—"

"Tell my ex-boss about his baby?" Keeping her voice low, not to waken the newborn baby sleeping in her arms,

Hallie glared at her friends. "After the way he treated me? Never!"

The other two women looked at each other. The three friends had been introduced months earlier at a single-moms support group, when a mutual acquaintance had realized that all three were pregnant with their first child, and, shockingly, none of them had yet told the fathers.

In Hallie's case, it was for good reason.

Her whole life, she'd tried to see the best in people. To be sympathetic and kind and good.

But she *hated* Cristiano Moretti. After what he'd done, he didn't deserve to know their three-month-old baby existed.

"But he's the father," Tess Foster said gently. A plump, kindly redhead who worked at her uncle's bakery, she cuddled her own tiny baby. "Hallie, you need help. It only makes sense to ask him."

"You're an idiot if you don't get child support," said Lola Price, who was blonde and fiery, and extra-irritable lately—which was saying something—as, unlike the others, she was still heavily pregnant. "Are you an idiot?"

Hallie ground her teeth. That question had already been asked and answered in her own heart. Yes, she'd been an idiot, letting her boss, a billionaire hotel tycoon, seduce her so easily into giving up her long-held dreams of a forever family, a forever home, for one night of passion.

One night? Ha! *Half* a night, since Cristiano had tossed her out of his bed at midnight and then had her fired from her housekeeping job the very next morning!

Who did that?

A selfish bastard with no heart, that was who. A man who'd ruthlessly thrown her into poverty and homelessness—since she'd also lost her company-paid housing—just because he'd wanted to avoid feeling awkward if he ran into her in the hallway of his hotel.

Hallie looked down at the sweet sleeping baby in her arms. Jack had been over nine pounds at birth, and he'd only gotten chubbier. She loved him with all the ferocious love in her heart. She'd always dreamed of having children. Now Jack was her only dream. Keeping him happy. Keeping him safe.

"You don't even have a place to stay tonight," Tess pointed out. "Unless you're going to call the police on your landlord."

"And you can't stay with me," Lola said, putting her hands over her huge belly. She didn't explain, but then Lola never explained anything.

"I wish you could stay with us, but my aunt and uncle would never allow it," Tess said mournfully. "They're already threatening to kick me out." She sighed. "If only you hadn't ripped up the check your boss stuck in the envelope with your severance pay."

Hallie lifted her chin. "I have my pride."

"But it was for a *hundred thousand dollars*," Tess said.

"And is pride going to feed your baby?" Lola said tartly.

Hallie's shoulders sagged. Lola wasn't sweet and comforting like Tess, but she sure had a way of forcing people to see hard truths.

After her supervisor had fired her, Hallie had stumbled out of the hotel in shock, then opened the severance envelope to discover a check signed by Cristiano personally. As if he thought paying her for taking her virginity would make it all right to toss her out like trash the next morning. Furious and heartbroken, she'd torn it into a million pieces.

Now Hallie realized painfully how that money would have changed her whole life—and Jack's. Because a year later, she had nothing.

But she hadn't known she would end up pregnant. She ran an unsteady hand over her forehead. So much for pride. She would have given anything to have that check back now.

"Come on." Lola stood up abruptly in the middle of the community-hall basement, surrounded by the folding chairs and a crowd of other single moms standing by a punch bowl and cookies that Tess complained constantly were stale. "We're going."

"Where?"

"To see your baby's father. Right now. It's your only option."

Hallie feared her friend was right. But thinking of facing Cristiano, her courage failed her. "I can't."

"Why?"

"I told you. I was just a notch on the bedpost. He was cruel—"

"Cruel?" Lola's eyes became fiercely protective. "You never said that. What did he do? Hit you? Threaten you?"

"Of course not," Hallie replied, taken aback.

"Then what?"

A lump rose in Hallie's throat. "He ignored me."

The blonde's shoulders relaxed slightly. "He's a jerk. But you're sure he's the father?"

"Yes, but I wish he wasn't!"

Lola's eyes were merciless. "Then make him pay. Child support, if nothing else."

Hallie thought of how desperately she needed money. The lump in her throat became a razor blade. "I can't."

"You don't have any choice. You have no family to help you. Are you seriously going to check into a homeless shelter while your ex lives at a luxury hotel, swilling champagne?"

Hallie sucked in her breath at her friend's frank words.

"And, you never know, he might be happy about the baby when you tell him," argued Tess, who was very tenderhearted. "There might be some perfectly good explanation why he kicked you out that night, then had you fired, then never returned your messages…"

Her voice trailed off. Even Tess couldn't quite overcome how ludicrous it sounded.

If only. Hallie gave her a wistful smile, then the smile slid away.

Tell Cristiano she'd had his baby?

Go back to the luxury hotel where she'd once worked as a housekeeper, to beg for the help of a selfish, ruthless tycoon, and this time give him the opportunity to reject both her and the baby in person? No way.

But looking down at her peacefully slumbering baby, his sweet little mouth pursing in his sleep, she knew Lola was right. Hallie had tried her best to survive on pride. But, after this latest disaster with her landlord today, she had nowhere else to go.

"All right," Hallie said in a small voice.

"You'll do it?" Lola's voice was tinged with relief. For all of the blonde's hard edges, Lola's protectiveness of her friends made Hallie suspect that on the inside she was every bit as kind as Tess but, for some reason, tried desperately to hide it.

"You're right," Hallie said glumly. "I have no choice."

The three of them, plus the two babies and Jack's folding stroller, all piled into a ride-share taxi. But by the time it dropped them off in front of the towering luxury hotel in Midtown, Hallie was already regretting her choice. Just half a night in Cristiano's arms had nearly destroyed her. How could she face him again?

Tess, with her own baby in a comfy sling against her chest, tilted her head back to look at the skyscraper that was the Campania Hotel. "He manages all this?"

"He owns it."

Both women turned to her sharply in the warm July night.

Lola wasn't easily impressed, but her eyes were wide as saucers. "Your ex is *Cristiano Moretti*?"

Hallie felt a little sick as she nodded.

"I thought it was the hotel manager," Tess said in awe.

"It doesn't matter who he is," Lola said fiercely. "Demand what is yours by right. For Jack."

Pushing the stroller, Hallie walked slowly past the neon sign of the Blue Hour glowing in the darkness. The hotel's jazz club had live music, and she'd once dreamed of performing there. Now, as she walked past the club, her failed singing career was the last thing on her mind.

What if Cristiano refused to see her? Or—worse—what if, when he found out about the baby, he demanded parental rights over Jack?

If only she could talk him into just blindly giving her that same big check she'd ripped up the year before!

She stopped, glancing back nervously when she saw her friends following her. "You're coming with me?"

"So you don't back out," Lola said.

"So you don't feel alone," Tess said.

With a deep breath, Hallie squared her shoulders and went through the enormous revolving door into the lobby.

The Campania's lobby was thirty feet high, gleaming with white marble floors and midcentury-modern furniture scattered around multiple fireplaces. One side held the long oak check-in desk, and at the very center of the lobby there was an elegant bar.

After going inside, Hallie stopped as well-dressed, wealthy guests passed them by on the busy summer evening.

"What's the problem?" Lola said.

"Can't you just go to his room?" Tess said.

"No," Hallie said. "There's security. You need a fingerprint on the elevator."

"Call him, then."

"I don't have his direct number. We never really talked before…" She hesitated.

Lola scowled. "You were just the hired help, huh?"

Hallie looked down, her cheeks hot. Even when she'd worked for him, there were about fifty levels of supervisors between a maid and the billionaire owner of an international hotel conglomerate. She said weakly, "I can try to leave a message with his secretary, or—"

Her voice cut off with a gasp.

Cristiano had just come out of the elevator on the second floor, open above the lobby.

The reaction was immediate, as if he were a movie star on the red carpet. Heads turned, people whispered and gasped. His entourage followed in his wake as he made his way down the stairs to the ground floor—a gorgeous, pouting model at his side, with two assistants and a bodyguard trailing behind.

But, for Hallie, everything else became a blur. Even her friends were forgotten.

All she could see was…him.

Cristiano Moretti was broad shouldered, dark and powerful, outwardly civilized in a perfectly cut tuxedo, but with a five-o'clock shadow on his hard jaw and glittering black eyes that hinted at a ruthless, brutal soul. Looking at him, Hallie shivered, caught between longing and fear, overwhelmed by memory of the night he'd seduced her. The night her whole world had changed.

As a trusted maid at the Campania Hotel New York, she'd occasionally been assigned the enviable task of cleaning and tidying the Italian tycoon's exclusive penthouse, used only when he was in town. Dusting pictures of Cristiano's gorgeous face as he stood beside famous politicians and celebrities, Hallie had developed a serious crush. She'd actually imagined that Cristiano wasn't just insanely handsome, he was also honorable and good.

Wrong.

She blinked now, looking at him. The way he smiled. So casual. As if he had not a care in the world. He was so arrogantly handsome, king of the world in his tuxedo, apparently off for a night on the town with a beautiful model. While she'd spent the last year struggling, looking for a new job when she was pregnant and trying to find a cheap place to stay in New York City.

For the last year, he'd been enjoying himself—swilling champagne, as Lola had said. He really had forgotten Hallie even existed.

As Cristiano turned to speak to the woman pouting beside him in a gold lamé minidress, Hallie breathlessly handed the stroller's handle to Lola.

"Keep an eye on Jack."

The blonde frowned. "The man will want to meet his own son."

Hallie set her jaw. "I will tell Cristiano in my own way."

"You're being irrational," Lola began, but Tess put her hand gently on Lola's arm.

"Let Hallie do it."

Hallie flashed the redhead a grateful look.

"Fine," Lola said, drawing back stiffly.

Swallowing hard, Hallie went toward Cristiano, planting herself in the middle of his path through the lobby. Her heart was pounding wildly.

It was funny, really. If she'd known when getting ready for the single-moms group that afternoon that she'd end up facing her old lover, she might have put on lipstick and worn something nicer than an old faded sundress that fit her post-pregnancy body. He'd probably take one look at her and wonder how she'd ever ended up in his bed in the first place. Well, there was no help for it now. And it wasn't like she would ever, ever, *ever* want to sleep with him again. Ever.

Putting her hands on her hips, she tried to hide her nervousness as she waited.

His bodyguard tried to smooth his way, holding out his arm. "Excuse us, miss."

Then, from behind him, Cristiano's eyes caught hers.

For a split second, he went completely still. Then his jaw tightened. "It's all right, Luther." He came forward. "What are you doing here, Hallie?"

He remembered her name. She was almost surprised. She hated the shiver that went through her at having him so close, towering over her in his tuxedo, nearly touching her. His dark gaze seared through her. She found herself wanting to blurt out everything, to tell him not just that she'd had his baby but that he'd broken her heart.

She forced herself to say, "I need to talk to you. In private."

His expression became distant. "That's not a good idea."

"I have something important to tell you."

"Tell me now."

"In the middle of the lobby?" Hallie's cheeks went hot. She could feel people watching them. Even the model, standing nearby in her high heels, was looking down at Hallie with scorn. They were all probably wondering why such a frumpy girl would dare talk to Cristiano Moretti. For a moment, Hallie's nerve faltered. She wanted to run away, to forget the whole thing.

Then she saw her friends watching from the other side of the lobby. Saw her sleeping baby cuddled in the stroller. That gave her courage. "It's important."

"Not interested." But as he turned to go, she stepped in front of him.

"Either you speak with me privately right now," she said, determined, "or I'll make a scene in this lobby you can't possibly imagine."

Cristiano stared at her for a long moment, as if assessing her. Then he held up his hand, halting the bodyguard's intervention.

"Go ahead to the gala, Natalia," he told his date. "My driver will take you. I'll see you later."

The woman's pout intensified. She glared at Hallie, then said, "All right, darling," and sashayed out of the lobby hips first, as if she were on a catwalk at New York Fashion Week. She was so obviously a model that even the sophisticated patrons of this luxurious hotel turned to watch her go. So did Hallie, a little wistfully. What would it be like to get that much attention wherever you went? *She* would be able to get an audition at the Blue Hour, for one.

"Follow me," Cristiano said, turning on his heel without waiting to see if Hallie followed.

She glanced nervously back at her baby and friends. Then, biting her lip, she went up the sweeping staircase, following the man she hated most on earth, to face him alone in his lair.

Cristiano Moretti's jaw was tight as he went to the wet bar in his private office on the second floor.

Lifting the lid off the crystal decanter, he glanced back at Hallie as she followed him hesitantly into the high-ceilinged room with its dark oak panels. "Scotch?"

Hallie shook her head, her beautiful brown eyes wide.

Turning back to the bar, he poured himself a short glass over ice. He could almost feel her vibrating with anxiety behind him. He put the lid back on the decanter, then drank the Scotch in one long, slow gulp. He realized he was playing for time.

But then, Hallie Hatfield had been Cristiano's biggest mistake. And at thirty-five years old, with his scandalous past, that was saying something.

He turned to face her. *"Va bene,"* he said shortly. "We are alone. What do you want?"

Hallie swallowed, blushed, hesitated. He could see her trying to formulate her words, but she didn't have to say anything. Cristiano already knew why she was here.

She'd come to demand money.

Silently he cursed himself. How could he have been so stupid?

He'd known this would happen. He was just surprised it had taken a year.

Hallie must have spoken with a lawyer who would have pointed out her excellent case for suing him for wrongful termination. His emotions had gotten the better of him the day he'd had her fired, because he'd never done anything so foolish, before or since.

Looking at her, he could almost understand why. Hallie had big, soulful eyes a man could drown in. And her curves! In a loose cotton sundress, her body was even more lush than he remembered. Her dark hair fell in waves over her full breasts, almost down to her tiny waist.

Cristiano could still remember how it had felt to have her in his arms, the sensation of her soft body sliding beneath his as their naked limbs tangled in the very bedsheets she'd made just an hour before.

He'd seduced her. There could be no doubt of that. Coming back to New York a day early, he'd heard her sweet, husky voice singing from the bedroom of his penthouse. Her wistful, heartbreaking melody had filled him with longing for things lost. Things he'd never had. Things he'd never dared even dream of.

Then he'd seen her, waving fresh sheets in the air with her arms spread wide. An incredibly beautiful, sensual brunette with an hourglass figure, leaning over to make his bed. Even that black housekeeping uniform had looked indescribably erotic on her.

A shocked sound had come from the back of his throat. She'd turned and looked at him. A tumble of emotions had cascaded across her beautiful face. Surprise, fear, delight. For a moment their eyes had locked, and he'd forgotten his own name.

Then he'd forced himself to give a casual smile. "You're not my usual housekeeper."

"Camille had to go home early today to be with her grandson, but she warned me not to let you catch me," she stammered. "I'm supposed to be invisible."

Coming forward, his eyes devouring every inch of her, he'd murmured, "You're anything but invisible. What were you singing?"

"Just an Appalachian folk song."

"It's beautiful." Coming close enough to touch her, he'd whispered, "So are you."

Her cheeks had gone rosy, her lips parting in unconscious invitation as she stood beside his enormous bed.

He'd reached for her.

Cristiano knew who was at fault. He'd wanted her. So he'd taken her. Without thinking of the consequences. If he had, he would have stopped himself. It was one of his rules: never sleep with employees.

But that wasn't the worst rule he'd broken. Hallie wasn't just an employee. She'd also been a virgin. Virgins were off-limits. He didn't toy with women who might mistake sex for love and become a problem later.

He'd known she was a virgin from the first time he'd kissed her, when he'd felt the tremble of her sweet lips. He'd felt her hesitation, her shyness, her inexperience. And he'd known. Somehow, this incredible woman was untouched.

It hadn't made him stop. He was a man who put few limits on his own behavior. But he had a code of honor. In Hallie Hatfield's case, he'd recklessly blown through his own rules like dynamite through a brick wall.

So it was no wonder he'd broken a third rule, afterward, and fired her for sleeping with him.

That wasn't the reason he'd given her supervisor, the head housekeeper, of course. But it had been obvious to Hallie. And clearly her lawyer, too.

But now, as Hallie stood across from him in his private office, biting her full, delectable lower lip, it was hard for him to think about lawyers when all he wanted to do was pull her back into his arms.

For a year, he'd done his best to forget her. He'd told himself he had. Now he knew that was a lie.

"Why are you here?" Cristiano demanded in a low voice.

"I came to…came to tell you…"

Her husky voice trembled, stopped. She looked at him.

Turning away, Cristiano set down the crystal lowball glass heavily on the dark wood bar. He clenched his hands at his sides to keep himself from the temptation of pulling her into his arms and kissing her to see if her lips were still as delicious as he remembered. He was drawn by the sweet sin of her mouth. Of her body. Of her deep brown eyes, luring him into their depths.

Possessing her once had not been enough. After he'd had her that night, he'd just wanted more. It didn't help that, naked and soft in his arms, she'd looked up at him in bed as if she were half in love with him already. She'd lured him like a siren to give him more than just his body. More than just his money.

But sex and money were all he could give any woman.

So he'd sent her away, tossing her from the warmth of his bed when his body was still aching for more. After she'd gone, he'd still longed for her, like a sweet, forbidden poison. First thing the next morning, he'd contacted her supervisor and arranged to have her fired. For her own good. And his.

But he had never stopped wanting her. And now, as he stepped toward her, his breathing was hard. And not just his breathing.

"Tell me what you want."

"I need to tell you something. Important."

"So you said." Cristiano's voice was low as he looked down at her. He came closer, almost close enough to touch her. His mind was scrambling for rationalizations as to why he should.

Perhaps if he slept with her just one more time…

Got her out of his system…

Stop, he told himself furiously.

Hesitating, Hallie licked her full, pink lips. He nearly groaned. Was she purposely taunting him?

"This…isn't easy to say," she whispered.

Gritting his teeth, he glared at her. "Let me say it for you, then. I already know why you're here."

Her caramel-brown eyes went wide.

"You know?"

He set his jaw. "You never cashed the check."

Hallie blinked, furrowing her forehead. "The check?"

"The morning after."

Her cheeks colored and she looked away.

"No," she said in a low voice. "I ripped it into a million pieces and threw it in the trash."

"Because you knew, even then, you could demand far more."

Hallie looked at him sharply.

"I can?" she whispered. "You'd give me money, just for asking? Why?"

"You want me to admit it aloud?" He pulled her roughly against him. She gasped as his hands suddenly moved over her waist, her hips.

"What are you doing?"

"Checking for a microphone." But even through the thin cotton of her sundress, touching her waist and hips without crushing her lips with his own felt like torture.

"Let me go," she breathed, not moving.

He released her. Stepping back, he leaned against the marble fireplace, folding his arms and keeping his voice very cold. "Who is your lawyer?"

"My lawyer?"

"Don't try to pretend you don't have one. You knew I'd want to keep this quiet. I'm not proud of it."

Her eyes widened. "Of—of what?"

"It would hardly improve the public image of my company if the CEO is sued for sexual harassment."

"Oh." Biting her lip, she looked away, staring for a long moment at the wall of leather-bound books he never read, and the leather reading chair he never sat in, both brought in by an interior designer to make his office look like a nineteenth-century gentleman's study. And all Cristiano could think right now was that he wanted to bend her back against the enormous dark wood desk, kiss her senseless, pull off her clothes and...

He had to get rid of her before he did something else he'd regret.

"Just tell me the amount," he said tightly.

"The amount?"

"How much?"

Licking her lips, Hallie said, "I want...the same amount as before."

"A hundred thousand dollars?" he said incredulously.

"I'll never bother you again. I give you my word."

Cristiano could hardly believe she'd ask for so little. Far less than he'd pay if they went to trial. Less than he paid his lawyers for a month. Was it some kind of trick? Or had she been given bad advice by the worst lawyer in the world?

Searching her face, he warned, "You'd have to sign a nondisclosure form."

"I'll sign anything you want," she said meekly, folding her hands in front of her like a nun at prayer.

Now Cristiano was really suspicious. "And a statement admitting that you were fired for cause."

"What does that mean?"

"You'd say it was your own fault you were fired." He gave a careless shrug, even as he watched her closely. "The reason can be anything you want. Tardiness. Stealing."

"Stealing!" Hallie repeated indignantly. Then her expression deliberately smoothed over and became meek again. "I will admit to being late. Yes. I was very, very late."

Something in Hallie's tone when she said *I was very, very late* rang true. And yet he knew it was not.

The morning Cristiano had decided to fire her, he'd asked the HR department to review her file, hoping to hear a legitimate reason she deserved to be let go. "Oh, no, sir," the HR head had chirped. "Miss Hatfield is one of our hardest-working employees. She works late and volunteers to work holidays instead of employees with kids. And she's never late!"

So he'd given the task of firing her to her supervisor, instead. Handing the head housekeeper a sealed envelope with a big check, he'd explained to the woman that he'd found Hallie intrusive and her singing annoying. The head housekeeper, whom Cristiano had never spoken to directly before, hadn't asked the same questions HR would have. She'd just followed his order.

So why would Hallie accept a hundred thousand dollars now, in lieu of a settlement that could have brought her millions? And want it so badly she was actually willing to defame her own character for it?

What kind of incompetent, useless lawyer would ever advise her to do such a thing?

Cristiano could barely restrain himself from telling her what a bad deal she was making. But his goal was to be rid of her before she caused him any more damage—personally or professionally.

"Fine." He turned to his enormous desk. Pulling out a standard nondisclosure agreement usually given to high-level executives, he pushed it across the desk toward her and scribbled something on a separate piece of paper.

"Might as well keep the lawyers out of it, and save us both time and trouble," he said carelessly. "Sign these and I'll write you a check."

Hallie looked at him sharply. "Give me the check first."

"What?" He gave a low laugh. "You don't trust me?"

"No." She looked at him with quiet determination. "Because I know what kind of man you really are."

His back snapped straight. "What kind is that?"

"You seduced me—" her dark eyes glittered in the shadows "—then had me fired. You took my job away, just to avoid the inconvenience of seeing me."

She was right. And he hated her for it.

"And now we both know what kind of woman *you* are," he said coldly. "The kind of woman who is willing to lie about herself for a hundred thousand dollars."

Her deep brown eyes held his, then dropped.

"Yes," she said in a low voice. "I suppose I am." She squared her shoulders. "But I'll still need the check before I sign."

"Fine." Turning away, he got his checkbook out of the safe. Scribbling the amount and signing it, he handed it to her.

Her hand trembled as she took the check. For a moment, she just looked down at it. Then she pressed it against her chest, looking almost near tears.

"Thank you," she whispered. "You don't know what this will mean to us."

"Us?"

"Me," she said quickly.

Obviously, she'd already found another lover. The thought bothered him. He pushed it aside. He had no claim on her, and she would have none on him once the deal was finished.

Setting his jaw, he held out the pen. "Now your side of the bargain."

"Of course." Taking the pen, she leaned over his desk to read the two documents—the nondisclosure agreement and an admission of fault. As she read, Cristiano's gaze traced unwillingly down her long throat to the dark hair tumbling down her back to the sweet fullness of her backside. Her breasts seemed fuller than he remembered.

He forced himself to look away.

Signing both papers with a flourish, she put the lid back on his pen, then handed it to him along with the signed papers. "Here."

She seemed strangely joyful, as if the weight of the world had just been lifted off her shoulders.

Cristiano barely restrained a scowl. His hand brushed hers as he took the papers and pen. Her cheeks went bright red, and she dropped her hand. "Thanks. Goodbye."

He watched incredulously as, without another word, she headed for the door.

"That's it?"

Hallie glanced back with a smile. "You wanted to be rid of me."

He couldn't believe it could be so easy for her to leave him when it was so hard for him to let her go. When it took all his self-control not to ask her to—

"Stay for a drink," he heard himself say. "Just one drink. To toast the future."

The corners of her lips curved into a humorless smile. "Isn't Natalia waiting for you?"

"Who?"

"Who?" She snorted. "The gorgeous supermodel you were taking out tonight."

"She's just a friend," he said impatiently. He knew the

Russian girl wanted more. But what did he care about her? Seeing Hallie today had brought back everything he'd tried to forget over the past year, everything he knew was forbidden but that he still wanted. "Share a drink with me."

For a second, Hallie hesitated. Then she straightened, glaring at him. "After the way you treated me, do you really think I would ever choose to spend more time with you?" She lifted her chin. "I never, ever want to see you again. Goodbye, Cristiano."

She turned away, clutching the check against her heart. She left him without looking back.

Cristiano stood in his private office, stunned.

Hallie would cause no legal trouble. The cost of his night with her had been minimal, one he'd been more than willing to pay. And now she was gone. For good.

His jaw tightened. It was what he'd wanted, wasn't it? He'd wanted to permanently rid himself of the temptation she offered. He'd never felt so attracted to anyone.

He'd slept with beautiful women before. The danger—the difference—was in Hallie's voice, so rich with heartbreak and longing. And in her deep brown eyes, which had looked at him with such frank joy. In her low, husky laugh that had melted him with her warmth and delight.

She'd made him feel things against his will.

Not with his body.

His soul.

So after he'd fired her he'd ordered his secretary to block Hallie's calls if she ever tried to contact him again.

Yet, tonight, he'd been the one who had asked her to stay. And Hallie, without any apparent difficulty or regret, had gotten what she'd wanted and easily walked away.

His pride was in shock.

As a matter of course, Cristiano always put his own selfish desires first. You had to look out for number one.

He'd just never imagined a kindhearted country girl like Hallie could do the same.

Rubbing the back of his head, he put his checkbook back in the safe. He told himself he'd go meet Natalia and spend the evening at yet another bland charity gala, but the thought seemed ridiculous.

Hallie had looked delicious, her body even more curvaceous than he remembered. She had a new maturity about her. Her dark eyes had become guarded, he realized. Not as honest and clear as he remembered. She'd held something back. Some mystery. Some secret.

Cristiano closed the safe, then stopped.

Something didn't make sense.

When Hallie had first met him in the lobby, she'd been nervous and tense. *I have something important to tell you*, she'd said. But what was it? Simply that she'd hired a lawyer?

Except she'd never actually said that. Cristiano had. She'd been slow to talk and so he'd filled in all the blanks. When he'd offered her money, she'd been surprised, even shocked. Surely that was why she'd asked to speak to him privately. Because her lawyer had told her to.

Unless she didn't actually have a lawyer.

Unless she'd come to him for some other reason. A reason she'd decided to forget once he'd offered her a check.

Cristiano's eyes widened.

He strode out of his private office and down the sweeping stairs that overlooked the huge, gleaming lobby with enormous chandeliers hanging from thirty-foot ceilings. His eyes scanned over the crowd of wealthy tycoons and beautiful starlets that filled the lobby and main bar of the Campania on a typical Thursday night.

He saw Hallie on the other side of the lobby, near the door, talking to two young women, a plump redhead and a pregnant blonde. Hallie smiled, her joy obvious even from this distance, as she reached out to take something from the blonde.

A baby stroller. Looking down at it, she smiled and cooed.

Cristiano's blood went cold.

A baby stroller.

A baby.

Later, he wouldn't even remember how he had reached her. His brain was blank, his body like ice as he walked through the faceless crowd toward Hallie Hatfield and the baby stroller she gripped by the handle. When he drew close, he heard her soft laughter as she turned to her friends. The other women's eyes went wide as Cristiano put his hand on her shoulder.

Hallie's face was still smiling as she turned. Then the blood drained from her face.

Cristiano looked from her guilt-stricken face down to the small, dark-haired, fat-cheeked baby drowsing in the stroller. He slowly lifted his eyes back to hers.

"Is this your baby, Hallie?"

The fear in her eyes told him everything he needed to know.

The other two women stared between them, wide-eyed.

"You didn't tell him?" the blonde said.

"Oh, Hallie," the redhead whispered.

"Please, just go," Hallie choked out to them. "I'll call you later."

The blonde looked like she intended to argue, until the redhead tugged on her arm and drew her away.

Standing alone with Cristiano in the crowded lobby of his flagship hotel, Hallie took a deep breath. "I can explain."

Cristiano looked back down at the baby. A baby with dark eyes exactly like his own. Suddenly he knew exactly why Hallie had come here today. And exactly why she'd changed her mind.

He controlled his voice with effort. "You have a baby."

She bit her lip. "Yes."

He lifted his cold gaze to hers. "Who is the father?"

Hallie said pleadingly, "Please, Cristiano, don't…"

"Who, damn you."

She flinched. When she spoke, her voice could barely be heard over the noise of the lobby. "You."

That single word exploded through him like a grenade. He had a child?

Heart pounding, Cristiano looked at the tiny, yawning baby. Emotions rose, choking him. Savagely repressing his feelings, he looked at her.

"You are sure?" he said flatly.

"Yes," Hallie replied in the same tone. "You know I was a virgin when—"

"I know," he bit out. "But perhaps after…"

"You think I rushed into bed with someone else after that?" Her expression tightened. "You are the only man I've ever been with. Jack is your son."

He had a child? A son?

His name was Jack?

Cristiano's throat tightened. "Why didn't you tell me you were pregnant?"

"I tried." Hallie's beautiful caramel-brown eyes narrowed. "I left two messages with your secretary."

Cristiano hadn't gotten those messages because he'd told his secretary never to tell him if Hallie called.

But he didn't want to hear reasons he might be at fault. He wanted to blame only her. "We used protection," he said accusingly. "How did this happen?"

She raised her eyebrows. "You are the one with all the experience. You tell me."

He ground his teeth. "You should have tried harder to contact me."

"After the way you treated me," she said, "I shouldn't

have tried at all. Why give you the chance to reject our baby like you rejected me?"

His shoulders tightened as her shot hit home.

"So you were just going to walk out of here tonight." His voice had a hard edge. His throat felt raw. "Once you had my check, you had no reason to tell me about my child. You were going to keep him a secret from me for the rest of my life, weren't you?"

Not meeting his eyes, Hallie gave an unsteady nod.

His hands clenched at his sides. "Why?"

"I've never known what it was to hate someone, Cristiano," she whispered. She lifted her gaze to his. "Not until you."

He was shocked by the fury and hurt he saw in her eyes. "I could not have hurt you that badly," he ground out. "We barely knew each other."

"You were so seductive. So tender. You made me think you cared, just a little." She ran an unsteady hand over her forehead. "But as soon as you got what you wanted, you showed me it was all a lie. You left me jobless, homeless. Pregnant and alone. I gave birth alone. I took care of him alone. Do you know how hard it is to look for a job when you have a newborn? I struggled to put a roof over Jack's head while you pretended we didn't exist." She looked around the luxurious lobby. "While you drank champagne and went to parties."

Her words made him feel oddly guilty. He didn't like it. "You never told me—"

"I came here to beg you for money, Cristiano." Her beautiful brown eyes were suddenly luminous. "To *beg*, so I wouldn't have to stay at a homeless shelter tonight. Can you imagine how that feels, asking someone you hate for help?"

No. Cristiano couldn't imagine lowering his pride to such an extent. Even when he'd been orphaned in Italy, desperately poor, he would have starved before he'd have done it.

But women were different, he told himself firmly. They didn't have the same fierce pride as a man.

"Then I offered you the check," he said, "and you decided to take the money and run."

"I'm doing you a favor," she said vehemently. "It's not like you'd want to be a father. So just forget I came here. Forget he was ever born."

Turning, Hallie started pushing the stroller away.

As he watched them go, the hotel's marble floor became suddenly unsteady beneath Cristiano's feet.

A flash went through him, memories of when he was six, when he was ten, of being dragged from one sagging apartment to the next, based on the preference of whichever useless new man his drunken mother had taken as her latest lover. He'd felt helpless as a child, lonely, never staying in one school long enough to make friends.

Most of the household's scant money had gone to alcohol. There had been very little for food and none for Cristiano's clothes, which the local priest quietly donated.

He'd never had a father, unless you counted Luigi Bennato, whom Cristiano assuredly did not. He'd never had a father to look out for him or protect him, even as a baby.

Without thinking, Cristiano stepped forward and grabbed Hallie's shoulder.

"I won't let you do this," he said hoarsely. "I won't let you take our baby away."

"Why?" she said scornfully. "Because you want to be a father?" Her eyes glittered. "Don't make me laugh. You're a selfish playboy, Cristiano. An indecent excuse for a man. You couldn't love someone if you tried, not even your own child. And now that I have enough money to support my baby, I don't want any part of you."

CHAPTER TWO

STANDING IN THE hotel's glamorous lobby with her arms folded, Hallie glared up at Cristiano as if she weren't in the least afraid. But the truth was her whole body was trembling with the effort it took to defy him.

She wished she'd followed her initial impulse when Cristiano had first come into the lobby, and turned and run.

But he'd have caught up with her before she'd even made it out the hotel's revolving door. A single glance at his supremely masculine, muscular body and the cold ruthlessness in his hard gaze was enough to tell her that.

Everything about Cristiano was dark, Hallie thought with a shiver. Dark hair. Dark eyes. Dark tuxedo. A five-o'clock shadow that stroked his hard cheekbones to the slash of his jawline and, most of all, his dark fury as he came closer to her, his hand still on her shoulder, his hulking body almost threatening.

"So this is what you think of me." His black eyes narrowed to slits. "That I'd coldly write you a check and abandon my child to your care."

She was quivering but refused to be cowed. "Money is all you could ever offer as a father. Why don't you just admit it?"

His grip on her shoulder tightened. "You lie to me, you take my money. Then you insult me to my face?"

He had a point, which made her want to throw the check back in that face. Her hand was already rising to do it when she remembered Lola's harsh words. *Is pride going to feed your baby?*

With an intake of breath, Hallie clutched the check more tightly. This money would be her baby's security and hope for the future. It would also give Hallie a chance to finally give up her stupid dream of becoming a singer and let her train for a real job, like an accountant or a nurse.

She wasn't going to let pride ruin her life. Not anymore.

Or Cristiano Moretti.

"You should thank me," she said.

He grew very still. "*Thank* you?"

"We both know, whatever you might say now, that you couldn't truly commit to anyone, even a child."

"How do you know?" he ground out.

"You, commit? For a lifetime?" She gave a choked laugh. "You couldn't even commit for a *night*." She tilted her head. "Were you that quickly bored, the night we were together? Or did you have another date afterward?"

His expression changed infinitesimally. "You think I sent you away because I was bored with you?"

Hallie thought of the glamorous supermodel she'd just seen on his arm. "What else?"

She couldn't let him see how badly that hurt her. When he'd first taken her in his arms that romantic night, she'd been so naive. She'd thought it was fate, an irresistible force drawing them together. She'd thought it was magic.

Hallie had been startled when he'd walked into his penthouse early that afternoon. She'd been warned to be invisible and that her cleaning must be spotless. After spending so much time dusting pictures of his handsome face, seeing Cristiano in the flesh had shocked her.

Cristiano Moretti was a dream come to life. A famous playboy, the self-made Italian hotel billionaire who dated princesses and heiresses.

And inexplicably, he'd wanted *her*.

One moment she and Cristiano had been talking by the bed; the next she'd been in his arms. After so many bleak years of anguish after losing her family and her home, when her handsome billionaire boss had lowered his lips to hers,

Hallie had imagined all the pain was behind her. She'd thought her life had just changed for the better.

And it had, in one way: her baby. Jack was all that mattered now.

"I'm leaving," Hallie said defiantly. "Once I cash your check, I promise you, we'll be gone for good."

Cristiano lowered his head until it was inches from hers. "And I promise you. You'll do nothing of the kind."

Her mouth went dry. As their eyes locked, her heart pounded in her throat as she realized her stupid, idiotic mistake.

She never should have openly defied Cristiano. Because he'd taken her words not just as a challenge but as an insult to his masculinity. To his honor, even.

All this time she'd been thinking about her pride. She hadn't considered his. And now he would make her pay for it.

"You don't want me," she whispered, her voice almost pleading. "You know you don't."

His dark eyes seemed like deep, fathomless pools as his gaze ripped into her soul. Then he straightened.

"You're wrong about that. I've wanted you for a year. And now I will have you."

"What are you talking about?"

His gaze fell to the stroller and his expression grew cold. "He's my child, Hallie. I'm not going to let him go." He focused on her. "Or you."

"I won't be your mistress, if that's what you mean," she said, struggling to keep her voice calm, not to show her rising fear.

"I know." Cristiano's black eyes suddenly glittered, and he smiled. "Because you're going to be my wife."

His wife.

Cristiano watched Hallie's eyes widen in shock.

It was strange, he thought. He hadn't known he was going to demand marriage until the words came out of his mouth. His whole life, he'd never once been tempted to marry. Of course he'd never imagined he'd be a father, either. And as he spoke the words, he suddenly realized he did want to marry her.

Call him an indecent excuse for a man?

Say he was incapable of committing for longer than a night?

Tell him he couldn't even love his child if he tried?

No.

Cristiano wouldn't abandon his newborn son to endure the same helpless childhood he'd known. Not when he himself had spent most of his adult life seeking vengeance on the father who'd abandoned him before he was born.

But he couldn't wrench his son away from Hallie, either. Mother and child were obviously bonded. Still, he needed to take control of the situation.

Marriage was the brutally simple solution.

"Marry you?" Hallie choked out, searching his gaze as if waiting for the punchline. "Are you crazy? I told you—I hate you!"

"And I'm none too fond of you." But as he put both hands on her shoulders and looked down at her, his nerve endings sizzled from the contact. He might be angry, but he'd told her the truth. He hadn't stopped wanting her for a year.

Her gaze fell unwillingly on his lips before she glared up defiantly. "Why would I marry you?"

Looking down at the baby, who was now awake and trying to grab his own feet in the stroller, he said quietly, "For our child."

"But...you can't seriously want to be a real father." There was a new nervousness in her voice. "If you want to see Jack, maybe we could talk about visitation—"

"No," he said coldly. Her expression looked relieved

until he continued grimly, "I will have full-time, permanent custody."

Hallie's beautiful face blanched. She whispered, "You'd try to take him from me?"

"No." He gave her a cold smile. "I want him to have two parents. Even though you didn't care about that."

Patrons and staff in the lobby had been staring at them for a while, but now they were coming closer, obviously trying to listen.

"I'm not having this conversation here," he said abruptly. "Come with me now."

She glanced around wildly, and he wondered if she was actually considering trying to flee. To help her avoid the temptation, he gently lifted the baby from the stroller.

"What are you doing?" she gasped.

"Holding my son," he said, and started walking. She immediately followed him to the elevator, as he'd known she would.

"Want me to come up with you, Mr. Moretti?" his bodyguard asked.

Cristiano shook his head. "Tell Natalia I won't be able to attend the gala after all. Give her my apologies."

"Sure, boss."

Cristiano continued into the elevator, with Hallie's stroller dogging his heels. Once inside, he pressed his fingerprint against the hidden button for the penthouse.

As they rode the elevator to the top floor, she watched him anxiously. He tried to act casual, as if he'd held a baby before, but he felt awkward. Even three-month-old Jack seemed to be looking up at him in disbelief, as if trying to decide whether to cry or not.

"You're doing it wrong. Hold his head like this," Hallie blurted out, positioning the baby differently in his arms. She shook her head impatiently. "Just give him to me."

"Forget it," he said crisply. Jack was his son and, in some

respects, until he secured her loyalty as his wife, Hallie was his enemy. There was no way he'd admit he didn't know what he was doing or give the baby back to her care in a sign of weakness and surrender.

The elevator door slid open onto a small hallway with a grand door and a smaller, inconspicuous one farther down. The top floor of the Campania Hotel was devoted exclusively to Cristiano's penthouse and terraces, with a small separate apartment for his bodyguard. He had a similar penthouse in his flagship hotel in Rome and smaller private suites in his hotels in Tokyo, Sydney, Rio, London and Berlin. He could have rented out the space to paying guests when he was away for an exorbitant amount, but he kept them to himself. Life was about little indulgences, or what was the point of being rich? A man, particularly a wealthy playboy, needed privacy.

Hallie followed him anxiously into the penthouse, as if she feared he might drop the baby. It was insulting. Especially as Jack gave a soft whimper in Cristiano's arms.

"Give him to me—now!" Hallie said.

Keeping his expression inscrutable and moving with deliberate slowness to show her that he was doing it as his own decision, not hers, he carefully handed her their son. Leaving the stroller in the foyer, she clung to the newborn as if they'd been separated for days.

"You bastard," she choked out. "Dragging us up here. It's practically kidnapping."

"Kidnapping?" He looked down at her coldly. "How about trying to steal my son from me for the rest of my life?"

Some of the anger in her gaze faded. "If you cared so much, you should have taken my calls when I was pregnant!"

He hated that she was right. With a low, bitter laugh, he turned away. "You remember your way around, I presume?"

She followed him into the enormous room with its starkly modern furniture and floor-to-ceiling windows that offered a magnificent view of the city's sparkling lights. To the left, an open-concept kitchen had all the latest appliances, none of which he'd ever used. There was a reason he chose to live in his own hotels.

He looked back at her. Hallie's cheeks were pink. He wondered if she was remembering when she'd cleaned here, as the maid. Or if she was remembering, instead, the night she'd helped him mess everything up again, tangling the bedsheets in a night of passion so hot it had burned past all barriers to create a child. A night he could never forget.

"Have a seat," he said coolly even as he fought the flash of heat at the memory. He indicated the white sofa that overlooked the spectacular view.

She tossed her head. "No, thanks. I don't intend to be here long enough to—"

"Sit down," he said more forcefully, and glaring at him, she obeyed, cradling the fussing baby in her arms.

Cristiano sat down in the white chair beside the sofa. He didn't need to see the city view; he knew it so well by now it bored him. He looked only at her.

"If Jack is truly my son, he belongs with me."

She set her jaw. "You're only saying that because I insulted your pride. You don't really care about him."

He narrowed his eyes. "Oh, you know that, do you? Because I'm an indecent excuse for a man? Because I couldn't love someone if I tried?"

She had the decency to blush. "I'm sorry if that was rude. But it's true."

He restrained himself from tossing a few insults back in her face, insults she richly deserved. "You don't trust me? Fine. I don't trust you, either." He looked down at the baby in her arms. "So from now on, my son is staying here."

"No."

"I will not allow him to disappear from my life just on your word that you'll take good care of him."

"And I won't let you turn our lives upside down, just because I injured your masculine pride!"

That was all she thought it was? Controlling his temper, he took a deep breath.

"I know from experience what it is like to grow up with no father and no name," he said slowly. "To live in poverty, with a mother too distracted by her own concerns to worry about mine. She moved us to a new town every time she took a new lover. Men who inevitably despised me as a burden, who thought I deserved to be screamed at, punched, starved."

The color drained from Hallie's face.

"What?" she whispered. "She didn't protect you?"

Cristiano shook his head. "She couldn't even protect herself. When I was eighteen, her last lover beat her almost to death. When I tried to intervene, she kicked me out." He gave a hard smile. "I learned my lesson. You can only look out for yourself."

Her soft eyes looked horrified, as if she'd never imagined any family could go so wrong. "I'm so sorry."

Cristiano hated the pity in her eyes. He regretted saying so much. He'd never spoken about his past to anyone. "I just wanted you to understand." He leaned forward in his chair. "I can't let you leave with him, then spend my life wondering if you're taking good care of my son, if you've taken lovers into your house who might hate him for crying, who might pick him up out of the crib and shake him hard until the crying stops—"

"I would never let that happen!"

"I know," he said grimly. "Because he's staying with me."

"But—"

"Did you give him my last name?" he interrupted.

"His last name is Hatfield, like mine."

"Something else that our marriage will rectify," he said.

Hallie looked down at her baby softly whimpering in her arms. Her voice was small as she said with visible reluctance, "I might be willing to talk about...about shared custody."

Why was she continuing to argue? Repressing his rising anger, he shook his head. "Marriage."

"But why?"

"I've given you the reasons." Suddenly he was finished trying to reason with her, trying to explain. He'd been far more patient and open with her than she deserved. For all the good it had done. He narrowed his eyes. "The discussion is over. We will wed. The decision is made."

"Made by *you*. But you're not my boss. Not anymore."

Cristiano tilted his head. He said in a deceptively casual voice, "You can refuse my proposal, of course."

"Then I refuse."

"Then our son stays with me."

Wide-eyed, she breathed, "Just because you're his biological father you think you have the right to take him from me? I'm his mother!"

"And I have an entire team of lawyers at my disposal. What do you have? Nothing. You've already indicated you're a liar and a flight risk. I'd request an immediate injunction from a judge to prevent you from ever leaving New York."

"Liar? When did I ever lie?"

"Just now. When you took a hundred thousand dollars from me under false pretenses, then tried to run away with my son without telling me he existed."

Hallie's face was deathly pale. The baby's whimpers rose to soft wails.

"I *am* a liar," she said suddenly. "You're not Jack's father, Cristiano. You never were. It was all a…a plot. To get money from you."

"You're the worst liar I've ever seen."

"I slept with five men right after you!" Her voice rose desperately. "Any of them could be his father. Here—take your money back!"

Pulling the folded check from the pocket of her sundress, she held it out to him.

Cristiano's lips curved.

"Why, Hallie," he said, without moving to take it, "are you trying to bribe me to give up my parental rights?"

Stuffing the check back in her pocket, she rose trembling to her feet. "I wish I'd never come here!"

His voice turned hard. "Sit down."

"And I don't care what you say." She lifted her chin. "Our justice system wouldn't take a baby from his mother!"

"So dramatic." He added with dark amusement, "You have a lot of faith in something you clearly know nothing about. How do you think judges and juries decide the truth? They believe the best lawyers with the best arguments. And what kind of lawyer would you find to represent you? An inexperienced pro bono attorney fresh out of law school? Some tired hack working on contingency? You'll have no chance. You will lose."

Cristiano watched the emotions struggle on Hallie's beautiful face. Remembering how she'd almost walked out with his child, he didn't feel sorry for her. At all.

He looked down at Jack, now loudly complaining in Hallie's arms. It had been so close. It scared him to think about it. If he hadn't been suspicious and followed her into the lobby, he never would have known. His son would have grown up believing his father had abandoned him. Rejected him.

Exactly as Cristiano's father had.

Hallie looked down at her wailing baby. "He's hungry," she said, avoiding his gaze. "Where can I go?"

"Right here."

"I'm not nursing him in front of you."

"I don't trust you not to run off."

"Fine," she bit out as the baby's wails increased. "At least turn around."

"Of course." He turned toward the wall of windows overlooking the city. The baby's crying ceased almost immediately, changing to soft, contented murmurs.

Cristiano's shoulders relaxed, and he realized that he'd been tense, feeling his son's unhappiness. He felt more sure than ever that his impulsive decision, demanding marriage, was right. It was the only way to ensure the baby's comfort and security.

His son's childhood would be completely different from his own. Jack wouldn't be abandoned by a father who cared only about his business empire, or left to the devices of a mother who cared only about her own selfish needs. He would never worry about getting beaten or having enough to eat. Jack would always have a stable home. And two loving parents.

Cristiano would do whatever it took, make any sacrifice, to make it so. And so would Hallie.

He would leave her no other choice.

Rising from the white chair, still with his back to her, he pulled out his phone, pressed a button and lifted it to his ear.

"Contact Dr. Garcia," he told his executive assistant, Marcia Lattimer, when she answered. "Tell him I'm bringing a woman and baby in twenty minutes for a checkup and paternity test."

"Yes, sir."

"What?" Hallie said in alarm behind him.

"Ask Matthews to pull the limo around," he continued.

He remembered the baby. "On second thought, the SUV. Have the concierge arrange a new baby seat to be sent down. Whatever is required for a three-month-old. I want it installed and ready by the time we're downstairs."

"Of course, Mr. Moretti," Marcia murmured. She was well paid to be on call around the clock. "Anything else?"

"I'll let you know," he said, and hung up.

"Paternity test?" Hallie's voice was low but enraged. "You don't even believe he's yours?"

"Can I turn around?"

"Yes."

He looked at her calmly. He was pleased to see the baby now sleeping contentedly in her arms. "You said he was mine. Then you said he wasn't."

She looked furious. "You know!"

"I believe he is mine, but I want proof."

She tossed her head. "What kind of quack doctor will do a paternity test in the middle of the night? It's after nine!"

Cristiano was amused that she thought of nine o'clock as the middle of the night. His own nights out often didn't start until eleven. "Dr. Garcia is my personal physician, one of the best in the city. He also appreciates that I fully fund his medical research."

She ground her teeth. "Is everyone in this city on your payroll? Do you always get what you want?"

"Yes," he said simply, to both.

Ten minutes later, they were seated in the back of a huge black SUV with tinted windows and a brand-new baby seat installed between them.

"Nice to meet you, ma'am," called Matthews from the driver's seat. "Cute little guy you've got there." He looked at Cristiano in the rearview mirror. "I understand congratulations are in order, sir?"

"Thank you," Cristiano said. He tenderly lifted a soft blue blanket against his sleeping baby's plump cheek. Feeling Hallie's gaze, Cristiano looked up. A current of electricity passed between them.

Biting her full, pink lower lip, she abruptly looked away. But his body was still aware of her. A new thought went through Cristiano.

He'd intended to marry her as a matter of honor and duty, but there would be compensations.

A year ago, he'd sent her away for her own good—and his. But fate had changed their lives. Now, through their child, they would always be connected.

Married.

And marriage would have other benefits. A wedding night. Endless sensual delights.

He wanted to kiss her. His gaze traced over the curve of her cheek, over the visible tremble of her pink lips as she stubbornly stared out the window into the dark city streets. He wondered how long it would take him to seduce her.

Would it be tomorrow?

Tonight?

Either way, Cristiano knew that nothing could now deny him the pleasure of taking Hallie to his bed. He would possess every inch of her. Every night. For as long as he desired.

Once they were wed, she would be his.

CHAPTER THREE

AS THEY LEFT the doctor's private office downtown later that night, Hallie was in despair.

She couldn't marry him. She *couldn't*.

But how could she not?

Closing her eyes, she leaned back in the seat of the SUV and tried to picture herself as Cristiano's wife. She imagined Cristiano in a tuxedo, striding through his luxury skyscraper while she trailed after him in a dumpy maid's uniform.

How could the two of them ever marry? What did they even have in common?

Just one thing. Her gaze fell upon the baby in the car seat beside her.

What would it be like for Jack to be raised as a tycoon's son, wealthy beyond belief? To go to all the best schools, with the best tutors? To be proficient at all the sports of the wealthy, like skiing, tennis, lacrosse? Every door in the world would be open to Jack.

A lump rose in her throat. But would her son be happy? Would he grow up to be a good, honorable man?

"Would you like me to take you home?" Cristiano said in a low voice.

Hallie looked at him over the baby seat in the back seat of the SUV. He'd taken off his tuxedo jacket and loosened his tie. His dark good looks and smoldering gaze burned through her.

"Home?" she whispered.

Cristiano lifted an eyebrow. "Whatever you might think of me, I'm not a total bastard. Now that I have proof of paternity I want you to be comfortable."

He was willing to take Hallie home? He'd given up his ridiculous plan of forcing her to marry him?

A rush of relief flooded through Hallie; it was so great she almost cried.

"Thank you," she choked out.

"Give Matthews your address."

Her address. Remembering what had happened with her landlord that morning, she gulped. She didn't want to face that horrible man again. Plus, if Cristiano saw where she'd been living, he might change his mind and refuse to let the baby live there. Hallie barely wanted to go back herself.

"Um…in the East Village," she said vaguely.

Cristiano looked at her expectantly, dark eyebrows raised. Reluctantly she gave Matthews the address.

I just won't let Cristiano go in, she told herself. The apartment building looked respectable enough on the outside. Plus, maybe her landlord was very sorry for what he'd done. Maybe.

She looked down at her baby, who'd been fed and changed at the clinic and was now happily babbling. She stroked his downy dark hair, looking into the eyes that were exactly like his father's.

Then she suddenly remembered. Reaching into her diaper bag, she grabbed her phone. Just as she'd expected, she saw multiple messages from her friends.

Are you all right? Is he being nice?

From Tess.

Did he agree to pay child support? How much?

From Lola.

Why aren't you answering?

Are you being held hostage?

Should we call the police?

Quickly Hallie typed out a response to them both.

All well. Just got a paternity test. He says he wants to be a father to Jack. More later.

She tucked her phone away. Rolling down her car window, Hallie took a deep breath, looking out into the warm, humid July night as their SUV drove into the Lower East Side. She felt sick at the thought of seeing her landlord, who wasn't a proper landlord at all, just a guy who'd been willing to rent her a room in his apartment at a cut-rate price.

But the man had made it clear to her that morning that he expected her to pay in other, less tangible ways. She gulped. She never would have wanted to come back here, except she'd left behind all her most precious possessions. Her old family photos from West Virginia. Her grandmother's homemade quilt. Her father's watch. It was everything she had left of her family now.

Hallie took a deep breath. She'd just pay the landlord off, take all her stuff and then she and the baby could check into a hotel.

"Um…" Hallie bit her lip. "Do you think we could stop somewhere so I could cash my check?"

"You waste no time." The corners of Cristiano's lips twitched. "You think some check-cashing store is going to count you out a hundred thousand dollars in twenty-dollar bills?"

"Maybe a bank…"

"The banks are closed. Why do you need money?"

"I've been having a small problem with the landlord," she said quietly. He stared at her.

"Are you under the impression that I'm leaving you and Jack at your apartment?"

She drew back, bewildered. "Aren't you?"

"We're getting your things. Jack's things. Then we're going back to my penthouse."

"Oh," she whispered.

"Put that check away. Rip it up, invest it, cash it tomorrow, whatever you want. But I'll be providing you and my son with everything you could possibly need."

His voice was autocratic. Clearly he thought he was still the boss of her. She felt shaken.

"I thought, now that you have the results of the paternity test—now that you have some legal rights—you wouldn't need to get married."

"You thought wrong." The SUV pulled up at the curb in front of the five-story building. "Get what you need for tonight. Tomorrow, I'll arrange for your lease to be paid in full. That should take care of your landlord. My staff will return to collect anything big or heavy. Cribs, furniture. Or we can leave all that behind and buy new. Whichever you prefer."

"Um," said Hallie, who owned neither a crib for the baby nor any actual furniture.

"I'll wait here with the baby and give you your privacy. Don't be long." When she didn't move, his gaze sharpened. "Well?"

Turning, she blurted, "I don't need anything. Let's just go straight to your hotel."

"But you need clothes—"

"No, I'm fine."

He looked at her as if she'd lost her mind. "But we're already here."

"I don't want to go in!" Her voice was shrill.

Cristiano looked at her for a long moment. When he spoke, his voice was surprisingly gentle.

"What's really going on, Hallie?"

With an intake of breath, she looked away. Even at midnight the street was busy, and the neon lights of pizzerias and Laundromats littering First Avenue lit up the sultry summer night.

"After you fired me," she said softly, "it was hard to find a job. I finally worked as housekeeper for a couple on the Upper West Side. The job included room and board. But when I brought Jack home from the hospital they let me go."

His eyebrows lowered. "Why?"

She gave a humorless smile. "They said Jack's crying was causing psychic trauma to their two Chinese Crested show dogs."

"Are you serious?"

"With a newborn, I couldn't find a new job. I've lived off my savings for the last three months. Even the cheapest apartments were too much." She looked down at her hands. "So last month, I rented a room in a stranger's apartment. From an online site. I was amazed it was so cheap. Then…"

She stopped, biting her lip.

Eyes narrowing, Cristiano leaned forward in the back seat.

"Then?" he demanded.

"The man wasn't bad at first. But over the last few weeks, he started brushing up against me in the kitchen. Trying to catch me coming out of the shower. That sort of thing." She looked away. It was surprisingly hard to go on. "This morning, he…grabbed me."

Silence fell in the SUV.

"He attacked you." Cristiano's voice was toneless. It gave her the courage to meet his eyes.

"Maybe *attack* is too strong a word." She tried to smile, failed. "He tried to kiss me and reach his hand under my dress. When I pushed him away, he told me I wasn't paying my fair share of the rent so I should pay in other ways."

Trembling, she looked away. "I grabbed the baby and my diaper bag and ran. He yelled after me that I'd signed a lease and he'd be keeping all my things as payment. The only reason I have the stroller is because I'd left it downstairs." She whispered, "He has everything I own. But I'm not sure I can face him again."

Silence.

Slowly she looked up.

Then Hallie saw Cristiano's expression. The fire in his dark eyes. The cold fury that threatened imminent death for the man who'd scared her.

"I'm fine. Really." Putting her hands on his taut arm, she said hurriedly, "I hardly own anything. All my clothes would fit in a single duffel bag. It's just family photos and an old quilt…" She realized she was babbling and took a deep breath. "He didn't hurt me. He never threatened the baby…"

His voice was low and deadly. "He tried to force himself on you."

"I got away. Everything's fine, we're all fine—"

"*I'm* not fine," Cristiano bit out, and got out of the vehicle. He looked back at her, his handsome face as implacable as granite. "Which apartment number?"

"Promise you won't hurt him—"

"His number," he ground out.

"Four C," she whispered.

His face was half-hidden in shadow in the gleam from the neon sign of a nearby bar. "Wait here."

He slammed the car door.

Hallie's wait seemed to last forever. She nervously watched the minutes pass by on the dashboard. She stroked her baby's cheek as he smiled up at her from the reverse-facing baby seat. "It's fine," she reassured Jack, who in response lifted his chubby arm to bat blindly at the giraffe toy dangling from the handle of his car seat.

Oh, she was being ridiculous. Most likely the two men were having a civilized chat, that was all. Cristiano was likely calmly writing a check—which was, after all, what he did best—and requesting that Mervin Smith, the man who possessed the rent-controlled apartment, would kindly pack up all her things and bring them down.

Right. Not even Tess would have believed that.

Nervously she looked up at Matthews, the driver, who was still sitting at the wheel. "I don't need to worry about what Cristiano might do, right? He wouldn't do anything violent. Right?"

Matthews peered up through his window at the building. "Luther's not here. That's a good sign."

"Luther?"

"His bodyguard."

Hallie brightened. "That's true."

"But Mr. Moretti was a brawler, back when he was young. He fought his way out of the streets of Naples."

"Oh." She swallowed. "But that was a long time ago. I'm sure Cristiano has changed—"

"And just last year—" Matthews stroked his beard thoughtfully "—two punks tried to jump him as he was jogging real early through Central Park. He put them in the hospital. And then there was the time—"

"That's good," Hallie said in a strangled voice, holding up her hand sharply. "You don't need to tell me more."

"Glad to help," the driver said, straightening his old-fashioned black cap. Then he sucked in his breath and got out of the vehicle.

Hallie jumped as her car door was suddenly wrenched open. She saw Mervin, with dried ketchup still on his chin and his too-tight T-shirt pulling up over his huge belly, on his knees on the sidewalk. He looked terrified.

"I'm sorry," he choked out. "I'm so sorry, Hallie—"

"Miss Hatfield," Cristiano corrected coldly, standing behind the man like a dark angel.

"Miss Hatfield," the man repeated desperately. "I brought down your stuff. Everything is there, totally perfect, I swear—"

"Thank you," she said anxiously. Her eyes lifted to Cristiano's. Even after what her landlord had done to her, she'd never wanted him humiliated like this. "It's all right now."

Cristiano looked down at the man with a sneer. "If I ever hear that you've attacked any woman ever again—"

"Never, ever, I swear," Mervin cried. Stumbling to his feet, he hurried into the building with one final terrified glance back.

As Matthews stacked the few boxes into the SUV's trunk, Cristiano calmly climbed into the back seat beside her and the baby. Matthews closed the trunk with a bang. Two minutes later, they were driving north through the streets of Manhattan.

Her heart was still pounding. "What did you do to him?"

Cristiano shrugged. "I asked him to apologize."

"You just...asked?"

"I asked nicely."

She thought about pushing the issue, then decided she didn't want to know. She hadn't seen visible signs of injury. That was the best she could hope for—and that the man had been sincere when he'd said he'd never try to force a kiss on any woman again. She took a deep breath.

"Thank you," she whispered. "I don't care about the clothes. But the pictures of my family mean the world to me."

He looked at her, then set his jaw. "I'm surprised you even care about your family after they turned their backs on you."

"What do you mean?"

"They left you and Jack to struggle alone."

Hallie blinked at him in surprise, and said gently, "They didn't have a choice. They died five years ago."

Cristiano's eyes widened. "Died?"

She swallowed over the lump in her throat. It was still hard to speak of it. "Back home, in West Virginia. I grew up in a tiny village in the mountains. I was nineteen, still living at home, working the overnight shift at a grocery store in a nearby town. A fire had burned much of the forest the previous summer. After a week of hard rain, one night a flash flood came down the mountain and ripped our cabin off its foundation. If I'd been sleeping in my bed, I would have died with my parents and brother." She looked down. "For a long time, I wished I had."

"I'm sorry," he said quietly.

Blinking back tears, Hallie looked blindly out her window. "I came home at dawn and found fire trucks where my house had been. It had floated down the river, knocked to one side, crushed into wood. They found my family later..."

She couldn't go on, remembering how she'd felt at nineteen when her whole world had fallen apart, when she'd lost her home and everyone she loved without warning.

Suddenly she felt Cristiano's hand over her own.

With an intake of breath, she looked up. His eyes were black as jet.

"My mother died when I was eighteen," he said quietly. "The night she kicked me out, I decided if she still wanted her lover even after he beat her, if she cared about him more than me, then fine, I'd go. But at three in the morning, I went back. I found the house on fire."

"Arson?" Hallie breathed.

He shook his head, his lips twisting. "Nothing so deliberate. Her lover had been smoking in bed. He passed out drunk, and they both burned to death." He gave her a crooked smile. "It's funny, really. Your family died of water. Mine of fire."

"Funny," she said over the lump in her throat. All this time she'd hated Cristiano, believing him arrogant and ruthless and cold. All of which he was. But she'd never stopped to ask why.

"I'm sorry." She twined her hand in his, trying in turn to offer comfort. "You know how it feels to lose family, too. To lose a home."

For a moment, he looked at her. Then he turned, pulling his hand away. Lights moved over them in patterns as they drove toward Midtown.

When the SUV pulled up to the grand porte cohere of the Campania Hotel, Cristiano lifted the baby's carrier from the back seat. Holding the handle with his powerful arm, he turned back to Hallie, extending his other hand to help her out of the car.

Nervously she put her hand in his. Just feeling his palm against hers as he helped her out made her shiver from her scalp to her toes.

He held her hand as they walked through the lobby with its soaring ceilings and elegant midcentury furniture. The space was filled with glamorous people, hotel guests and patrons of the lobby bar or the jazz club. She saw a sexy sheikh, pouting models and starlets.

All of them turned to stare at Cristiano as he passed. Then their gazes slid in confusion to Hallie, makeup-free and wearing a limp cotton sundress. Even more shocking was the baby carrier hanging from Cristiano's arm.

People stared and whispered as they passed. A few dared to approach Cristiano with questions in their eyes. He just nodded at them and kept walking.

He stopped only briefly to speak to Clarence Loggia, the hotel manager, as Matthews and a porter headed for the elevator with Hallie's boxes.

"Good evening, Mr. Moretti." Mr. Loggia was too well

trained to show even the slightest surprise at seeing either a baby or a former hotel maid on his employer's arm.

"How is it tonight, Clarence?"

"I am pleased to report the hotel is currently at ninety-six percent capacity. The Sultan of Bataar just arrived. He's taken the presidential suite for the entire summer, along with the rest of the floor for his entourage."

"Excellent. Please send him my regards and a collection of his favorite brandy and cigars with my personal compliments."

The man smiled. "Already done, sir." He hesitated, then lowered his voice. "Also, I thought you would want to know. Prince Stefano Zacco di Gioreale just checked in."

"Why does he insist on staying here?" A shadow crossed Cristiano's face, then he shrugged. "I suppose his money is as good as any other's."

"I thought you'd say that." The manager gave an impish smile. "But in light of your past history with the gentleman, I did take the liberty of adding a surcharge to his nightly rate."

"He deserves it, the Sicilian bastard. Nicely done, Loggia. Anything else?"

"Nothing that requires your attention."

"I see I'll be leaving the hotel in good hands when I depart. *Buonasera*."

"Good night, sir."

Cristiano turned back to her. As they walked to the elevator, suddenly Hallie felt very tired. Without a word, he stepped ahead of her to press the elevator button.

"Hallie Hatfield!"

A woman's shrill voice behind her made her jump. Turning, she saw Audrey, who'd once been her supervisor. Not just that. She'd once been a trusted mentor and friend.

"What are you doing here, Hallie?" the other woman demanded. "Looking for another rich man to seduce? You're no longer employed here and not allowed to be loitering in the lobby with the guests. Get out before I call the—"

Audrey sucked in her breath as Cristiano suddenly turned around.

"Hallie's with me," he said mildly. "And I own the hotel, so that makes it all right, does it not, Ms...." He looked at her name tag. "Ms. Johnson?"

Audrey's shocked face went white, then red.

"Yes, of course. I'm so sorry, Mr. Moretti," she stammered, backing away. She bowed her head repeatedly. "I didn't realize Hallie was with you. I'll, um, return to my duties—"

The woman fled. As Hallie and Cristiano got into the elevator with their baby, he frowned. "That was your old supervisor."

"Yes."

"Did she always treat you so poorly?"

She gave a brief smile. "No."

"Do you want me to fire her?"

Hallie gaped at him. She couldn't tell if he was joking, but just to be safe she quickly said, "No, of course not. I feel bad for her."

"Why?"

"When you ordered her to fire me directly, without going through HR, then gave her the mysterious severance envelope she wasn't allowed to read..." Hallie shrugged. "She's not stupid. She guessed we'd slept together."

"Why would she care?"

Did he really not know? "Because she's in love with you."

"Is she?" he said carelessly. Hallie gave him a wistful smile.

"Most women are, I imagine. Even I almost was, once."

Cristiano focused abruptly on her. She felt the intensity of his gaze burn through her soul. "You were in love with me?"

She swallowed.

"For a year, I often cleaned your penthouse—did you know that?"

He shook his head.

"Anytime your regular housekeeper, Camille, was sick or needed to take her grandchildren to school." She gave a wistful smile. "Dusting your pictures, I used to look at your face and wonder what it would be like to…"

"Yes?" he said, drawing closer, putting his hand on her bare shoulder above the straps of her sundress. A hard shiver went through her.

The elevator reached their floor, and the door slid open with a ding.

"But that was before I knew you," she said steadily. "Now nothing on earth could make me love you again."

She walked out of the elevator, head held high. Cristiano reached past her to unlock the penthouse door with his fingerprint, still holding their baby's carrier on his arm.

The city skyline, sparkling through floor-to-ceiling windows, was the only light in the penthouse.

The darkness was suggestive. Intimate. Setting down the baby carrier, Cristiano turned to face her.

"I don't know about love," he said in a low voice. "It's not something I've ever felt, or wanted to feel." Reaching out, he tucked a tendril of Hallie's hair behind her ear. "But from the moment I first heard you sing, I knew you were different from any woman I'd ever known."

"Thank you." Shivering from his brief touch, she tried to smile. "That's why I came to New York. Did you know? I dreamed of becoming a world-famous singer."

For all his praise, he looked surprised. "A singer?"

Hallie gave a low laugh. "Did you think I came all the

way from West Virginia because my big dream was to be a maid in your hotel?"

"No?" Cristiano smiled. "You certainly have the voice, *cara*. The heartbreak and longing of your song—you made me feel it. Your voice was the first thing I noticed about you." His eyes slid over her face, to her bare shoulders, down her curvy body beneath the cotton sundress. "Do you want to know the second thing?"

A wave of heat went through her. Her cheeks burned as she whispered, "No."

Maybe he wasn't doing it on purpose, she thought. Maybe he flirted without thinking, like breathing. He couldn't really still want her. But something in his eyes made her think—

He turned away, picking up the baby carrier. Beckoning Hallie to follow, he pushed open the first door down the hall.

"You can sleep here tonight."

Confused, she followed him into the pristine guest room that she'd cleaned many times long ago. "Who's in charge of cleaning this now?"

"Still Camille. I have no idea who her backup is." He gave her a crooked grin. "They're more careful than you were not to be seen."

With a snort, Hallie looked around the guest room. "Every time I changed these sheets, they seemed untouched. I used to wonder if the room was ever used."

He set the baby carrier gently on the floor. "It isn't."

Frowning, she turned to look at him. "Never?"

"You're my first guest."

"But surely you've invited family, friends—"

"I have no family," he said. "When friends visit, I give them their own suite downstairs."

"Oh." *No family*, she thought. And though he lived in a luxurious hotel, he had no real home. In some ways, they were the same. Strange. For a moment their eyes met. Then she saw the boxes stacked neatly in the corner. "My things!"

She rushed over and started digging through the boxes. Relief poured through her as she found the family pictures, her father's watch, her brother's old baseball trophy, her mother's music box. All the photos, still warped and faded, found on the banks of the river. Blinking away tears, she leaned back on her haunches and looked up at Cristiano.

"Everything is here. Thank you." Her voice choked. "You don't know what this means to me."

"So I'm not still an indecent excuse for a man?"

She blushed. "I never should have said—"

"It's all right." He turned away. "I'll leave you and the baby to rest."

"You're not afraid I'm going to try to run away with him in the middle of the night?"

He glanced back. "Are you planning to?"

Hallie thought of the fierce joy in Cristiano's face when he'd gotten the paternity test results that proved Jack was his son. How he'd been so protective of her. How he'd gotten her precious possessions back for her. He, too, had experienced the pain of losing family and home.

She could no longer imagine stealing Jack away when Cristiano wanted so clearly to be part of his life.

"You're Jack's father," she said in a small voice. "I wouldn't try to hurt you."

His shoulders relaxed. He motioned around the guest room and en suite bathroom. "It should be equipped with everything you require."

"And then some," she said, noticing the crib and a co-sleeper both set up on the other side of the king-size bed.

Following her gaze, Cristiano said awkwardly, "I didn't know how you and the baby prefer to sleep. My assistant said both of those were popular with new mothers."

"Thank you." She gave him a smile. "It'll be fun to use a co-sleeper that's new. The crib looks nice, too."

He gave a brief nod. "If you get hungry or need anything, just lift up the phone and dial one. It's an express line to the front desk and will be prioritized above all other calls. The staff pride themselves on answering on the first ring." Coming forward, he put his hand gently on Hallie's bare shoulder. She felt his touch race through her entire body, setting her nerves aflame.

"Until tomorrow," he said in a low voice.

After Cristiano left, closing the door behind him, Hallie took the baby carrier with her into the en suite bathroom. As Jack babbled contentedly from his carrier nearby, she took a quick, hot shower. She let all the sweat and anxiety of the long day wash off into steamy bliss. She washed her hair with the expensive shampoos and conditioners she'd once just stocked as a housekeeper. Afterward, she stepped into a soft, thick white terry-cloth robe from the heated stand. Her skin was pink and warm with steam as she came out and saw Jack was still happy in his baby carrier, cooing at the soft giraffe dangling from the handle.

"Now your turn, little one." Unbuckling him from the carrier, she cuddled him close, kissing his soft head and chubby cheeks. She gave him a warm bath in the baby bathtub she found in the bathroom cabinet along with baby shampoo. Drying him off, she put him in a new diaper and clean footie pajamas.

Cuddling her baby close, she went to the soft new glider chair by the bedroom window and took a deep breath, relishing Jack's sweet, clean baby smell. After reading him a short baby book from a collection on the shelf, she fed him and rocked him to sleep, then tucked him snugly into the co-sleeper.

Hearing her stomach growl, Hallie tried to remember the last time she'd eaten. A stale cookie at the single mothers support group? It seemed a year ago. Which reminded her. She grabbed her phone from her bag and messaged Tess and Lola.

I'm staying at his penthouse tonight. He got everything back from the landlord. I think everything's going to be fine.

Plugging her cell phone in to recharge, she turned to the bulky phone plugged in to the wall. Hungry though she was, she couldn't imagine calling room service, especially so late. She'd never ordered it herself, but her parents had told her about room service after they'd gone to a hotel in Cincinnati for their twenty-fifth anniversary.

"It was so expensive!" her father had exclaimed.

"With a required twenty-percent gratuity," her mother had breathed in shock, "and a delivery fee on top of that!"

"And the food arrived cold!" he'd added indignantly. "Room service is for suckers who want to burn money!"

Hallie smiled at the memory. Her smile faded as she felt all over again how much she missed them. Then she shook her head decisively. No room service. She'd just have to find something in Cristiano's kitchen.

Tightening the belt on her white terry-cloth robe, she peeked out into the penthouse's dark hallway, telling herself that Cristiano was already asleep in his own bedroom. But when she crept into the kitchen, she saw him sitting on the white sofa in the great room, his handsome, intent face shadowed by the glow of his laptop.

Looking up, he saw her, and the smile that lit up his hard, handsome features made her heart skip a beat.

"Can't you sleep?" Closing his laptop, he rose to his feet. He must have taken a shower, because his hair was wet. His chest was bare, revealing the defined curves of his muscled torso in the moonlight streaming through the windows. He wore only low-slung drawstring pajama pants. *Very* low-slung, clinging to edges of his hips, revealing the trail of dark hair on his taut belly.

Her mouth went dry. She had to force her eyes up.

"I'm, um, hungry," she croaked, praying he couldn't read her thoughts. Licking her lips, she gazed around the room, desperate to look anywhere but at his powerful bare chest, the flat plane of his stomach or the drawstring pants barely clinging to his hips.

"Did you call room service?"

What did room service have to do with anything? Oh, yes. She'd said she was hungry. Her eyes met his, and he gave her a sensual, heavy-lidded smile. She blushed to realize that he had caught her looking after all.

"It's not necessary. I'll just rummage in your fridge if that's all right."

Cristiano looked amused. "Go right ahead."

But as she opened the door of his sleek, commercial-grade refrigerator, she was disappointed to see only an expensive bottle of vodka and some martini olives.

She turned back with a frown. "Where is your food?"

"I don't cook."

Peeking in his freezer, she saw ice cubes. That was it. No ice cream or even frozen broccoli past its sell-by date.

She'd known from her time cleaning the penthouse that Cristiano Moretti wasn't exactly a chef, but the level of emptiness shocked her. Hallie looked through the cupboards with increasing desperation. They were empty except for a few items that belonged in a wet bar. Disappointed, she looked at him accusingly.

"Don't you even snack?"

He shrugged. "I lead a busy life. Why own a hotel if I don't use the amenities?"

"No one can hate cooking this much."

He gave her a sudden grin. "I prefer to think of it as quality assurance. What can I say? I'm a workaholic."

"I know," she sighed.

"Get room service."

She shook her head. "It's the middle of the night. And do you know how much it costs?"

He looked amused again. "You do know I own this hotel?"

She tried not to stare at the curve of his sensual lips. Then she realized she'd just licked her own. Her blush deepened. She croaked, "That's no excuse to—"

"I'll order it for you." He went to the kitchen phone on the marble counter. Picking it up, he looked at her in the shadowy kitchen. "What do you want?"

Want? What a suggestive question. Hallie's gaze lingered on his broad shoulders, his powerful arms, his muscular chest dusted with dark hair. She could see the outline of his powerful thighs beneath the thin knit fabric of his drawstring pants. He gave her a wicked smile. She realized he'd caught her looking again.

Quick, say something intelligent to distract him! she told herself desperately.

"Um…what do you recommend?"

No!

His eyes gleamed. "Shall I tell you?"

Her heart was pounding in her throat. "I'll have a cheeseburger and fries," she said quickly. "And a strawberry shake."

Cristiano's sensual lips curved, as if he knew exactly how her blood was racing and her heart was pounding. She was suddenly afraid to even meet his gaze. Turning to the phone, he gave the order swiftly, then hung up. "Your dinner will be here in nine minutes."

Hallie looked at him incredulously. "Nine minutes? That's impossible."

"Know all about room service, do you?" He sounded amused again.

"My parents told me horror stories. Cold food, small portions, no ketchup, then a big bill."

"Let's test out your theory." He lifted an eyebrow. "Care to place a friendly wager?"

"What kind of wager?"

Going back to the sofa, he sat down and patted the cushion beside him.

She sat down hesitantly beside him, perching awkwardly on the edge of the sofa. She was suddenly aware that she was naked beneath her bathrobe. Nervously she pulled it a little tighter around her. "What do you have in mind?"

"If your food arrives within—" he glanced at his platinum watch "—seven minutes and forty-eight seconds, I win. If it doesn't, you win."

"What do I win?"

His eyes flickered. "What if I cook breakfast for you tomorrow?"

She snorted. "Cereal?"

Cristiano shook his head. "Eggs and bacon. Belgian waffles. Anything you want."

She was impressed in spite of herself. "But you hate cooking."

"I won't have to do cook."

"You won't?"

"Because I'm not going to lose."

The man had confidence, she'd give him that. "And if you do win, what would you want from me?"

His dark eyes glinted wickedly.

"A kiss."

A rush of need crackled through her body as her lips tingled in anticipation. She croaked, "What?"

"You heard me."

She couldn't risk placing this bet. She hated him. Didn't

she? Not exactly. Not anymore. But she definitely didn't want him to kiss her. Did she? Okay, maybe she did, but she knew it would lead to disaster. On that, her body and brain and heart agreed. *She could not let him kiss her again.*

Yet Hallie was unable to look away from his hungry gaze. "Why would you want to kiss me?"

"Why not?" he said lazily.

Was he bored? Or just suggesting it to throw her off-kilter and make clear his power over her? "No, thanks. I'm not the gambling kind."

"I think you are. If you refuse my wager, then you're admitting that you might be wrong." He leaned toward her on the white sofa, almost close enough to touch. "And I might be right."

Her heart was in her throat. "About room service?"

"About everything," he whispered, his lips almost grazing her cheek.

She shivered at his closeness. Then she realized what he was saying and that he was talking about far more important issues than food.

"I admit no such thing." Still, as she drew back sharply, his gaze fell to her knee, and she realized that her robe had slipped open to reveal her crossed leg all the way to her thigh. Cheeks aflame, she covered her legs.

His eyebrow lifted. "Then take the bet."

"Fine," she snapped. "I'll enjoy watching you cook for me tomorrow." She lifted her chin. "But in addition to the food being delivered on time, to prove me wrong it also has to be the best cheeseburger, fries and shake I've ever had."

"It will be," he said without hesitation, and held out his hand. She stared at it for a moment, then shook it as quickly as she could, desperately ignoring her body's reaction at that brief touch.

And so it was that exactly five minutes and four seconds later, a full fifteen seconds before the deadline, she found herself looking despondently at the white linen-covered room-service tray resting on the coffee table. As Cristiano got up to chat with the smiling room-service waiter, she sighed. Even the incredible smell of hot French fries wafting through the air could offer no comfort. She knew she was about to lose their bet.

A kiss.

Hallie put her hands on her forehead. Why had she ever agreed to it? *Why?* How could she have been so stupid? Cristiano got room service all the time! He knew how long it took! He knew how good the food was!

Did she *want* him to kiss her?

But that was a question Hallie didn't want to answer, not even to herself, as the waiter left and Cristiano came back. Turning on a lamp, he looked down at her. His cruel, sensual lips curved. "Don't look so frightened."

She lied. "I'm not."

"You're terrified." Lifting the silver lid off the tray, he said idly, "Do you think I intend to take my kiss now, and ravish you against the wall?"

With a flash of heat, images came to her mind. Mouth dry, she croaked, "I—"

"Why don't you try it?" he murmured, sitting beside her on the sofa. "See if you like it?"

Her heart nearly stopped. She looked at him, lips parted.

He held out a French fry.

"Decide," he said huskily, "if it's the best you've ever had."

She stared from the French fry to the challenge in his eyes. Snatching the fried potato from his fingers, she licked off the salt, then popped the whole length into her mouth. It was so hot, salty and delicious that she gave an involuntary groan of pleasure.

"So…good…" she breathed, briefly lost in ecstasy.

A strangled noise came from the back of his throat. Looking up, she saw his handsome face looked strained.

Clearing his throat, he rose from the sofa. "I'll leave you to enjoy it."

"Wait. I haven't tried the rest." Although she knew, even before she picked up the cheeseburger, that it would be the best she'd ever had. She took a big bite, licking a splash of ketchup and mustard off her lips, then washed it all down with a milkshake of fresh strawberries whirled into vanilla ice cream. The milkshake was so thick she had to suck hard on the straw.

Finally she looked up, defeated. "All right, you win—"

Her voice cut off when she saw his face. He looked hungry, ruthless. Something in his eyes was dark and wild. He took a step toward her, his hands gripped at his sides, and the memory of his words flashed in her mind.

Do you think I intend to ravish you against the wall?

She shrank back from the fire in his eyes. "No."

That one word, whispered soft as a breath, seemed tangible in the air, like a wall between them. He blinked. His expression changed as if a shutter had gone down. His civilized mask slid back into place.

"Good night," he said hoarsely. Turning, he hurried down the hall toward the master bedroom.

Hallie sat alone on the sofa, shivering from what had just happened. Except nothing had happened, she told herself, struggling to calm her breath. Nothing at all.

After turning off the lamp, she stared out blankly at the lights of the moonlit city. Woodenly she ate the rest of her meal. All she could think about was how badly she'd wanted him in that moment. But the word that had escaped from her lips was *no*. Because she was afraid.

Before her night with Cristiano, Hallie had barely been kissed. She'd had a few awkward kisses with her boyfriend in high school, who'd never tried to press the issue—with good reason, as it turned out, because as soon as he left for university he announced on Facebook that he was gay. And one time, Joe Larson, the mine owner's son, had tried to force his tongue down her throat at a company Christmas party. Before Cristiano, that had been the sum total of her sexual experience.

And now he wanted to kiss her?

Now he wanted to *marry* her?

She was way out of her league.

Rising from the sofa, she walked heavily back to the guest room, where she found Jack sleeping peacefully. Putting on underwear and pajamas, she brushed her teeth and crawled into the bed next to her baby, knowing she wouldn't sleep a wink.

But, somehow, she did. She rose only once in the night, to feed the baby. When Jack next woke her with a hungry whimper, she saw golden light flooding the window. She sat up in shock, realizing that she'd just had the best night's sleep in months. How was that possible?

"Good morning, sweetheart," she said, smiling at the baby, who gurgled and waved his arms at her.

When mother and baby came out into the main room some time later, both of them were dressed—Hallie in a soft pink sundress of eyelet cotton and sandals, the baby in a onesie and blue knit shorts. She stopped when she saw Cristiano sitting at the kitchen counter. Her cheeks went hot at the memory of last night. *But why?* she said to herself. Nothing had happened!

"Good morning." Cristiano's voice was gravelly as he set down his newspaper. "I trust you slept well?"

Hallie shifted her baby's weight on her hip as she stood uncertainly in the kitchen, beneath a shaft of golden light from the windows. His eyebrows lifted as he waited. His handsome face was courteous, his dark eyes civilized. Nothing like he'd looked last night…

She shivered.

"Hallie?"

She jumped. "I slept well. Thank you."

Hallie wondered when he would kiss her. She felt the weight of that debt between them. *It's just a kiss*, she told herself, but she couldn't quite believe it. She tried to tell herself that now that he'd had time to recover from the shock of learning he was a father, Cristiano probably wouldn't repeat his demand for marriage. But looking into his hard-edged face, she couldn't believe that, either. Cristiano Moretti was the kind of man who would stop at nothing to get what he wanted.

He wanted to secure possession of their child. She knew that. But now she knew he wanted more.

He wanted her.

Nodding toward the marble countertop and holding out a china cup edged with fourteen-karat gold, he said gruffly, "Have a seat."

"Thanks." Sitting down on one of the high barstools, keeping her baby securely in her lap, she watched in surprise as he poured her a cup of steaming hot coffee from a silver carafe. "You made coffee?"

"Room service." He nodded at the tray. "There's cream and sugar."

"Thanks." Too late, she saw the wheeled carts nearby and felt foolish. Adding copious amounts of cream and sugar to her coffee, she took a sip and sighed with pleasure. Glancing at him, she said shyly, "Would you like to hold the baby?"

Cristiano hesitated, looking down at the plump, babbling three-month-old. He shook his head. "Maybe later."

"All right." She was surprised anyone could resist holding Jack, with his adorably goofy smile and his fat little cheeks.

"I ordered you a breakfast tray. It's been here an hour, so it might be cold." Cristiano turned back to his newspaper.

"Thanks." She didn't feel hungry at all. She gave him a sideways glance. "You're reading in Italian."

He didn't look up. "Yes."

"And on paper rather than on a tablet."

"So?"

"It's very retro," she ventured.

He didn't answer. He seemed barely aware of her, while her hands were shaking from being this close to him. Had she somehow imagined the way he'd looked at her last night? Had he already forgotten that he'd demanded a kiss—and marriage?

Sitting at the marble counter that separated the sleek kitchen from the great room, Hallie looked slowly around his penthouse. Modern art was splashed across the walls. Strange, heavy sculptures were displayed on columns. Once Jack started to pull himself up and walk, those would be dangerous.

But such unimaginable luxury and style. So different from how she'd grown up. A flash of memory came to her of the cabin in the West Virginia hills, with its worn wood exterior, sagging furniture and peeling linoleum.

But so comfortable for all that. So full of love. Her beloved home. Her parents. Her older brother.

Gone. All gone.

They would never know her son.

A sudden pain, like a razor blade in her throat, made her gasp as fresh, unexpected grief ambushed her.

Setting down his newspaper, Cristiano looked at her sharply. "What is it?"

Blinking fast, she looked at him. She swallowed. "I was just remembering…"

"What?"

Jack fussed a little in her arms. She was grateful for the excuse to turn away. "Nothing."

Getting up, she set the baby down in his new play gym with a padded blanket on the floor, so he could bat at the brightly colored mobile overhead. She felt Cristiano's gaze on her as she went to the room-service carts and lifted a silver lid. Taking the plate of food and silverware, she returned to sit beside him at the counter. She forced herself to take a bite, then another. The waffles and bacon were indeed lukewarm, and all she could feel was sad.

"Can I ask you something?" Cristiano asked, setting his fork down on his own empty plate.

"What?"

"Why did you refuse my marriage proposal yesterday?"

She glanced at him. "I told you—"

"That we hate each other. I remember." He took a drink of black coffee. The dainty china cup looked incongruous in his large, masculine hands. "It's just funny. I always thought if I ever asked a woman to marry me, the reaction would be very different."

"But you didn't ask. You told." Hallie looked at her limp waffles. "And I'm not convinced you know what commitment means."

"How can you say that?"

Setting down her fork, Hallie stared out at the view of the city and bright blue skies. "My parents married straight out of high school. They fought all the time, but never threatened to leave. We were a family. And family means sticking together, no matter what." Her voice choked, and she looked down at the marble floor. "After they died, it was all I dreamed about. Having a family again. A home."

"That's why you were still a virgin when we met," he said slowly. "You were waiting for the man you could give your life to. Not just your life. Your loyalty."

She nodded, unable to meet his eyes, bracing herself for his cynical, mocking response.

Instead, his voice was quiet. "I destroyed all your plans by seducing you."

Hallie's gaze lifted to his. Then she looked at their baby in his play gym. Jack was stretching out his chubby arms, waving them like a drunken sailor as he tried to reach the mobile hanging over his head. With a trembling smile, she shook her head.

"How can I blame you, when that night brought our baby? Besides." She stared down at her hands. "What happened wasn't just your fault. It was also mine." With a deep breath, she said, "If I had really wanted to wait for marriage, I wouldn't have let you or anyone else change my mind. No matter how badly I wanted you. Because I knew even then that I could never be more than a one-night stand to a man like you."

"You're wrong." His voice was low. "You were always more than a one-night stand to me."

"So that's why you had me fired and tossed out of the hotel?" Her lips lifted humorously. "Because you wanted to spend more time with me?"

"You were an employee. A virgin. But from the moment I first heard you sing, from the moment I saw you, floating my sheets softly through the air, I had to have you. I smashed every rule."

"You knew I was a virgin?" she breathed.

He gave a slow nod. "I could tell when I kissed you. But I still couldn't stop myself from taking you to my bed. And once I had you," he said softly, "I only wanted more."

"Then why did you send me away?" she said, trembling.

His eyes met hers evenly. "I was afraid you'd want a relationship. That you'd ask for a commitment."

His words burned her pride. "But I didn't."

"No," Cristiano agreed. He leaned toward her at the

counter. "But now I'm asking you. I want us to give our son a home. To be a family." Leaning forward, he took both her hands in his own, his eyes intense. "I'm asking you to marry me."

She sucked in her breath as all her childhood dreams clamored around her. Could it truly happen? Could a night of passion turn them unexpectedly into a family?

A home.

Loyalty.

Family.

He was offering her everything she'd ever wanted, and unimaginable wealth and luxury, too.

For a moment, Hallie was tempted. Then she shook her head slowly.

"Why?" he demanded.

She turned away from his arrogant gaze, busying herself with tackling a thick, salty slice of bacon. "A marriage of convenience? How would that even work?"

"I never said it would be a marriage of convenience." His black eyes pierced hers. "Our marriage would be very real, Hallie."

Beneath his gaze, she felt hot all over. She swallowed the bacon, barely tasting it. Her full breasts were suddenly heavy, her nipples aching and taut. Tension coiled, low and deep, in her belly.

Swallowing, she pushed the plate away. "You could have any woman for the asking." She looked at Cristiano's elegant penthouse, and the wide windows that showed all New York City at his feet. "Why not wait for someone you love? Someone—" her voice faltered "—who loves you?"

"I'm thirty-five years old, and I've never loved anyone. I never thought I had the ability." Cristiano looked at Jack, wriggling happily on the soft quilted mat of the baby gym. "Until the day I found out I had a son."

Hallie felt her heart constrict as she saw the way he

looked at Jack. In their intense love for their child, they were the same.

He turned back to her. "And now I know this. My duty is to protect you both. To provide for you. To give you a home. To give you my name. I offer you my loyalty, Hallie. For a lifetime."

"Your loyalty," she whispered.

Cristiano looked at her, his eyes black as night. "I will protect our son. No matter the cost."

His words sounded strangely like a warning. But that didn't make sense. Why would he warn Hallie that he intended to protect their son?

So much she'd thought about him was all wrong. He actually wanted to commit to her. To be a father to Jack.

Her son would have financial security, the best schools, the promise of a brilliant future.

And, even more importantly, Cristiano would always protect him and watch his back. If anything ever happened to Hallie, Jack would still be safe. She'd learned the hard way about loss.

Cristiano was offering her everything and, still, some part of her hesitated. "You're asking me to give up love— all hope of it forever."

"Have you ever been in love?"

"No," she was forced to admit.

"Then how can you miss what you've never had?"

His words were starting to make the impossible seem reasonable. "A marriage implies faithfulness…"

"Which I would be."

Her breath caught in her throat. She hadn't expected that. Cristiano Moretti, the famous billionaire playboy, was promising total fidelity. To her.

That thought was too outlandish to believe. She shook her head, her lips curving up at the edges. "Have you really thought this through? No more Russian supermodels?"

"You persist in underestimating me," he said softly. Reaching out, he tucked hair behind her ear. "When will you learn the truth?"

Hallie swallowed. "What's that?"

His gaze cut through her. "I want only you."

Her heart was pounding. A year ago, when he'd tossed her to the curb, she'd thought she'd made the worst mistake of her life. For the last year, she'd barely held on sometimes, trying to keep a roof over her baby's head. Security had seemed like a fairy tale.

Now Cristiano was offering her everything she'd dreamed of. She could secure her son's comfort and give him two parents and a stable home for a lifetime.

The only cost would be her heart. Their marriage would be about partnership and, yes, passion. But not love.

Could she accept that? For the rest of her life?

Or would her heart shrivel up and die?

Getting up from the barstool, Hallie crossed the great room uncertainly. She looked down at her sweet baby, cooing and playing happily. Holding her breath, she stared out the windows at the gray city and brilliant blue sky.

Silence fell in the penthouse. She felt the warm morning sun against her skin, the rise and fall of her own breath. Then she heard him cross the floor. Putting his hands on her shaking shoulders, he turned her to face him. His dark eyes burned like fire.

"One more thing," he said in a low voice. "Before you decide."

And pulling her roughly against his body, he lowered his mouth to kiss her.

CHAPTER FOUR

His lips were hot and yearning, burning through Hallie's body and soul. This kiss was different from the hungry, demanding passion of their first night. This time he tempted rather than took. He lured rather than ravished.

His hands tangled in her dark hair, stroking slowly down her bare shoulders and back. Shivers of need cascaded through Hallie's body. She could not resist his embrace, as wistful and tender as his whispered words, which still hung between them like mist.

When will you learn the truth?
What's that?
I want only you.

Her mind scattered in a million different directions, the penthouse whirling around her. She felt his desire for her through his low-slung pajama pants. She gripped his naked, powerful shoulders, feeling that Cristiano was the only solid thing in a world spinning out of control. His skin felt warm, his body solid and strong. This kiss, the sweet dream of his lips on hers, was all that felt real.

He deepened the embrace, pushing her back against the white sofa, his hands running over her body—over her naked arms, the spaghetti straps of her sundress. As the kiss intensified, hunger built between them until she kissed him back desperately, her whole body on fire. She gripped his shoulders, his mouth hot and demanding against hers. Feeling the sweet weight of his body over hers, the hard warmth of his muscular chest, she would have done anything—agreed to anything—to make this moment last…

"Say you'll marry me," he whispered against her skin. "Say it—"

"Yes," she choked out. She didn't realize she'd spoken until he pulled back, searching her gaze.

"You won't take it back? You won't change your mind?"

She shook her head. "It's what I want most. Loyalty. Family. Home."

"And this." And Cristiano kissed her, consuming her, until all that was left of her was fire and ash.

Cristiano had to take her to bed. Now.

If he didn't have her, now that he knew she was going to be his wife, he thought he might explode.

"You've made me so happy, *cara mia*," he whispered, kissing her forehead, her cheeks. The sweet intoxication of her lips. He started to lift her in his arms, intending to seal the deal immediately in his bedroom.

Then his baby son gave a low whimper.

"Jack," Hallie said immediately, and the sensual spell was broken. Looking at each other, they both gave a rueful laugh. Moving back, he let her get off the sofa.

After hurrying across the room, she scooped Jack up from his play gym. The baby immediately brightened in his mother's arms. "But I'm being greedy." Walking with him back to where Cristiano stood, she gave him a shy smile. "Do you want to hold him?"

He shook his head. To be honest, the baby seemed happier with his mother. And he couldn't blame Jack for preferring her. What experience did Cristiano have with children? He couldn't bear the thought of his son crying. What if he held him wrong again and Hallie scorned him for being a clumsy fool?

"Are you sure?" Hallie said, looking disappointed. But she didn't wait for an answer. She just smiled down at her son, crooning, "How are you, sweet boy?"

Cristiano's heart expanded as he looked at them, his tiny baby son with the chubby cheeks, held by his incredibly loving, sexy bride-to-be. Reaching out, he put his hand on his son's soft, downy hair. His eyes locked with Hallie's and he felt a current of emotion.

It was too much. Feeling his heart in his throat, he abruptly turned away. "We've been stuck in this penthouse long enough. I want to buy you an engagement ring."

"It's not necessary."

"But it is." He'd buy her the most obscenely huge diamond that the world had ever seen. "And our wedding must be arranged quickly, before I leave for Italy."

"You're going to Italy?"

"Tomorrow night."

"So soon!"

He turned to her with a frown. "I will visit my hotel in Rome. Also I'm building a new hotel on the Amalfi Coast and want to supervise the final preparations before the grand opening next month."

"How long will you be gone?"

"It doesn't matter, because you're both coming with me."

Hallie's eyes became round as saucers. "You want to take me and Jack to Italy?"

"Is that a problem?"

"I don't have a passport."

"Something we'll fix today, after we go to the jewelry store—and get our wedding license."

"You want us to be married in Italy?"

"That would take too long. The laws there are complicated."

Her lips parted. "You want us to be married before we leave?"

"Yes," he said roughly.

"A wedding? In *two days*?"

"Tomorrow," he said.

Hallie looked shocked. Coming forward, he took her in

his arms and kissed her. "Everything will be perfect," he whispered, cupping her cheek. "I swear to you."

"All right." Looking dazed, she gave him a crooked smile. "I'll take your word for it. After all, you were right about the room service."

He returned her grin. "I'll go get dressed." His body protested at the thought of putting on clothes instead of taking Hallie's clothes *off*. Still, he could wait the few hours until they were alone, until they weren't being watched so keenly by their three-month-old chaperone. Glancing down at his pajama pants, he turned toward his bedroom, intending to find a shirt and trousers. "We'll leave in five minutes."

Behind him, Hallie gave a laugh that came straight from her belly, deeper and more heartfelt than he'd ever heard from her before. "Oh, we will, will we?"

Frowning, he turned back.

"What's so funny?" he said suspiciously.

"Nothing." She gave him a grin. "Except you're used to people always being ready whenever you want them to be, aren't you?"

"I'm a busy man. Others wait for me. I don't wait for them."

"Not anymore." She giggled. "Now you have a baby."

She was right. It was, in fact, over an hour before they left the penthouse. In that time, the baby was fed, then he'd cried, and then they had to change his clothes when he spit up all over his onesie. He was burped a little more and cried some more. Then the real reason for Jack's earlier fussiness was revealed—a blowout needing a diaper change and yet another new outfit. Hallie calmly repacked everything in her diaper bag. Finally, just as they were about to leave, the baby let out a whimper and needed to be fed again.

Through it all, Cristiano was impressed with Hallie's infinite patience and skill. He wouldn't have had a clue what to do. When she'd looked up at him with a gentle smile and asked if he wanted to help burp or change the baby, he had been filled with alarm. He'd shaken his head. What did he know? Better to leave it to the expert. Patient and loving, Hallie was clearly born to be a mother.

Once again Cristiano congratulated himself on securing his possession of her.

By the time they were out of the hotel and on the street, he took a big breath of fresh air. Yellow taxi cabs raced down the avenue as backpack-carrying tourists fought for space on the sidewalk with lawyers in suits and food carts selling everything from hot dogs to cupcakes to falafel. The summer morning was warm and fresh, and the sunlight spilled gold on the streets of New York.

But the brightest glow of all came from Hallie's sparkling eyes as she snapped their baby's carrier into his expensive new stroller.

"Thank you for this, by the way," she said, nodding at the stroller.

He'd told Marcia to send the best one. "Does Jack like it?"

She turned it toward him. "See for yourself."

Peeking down, he saw that his baby, who'd spent the past hour causing a fuss, was nestled in the stroller cozily, smiling.

Cristiano's heart swelled in his chest as his son stretched up his chubby little hands, as if reaching for the towering hotel.

"All yours someday," he told Jack softly in Italian. Then he looked at Hallie's beautiful face as she pointed up at the top of the hotel in the clouds, talking tenderly to their son. Under his breath in the same language, he added, "All mine."

Hallie turned to him quizzically. "Did you say something?"

"Just that our first stop this morning is to get our marriage license." As they waited briefly outside the hotel, he took her hand. He felt it tremble at the intimacy of the gesture.

The black SUV with tinted windows pulled up. Matthews was at the wheel and Luther, the bodyguard, sat beside him in the front.

As Matthews folded the stroller into the trunk, Cristiano opened the door for Hallie. He snapped the baby carrier securely in the back seat, then followed her inside.

"Where to, sir?" Matthews said cheerfully as Hallie smiled down at the chattering baby.

"The city clerk's office downtown."

An hour later, they left with their marriage license. Cristiano exhaled deeply. *One step closer.* In twenty-four hours it would be permanent. He would give Jack his last name. And not just the baby…

His eyes lingered on Hallie as she climbed back into the waiting SUV, tucking their smiley baby into his car seat.

He could hardly wait to possess her in bed. Tonight. This afternoon. He paused. Or he could wait to make love until their wedding night, as Hallie had once wanted.

Could he give her that? Could he wait until she was legally his to bed her? Knowing that, after tomorrow, she would be his forever?

No. He couldn't.

"Now where, sir?"

Leaning forward in the SUV, Cristiano named the most exclusive jewelry store on Fifth Avenue. He glanced at Hallie to see if it met with her approval, but she was busy playing peekaboo with the baby.

When they arrived, Hallie stared out of the window, wide-eyed at the sight of the luxury jewelry store. "Here?"

"Here," he said firmly. He intended to woo her. Perhaps

he couldn't do love, but he knew about romance. Though he'd never shopped for an engagement ring before.

As Cristiano got out, he saw Hallie unbuckling their baby from the car seat. "You're bringing him with us?" he asked in surprise.

"Of course I am." As Matthews got the stroller from the back, she smiled down at her baby, tucking him inside it. "What would you expect me to do, leave him alone in the car?"

"He wouldn't be alone," Cristiano said, nonplussed. He'd intended to romance her, and even with his limited experience of babies, he'd already seen that they could be a distraction from romance. He'd told Luther to remain in the SUV, as bodyguards also could impinge on intimate moments. "Matthews and Luther could watch him."

She glanced back at the two burly men, and her lips curved. "Not exactly trained baby professionals. No offense."

"None taken, ma'am," Matthews said.

"None whatsoever," Luther said.

"Va bene." Cristiano gave in with grace. Perhaps Hallie was right, anyway. The engagement ring wasn't meant to cement just the two of them as a couple, but the three of them as a family. Still, he made a mental note that they should acquire a—what had she called it?—a *trained baby professional* as soon as possible. Because he had sensual plans for Hallie, and he knew she wouldn't be able to linger in his bed unless she was certain Jack was being well tended.

"We won't be here long," he said, as they pushed the stroller past the doorman and security guard into the gilded jewelry store. Smiling down at Hallie, he said huskily, "I already know what I want."

"I think you've made that clear," she said, her cheeks a charming shade of pink. So were her lips.

Cristiano stopped abruptly inside the entrance, beneath the stained-glass cupola high overhead. Not caring who might see, he pulled Hallie into his arms, her pink sundress fluttering behind her.

Ruthlessly he lowered his mouth to hers, kissing her long and lingeringly. The stained-glass cupola dappled them with colored light. He heard whispers and romantic sighs as some customers walked by, as well as the irritated grumbling of men as their partners hissed, "Why do you never kiss me in public like that?"

When Cristiano finally pulled away, he looked down, relishing the dazzled look in Hallie's brown eyes. Gently he traced her swollen bottom lip with his thumb.

"Soon," he whispered. "Very soon."

Hallie sucked in her breath as if still in a trance. Taking a step, she nearly stumbled. He felt a surge of supremely masculine satisfaction.

"Let me help." With a wicked grin, he took the stroller with one arm and her hand with the other. "Let's have some fun."

He already knew exactly the ring he wanted: the biggest diamond in the store. Maybe Hallie didn't care about luxuries like room service, but every woman wanted an amazing engagement ring. And Hallie would have the best.

The store manager's face lit up upon seeing Cristiano, who, though he'd never bought a ring, had purchased expensive bracelets and necklaces for various mistresses in the past. The man took them swiftly to a private room, where he spread out a selection of diamond engagement rings across a black velvet tray.

"Which would the lady like to see first?" purred the manager, who was short and sophisticated in a designer suit.

"Which is the best?" Cristiano said.

With an approving smile, the manager pointed at a middle ring, an enormous emerald-cut canary diamond set in platinum. Cristiano nodded. "That's the one."

He was surprised to see Hallie frown, her eyebrows furrowed. "But it's yellow."

"A special type of diamond, very rare and beautiful," the manager intoned, "for a rare and beautiful woman."

Staring at him, Hallie burst into a laugh. "And here I was thinking that since the color's off, we might get a discount."

The manager's smile froze in place. "It's the most luxurious diamond we possess, with a cost that is, of course, commensurate with its rare beauty."

"Try it on," Cristiano said.

Biting her lip, Hallie allowed him to slide it over her finger. Her eyes were huge as she stared down at the ring. The rectangular yellow diamond was so huge it extended over her ring finger to partially cover the two adjacent fingers.

"Twenty and a half carats," said the manager reverently.

Her hand shook visibly, and she yanked it off suddenly and placed it back on the black velvet tray.

"You don't like it?" Cristiano asked, confused.

Hallie shook her head. "It weighs like a billion pounds! It's cold! And the setting scratched my skin. What if I scratched the baby?"

"Hurt the baby?" he said incredulously. Any other woman he'd known would have grabbed the million-dollar ring with a fervent *thank you*.

Hallie shook her head. "I wouldn't want to worry about gouging out someone's eye with that thing." She tilted her head. "And since we're getting married tomorrow, why do we even need an engagement ring? It seems silly."

There was a suppressed scream from the other side of the counter. The manager looked as if he might have the vapors.

Cristiano turned back to her with a frown. "You don't want a ring?"

She put her hand in his.

"I'd rather just get a plain gold wedding band. For each of us."

Now he was really confused. "Doesn't a diamond symbolize forever? Exactly as you wanted?"

"It does," agreed the manager, nodding vigorously.

"Not for me." She entwined her smaller hand in his. "My parents just had gold bands. I don't need a big diamond or a big wedding. It's the commitment I care about. Knowing the baby's safe. That I am, too."

Her big, brown eyes were like pools to drown in. Cristiano could not argue with her. He turned to the manager.

"You heard the lady. Get her what she wants."

The manager's face fell at seeing his easy million-dollar sale slip through his fingers. Then he seemed to recall that a man such as Cristiano would be likely to buy other expensive trinkets for his wife over time, and he recovered.

"I know just the thing," the man said.

Ten minutes later, Cristiano walked out of the jewelry store into the sunshine with his beautiful bride-to-be pushing the stroller. From her wrist dangled a small red bag, which held two simple wedding bands in shining gold.

Calling an enormous diamond ring silly? Cristiano shook his head with wonder. Truly, Hallie was one in a million. But, seeing her smile, he was glad he'd let her have her way.

He had another surprise for her, too.

"Now we need to get you some clothes," he said after the SUV picked them up. He hid a smile. The surprise had taken some effort to arrange.

"Why?" Hallie looked puzzled. She looked down at her faded pink sundress and her slightly scuffed sandals. "What's wrong with this?"

"You'll need a wedding dress. We'll get the rest of your trousseau in Rome."

She gave a laugh. *"Trousseau?"*

Her expression made him feel old-fashioned, or at least *old*. "That is the word, is it not, for the traditional new wardrobe for a bride?"

Her grin widened. "That's the dumbest thing I ever heard. Why would I need new clothes to be a wife?"

"Because you're going to be *my* wife. There will be certain expectations."

"What expectations?"

She was blushing, as if she assumed he was speaking of sex. But he would hardly talk dirty with his driver, his bodyguard and their innocent baby all listening in. His lips quirked. "I am the owner of twenty-two luxury hotels around the world. That makes me the advocate for my brand. As my wife, you will be, as well."

"So?"

"So you need new clothes."

"You mean sexy? Expensive?"

"Sleek. Cosmopolitan." He ran his fingertips slowly down the side of her dress. The cotton fabric was rough and pilled from repeated washings. "I can't have my wife's clothes looking like they were bought at a discount shop. What would my shareholders think?"

"That I'm good with money and know how to get good value?" she replied archly.

He snorted. "In private, of course, you can wear whatever you want. I like the look of you in everything." Leaning forward, he whispered for her ears alone, "Or nothing."

He felt her shiver, felt his own body rise. He had to fight the urge to grab her and kiss her again. *Soon*, he promised himself hungrily. *Tonight*.

Cristiano leaned back against the SUV's soft leather seat. "You will need clothes that you can wear to events where you will be photographed and appear in newspapers as a symbol of the Campania brand."

"I didn't sign up for that."

"And yet it is so." He tilted his head curiously. "Most women would not object so strenuously to a new wardrobe."

"I'm remembering something I read in high school… that you should beware any relationship that requires new clothes."

His lips lifted. "You're talking about Thoreau. He didn't say beware the new relationship, he said beware the new enterprise."

"Marrying you, it doesn't sound like there's a difference," she said grumpily. The SUV stopped, and she frowned. "What are we—"

Then Hallie turned, and her jaw dropped when she saw Cristiano's surprise.

CHAPTER FIVE

HALLIE STOOD IN front of a full-length mirror, turning to look at herself from all angles. This wedding dress was deceptively simple, made of duchess satin with a bias cut. It made her post-pregnancy figure look amazing in a way that even she couldn't deny.

"That's it!" Lola yelled. "That's the one!"

"It's perfect," Tess said dreamily. "You look like a princess."

Hallie had been shocked to see Lola and Tess waiting for her on the curb in front of the luxury bridal shop on Fifth Avenue. Amazed, she'd stared back at Cristiano in shock. "What did you… How did you?"

He'd given her a wicked smile. "Your friends called the front desk of the hotel this morning, demanding to know if I'd kidnapped you, since you weren't responding to their messages."

"Oh," she'd said sheepishly. She had turned off her phone last night and forgotten to turn it back on.

"I told them to come see you for themselves. They're going to help you pick out a wedding dress. If you want."

"Are you serious?"

His smile widened. "Then you all have appointments for spa treatments next door."

She'd beamed at him, then her joy had faded. "But who will watch Jack?"

"He's coming back to the penthouse with me," Cristiano said gravely, "for a little father-son time."

He'd looked at her steadily, as if daring her to object. Hallie had felt it was some kind of test. "But," she said helplessly, "how will you know what to do?"

"I'll keep your diaper bag. Bottles, diapers. Everything I could need, right?"

"Right," she said doubtfully.

He lifted an eyebrow. "I run a billion-dollar company, Hallie. I think I can handle watching my own son while he sleeps for a few hours."

Put like that, she'd been forced, reluctantly, to agree. Giving Jack one last kiss on his plump cheek, she'd slowly gotten out of the SUV. Then she'd turned back anxiously. "I'll be back in two hours."

"Take all afternoon. Take as long as you want. Enjoy yourself. We'll be fine." Leaning forward, Cristiano had given her a goodbye kiss that had left her knees weak, and then he'd smiled. "Have fun."

And, somewhat to her surprise, Hallie had. For the last hour, she and her friends been pampered like royalty at the designer bridal store. Cristiano had already won the loyalty of both her friends.

Tess admired him for demanding marriage immediately. "It's so romantic, practically an elopement! And next he's whisking you off to Italy!" She'd sighed. "So romantic!"

Lola had liked that Cristiano had left them an open credit line and told her and Tess, as bridesmaids, to get new outfits, as well. "Even shoes!"

The bridesmaid dresses were already chosen. Looking at herself now in the mirror, Hallie knew that this wedding dress was the one. It fit her perfectly, no alterations required, and made her look, as Tess had said, like a princess.

Nervously she charged it to Cristiano's account, half expecting the manager to laugh in her face. Instead, the manager rang it up, then talked her into also buying demure white high heels, an elegant veil and bridal lingerie that made her blush. Once all her purchases had been packed and sent off to the penthouse, the three girls headed next door to spend a precious hour at the day spa.

"This is the life," sighed Tess, stretching out her legs as a pedicurist massaged her feet.

"Who's watching Esme, Tess?"

The redhead gave a guilty smile. "My cousin. Don't get me wrong, I love being with my baby. But a few hours to myself feels like a vacation."

"Yeah," Lola said, selecting a chocolate-covered strawberry from a nearby silver tray. "This fiancé of yours is not so bad."

Hallie snorted. "You're just saying that because he told you to spare no expense on the bridesmaid outfits."

"I want your wedding day to be perfect," Lola said demurely, rubbing her heavily pregnant belly as she smiled at the shopping bag that held her new thousand-dollar shoes.

"I just wish Lacey could be here," Tess sighed. "We tried to invite her."

"Lacey!" Hallie smiled at the memory of the energetic young woman who'd invited each of them to the single-moms group, then introduced them to one another. "I owe her a lot."

"Me, too. Because of her, I got to meet you losers." Lola's smile was fond. She held up her champagne glass for another refill of sparkling water from the hovering spa attendant. "Lacey's traveling the world happily with her husband and baby. She sends her love. And promised to send a wedding gift."

"I don't need a gift."

"Of course you don't," Lola said. "You're marrying one of the richest men in the world."

"She doesn't care about his money," Tess protested. She turned to Hallie, her eyes shining. "It's love that brought you together. Pure, perfect love. That's the only reason anyone would marry."

"Um," said Hallie, feeling awkward. Love had nothing to do with it. They were just getting married to give their baby a good home. But she didn't want to disillusion Tess, who was looking at her with dreamy, happy eyes. It made Hallie feel uneasy. She'd told herself that there was nothing wrong with a loveless marriage. Their arrangement would be both practical and sensible.

So why did her throat close at the thought of explaining that to her friends?

"Your baby's father reacted just like I said he would. As soon as he knew about Jack, he realized he loved you and begged you to marry him," Tess said joyfully. "So who knows? Maybe my baby's father will do the same."

"Give it up," Lola said, rolling her eyes. "He's never coming back, Tess."

The redhead sucked in her breath, looking like she was going to cry.

"We don't know that," Hallie said loyally, though she understood Lola's irritation. For as long as they'd known her, Tess had spoken constantly of the man who'd seduced her and disappeared. She'd spun out endless reasons why he might not have returned—ridiculous reasons, like his plane crashing on a desert island, or being kidnapped in Antarctica, or that he'd developed amnesia.

Privately, Hallie agreed with Lola. The guy was obviously a jerk and gone for good. But telling Tess that seemed like kicking a puppy.

Hallie gave the redhead a sympathetic smile. "It could happen, Tess. He could come back."

Her friend gave her a grateful smile. "You think so?"

"Stop encouraging her," Lola snapped. Unlike the other two, she'd never once spoken of the man who'd gotten her pregnant, no matter how many times they'd asked. "It'll just hurt her more in the end."

"Shush," Hallie told her, and turned to Tess. "He— What's his name again?"

"Stefano," Tess murmured. She blushed. "I never learned his last name."

"Stefano." Where had she heard that name recently? She tried to remember, then gave up. Hallie leaned back in her spa chair, closing her eyes. "He could be on his way to you already."

But as the facialist covered her eyelids with cool cucumber slices, a faint hint of memory teased her. Where had she heard that name?

"This is nice," Lola said, and sighed from the next chair. "You should put something about spa days in your prenup, Hallie."

"My what?" Hallie yawned.

"Your prenuptial agreement."

"Cristiano hasn't asked for one."

"He will. Trust me. Rich men always look out for themselves. He'll want a legal contract. Read your prenup carefully."

"A contract for marriage? That's silly," Hallie said, already half-asleep as the pedicurist massaged her feet. "Marriage is forever. We're going to take care of each other."

Two hours later, as Hallie walked back through the soaring lobby of the Campania Hotel, she felt so relaxed she glowed. For the first time since Cristiano had taken her virginity and kicked her out of the hotel, she felt...happy.

Cristiano had done that, she realized. He'd arranged everything.

He was so different from the selfish, arrogant bastard she'd once thought him to be. He'd gotten her the simple gold ring she wanted, instead of the enormous diamond. He'd invited her friends to join her for a spa afternoon. He hadn't once said the word *prenup*. And, even now, he was taking care of their baby.

"Hallie!"

She turned around, and all the relaxed, good feelings in her body fled.

Cristiano was sauntering through the lobby with a briefcase, Luther behind him. Coming up to her, he kissed her cheek softly. "Did you have an enjoyable afternoon?"

"Yes." *But where—where was—* Hallie looked all around with rising panic, her eyes wide. Her heart lifted to her throat. "Where's Jack?"

Cristiano gave a low laugh. "Upstairs in the penthouse. Safe. In the best of hands."

"Whose?" she choked out. "Why isn't he with you?"

Cristiano started walking toward the elevator, in no particular hurry. "I had to go to my lawyer's office, to collect the prenuptial agreement."

"The *what*?"

His handsome face looked down at her quizzically. "The prenuptial agreement, *cara*. Of course we must have one."

Hallie's jaw tightened. Turning away, she pushed the elevator button multiple times. When the elevator finally opened, she rushed inside. He followed her, frowning.

"Are you in a rush?"

"How can you ask me that?" She frantically tried to push the button for the penthouse floor, but it didn't work until he placed his finger against the keypad, after which the elevator door slid closed.

"Are you upset at the idea of a prenup? You surely cannot think I would marry you without one, exposing me to the risk of New York's divorce laws and the possibility of losing half my fortune."

She whirled on him. "You think I care about money?"

He looked at her evenly. "Everyone cares about money."

"You left our son with a stranger!"

Cristiano's shoulders relaxed. "He could hardly come with me to the lawyer's office. But you don't need to worry. I left him in the care of the best nanny in the city."

He didn't get it, Hallie realized. She'd been a fool to let herself be lulled into trusting him with her baby, even for an afternoon!

Her fears proved right. Even before the elevator opened on the top floor, she could hear her baby crying.

Wailing.

With no one apparently trying to comfort him.

Hallie rushed to the penthouse door. She was ready to kick it open, to scratch it with her hands. "What kind of home is this if I can't even open my own door?" she said furiously.

Wordlessly Cristiano opened the door with his finger-print, and she rushed through it. Her baby's crying came from the guest room, but as Hallie rushed forward, a stern older woman in a uniform blocked her path.

"Get out of my way," Hallie thundered, pushing past her into the bedroom.

Picking up her tiny sobbing infant from the crib, she held him close to her heart, whispering and singing softly. The baby's wails subsided. Once she'd sat down in the glider and loosened her top, the baby was able to suckle, and his crying stopped abruptly and completely.

"You're making a mistake," the uniformed nanny said, watching dispassionately from the doorway. "It is a mistake I see with many of my ladies. If you give in to your baby's demands now, you'll be his slave. The only way to have a calm household is to get the child on a feeding schedule. You must let him cry it out, madam."

"Cry it out? Cry it out!" Hallie had never been much for swearing, but she suddenly let loose every curse she'd ever heard from her father, who'd been a coal miner and a serious overachiever in the field of swearing. "I'll cry *you* out!"

The woman blanched. "I was hired by Mr. Moretti himself," she said unfeelingly. "I have worked for princes and kings, and I am not going to be insulted by the likes of you."

"Get out," Hallie said, cuddling her baby.

"I'm not going to take orders—"

Her voice became shrill. "Get! Out!"

"Do as she says," Cristiano said in a low voice from behind the nanny, who whirled to face him. His dark eyes glittered in the shadows.

"Fine," she said stiffly. "But I expect to be fully paid for—"

"You'll be paid," Cristiano said. "But if you ask for a reference, don't expect any more princes or kings to hire you."

The woman left with a sniff. Cristiano went to Hallie, who was still sitting in the glider, trembling as she cuddled their baby. He put his hand on her shoulder.

"I'm sorry," he said quietly. "She came highly recommended."

Hallie took a deep breath. She had to force her voice to remain calm. "You have no experience with children."

His eyes flashed to hers, and his expression changed.

"No," he said finally.

She lifted her chin. "You have to learn."

His grip on her shoulder tightened infinitesimally.

"I was told she was the best in New York."

"The best? He was hungry and she was deliberately choosing not to give him a bottle!" She glared up at him. "How can I trust you after this? You convinced me to leave the baby in your care. *Yours*, Cristiano. Not some stranger's!"

For the first time, he looked uncertain. His arms fell to his sides as he muttered, "I told you. I had something to do."

"Yes—watching our son! The son you supposedly care about so much that sharing custody wasn't enough for you—you had to demand marriage! You insisted you wanted to be a father. Was that all just a lie?"

"No," he ground out.

"So why would you immediately desert him?"

"I did not desert him!"

"If you don't want to actually raise him, then what are we even doing?"

Folding his arms, he paced three steps. "You are being unreasonable."

Hallie took a deep breath. "No," she said steadily. "I'm not. If you want us to live with you…if you want me to be crazy enough to marry you tomorrow, then—" she lifted her chin "—I'm setting some rules."

He looked at her in disbelief. "*You're* setting rules?"

"Yes." She added coolly, "We'll even put them into that prenup of yours if you like. Just to make it all official."

He stared at her, clawing his hand through his dark hair. "Fine," he said, his eyes glittering. "Tell me these ridiculous rules."

"First. You will stop being so afraid of the baby."

"Afraid?" he said incredulously. "I'm not afraid!"

"You will learn to be a father to Jack," she continued, ignoring him. "You will learn how to hold him, change him, give him a bottle and bath and rock him to sleep."

His expression darkened. For a second she thought he would refuse. Then he said tightly, "Continue."

"Second. We will spend time as a family. You will join us for at least one meal every day—no matter how busy you are with your company."

"I don't intend to neglect you and Jack," he ground out. "Why would you want that in the prenup?"

Hallie looked at him evenly. "I don't intend to divorce you and steal half your fortune. But, strangely, you still want that written up in a contract."

His jaw looked so tight she wondered if he was hurting his teeth. "Fine."

"I prefer dinner, but if you have to work late, breakfast or lunch is all right, too."

"Anything else?"

Hallie glanced down at her tiny baby son, who had already fallen asleep in her arms. She thought of all her hopes, all her dreams. Only one really mattered.

"Third," she whispered. "You will love him and protect him with your life. As I do."

He stared down at her in the shadowy quiet of the guest bedroom.

"I accept your terms," he bit out. Going to his briefcase, he removed a legal document ten pages long. After turning to the last page, he scribbled something. He handed her the papers.

"Read," he said. "Then sign."

Hallie skimmed the document swiftly, elated to see he'd written all three of her rules exactly as she'd wanted, squeezing them in above the signature lines. As she read through the rest of the pages, the tiny font and legal jargon started to swim before her eyes.

Read your prenup carefully.

The memory of Lola's voice floated back to her, and Hallie wondered if she should get a lawyer to explain the details to her. But she didn't know any lawyers, and it all seemed like too much trouble when she just wanted to snuggle her sleeping baby and maybe take a nap herself, right here in the chair.

Besides, what was the point of getting married if she couldn't even trust Cristiano? He'd admitted his mistake. He intended to rectify it. She could forgive him. She wanted them to be a family. She wanted security for her son, and a home. Why else would she agree to a loveless marriage?

He'd agreed to her own rules. If he followed them, why would they ever divorce?

But, as she started to sign her name, she heard the echo of Tess's voice.

It's love that brought you together. Pure, perfect love. That's the only reason anyone would marry.

She hesitated, then gripped the pen. Her hand shook a little as she signed her name. She gave him back the document.

"Here," she said a little hoarsely.

"Thank you." His voice was clipped. Setting the papers down on the end table, he signed them without another word.

Hallie wondered what he was thinking. His handsome face seemed closed off, remote.

A rush of insecurity went through her. Were they making a mistake? In settling for a loveless marriage, were they just being practical—or were they selling their souls?

She swallowed and looked up at him. "Cristiano, are we doing the right thing?"

Straightening, he stood over the glider, looking down at her and the sleeping baby in her arms. His voice was cold. "What do you mean?"

"Settling for a loveless marriage..."

"Don't second-guess it," he said harshly. "The decision is made."

He turned away.

"Where are you going?" she said, astonished.

Cristiano stopped at the doorway, his handsome face in shadow. "I have work to do."

"Tonight?" Hallie yearned for him to give her reassurance—a kind word, a smile. "Can't you take the evening off? Tomorrow's our wedding."

"I have taken too much time off already. There are details to finalize before I leave New York."

"But—"

"Get some rest. After the wedding reception, we'll leave for Rome." His voice was brusque, as if she were one of his employees and he was giving her instructions. "You know how to order room service. I'll see you in the morning."

With that, he left, closing the door behind him.

Hallie shivered, looking out the window into the early-evening light, cradling her sleeping baby in her arms.

She should have been proud of herself for standing up to him over the prenuptial agreement and setting her own terms. Instead, she felt as if she'd just agreed to the terms of her employment.

Stop it, she told herself angrily. Once they were married, they'd be a family. Jack would have a secure home. His childhood would be happy, as Hallie's had been.

But something didn't feel right.

With a deep breath, Hallie pushed the feeling away. Tomorrow, she would leave the only country she'd ever known and set off into the unknown.

Tomorrow, she would be Cristiano Moretti's bride.

"Do you, Hallie Jane Hatfield," the judge intoned, "take this man to be your lawfully wedded husband?"

Cristiano looked down at Hallie as they stood in a quiet, elegant salon on the third floor of his hotel, with chandeliers, a frescoed ceiling and high windows that overlooked the wide avenue below.

"I do," she said, her face pale.

Cristiano's eyes traced over her voluptuous figure in the deceptively simple ivory satin wedding gown. Her dark hair was pulled back beneath a long, elegant veil. She held a bouquet of pink roses. Her beautiful brown eyes were emotionless.

"Do you, Cristiano Moretti, take this woman to be your lawfully wedded wife?"

"I do," he said, and marveled that he didn't have trouble speaking the words. He'd always thought making a lifetime commitment would feel like facing a firing squad. But he felt nothing.

Everything about this wedding had been easy. His executive assistant, Marcia, with the help of the Campania's stellar wedding planner, had pulled the ceremony together in twenty-four hours, so quickly and quietly that the paparazzi had no idea.

Just a few guests were there to mark the occasion. Hallie's two best friends were bridesmaids, each dressed simply in blue and holding a single rose, as requested by the bride. Two babies were also in attendance—tiny newborn Esme, the daughter of the redheaded bridesmaid, and Jack, who was dressed in a miniature tuxedo and held by the other bridesmaid, the pregnant blonde.

His own friend, Ares Kourakis, was there as best man. The Greek owed him that much, as Cristiano had once blindly supported him through a similar endeavor. His bodyguard, Luther, was there with his girlfriend, and Marcia was with her husband. Even Clarence Loggia, the manager of the hotel, had brought a date.

But looking down at his bride, Cristiano had eyes only for her. His gaze traced to her full breasts, pushed up against the bodice of the bias-cut satin, and his body stirred. Angry as he was, he still wanted her.

Last night, when she'd demanded he agree to her rules, he'd been astonished. His original prenuptial agreement had been entirely appropriate, standard among the wealthy. He'd assumed Hallie would sign it without demur. Instead, she'd demanded that he add clauses legally forcing him to learn to take care of their child and always come home for dinner. Seriously?

He didn't necessarily have a problem with either of those things. But he wanted them to be requested, not required. No man wanted to be blackmailed by his own wife the night before the wedding.

And then, as if that weren't enough, once he'd signed, she'd wanted emotional reassurance that their marriage was a good idea. With the wedding arrangements made and the gold rings bought, she'd wanted him to waste another night rehashing the reasons for their marriage!

Cristiano had seen many last-minute hardball negotiating tactics in the business world. He'd just never expected them from the mother of his child.

Hallie had gotten what she wanted. What more had she hoped to accomplish last night, asking for reassurance? Had she wanted to hear him beg?

Not in this lifetime. Cristiano glowered down at her.

"Then, by the power vested in me by the state of New York, you are now husband and wife. You may kiss the bride," the retired judge finished happily.

Hallie's emotionless gaze flashed up to his, the sweep of her dark eyelashes fluttering against her pale cheeks. She was breathing rapidly, and he noted the quick rise and fall of her breasts.

Cristiano was already hard for her. His hands tightened. There would be no more pleading, no more reasoning.

Hallie was his now. Forever.

After a year, his restraint could end. At last, he could claim his prize.

He pulled her into his arms. Lowering his head, he crushed his mouth to hers.

Their lips joined in a flash of heat that ripped through him like a fire. She gasped, then her resistance melted and she kissed him back, matching his desire with her own. As her hands reached up around his shoulders, he heard her bouquet fall to the floor.

The guests applauded and whistled. He took his time, relishing his possession.

When he finally let her go, Hallie's deep brown eyes were shocked and wide. She looked dizzy as they turned to face the cheers of their friends. Stepping forward, she stumbled and he grabbed her arm to steady her. The truth was, though he was better at hiding it, he felt exactly the same way. He wished they were alone so he could take her straight to bed. As it was, he had to adjust the coat of his morning suit to hide the blatant evidence of his desire.

While they accepted the congratulations of their well-meaning friends, Cristiano hummed with impatience. As they enjoyed lunch in a private room of his hotel's elegant restaurant, it was all he could do not to tell his friends to get the hell out.

Midway through their friends' champagne toasts, Cristiano could take it no longer. He cut them off, rising to his feet.

"You'll have to excuse us," he said perfunctorily. "My bride is tired, and needs time for a nap before our flight to Rome."

Everyone looked at Hallie, who appeared astonished.

"Thank you for coming," Cristiano said firmly. Rising to his feet, he reached his hand out to Hallie. "Please feel free to stay as long as you want and order whatever you like." He turned to the pregnant bridesmaid, who was holding Jack. The baby was happily smiling and clapping his hands. "Would you mind watching the baby for an hour?"

"Sure," she said, a glint of wicked amusement in her eyes.

As he pulled his new bride out of the private dining room, he saw the bridesmaids look at each other with a knowing grin, and even Ares Kourakis gave him a smug smile, as if to say, *See? It happened to you, too.*

Cristiano didn't give a damn. After all this time, Hallie was his wife. She was his by right.

He intended to make her so—in every way.

"You were rude," Hallie snapped once they were alone in the elevator. He pushed the button, then turned to her.

"Do you want to go back and make my excuses?" he said in a low voice, running his hand softly over her ivory satin wedding gown, up her arm, to her neck, to her sensitive earlobe and her cheek. He felt her shiver.

"You're a brute," she whispered.

"Yes," he growled. "And now you're mine."

"I'm not—"

Lowering his head, he cut her off with a rough kiss. Pressing her against the wall, he cupped her breasts, kissing down her throat. With a soft gasp, she surrendered, closing her eyes as her head fell back. With her in his arms, he was lost in a sensual haze. He'd almost forgotten they were in an elevator when he heard the bell ding and the door slide open on the top floor.

Lifting her in his arms, he carried her into the penthouse, kicking the door wide over the threshold. Once inside the bedroom, he set her down on her feet, letting her body slide slowly over his so she could feel how hard he was for her.

"Mrs. Moretti," he whispered, and felt her shiver at hearing her new name. In front of the windows revealing the shining New York skyline, with deliberate slowness Cristiano pulled out the pins holding her veil. Her lustrous dark hair fell tumbling down her shoulders.

"You're so beautiful," he said hoarsely.

Reaching up, she loosened his tie. Her brown eyes were soft and inviting. Tossing his black morning coat on the white sofa, he pulled her in his arms.

"You're mine now, Hallie," he said, fiercely searching her gaze. "You know that, don't you?"

"Only if you admit you're mine."

"Yes," he whispered. "Forever."

He lowered his mouth to hers, crushing her body against his own. Sensation and yearning and desire ripped through him, and in that moment he simply let go.

Let go of his anger. His self-control. His reason. He let go of his need to guard himself from everyone and everything.

All that mattered was her.

All that mattered was this.

He slowly unzipped her wedding dress, letting it drop to the floor. He took a ragged breath when he saw her in her wedding lingerie—a white lace bra and tiny panties that clung to her deliciously full hips.

Lifting her up with a growl, he lowered her reverently onto the bed.

Never taking his eyes off her, he loosened his platinum cuff links and unbuttoned his white shirt, then dropped it onto the floor. Pulling off his black trousers, he climbed beside her on the enormous bed, pulling her against his body.

"I've wanted you so long," he whispered.

Her eyes were luminous, and, like a miracle, she lifted her lips to his.

A rush of overwhelming need poured through him, and he crushed her violently against his hard body, plundering her mouth with his own. He yanked off his silk boxers, intending to roll her onto her back and push himself inside her, to impale with a single thrust.

Then he remembered that he had to be gentle. Even though his body was raging with the need to take her, she'd just had his baby three months before. A low curse escaped his lips. He might be a brute, but he wasn't a…a *brute*.

Gentling his embrace, he lingered, naked against her lingerie-clad body, kissing her slowly and thoroughly. Their tongues touched and intertwined in their kiss until he heard her soft sigh, until he felt her body rise. He stroked her face, lightly kissing her forehead, then caressing slowly down her cheek to suckle her ear. He gloried as he felt her shiver beneath him.

Moving down her body as she lay stretched on the bed, he cupped her breasts over the white lace, then with agonizing slowness, removed her bra. He nearly groaned at the sight of her magnificent breasts. He felt their naked weight, before he kissed down the sharp crevice between them, down to the sweet slope of her belly.

For a moment, he teased her with the warmth of his breath. Then he moved lower, and lower still. Finally, gripping her hips, he lowered his head between her legs, teasing her thighs with his breath.

Her hands gripped his shoulders, as if she were afraid of what he might do next, or afraid he might stop.

He ran his tongue along the edge of her white lace panties, letting the tension build in her. Then he ripped the lace off her body entirely.

Lowering his head, he tasted her, caressing her with the hot, slick pressure of his tongue. As she gasped beneath him, he spread her thighs wide with his hands. Ruthlessly, he pressed his mouth against her hot wet core, working the taut nub of her pleasure with his tongue. She gasped, then held her breath.

Then…she exploded.

Fierce joy filled him at seeing her ecstasy.

Moving quickly, he covered her naked body with his own. Lowering his head, he pressed his lips to hers, swaying his hips sensuously against hers. Still lost in pleasure, she accompanied him, her body rising anew. With deliberate slowness, he positioned himself between her legs. He watched her face, keeping himself under control as he finally pushed inside her, filling her inch by delicious inch. He heard her shocked gasp of pleasure. She wrapped her hands around his shoulders, pulling him down harder against her. And, with a groan, he obliged her, thrusting deeper until he was all the way inside her, all the way to her heart.

He was deep, so deep inside her.

Still dazzled by the pleasure he'd given her with his mouth, Hallie moaned softly as he entranced her anew, filling her so completely. She tried to remember when she'd ever felt such intense pleasure. Even their first night together, as incredible as it had been, hadn't been like this. What was the difference? Was it that they were wed, bonded together forever as man and wife?

Or was it something more, something she felt in the deepest corner of her soul—that he belonged to her, and she to him?

But, as he filled her so slowly and deeply, it wasn't just her body that ached desperately for release.

She wanted to love him.

That was the one thing she couldn't do. The one thing that could only lead to ruin: loving her husband.

For a moment, she looked up at his handsome face looming over hers, at his heartbreaking dark eyes. She closed her eyes, turning away as he kissed slowly down her throat.

Slowly, deliberately, he began to ride her. And all she wanted was more. She gasped, clutching at the white comforter beneath her, wrapping her legs around his hips. His thrusts seared her, hard and deep.

Gripping her shoulders, he pushed into her with increasing roughness until their bodies were sweaty, their limbs tangled. Her fingernails tightened into his shoulders, her back rising off the bed, until she exploded, flying even higher than before, higher than she'd ever imagined. Pleasure overwhelmed her in waves so intense she almost blacked out.

With a low growl, he thrust one last time, then roared as he exploded with her.

Gasping, they clutched each other, eyes closed. She struggled to catch her breath. He collapsed beside her, holding her as if she were the only thing that existed. They held each other, tangled in the shadowy bed, for what could have been minutes or hours.

When Hallie finally opened her eyes, she saw Cristiano was pulling away from her, sitting up.

"Don't leave," she pleaded, reaching for him. "We still have a few hours."

He smiled down at her, taking her hand and kissing it tenderly. "It would be good to arrive in Rome early. My jet is already waiting. We should go."

"But our friends…"

"Our friends will understand." Leaning down, he kissed her naked shoulder with a sudden wicked grin. "And there's a bedroom on my jet."

Shivering with need, exhausted with desire, Hallie grinned at him. She blushed, shocked at her own wantonness.

Lowering his head to kiss her one last time, he whispered, "You are magnificent, Mrs. Moretti." Getting up from the bed, he headed for the en suite shower.

Once he left her, she felt suddenly cold, bereft. She wanted him back in bed. Beside her. For always. And not just that.

With an intake of breath, Hallie realized how easy it would be to give her husband—the man who'd told her outright that he could never love her—not just her body, but her soul.

CHAPTER SIX

As the Rolls-Royce drove from the private airport into the crowded and winding streets of Rome, Hallie's head was twisting right and left. She knew she was gaping like a fish, but she didn't care.

After five years in New York, she'd thought no city could easily impress her; yet she'd never seen anything so beautiful, so decadent, so ancient, as the Eternal City.

She looked out the window at a red sports car zipping by, at a young girl in a scarf clinging to a smiling boy on the back of a cherry-colored moped. Down the street, she saw a passionate young couple gesticulating angrily at each other in front of a sidewalk café, before the man swept the woman up into a hungry kiss.

Roma. Hallie felt the city like a thunderbolt. It was like, she thought, a huge, sexy party, with food, wine and dancing—all on top of an ancient tomb. The city itself seemed to cry out: *Take every bit of joy today, for someday you will not be at the party, but below it.*

"What do you think?" Cristiano looked at her over the baby's seat in the back of the limo.

She shivered at the frank sensuality of his gaze. She could hardly believe that she was his wife. Cristiano was her husband. Good thing, too. What he'd done to her last night…

After their passionate interlude at the penthouse, they'd made good use of that bedroom on his private jet. Any time the baby slept, he drew her into his bed, into shockingly sensual delights so new she still shook at the memory.

He smiled, his eyes amused, as if he knew exactly what she was thinking about.

Blushing, she turned back toward her window, marveling as their Rolls-Royce sped down slender, crowded roads, following traffic laws she didn't understand. They'd been met at the airport that morning by their new Italian driver, who was called Marco, and new bodyguard, Salvatore. She gaped as they drove past one incredible ancient monument and cathedral after another. Finally, they arrived at the Campania Hotel Rome, a magnificent Mediterranean-style edifice near the top of the Spanish Steps.

Tilting back her head, she gaped when she got out of the Rolls, staring up at the glamorous hotel. She held her breath as she turned to see the view. All of Rome was at their feet.

"Like it?" Cristiano murmured lazily.

"I've never seen anything like it."

"Of course you have not." He grinned, looking pleased. "Campania is the best luxury hotel brand in the world. And the Campania Roma is the best of them all."

As Marco and Salvatore collected their bags, Hallie and Cristiano strolled hand in hand. Baby Jack, pushed by his father in the stroller, didn't seem nearly as impressed by their surroundings. He chewed on the stuffed giraffe clipped to his shirt.

Hallie looked down at the letters imprinted on a manhole cover near the sidewalk. "What is SPQR?"

"It's Latin. *Senatus populusque Romanus*—the Senate and People of Rome. You'll see the emblem everywhere in the city."

"Wow. This city is really old," she said in awe, and flashed him a grin. "Almost as old as you."

He lifted an eyebrow. "Am I old?"

She liked teasing him about the eleven-year difference between them. She countered, "You're teaching me Latin now?"

His dark eyes simmered. "Let me take you to our room, *cara*. And I'll teach you other things. All night long."

Her cheeks burned as a smiling, dark-eyed doorman held open the hotel door. Pushing the stroller ahead of them, they walked into the soaring lobby.

Hallie sucked in her breath. The opulence was unbelievable. Gilded Corinthian columns stretched up toward the Murano glass chandeliers high above.

"I didn't think it possible," she breathed. "This place is even more amazing than your hotel in New York."

He smiled at her. *"Grazie."*

She turned to stare as a chic fortysomething woman passed by, dressed to the nines in six-inch heels and a velvet skirt suit so well crafted the jacket was like a corset, and perfect scarlet lips. At the woman's side was a man in a well-cut suit who paused to let his eyes caress Hallie before he continued past. Hallie blinked in amazement, staring after them. "And the people…"

"What about them?"

"All the women look like movie stars. And the men like James Bond. Everyone dresses as if they're about to meet the love of their lives. What is this place?"

Cristiano gave her a sudden wicked grin. "Roma."

She shook her head in awe at a city where everyone, from teenagers to octogenarians, seemed to claim eternal sensuality as both a privilege and a duty. "You grew up here?"

"I lived here briefly."

She knew so little about his past. "You were born in Rome?"

His gaze shuttered, as if he could sense her probing.

"Naples," he said flatly. Clearly he wasn't interested in saying anything more.

Mr. Moretti was a brawler, back when he was young. He fought his way out of the streets of Naples.

His driver's words came back to her. Not for the first time, she wondered how a fatherless, penniless boy, neglected then orphaned by his mother, had made his fortune, turning himself into an international hotel tycoon.

"Look." Cristiano pointed at the lobby ceiling. She gasped, tilting back her head to look up.

On the ceiling, gold-painted stars decorated a midnight sky. Across the lobby, she saw huge vases filled with red flowers beside marble fireplaces carved with cherubs. The enormous sweeping staircase had an actual red carpet.

She'd never seen anything so incredible, not even in a movie. She stopped, feeling she was in a dream. "It's— it's—"

"I know," Cristiano replied. "The building was once a *palazzo* gone to ruin. I was only twenty-two when I convinced the *contessa* to sell it. It took two years to rebuild and restore it. I gambled everything I had—my reputation, my future. This place," he said softly, looking around them, "was the making of me."

His voice was deep with emotion. Hallie looked at him, her heart in her throat.

Coming back to himself, he smiled at her. "Come."

As they walked through the hotel lobby, everyone beamed at Cristiano, and not only him.

Somehow, weirdly, everyone in the hotel seemed to already know Hallie. As if, simply by marrying Cristiano Moretti, she'd suddenly become a celebrity in her own right—famous, beautiful and adored. They all beamed at her.

"Buongiorno."

"Buongiorno, signor e signora."

"Benvenuto, Signora Moretti."

After three different people of different ages greeted them, Hallie turned to Cristiano in bewilderment. "They know who I am?"

He gave her a crooked grin. "Of course they do. We were

married yesterday. By now everyone in Rome knows you are my wife. You're a celebrity here, *cara*."

"Why would I be a celebrity?" Then, looking at his face, she gave him a sheepish grin. "You're teasing me."

"I don't tease," Cristiano said. Taking her hand, he brought it to his lips for a brief, hot kiss, then whispered, "At least not that way."

She shivered until he released her hand.

"Be serious," she pleaded. She saw several people in the lobby covertly lifting cameras to take her picture. Why? Was something wrong with her? She looked down at the simple outfit that Cristiano's concierge had packed for her in New York. It was sleek and severe, less comfortable than her beloved sundresses: a black dress with a sweetheart neckline and black high heels.

Cristiano had assured her that the outfit would be appropriate in Rome. Now, her heart pounded at all the curious eyes staring at her. "Why is everyone looking at me?"

"Because many Italian women want to know your secret."

"What secret?"

His dark eyes flickered. "Of how you hooked me into marriage."

"Um, by letting you accidentally knock me up?"

With a snort, he said mildly, "In New York, I am not that unusual. There's a Sicilian tycoon in my hotel who is a well-known playboy, in addition to being a cold bastard. Even Ares Kourakis, my best man at the wedding, was called uncatchable before he fell for some little waitress from the West last year. But here, in Rome and Naples, everywhere in southern Italy, I am famous." He looked down at her, caressing her with his eyes. "And now, so are you."

Butterflies skimmed through Hallie. As he led her to the extravagantly gilded elevator, and they rode it to the top floor, the butterflies only increased. Marco and Salvatore went ahead of them, carrying their luggage.

Cristiano stopped at the penthouse door with the stroller. "Welcome to our home."

"Our home?"

He smiled. "For now."

Following him inside, Hallie saw a large suite of rooms, all decorated as lavishly as the lobby. The baby's blue-walled room was furnished with every luxury and comfort, with books and lavish toys. Next to that, she saw the enormous master bedroom, with a huge bed and walk-in closet.

Through sliding doors, she walked out onto a terrace. Purple flowers laced the edge of the railing and she felt the hot Italian sun beating down from the blue summer sky. Looking out, she gasped at the panoramic view, gaping in wonder at the old buildings, domed churches and Roman temples spread out across the seven hills.

Coming from behind, Cristiano wrapped his arms around her, pulling her back against his chest, nuzzling her neck.

"It's so beautiful," she whispered, and turned around in his arms, feeling she was in a dream.

He smiled. "You're beautiful, *cara mia*," he said huskily, lowering his head to hers. "And now that you're my wife, I intend to give you the world..."

For the next two weeks, whenever Cristiano wasn't working, checking every detail of this hotel—which had prepared strenuously for his inspection—he took Hallie and the baby to explore the city.

First, he insisted on taking Hallie shopping. With the new burly bodyguard at their side, they visited all the grand shopping streets of Rome, starting with the expensive boutiques near the Spanish Steps.

"More shopping?" she'd protested in dismay. "Is that really necessary?"

"One must be conscious of *la bella figura* in Rome. Even more than in New York. And it will help you relax, knowing you fit in."

"How would you know?" she grumbled. "You fit in everywhere."

Looking at her, he said quietly, "I came to Rome as a young Napolitano. I changed my clothes and changed my fate."

Hallie waited breathlessly for him to continue, to tell her more of his hard childhood and how he'd made his fortune. But he did not.

Sighing, she gave in, rolling her eyes. "Fine. Take me shopping."

She was relieved when the clothes were purchased and they could do what she really wanted—explore the city. They bought Jack a wooden sword and shield at the Colosseum and laughingly tossed coins in the Trevi Fountain. They drove past an enormous white-columned building that looked like a wedding cake, and the endless Roman ruins scattered around the city as casually as food carts in New York.

In the evenings, they had room service sent up to their penthouse for dinner, but once Cristiano took them out, to a simple outdoor trattoria with a private courtyard near the Piazza Navona. As the sun set, with flowers everywhere and fountains burbling, Hallie wistfully watched musicians sing and play guitar, remembering her old dream of a singing career. Cristiano had observed her, then had a quiet word with the trattoria's owner.

A moment later, the musicians spoke into the microphone and invited Hallie to come up on stage and sing. Embarrassed, she'd tried to refuse until Cristiano had said, "Please, do it for me."

Staring at his handsome face, she couldn't deny anything he asked of her. She'd gone up on stage and sung an old Appalachian folk song a capella.

Applause rang in her ears as she returned to their table. As she passed by, an American man claiming to be a record executive even gave her his card. Laughing, she showed it to Cristiano when she sat back down at the table.

"I told him thanks, but no thanks. My days of trying to get singing gigs are over."

"Are you sure?"

Remembering all the painful years of rejection, she nodded fervently.

"Good," he said huskily. "You'll sing only for me."

For the rest of the evening, Hallie ate pasta and drank wine and watched her new husband learn to be comfortable holding their baby. Seeing Jack tucked gently and tenderly in Cristiano's arms, she felt a rush of happiness, like everything was right with the world.

But once they left the trattoria's private courtyard, Salvatore had to hold back the rush of onlookers and paparazzi eager to take pictures of their family. It made her scared to go out on the street with the baby.

Each night, she sang lullabies to Jack, the same lullabies her mother had once sung to her, passed down from her grandmother and great-grandmother before. That night, when her baby finally slept, with his plump arms over his head, she turned and saw Cristiano silhouetted in the doorway, his face in shadow.

"Those songs you sing," he said in a low voice. "They break my heart."

Drawing her out of the nursery, he kissed her and pulled her to their bed. Then he made her heart break, too, with the purest happiness she'd ever known.

However, after living in a hotel for two weeks, she'd

started to feel trapped, unable to leave the penthouse without Cristiano and the bodyguard.

One afternoon while he was working, Hallie took her baby out onto the penthouse terrace to enjoy the warm summer sun. Watering the purple flowers that decorated the terrace railing, she tried to pretend she was back in West Virginia, in their old garden. Her mother had loved to spend hours taking care of their plants. As she watered the flowers, she would sing.

"Why did you never leave, Mama?" Hallie had asked her once in the garden, the year before she'd died. Hallie had just graduated from high school, and what the world was telling her she should want and what she actually wanted seemed to be two different things. "Why did you never go to New York and become a famous singer?"

"Oh, my dear." Turning to Hallie, her mother had caressed her cheek tenderly. "I did think of it once. Then I met your father and traded that dream for a better one."

"What?"

"Our family." Her mother's eyes had glowed with love. "Your whole life is ahead of you, Hallie. I know whatever you decide to do, you'll make us proud."

And so, after she'd lost everything—her mother and father and brother and home—Hallie had taken her father's meager life insurance and gone to New York. To try to make her family proud.

"Hallie?"

Lost in thought, standing on the terrace watering the flowers, Hallie jumped when she heard Cristiano's voice behind her.

Turning, she saw him, devastatingly handsome as always in a sleek suit. He wasn't alone. Behind Cristiano was an older woman, plump, white-haired and simply but perfectly dressed.

"*Cara*, I have someone I'd like you to meet." He looked

over Hallie's tank top and capri pants as she stood holding a glass pitcher from the kitchen. "Are you watering the flowers?"

She could hardly deny it, since he'd caught her redhanded. "Um, yes?"

"You must not. We have hotel staff who are paid very well to do it and who are supporting families. You would not wish them to be out of a job?"

"I suppose not," she said, crestfallen. With a sigh, she set down the glass pitcher on a nearby table. "I can't wait until we have a house of our own."

He frowned. "A house?"

"When we go back to New York."

"I thought you liked Rome."

"I do, but…" She thought of her friends with a pang. "Tess sent me a text that Lola had her baby yesterday. I miss my friends. I'm looking forward to when we can settle down and have a proper home."

A strange expression crossed Cristiano's face. "Well, we'll talk about that later." Clearing his throat, he motioned to the white-haired woman behind him. "I'd like you to meet Agata Manganiello. She lives in Rome and used to work for me. She was my first secretary, long ago."

"Hello…um…*buongiorno*," Hallie said.

Smiling shyly, the woman said in careful English, "Hello, Mrs. Moretti. I am pleased to meet you."

"I'm pleased to meet you, too," Hallie said, then turned inquisitively to Cristiano.

"I have known Agata for almost fifteen years," he said. "She is careful, responsible. She's very good with children."

"I raised six of my own," Agata said proudly, "while working for Cristiano." She tilted her head thoughtfully. "I think caring for you was harder than the other six put together."

Cristiano gave a good-natured laugh. "You were a miracle worker," he said affectionately.

Hallie looked at him in amazement. He sounded so relaxed. And the Italian woman had called Cristiano by his first name. She'd never heard any of his other employees do that, not even Mr. Loggia, the manager.

Cristiano was treating this woman like…family.

"You're thinking of hiring her to watch Jack," Hallie said slowly. "Aren't you?"

His gaze met hers. "I'd like you to consider it."

"But I don't want a nanny."

"Not a nanny. A babysitter. Occasionally, I'd like to take you to dinner, just the two of us. And once my new hotel opens on the Amalfi Coast, there will be a grand ball to celebrate. We will sometimes need help. And I'd trust Agata with my life."

He waited, watching her. Biting her lip, Hallie considered. It felt very different from when he'd tried to force that last awful nanny on her by surprise.

Reluctantly she turned to the older woman. "You raised six children?"

Agata nodded. "And now I have five grandchildren."

She has kind eyes, Hallie thought. Cristiano said he trusted her with his life.

Slowly she asked, "Would you like to hold Jack?"

The woman smiled. *"Sì, naturalmente."*

Picking up the baby from the thick quilt on the terrace, Hallie placed him in the woman's capable arms and waited for him to fuss. He simply gurgled happily, reaching a flailing arm toward Agata's nose.

"I was thinking Agata and the baby could get to know each other this afternoon," Cristiano said. "If it goes well, I'll take you out to dinner tonight. Just the two of us."

Hallie opened her mouth to argue. Then she heard Agata crooning some Italian song as she snuggled Jack in her plump arms, to the baby's delight. She looked at them. Jack seemed happy and content.

"I'll think about it," she said grudgingly.

"Va bene." Cristiano kissed her lightly on the forehead. "I will be back in a few hours to spend time with Jack, then you and I will have dinner. As per your rules. Speaking of which—" he angled his head "—I've been thinking about making some new rules of my own."

She frowned. "What rules?"

His smile transformed into a grin. "Wait and see."

Hallie watched the Italian grandmother carefully that afternoon, telling herself she'd send Agata away the instant Jack seemed unhappy. But the baby seemed to love her, and Agata was easy to have in the penthouse, kindly and unobtrusive. It was almost, Hallie realized, like having…no, not her mother, but some kindly great-aunt come to watch the baby. Maybe it was the fact that Cristiano—who didn't trust anyone—seemed to trust her, for it made Hallie trust her, too.

Later that evening, with the baby safely fed and sleeping in his crib, she left capable Agata in charge and went out on a dinner date with her husband for the first time.

Hallie dressed carefully in a new, sexy black dress with a bare back that he'd bought her. Trying to match the drama of the dress, she pulled her long, dark hair into a high ponytail that hung down over her naked back. Going to the internet for makeup tips, she lined her eyes with black kohl and mascara to make them smoky and dramatic, then put on scarlet lipstick.

As she came out of the bedroom, she was nervous that Cristiano wouldn't like her new look.

But, when he saw her, his jaw dropped.

"You make me want to stay home," he growled, coming closer. In his own well-cut black button-down shirt and trousers, his dark hair rumpled and sexy, he looked amazing to her, as always.

"Please, take me out," she whispered.

"As you wish." Catching her hand in his own, he lifted it to his lips. His breath against her skin made her shiver all over. "I'll take you out." He gave her a sensual smile. "Then I'll take you in."

He never let go of her hand as they descended the elevator into the lobby. Past the crowds, she saw a bright red Ferrari waiting for them in front of the hotel.

"What about Salvatore?" she asked, looking at the two-seater car.

"I want to be alone with you tonight," he said, opening her door.

As Cristiano drove her through the streets in the fast sports car, she looked out her window at the sensuality of Rome at night. So mysterious and dangerous, the city seemed to whisper two words: *sex* and *death*. She felt his hot gaze on her. Then he punched down hard on the gas, racing over the hills of the city.

Eventually he parked in front of a nineteenth-century brick building tucked back on a quiet street. There was no sign it was a restaurant except for two valets standing mysteriously in front.

"What's this?" she asked as he helped her out of the car.

Cristiano smiled. "It's by invitation only."

Once inside, a maître d' escorted them through the building and out into a lush garden courtyard. Scattered at ten small tables, she saw people she recognized—famous performers, politicians and athletes. Her eyes widened as they walked past someone that Hallie knew had millions of social-media followers.

"What is this place?" Hallie whispered to Cristiano. His hand tightened on her arm as other patrons turned to look at them with similar interest.

"A Michelin-starred chef runs the restaurant as a hobby. He invites only friends, or friends of friends."

She looked at the ruined walls on the other side of the courtyard. They looked ancient. "How old are those?"

Cristiano glanced casually at the ruins. "Fifth century, I'd imagine."

They were escorted to the best table, beside an old stone fountain. She looked up. The only ceiling was the dark velvet of the Italian sky, twinkling with stars. Fairy lights were strewn against the rough, ruined walls, illuminating red flowers and greenery proliferating amid the cracks.

"Incredible," she breathed.

Cristiano reached for her hand over the table. His gaze was hungry. "You're incredible."

After fully enjoying each other every night over the last two weeks, she felt deliciously sore all over. And aware. So aware. Just his hand on hers made her body tighten and shiver. When the tattooed waiter spoke to Cristiano in Italian, she thought again how easy it would be to love her husband.

But she couldn't. It would be a horrible mistake. Because he would never love her back, and, eventually, that would make her love turn to hate.

Their meal started with a cocktail, the ubiquitous Aperol spritz, a light bubbly drink blending Prosecco, soda water and orange liqueur over ice and orange slices, but with an added twist of rosemary. Sipping the drink, Hallie felt the other celebrities staring at them. She glanced down at herself self-consciously. She whispered, "What's wrong with me?"

"Why do you think something's wrong?"

"Why would they—" she waved her arm toward the powerful, fascinating people at the other tables "—stare at me?" She bit her lip. "It's my makeup, isn't it? The bare back of my dress? I look weird, don't I?"

He leaned forward. "You are," he said huskily, "the sexiest woman in Rome."

She felt the weight of that compliment and saw, from the expression in his eyes, that he meant every word.

As their eyes locked, a pulse of heat rushed through her. Turning away, she took a sip of the light, bubbly cocktail to try to cool down. She cleared her throat. "But there are so many beautiful people here. Famous people. Why would they bother looking at me?"

"You're famous now, too. And unlike all of them—" he dismissed his fellow patrons with a glance "—no one knows anything about you."

Hallie gave an incredulous snort. "I'm just a regular girl from rural West Virginia."

Wordlessly Cristiano drew his phone from his pocket. Pressing a few buttons, he handed it to her.

Hallie stared down at the screen in amazement.

"See? You're a star," he said softly.

Looking at his phone, she realized it was true. Pictures and stories about her had exploded all over the internet. She was on news websites. Celebrity gossip pages. Someone had started a fashion blog in Italian, with a photo of her every time she'd come out of the hotel over the past two weeks, with a listing of each day's clothes, who'd designed them and where to buy them. There was even a page devoted to Jack's clothes. Her baby had somehow become a fashion icon.

It was jarring to see pictures of herself, taken without her knowledge, and pictures of her baby, too, all now online for the world to see.

She sucked in her breath when she saw a video of herself singing at the trattoria, posted on YouTube a few days before. It had already gotten over a hundred thousand hits. *A hundred thousand.*

Her mind boggled.

But not all the attention was positive. Some of the posts were downright mean. Strangers were calling her a gold-digger. And, apparently, Hallie's family tragedy made excellent news fodder. Many news stories breathlessly reported that Hallie was a failed folk singer from a poor Appalachian family who'd all died tragically in a flash flood, but then she'd gotten pregnant and was now married to an Italian billionaire, so wasn't she the luckiest girl in the world?

The words and pictures swam before Hallie's eyes. Her stomach clenched. Abruptly she gave him back his phone.

"You see why," he said quietly, "I want you always to take Salvatore with you when you're out on the street."

Hallie shivered. As a girl, she'd wistfully dreamed of growing up to be somehow special. Hadn't she even gone to New York hoping to become a star?

Now she found that being the center of attention just made her uncomfortable. Feeling the warm night breeze against the bare skin of her back, she tried to smile. "You didn't bring Salvatore with us tonight."

"This restaurant is exclusive. The patrons are mostly famous themselves." His eyebrow lifted. "Besides, I can protect you."

Remembering the night he'd forced her landlord to return her precious possessions, Hallie could well believe it. Biting her lip, she ventured, "Matthews said that you were a street fighter in Naples when you were young."

His expression closed up. "That is one way of saying it. I had no money. So I fought."

"And now you are a billionaire, with the most luxurious hotel chain in the world."

"So?"

"How did it happen? How did you build your fortune?"

Cristiano stared at her, his handsome face shadowed against the soft lighting of the garden.

"I was lucky," he said flatly. "I met a man who owned a small hotel chain in southern Italy. I convinced him to hire me and teach me everything he knew. Then I betrayed him."

Shocked, Hallie stared at him. With a cold smile, he took a sip of his drink, then looked up as the waiter arrived and, in both Italian and English, listed the five choices on the evening's menu.

Cristiano ordered the veal, Hallie the *spaghetti alla vongole*—pasta with clams in a light wine sauce. She added, "And could I get that with lots of Parmesan cheese, please?"

Both Cristiano and the waiter stared at her with identical horrified expressions.

"Clams...seafood...these you should not eat with cheese," the waiter said patiently, as if explaining to a toddler she shouldn't run into traffic.

Hallie smiled, but held her ground. "I still like them."

"But it is not done!" The waiter looked at Cristiano for support, but he just shrugged, as if to say, *Americans, what can you do?*

When the pasta arrived, Hallie covered it with Parmesan and thought it was delicious. She washed it all down with a glass of red wine, causing another shocked gasp from the waiter, at the thought that she'd drink red wine with seafood, not white. Hallie decided that maybe she enjoyed shocking people, because she didn't care.

As the evening lengthened, a pleasurable sensation seeped into her bones. Maybe it was the delicious dinner or the sensual wind against her bare skin. Maybe it was the fragrance of the flowers or sitting with Cristiano amid a fifth-century ruin beneath the starry sky. But she felt strangely like she was in a dream.

"When are we going back to New York?" she asked.

"I'm not sure." Cristiano watched her. "After I'm done in Rome, I'll need to go to the Amalfi Coast for a few weeks to oversee the finishing touches on the new hotel opening in Cavello. The grand opening gala is next month."

She brightened. "I've always wanted to see the Amalfi Coast."

"You and the baby will remain in Rome. I'll commute via helicopter."

"What? Why?" she said, dismayed. More weeks spent cooped up in the penthouse, afraid to go out alone on the streets of Rome didn't sound appealing. A prison was a prison, no matter how luxurious. "That's not what the rules say. What about our family time?"

"Rules are made to be broken."

"Not my rules. You gave your word."

He ground his teeth. "I cannot bring you with me. The Campania Cavello isn't yet ready for guests, and I can hardly let it be known that Cristiano Moretti's bride is staying in a rival's hotel."

"That would be bad," she agreed. She looked down at her empty plate. "Still, you must find a way," she said in a small voice. "I don't want to be separated from you."

"You won't be." His leg brushed hers beneath the table, and she looked up. The air between them changed.

Sitting across from Cristiano in the sexy black dress, defying the tattooed Italian waiter and even her own husband to enjoy her meal exactly as she pleased, Hallie realized she wasn't the same shy girl she'd once been. She felt stronger. Braver.

Becoming Cristiano's wife, living in Rome, wearing this sexy dress, with dark eyeliner and bright red lips, she felt bolder somehow. She didn't know why, but she suddenly felt powerful. Like his equal.

Maybe that was what gave her the courage.

"I need to know when we can go back to New York and buy our own house."

Taking a bite of veal, he frowned at her. "We have twenty-two houses."

She blinked, taken aback. "You mean your hotels?"

"Yes." He swirled his wineglass. "The hotels. All of them fully staffed in the most beautiful locations. The perfect way to live. We never need to settle. We'll never get bored. And I can run my company and build my empire."

"Your hotels are amazing, but…" How could she say it? "They're not home."

"A home, a home," he repeated irritably. "I'm tired of hearing you ask about it."

She looked at him in surprise. "I've barely mentioned it."

"For days now, all the lullabies you sing to Jack have been about finding home and losing home and longing for home."

She drew back, genuinely surprised. "Really?"

He scowled. "Plaintive, heartbreaking folk songs. Are you trying to wear me down?"

"I didn't realize…"

"From now on, sing happy songs to our baby," he ordered.

"Okay," she said, biting her lip. The songs she knew were mostly old Scottish-Irish ballads, a repertoire that didn't exactly specialize in "happy" songs. "Um… I'll try to think of some."

"And we don't need to buy a house. You should be happy living all over the world in penthouse suites with spectacular views, waited on hand and foot by staff. That should be enough."

She paused.

"It's…nice," she said carefully. "For a honeymoon. But we need a permanent place of our own. Maybe with a garden."

"A garden? In Manhattan?"

"They exist," she said defensively. "I worked once at

this amazing house on Bank Street. There was a garden tucked in back."

"By *garden*, do you mean a few pots on a stoop?"

"A real garden," she said indignantly. "My employers let me go because the owners lived overseas and were never there. They were going to put it up for sale."

"We would never be there, either," he said. "My work requires constant travel, and I want you with me."

"But soon Jack will go to school…"

"Truly you think our son is a prodigy if he needs to go to school when he has not yet learned to roll over."

Defiantly Hallie lifted her chin. "You talk about building an empire. I want to build a family." She hesitated. "I'd prefer New York, but I can compromise. If you want to live in Italy, I can make it work. I'll learn Italian and try to make friends—"

"We're not staying. After the new hotel is launched in Cavello, we'll spend a few weeks in Tokyo, then Seoul, Sydney and Mumbai."

"All those places," she said faintly. Beautiful places she'd only imagined. Normally she would have been thrilled at the thought of seeing them with her own eyes. But tonight, she thought longingly of her friends. Lola's baby, now one day old. "After that, we'll go back to New York?"

"Briefly. Then Paris, London and Berlin." He paused. "I have twenty-two hotels, and they all need my attention."

Her heart sank. Circling the world, she would barely see her friends. And forget about a garden. Her eyes fell forlornly to her plate. "Oh."

Cristiano scowled at her. "Surely you're not complaining about traveling around the world in a private jet, staying in luxury hotels."

But a life of luxury had never been Hallie's dream. Licking her lips, she said, "I'm sure all those places are amazing, but…"

"But?"

"How can we ever have a home if we never stay in one place for long?" Her voice was small. "How will I make friends? How will Jack?"

"Learn all the languages, as I have. Be a citizen of the world."

"A citizen of nowhere."

"Everywhere," he corrected coldly.

Angry tears lifted to Hallie's eyes, though she didn't want to fight, not on their first baby-free date. She tried to keep her voice calm.

"Traveling is fine, but eventually we need to stop and have a home!"

"What you call home I would describe as a prison. I'm not buying you a house, Hallie. It would be a waste of money."

The warm summer night suddenly felt cold.

"So you'll waste money on everything but the one thing I actually care about?" Folding her arms, she turned away stonily. By now, as the night grew late, many of the tables had emptied.

"Hallie." His voice changed, turned gentle. "Look at me."

Grudgingly she did and saw his dark eyes were tender.

"Tell me why a house means so much to you," he said. "Because I truly do not understand."

Hallie took a deep breath.

"The house I grew up in was built by my great-grand-father. By his own two hands." She tried to smile. "The songs I sing to Jack, the songs you love so much, they were the ones my mother once sang to me. My family lived for generations on the same mountain. I had close friends. A place in the world."

"If you loved it so much," he said quietly, "why did you leave?"

With an intake of breath, she looked away as a rush of pain filled her heart. Even after five years, grief often still caught her like this when she wasn't looking. "Everything was suddenly gone. My family. My home. I couldn't stay. I felt lost." Her hands twisted together in her lap. "My parents always said I should be a singer. Even my brother said it. So I tried. For five years."

"That's a long time."

She gave a choked laugh. "So many people try to break in as singers in New York. All so talented, better than I'll ever be."

"I doubt that very much."

"The harder I tried to succeed, the worse I felt." Looking down, she said softly, "And it didn't bring them back."

Silence fell across their table. She heard the clank of silver against china from a few remaining patrons and the distant sound of traffic and birds crying in the night.

"So why," Cristiano said slowly, "would you ever choose to leave yourself vulnerable to such pain? After losing so much, I'd think you'd never want a home again."

Hallie looked at him. "Is that why you live in hotels?" she said softly. "Never stopping. Never staying."

Cristiano's eyes widened slightly. Then he drew back, his jaw tightening. Rising to his feet, he held out his hand. "Come. The night is growing cold."

It was quiet in the sports car as he drove them back through the city after midnight.

How did you build your fortune?

I was lucky. I met a man who owned a small hotel chain in southern Italy. I convinced him to hire me and teach me everything he knew. Then I betrayed him.

Hallie looked at him sideways, wishing she had the courage to ask him who the man was and why Cristiano had betrayed him. She stayed silent.

Before their wedding, she'd convinced herself he was a good man, deep down. But now that they were married she was starting to see a darkness inside Cristiano she'd never glimpsed before.

She was suddenly afraid of learning things about him she didn't want to know.

When they arrived back at the hotel, they found Jack sleeping in his crib and Agata snoozing nearby on the sofa, her knitting folded neatly in her lap. After they'd thanked her and she'd left for the night, Hallie and Cristiano tiptoed into the darkened nursery. For a moment, they just stood together looking at their slumbering child.

Then Cristiano took her hand. Wordlessly he led her to their bedroom, and even though a corner of her heart was still angry, she could no more resist him than stop breathing.

Once in their bedroom, he pulled her against him. In the slanted moonlight coming through the blinds, his eyes burned through her. So did his fingertips, lightly stroking down the top of her sexy black dress, the bare skin of her back.

"I have followed all your rules, have I not?" he said in a low voice.

Confused, Hallie nodded.

"I've shared a meal with you both every day? Learned how to care for our son? Loved him?"

"You know you have."

"Now it is time for you to learn some lessons, also." Pulling her close, Cristiano nuzzled her throat, kissing the sensitive hollow at her shoulder before suckling the tender flesh of her earlobe. She shivered beneath his touch. Her heart was pounding.

"L-lessons?"

He stroked his hand along her cheek, rubbing his thumb against her lower lip. "How to truly please me."

Hallie's eyes went wide. "Have I not pleased you?"

He placed a single finger against her lips.

"You have, *cara*," he said huskily. "But I want more. Not for me. For you."

"There's more?" she whispered.

He smiled. "Even after two weeks of marriage, you are still so innocent." His hungry eyes met hers. "I will teach you how to know what you want and how to get it. I will teach you," he whispered, cupping her cheek, "how to experience a different level of pleasure entirely."

He kissed her, leaving her breathless and clinging to him. Reaching back, he pulled out the elastic of her ponytail, and her dark hair tumbled down her bare back. Roughly he yanked down her black sleeveless cocktail dress, dropping it to the floor. She stood shyly before him in only her tiny black lace panties, her naked breasts heavy and full.

With a low growl, he pushed her back against the window. Behind them was a vision of Rome, the sweep of cathedrals and Roman ruins spread across the hills, illuminating the darkness at their feet.

"The first rule is," he said in a low voice, "don't hold back."

He pushed his knee between her bare legs, gripping her wrists against the window as he kissed down her throat. She gasped with pleasure.

This is wrong, she thought, *so wrong*. Anyone could look up and see them through the window. She should put a stop to this. Be modest. Be…

Sensual kisses caused swirls of pleasure to cascade down her body. She wanted more. She wanted to wrap her arms around him, to feel him.

The first rule is don't hold back.

Yanking her wrists from his grasp, she folded her arms around his shoulders, drawing him against her. She kissed him back hungrily, matching his fire. But unlike her, Cristiano was still fully clothed. It didn't seem fair.

Grabbing the top of his shirt, she ripped it down the front, scattering buttons against the floor. She sighed in pleasure as her hands roamed the warm satin of his skin over the hard muscle of his chest, laced with dark hair. She squeezed his nipples and luxuriated in the sound of his gasp, followed by a low masculine growl.

He wrapped his hands over the back of her black lace panties, which had cost three hundred euros at a very nice lingerie shop on the Via Condotti. As she felt his hand move forward between her legs, she was wet and aching. Pulling him closer, she kissed him hard.

With a growl, he ripped off the black panties, leaving them a pile of crumpled lace on the floor.

"Please," she whispered. Amazed at her own boldness, she reached down to unzip his black trousers.

He gave a jagged intake of breath. With a single motion, he pushed down his silk boxer briefs. Using both hands, he lifted her backside, pushing her up against the window, as her legs wrapped around his hips.

Then he pushed inside her with a single, deep thrust.

Feeling him so thick and hard inside her, she moaned, closing her eyes and letting her head fall back against the glass. Her hair tumbled around them as she gripped his shoulders. As he moved, she didn't care anymore who might be watching. She didn't even pause to wonder if the window could break. She knew only she couldn't let him stop.

Her arms wrapped around his shoulders as he pumped inside her, hard and fast. Her full breasts pushed against his hard muscles, the hair of his chest rubbing against her sensitive nipples. She gasped with pleasure as, with each thrust, he filled her more deeply. Her legs tightened around his hips as she built higher and higher until, with a gasp, he exploded into her the moment she screamed his name.

Screamed quietly, of course, so as not to wake the baby. Even lost and frantic with abandon, though she might have been willing to risk shattering the window to fall to her death on the streets of Rome, she wasn't going to risk waking their sleeping infant. She was wanton, she was bold. But she wasn't insane.

For long moments afterward, sweaty and panting for breath, they held each other, collapsing against the enormous bed, their naked bodies intertwined.

"All right," Cristiano said in a low voice.

"What?" she said sleepily, lifting her head from his shoulder.

His expression was blank, his handsome features half-hidden in shadow. "I'll buy you a house."

Joy filled her heart. "You will?"

"But you must let me choose where."

"I don't even care where," she lied, pushing away her longing for her friends in New York. What difference did the location make? As long as their family had their own place with a garden, and they could live in one place long enough to make friends and really settle in, what did she care?

"You won't be sorry," she said tearfully. "We'll be so happy. You'll see. You won't regret it."

Cristiano looked at her, his eyes glittering in the shadows. "I regret it already."

CHAPTER SEVEN

CRISTIANO RARELY DID things for others, and he never did anything he did not want to do.

But perhaps there was something in do-gooding after all. Because the moment he decided to buy a house to please his wife, he'd discovered one for sale on the Amalfi Coast that was spectacularly satisfying for him to acquire. Especially at a cut-rate price.

Just weeks after he'd made his promise to her, their Rolls-Royce approached the magnificent estate on the rugged cliffs of the Amalfi Coast a short distance from the village of Cavello. A wave of euphoria went through Cristiano.

It was his.

He remembered the first time he'd passed through this same tall wrought-iron gate, surrounded by old stone walls. He'd been young then, newly orphaned, utterly penniless. And obsessed with revenge.

Luigi Bennato had been kind from the beginning. Strange for a man who'd ruthlessly rejected his infant son, in order to focus on building his small luxury hotel chain. But Cristiano had been coldly determined to impress him. And he had. Bennato had seen something in eighteen-year-old Cristiano, something no one else had.

But he didn't detect everything. He didn't see that Cristiano was his long-abandoned son.

Why would he? Even if he'd remembered Cristiano's mother, her name then had been Violetta Rossi. *Moretti* was the name of the man who'd been her husband when Cristiano was born. Her first husband. Her second husband had been an Englishman, her third an American. Both horrible stepfathers, whose only gift to Cristiano had been teaching him English. After a third screaming divorce, his mother had given up on marriage and focused on love affairs that were increasingly short, violent and toxic.

But Luigi Bennato was the man who'd destroyed her first. According to Violetta, before she'd met him, she'd been an innocent virgin who'd never tasted wine. Bennato had seduced her, then tossed her out of his life when she'd fallen pregnant and refused to have the abortion he demanded.

His mother had told Cristiano the story repeatedly when he was growing up. She'd always ended it the same way. "And Luigi was right," she'd say with a swill of bourbon and a raspy cough. "I should have done what he wanted. Then I'd be happy!"

After his mother's death, eighteen-year-old Cristiano had stood at her grave and felt nothing. What kind of man would feel nothing at the death of his own mother?

It was then that he knew himself for a monster.

But, standing in the rain, he'd had a new thought, one that lit a fire deep inside him. One that made him feel warm for the first time in his life.

Revenge. He had let the word settle against his lips, caressing it like a lover.

Vendetta. He'd loved the rhythm in his mouth.

Rivincita. He'd felt his tongue brush softly against his teeth.

He would have his revenge on the man who'd first made his mother a monster, so she in turn could make one of Cristiano.

And he'd had his revenge. In just three years, Cristiano got his vengeance. He'd claimed the ruined *palazzo* in Rome for himself, with Luigi's rival as his investor. He'd left Luigi's company in tatters.

Cristiano marked his adulthood from that moment. His revenge had been the act that had defined his life. The first step on a path that had made him richer than his wildest dreams.

The truth was it had been almost too easy. He still couldn't believe how quickly and completely Bennato had trusted him. It was almost, he thought sardonically, as if the man had *wanted* to be destroyed.

Now Cristiano was more powerful than Luigi Bennato had ever been. He was famous. Better in every way.

It still wasn't enough. Some part of him craved more, wanted to crush the ashes of the man's life smaller still. Which was why he'd chosen Cavello as the site of his newest Campania Hotel.

The old man's business had long since gone bankrupt, without enough capital to refurbish the hotels to satisfy the constant demands of perfection that a wealthy clientele required. Bennato's three small luxury hotels, once the jewels of Capri, Sardinia and Sorrento, had all long been demolished and replaced.

Several times over the years, Luigi had tried to contact him. Cristiano had never responded. He had no interest in listening to the man's angry recriminations. Let the man figure out for himself why Cristiano had destroyed him.

It was now seventeen years after he'd first entered the stately villa once owned by Bennato, and Cristiano had bought it for himself. The bankrupt, lonely old man was living in the former housekeeper's tiny house outside Cavello.

Life could be full of unexpected joys, Cristiano thought with satisfaction. As the Rolls-Royce pulled up in front of the grand courtyard of the elegant nineteenth-century villa, he smiled to himself, glancing at Hallie, waiting for her reaction.

Her eyes were huge as she looked from the villa to the terraced, manicured gardens overlooking the sea. *She's in shock*, he thought smugly. He was already keenly anticipating the sensual expressions of her gratitude later.

Their driver, Marco, opened the door and helped Hallie out of the car with the baby. Behind them parked an SUV carrying Agata, Salvatore and all the luggage.

Hallie's mouth was open as she looked out over the vastness of the estate, which had once been owned by the King of Naples.

"Welcome to your new home," Cristiano said. He waited for her cries of joy, for her to fling her arms around him and kiss him with the intensity of her delight.

She simply held their baby, looking up blankly at the palatial villa.

"Our home," he said encouragingly. "Just like you wanted."

Looking at him, Hallie shook her head. "This wasn't what I had in mind at all."

"It's the grandest house on the Amalfi Coast. What can you possibly dislike?"

"It's too big."

"Too big?" he said incredulously. How could anything be too big?

Hallie looked at him. "It's like a hotel."

"We'll be the only ones living here."

"We'll need a megaphone to find each other."

He frowned. "And the gardens—what do you find wrong with those?"

Slowly she looked around the manicured gardens, from the formal hedge maze to the perfectly arranged flowers and palm trees overlooking the blue Tyrrhenian Sea.

"It's…like a park," she said. Turning back to face him, she shook her head. "How can I possibly take care of it all?"

"We'll have staff, of course."

"Oh." She looked oddly dejected. Not exactly the reaction he'd been hoping for.

"Would you prefer a sad, broken-down apartment?" he said shortly. "Where you can hear neighbors screaming and your windows get smashed by thieves? Where the electricity is often out and even your few, most precious possessions can disappear at any moment to pay for—"

For your mother's whiskey, he'd almost said. He caught himself just in time.

"No. Of course not." Putting her hand on his arm, Hallie gave him an apologetic smile. "You're right. I'm being a jerk."

He didn't respond. He was suddenly picturing his mother the last time he'd seen her. Violetta's face had been bruised and bleeding from her lover's fists, and she'd been screaming at Cristiano for trying to defend her. That was his last memory of her face. He'd returned hours later to find her house ablaze.

He could still feel the searing pain of the flames when he'd nearly died trying to get inside to save her. He could hear the crackle of the fire and the furious howl of grief that rose to the dark sky when they brought her body out of the embers and ash.

"I'm so sorry." Feeling Hallie's hand against his cheek, he focused on her again. "I've made you upset, haven't I?"

"No," he bit out.

"I can see I have. I'm sorry for sounding so ungrateful. The house is beautiful. Thank you."

Reaching up on her tiptoes, she kissed him. Taking her roughly in his arms, he kissed her back hungrily until their baby, still held on Hallie's hip, complained about the close quarters, and they both pulled away with rueful laughs.

Tilting her head back to look at the palatial villa, she said, "I'll try to get used to it."

Cristiano took her hand. "Come see inside."

As they walked through the long hallways, over the tiled floors and past the antique furniture and tapestries, Hallie obligingly oohed and aahed over every detail he pointed out. Having gotten over the initial shock, she seemed determined to be pleased.

He'd arranged for new furniture to be put in the master bedroom and the baby's nursery next door. Finally they walked out onto the villa's wide terrace and Hallie approached the railing. Beneath the hot August sun, hungrily she drank in the incredible view as soft sea breezes lazily blew tendrils of her hair.

"Wow. Maybe this place isn't so bad." With a laugh, she glanced back at him with sparkling eyes.

But Cristiano didn't return her smile. As he looked out at the magnificent view of the sea and the village clinging precipitously to the rugged cliffs on the other side of the bay, he was overwhelmed by the memory of the last time he'd stood on this terrace. He could still see Luigi's bright eyes, the man's chubby cheeks smiling as he'd said, "My boy, this *palazzo* in Rome, this is going to be the thing for us! It will take our company global!"

Our company, Luigi had said. *Our.* The memory was like a rough piece of cut glass on Cristiano's soul because, after three years of working for the man, Cristiano had started to like him, even respect him. Bennato had been generous, kind. He'd treated Cristiano almost like a son.

He shook the memory away angrily. If Bennato had wanted a son, he shouldn't have thrown Violetta and Cristiano away like trash. The old man deserved what he'd gotten. Bennato was the one who'd taught Cristiano the lesson: Life meant every man for himself.

And yet, suddenly, Cristiano didn't enjoy owning the villa as much as he'd thought he would. Thinking of the times he'd ignored Luigi's calls over the years, he wondered what the old man would have said.

"The view is incredible," Hallie whispered. She wiped her eyes surreptitiously. "Thank you. You don't know what this means to me. You don't know how I've longed to have a real home where we can stay forever and ever."

He opened his mouth to inform her that after the Cavello hotel opened in two weeks, they would still be traveling to Asia on schedule. He'd bought this house as a temporary amusement, perhaps a long-term investment. But he doubted they'd return to Italy for another six months, or perhaps even a year.

As he looked down at her, though, the happiness in Hallie's face made him change his mind. Her caramel-brown eyes glowed at him.

He didn't want her to stop looking at him that way.

"You're welcome," he said softly, taking her hand. Together they looked out at the picturesque rocky coastline plummeting into the blue sea.

Later that night, as they slept together in the palatial master bedroom, with the windows open to salty sea breezes scented with tropical flowers, Hallie made him very, very glad that he'd made her so happy.

But he could make her happy anywhere, Cristiano told himself afterward, as she slept so contentedly in his arms. He had nothing to feel guilty about. Yes, he'd bought her a house. He'd never promised they would stay.

Cristiano looked toward the terrace, toward the moonlit sea. His arms tightened around his wife. He had promised himself long ago never to sacrifice his own needs for another's. And he never would.

Life meant every man for himself, he thought. Even in marriage.

After just two weeks of living in her new home on the Amalfi Coast, Hallie felt she had fallen into sunshine and joy.

She sang all the time. Songs about dreaming of love and falling in love and being in love.

For no particular reason, of course.

Hallie was thrilled to have a home at last. A place, as she'd told her husband, where they could stay forever and ever. Even as formal as the villa was, with its endless gardens, the view was breathtaking from every window, looking out with a sharp drop to the sea. And when she went outside the villa's gate, no one bothered her here. No paparazzi. No fashion bloggers sneaking pictures of Jack. Here, Hallie could just be herself.

It was true that Cristiano hadn't been around much. He often worked eighteen-hour days, personally overseeing the final touches of the lavish new hotel in Cavello, on the opposite cliff, while still running his worldwide empire.

And if he'd broken her dinner rules a few times, disappearing from the house before dawn and not returning until well after midnight when she and Jack were asleep, well, she'd decided to bend the rules. He was busy. Hallie could understand. He'd given her what she wanted most—a home, and she'd tried to be flexible. She hadn't even complained.

But she was relieved it was almost over. Tonight, the Campania Hotel Cavello would have its grand opening gala, and then Cristiano would be able to spend more time in their new home. They could finally be together as a family.

His constant absence had to be why, in spite of the beauty and comfort, this villa still didn't feel quite like home to her. Maybe it would just take time. But she still didn't have the feeling of home she'd had as a child, living with her family in the rickety wooden house in the mountains.

True, there was a staff of four to oversee the house and gardens. It sometimes made her uncomfortable having servants cook and clean and pull weeds for her, but she'd told herself she'd get used to it. She should be grateful. All she had to do was care for her baby, decorate her home as she pleased, bake cookies if she felt like it, and water any flowers she wished.

Still, in spite of being surrounded by servants and having Jack with her, sometimes her days felt lonely.

Since they'd arrived on the Amalfi Coast, she'd seen Cristiano only at night, in the dark, when he woke her up to set her body on fire with bliss. Then, in the morning, when she woke, he was always gone. Like some tantalizingly sweet dream.

Strange she should feel lonely when she was never alone. Even when she walked to the village with the baby, Cristiano insisted she take Salvatore with them. It bewildered her because there were no paparazzi here, and it was hard enough trying to make new friends, given her lack of Italian, without also having a hulking bodyguard standing behind her, scowling behind his sunglasses.

But the villagers were friendly and interested in meeting the wife of the man who'd brought so much new employment to the area. And baby Jack, with his bright smile and chubby cheeks, charmed everyone he met, even on the rare occasions when he cried.

Hallie was slowly learning Italian from Agata, who was very patient with her. Living in a brand-new country where she didn't speak the language, she was trying her best to settle in, make friends, to find a dentist and doctor and grocery store, and do everything she could to make the Amalfi Coast feel like home.

Except for the wistful memory of her childhood home, Hallie didn't miss West Virginia. She missed New York. But she tried to push that feeling away. Hadn't she told Cristiano that their home could be anywhere? If Italy was the place he loved most, then she would be happy here. She would try to forget New York, especially since every time she tried to text or phone Tess and Lola lately, they seemed distracted. No wonder, with newborns.

But she missed their friendship.

The afternoon before the gala, Hallie played with Jack in the huge formal salon, kissing his fat baby feet as he lay stretched out on a blanket beneath a flood of afternoon sunshine. Soon, Cristiano would come home and they'd get ready to go to the gala together. As she sang yet another song about true love, she knew tonight would be magical. After tonight, their lives could truly begin.

Her voice suddenly choked off as she realized she did know happy songs after all. Love songs.

Wide-eyed, Hallie looked out the wide windows at the palm trees and blue sky. She stared down at her cooing baby, his dark eyes exactly like Cristiano's.

And she gasped aloud, covering her mouth with her hand.

There was a reason she'd been singing only happy love songs lately.

Because she felt them.

She was in love with Cristiano.

Her husband. Her ex-boss. The man she'd once hated. The man she'd never thought she could trust.

She trusted him now. He'd become a real father, a real husband. He'd brought her home. He'd given her what she'd dreamed of most: *a family.*

She loved him for everything he'd done for her. For the way he'd made her feel. For the person he'd encouraged her to be. Bold. Fearless.

Was she fearless enough to tell him she loved him?

Hallie gulped.

If she did, would his handsome face light up? Would he say, "And I love you, *cara mia*," then kiss her senseless?

Or would he just look at her coldly, and say nothing?

Love had never been part of the deal. Cristiano had told her outright he didn't think he was capable of it.

Yet, he treated her as if he did love her. Marrying her. Buying her this magnificent home. Giving up his lifestyle of constantly traveling in order to remain here, in one place. Just to make her happy.

She put her hand on her forehead. What should she do? Should she remain silent and keep things safely as they were?

Or should she take the chance and risk everything in their marriage to tell him she loved him?

"It's just arrived from Rome, *signora*," said Agata, coming into the salon with a designer garment bag in her arms.

"The dress," Hallie said, rising unsteadily to her feet. "Cristiano told me he'd called in a favor with a designer, to send me a special dress to wear tonight."

"Sì." The Italian woman didn't meet her eyes, but Agata had been acting strangely all day. Taking the garment bag from her, Hallie laid it across the elegant sofa. Unzipping the bag, she discovered a breathtaking strapless red ball gown with a sweetheart bodice and full skirts. It was a dream dress. A Cinderella dress.

Hallie touched the fabric in awe.

"Maybe he does love me," she whispered.

Agata made a strange noise.

"What?"

The Italian woman cleared her throat. "Cristiano told me not to say anything. He intends to tell you himself."

"Tell me what?" Hallie said, holding up the beautiful red gown and looking at herself dreamily in the mirror. Maybe she'd tell him she loved him tonight, while they were dancing at the gala. If she could just be brave enough, maybe she'd be rewarded. Maybe against all odds, he'd pull her closer in his arms and—

"You are a good woman, *signora*. What he is doing is not right, keeping it from you."

Hallie turned in bewilderment. "What are you talking about?"

"Then again, I understand why he hates this house and wants to be away as soon as he can."

Hallie sucked in her breath. "Cristiano doesn't hate this house!"

The older woman looked at her sadly. "He does, *signora*. Because of the man who used to own it." She turned away. "And that is why, while you are at the ball tonight, he has ordered me to pack all your things. Tomorrow, you leave for Asia. Me, I have refused to go. I will return to Rome, close to my grandchildren."

"Leaving?" Hallie drew back. "But we just got here! It's our home! We're not leaving our home. And I don't want you to leave us!" Agata had started to feel like family.

"I'm sorry, *signora*. He said to pack everything," she said quietly. "I doubt you're ever coming back."

Anguish went through Hallie. It couldn't be true.

And, in a flash, she knew it was.

She'd thought Cristiano had changed, that he'd been willing to sacrifice his restless travel for her and actually settle down in one place.

But he hadn't changed at all. This so-called home was temporary, like everything else in his life.

And Cristiano had told Agata first. Before his own wife.

Hallie's hands clenched at her sides. While she'd been trying to compromise, to make this place her home, he'd been lying to her. He'd never intended to settle down at all.

Hallie looked around the villa. This antique furniture wasn't to her taste. It was too big, too fancy, but since they'd arrived, she'd convinced herself to overlook that, so badly had she wanted a home.

Now he wanted to drag her and the baby back to his empty lifestyle of moving from hotel to hotel to hotel?

All she wanted, all she'd ever wanted since her parents and brother had died, was a home. A family. A place in the world.

Hallie choked out, "If he hates this villa, why did he buy it?"

Agata looked at her sadly, her wrinkled eyes mournful. "He bought it for the same reason he hates it. Because the man who once owned it was his friend, then his enemy. Luigi Bennato was the first to give him a real job. He taught him how to run a hotel. Then Cristiano turned on him. Ruined him."

Hallie shivered as she heard the echo of Cristiano's voice. *I met a man who owned a small hotel chain in southern Italy. I convinced him to hire me and teach me everything he knew. Then I betrayed him.*

She wasn't sure she wanted to know more. In a small voice, she said, "What happened?"

"I worked for Luigi," Agata said. "Before I worked for Cristiano. I still don't understand. For three years, they worked together, as close as father and son. Cristiano used his charm and Luigi's money to convince a widowed countess to sell her *palazzo* in Rome. Then, instead of developing the hotel together as they'd planned, at the last minute Cristiano took the information to one of the international hotel chains. He cut Luigi out of the deal. Left him bankrupt."

Hallie stared at the older woman, cold with shock. "But why?"

"I still do not know. Yet, even after Cristiano betrayed him, Luigi tried to protect him. He even convinced me to accept Cristiano's job offer in Rome. 'The boy's still so young,' Luigi told me. 'He'll need someone he can trust.' So I left Luigi's hotel for Cristiano's. And now he's a broken man. He has no family, no money. He lives in an old shack. I feel badly for him."

"Why are you telling me all this?" Hallie whispered.

Agata looked at her. "He wants to talk to you."

"Who?"

"Luigi Bennato."

Hallie stared at her in shock. "Why would he want to talk to me?"

"I do not know." The white-haired woman looked at her steadily. "All I know is your husband owes him a debt."

Meet the old man Cristiano had betrayed? Hallie felt caught between fear, curiosity and loyalty to Cristiano. "I couldn't. Besides," she said hesitantly, "how do I know he wouldn't attack me or something?"

"Luigi?" Agata gave a low laugh. "He has a good heart. Better than Cristiano's. Luigi is no risk to you. He's waiting in the forest on the other side of the gate."

A trickle of fear went down the back of her neck. "He's here? Now?"

"Tomorrow you leave Cavello, possibly never to return. He might not live until your next visit. I told him I would ask you. If you wish to see him, it is your choice."

Hallie stared at her, a lump in her throat.

"I'll leave you to get ready for the gala. I need to pack for your trip." She sighed. "And my own back to Rome. Tonight will be my last time watching Jack, while you're at the gala." Agata smiled sadly. "I will miss you both."

"Won't you come with us?"

"I'm sorry." The older woman's eyes lifted apologetically. "I do not want to leave Italy. It's my home. My place is here."

Hallie hugged her hard. After Agata left her in the salon, she was still blinking back tears, but she couldn't blame the older woman for not wanting to endlessly circle the globe. Hallie didn't want to do it, either.

She wanted a real home. She wanted to be surrounded by the people she cared about and who cared about her.

She wanted to love her husband, and she wanted him to love her back.

Hallie sucked in her breath. What would she do about Luigi Bennato?

Her eyes fell on her baby, playing happily on his blanket. She couldn't go behind Cristiano's back to talk to the man he'd betrayed. He wouldn't like it. At all.

But then—Hallie's face suddenly hardened—he'd done a few things lately that she didn't like, either.

She picked up her cooing baby. Crossing to the foyer, she grabbed the stroller in quick decision. If Cristiano wouldn't explain anything to her, if he wouldn't tell her about his past or open his heart, she would find out without his help.

If she loved him, she had to try to understand.

"Going somewhere?" Her bodyguard, Salvatore, stood in the doorway, looking at the stroller.

Blushing, she said quickly, "Oh, no, I just wanted to clean the stroller."

"All right. I'm going to lunch."

Hallie waited until the bodyguard had gone into the kitchen to have his usual lunch and flirtation with one of the maids. Quickly she tucked Jack into the stroller, along with a pacifier, a blanket and an extra diaper just in case, and crept quietly out of the villa.

It felt scary and exhilarating to go by herself. She realized that this was the first time she'd gone out alone since the day she'd told Cristiano about the baby, back at his hotel in New York.

Jack cooed happily in the sunshine as she walked swiftly toward the rough stone walls leading to the gate. Around the side, some distance up the hill, she saw an old man peeking through the trees. She stopped, wondering if she was making a mistake.

Gathering her courage, she took a deep breath and pushed the stroller forward.

"Signora Moretti—you are she, yes?" said the old man anxiously as she came forward. He was plump, and his hair was gray, and there was something about him that seemed oddly familiar.

Hallie took a deep breath. "You wanted to talk to me?"

She was startled to see tears in the old man's rheumy eyes. "Cristiano's wife," he whispered. "I have seen pictures of you." His gaze fell to Jack, who was waving his fat arms, as he whispered, "And his son?"

He'd seen pictures of them? Oh, yes, right—she was famous. "I'm so sorry, Mr. Bennato. I don't know the whole story between you. But I know my husband betrayed you. You must hate him for what he did to you."

"Hate him?" The old man's dark eyes looked strangely familiar. She tried to think who they reminded her of. He shook his head. "I am proud of him for doing so well. I am glad for him to have my villa."

Her lips parted. Surely no one could be *that* kind, no matter what Agata had said. "That is very generous…"

"An old man like me, I don't need a big house." He looked at the baby with longing, then lifted his tearful gaze. "I'm so happy to meet you both."

"But why? After the way Cristiano betrayed you, why would you…?"

Then she looked more closely at the old man's eyes. Black, like obsidian. Like her baby's.

Like her husband's.

"Cristiano's your son," she whispered. "You're the father who abandoned him."

Luigi gave her a tearful smile. "I saw a picture of Violetta in the paper after she died in the fire. Her last name had changed, but I recognized her. When I read she was survived by an eighteen-year-old son, I was desperate to find him. Before I could—" he took a deep breath "—Cristiano himself showed up at my hotel, asking for a job."

"You knew he was your son?"

"I thought…maybe. He looked like I did when I was young. And Violetta had told me she was pregnant with my child. But sometimes she lied to me, especially when she was drinking. One day, I could take it no longer and told her we were through. She said she was pregnant, so I tried to make it work. I made her stop drinking. But she screamed I was making her a prisoner. When she was six months pregnant, she disappeared. I never saw her again."

"Why didn't you tell Cristiano? He thinks his father abandoned him!"

"I did abandon him." The old man's voice trembled. "I tried so hard to find them. But I should have tried harder. I never should have given up. What I read about the life Violetta was living before she died…" He shuddered. "I cannot imagine what that boy went through as a child. When Cristiano showed up at my door asking for a job, he seemed to have no idea I might be his father. He said he just wanted to work at the best boutique hotel in Italy. I thought it was a miraculous coincidence."

"Why didn't you tell him?"

"I decided I couldn't reveal myself as his father, not until I was sure it was true. But I kept putting off the test. I think I was afraid," he said quietly. "By the time I finally stole a hair off his brush and sent it in for the test, it was too late. The day he betrayed me…" His voice trailed off as he looked out at the sea. "That was the same day I got proof he was my son."

"So why didn't you say something?" Hallie cried. He gave her a small smile.

"It was too late. I didn't want to cause him pain. He had no idea I was his father when he betrayed me. And I thought…perhaps I deserved it. So I let him go."

Closing her eyes, Hallie took a deep breath, pain filling her heart. She looked down at her happy baby. She couldn't imagine the pain of losing him. "Why are you telling me all this?"

Luigi gave a wistful smile. "He has done well, my boy. He's built his own hotel empire over the last fifteen years. He's been more successful than I ever was." He blinked fast. "He is my only family. When he refused to answer my phone calls, I tried to accept it. But then I read about him having a wife and child…" More tears filled his rheumy eyes as he gently stroked Jack's head. "He's my grandson. You're my daughter-in-law. But my son…" He lifted his gaze. "Please. You must convince him to speak to me."

Hallie hugged the old man tightly, wiping away her own tears. "I'll make this right," she said softly. "I swear to you."

When she finally returned to the villa, the afternoon was growing late. Hallie was still shivering with emotion and regret. How would she tell her husband that the man he'd betrayed had been his own father?

Her baby had fallen asleep in his stroller so she left him in the foyer when she heard Cristiano calling her from the salon. Nervously she went to see him.

She found Cristiano pacing angrily. When she entered the salon, he turned to her, his expression furious.

"Where have you been?" he said tersely.

She stopped. "On a walk."

"I told you to always take Salvatore!"

"I wanted to be alone." She bit her lip, trying to think of how to break the news to him. She wanted to do it gently and couldn't. Her brain was exploding. "I met your father."

"What?" Eyes wide, Cristiano stumbled back. "What are you talking about?"

"I got a message that a man wanted to meet me. So I went to talk to him." She looked at her husband anxiously. "Perhaps you should sit down…"

He didn't move. "You met my father?"

"I'm afraid this is going to be a big shock." She took a deep breath, then said very gently, "Cristiano, your father is Luigi Bennato."

For a long moment, he stared at her. Then he turned away, his shoulders shaking. At first, she thought he was crying. Then she realized he was laughing. His laugh was harsh and strange.

Hallie stared at him, wondering if the shock of the news had disjointed her husband's mind.

"Don't you understand, Cristiano?" she said in a low voice. Reaching out, she put her hand on his shoulder. "The man you betrayed—he's your father. I'm so sorry. Such a horrible coincidence—"

"Coincidence?" He whirled on her, silhouetted in front of the windows overlooking the sea. His dark eyes glittered. "I knew Bennato was my father. Of course I knew! And from the moment my mother died, I vowed to make him pay!"

Hallie drew back, astonished. She whispered, "You knew?"

"My mother told me how he ruined her life. She was just an innocent girl when he seduced her. He gave her her first drink, and when she got pregnant, he told her to go to hell!"

Hallie thought of Luigi's heartsick face, at the tears in his wrinkled eyes when he said, "I tried so hard to find them. But I should have tried harder. I never should have given up."

"Luigi told me, after Violetta got pregnant," she said slowly, "he tried to make her stop drinking. But she hated that, and she ran away. He said he tried so hard to find you—"

"He was lying," Cristiano said coldly.

She shook her head. "I believed him."

"Of course you did." His lips twisted in a sneer. "A

man as devious as Bennato could easily twist your innocent little heart."

His scorn made her shiver. She lifted her chin. "You're wrong. If you'd only speak to him—"

"What else did he say?" He came closer to her, his face like stone. His powerful body left her in shadow.

Hallie saw the cloud of darkness around him, and for the first time she was afraid.

This was the darkness she'd feared. The darkness she hadn't wanted to see.

"You'll never talk to him, will you?" she whispered. "You hate him beyond all reason. You'll never be free."

Cristiano's black eyes narrowed into slits as he repeated dangerously, "What did he say?"

"He regrets not protecting you when you were a child. He's all alone now. He wants to make amends. He wants a family."

"He wants money."

"No." She shook her head eagerly. "If you'd seen his expression when he touched Jack's head—"

"Jack?" His expression changed, then his folded hands dropped to his sides as he roared, "You let him touch our son?"

"Of course I did. He's Jack's grandfather!"

"Don't call him that!" Furious, he turned away. "Where is Jack?"

"Sleeping in his stroller. In the foyer—"

Cristiano strode out of the salon. When she caught up with him in the foyer, she found him cradling their sleeping baby tenderly against his powerful chest. When he looked up at Hallie, his dark eyes glittered.

"You will never," he said in a low voice, "talk to that man again. Or allow our son anywhere near him."

His voice frightened her. "You're being ridiculous!"

"You will give your word," he ground out. "Or I'll never

allow you to leave my sight again without six bodyguards at your side."

"You won't *allow* me?" she cried.

His jaw clenched. "It's a dangerous world. I have enemies. Luigi has good cause to hate me and he could choose to take it out on you. Or our child."

"How can you think of the world like that?"

"Because that's how it is," he said grimly.

Hallie stared at him in horror. He was refusing to even consider that he might be wrong about Luigi. Justifying his own selfish actions by trying to punish a sweet old man who hadn't done anything wrong.

"It's not true." The lump in her throat became a razor blade as she whispered, "The world is full of second chances. It's full of love if you only—"

Still cradling their sleeping baby, Cristiano turned away. "I'm done talking." He looked at his platinum watch. "I'll take Jack upstairs to Agata. Go get ready for the gala."

"Why are you acting like this?" she whispered.

"It's my responsibility to protect my family."

"But not to tell us anything." Anger filled her. "Agata told me that we're leaving Italy tomorrow."

He looked off-kilter. "She told you?"

"Did you think I wouldn't notice when she started packing all our clothes?"

"Yes. We're leaving for Tokyo." He lifted a dark eyebrow. "So?"

Swallowing over the pain in her throat, she choked out, "You said this was our home."

"And the next place will be, as well. And the place after that."

Hallie stared at him. "You spent millions on this villa, just for us to live here a few weeks?"

"And if I did?" he said coolly. "I can buy you ten more

houses anywhere around the world. I can always sell them again. What does it matter?"

Hallie looked at him, stricken. "You said we'd have a home. You said we'd be a family."

"And we are. But we're doing it my way."

"And your way is to drag us around the world at your beck and call, and tell me who I can and cannot speak with?"

Holding their baby against his chest, Cristiano set his jaw. "Either you're with me, or against me. Either you're my partner—"

"Your prisoner!" she cried.

"Or you're my enemy." His eyes glittered. "Decide carefully, *cara mia*, who you want to be. Now get ready." He gave her an icy smile. "You must sparkle like a star tonight."

And he left her.

Numb with shock, Hallie went back into the salon. She collected the red Cinderella dress. But as she carried it upstairs, it felt heavy in her arms.

As she got ready that night, putting on exquisite lingerie and the gorgeous designer ball gown, she felt cold inside. She brushed her dark hair until it shone, then stopped, looking at herself in the mirror.

When she tried to defy him, to fight for their happiness, he saw her as an enemy instead of recognizing it for what it was—love.

How could it be otherwise, when he'd never known what it was to be really, truly loved by another?

Either you're with me, or against me.

How could she get through his darkness, the pain of his childhood that still enveloped him like a shroud?

How could she show him that the world was more than danger and betrayal and cruelty and regret? Could she show him that she wasn't his enemy, but that she was fighting for his happiness, as well as her own?

Cristiano had given them his name, his wealth, his status. But Hallie and their son would never be more than possessions to him. He would never give them a home. Unless...

She took a deep breath.

There was only one way to break through. One risk she had to take, to win or lose it all.

Putting on lipstick, Hallie met her own scared eyes in the mirror.

Tonight she would tell him she loved him.

CHAPTER EIGHT

WEARING HIS TUXEDO, Cristiano paced furiously at the bottom of the villa's sweeping stairs. They were already five minutes late to his own hotel's grand opening gala.

Another transgression to add to the list. A low curse escaped his lips.

He could not believe Hallie had gone behind his back to speak to his father, his mortal enemy.

He'd thought he could trust her. Their marriage had been going so well. Living in this lavish villa overlooking the sea, as he'd been busy overseeing the Campania Cavello's final preparations, Hallie had been the perfect wife: beautiful, patient, supportive and uncomplaining. She'd been an excellent mother to their son by day and a hot temptress in Cristiano's bed by night. In his opinion, it was the perfect relationship.

Then she'd snuck out to meet Luigi Bennato behind his back.

Cristiano ground his teeth. He would send Salvatore to visit the man and warn him off. No, better yet, he'd send a lawyer. Send a cease-and-desist letter. Get a restraining order. Yes. Then he'd take Hallie, leave Italy and never return.

But the world was a small place. What would stop Bennato from contacting Hallie again if she wanted it? Pacing, he clawed his hand through his dark hair.

If Hallie wouldn't obey his rules, how could he protect her? How could he keep Hallie and the baby safe? How could he make sure he never lost them?

His eyes narrowed. He hoped she now realized the error

of her ways. He expected her to apologize tonight. He would try to forgive her.

He would also make sure she never had the chance to betray him again.

"Am I late?" He heard her sweet voice from behind him.

Turning, Cristiano looked up and sucked in his breath.

Hallie was at the top of the stairs, her glossy hair pulled up in an elegant bun. Her red ball gown fit perfectly, from the tight bodice to the full skirts. He held his breath as he watched her come down the stairs, in awe at her beauty.

"You are magnificent," he said in a low voice. She smiled, her cheeks turning a pretty shade of pink.

"You are too kind." But she gave him a troubled glance from beneath her dark lashes. Her lips were full and red. His eyes widened, then fell lower to the round curve of her breasts, plump and ripe beneath the corset-style bodice.

Even as angry as he was, he was tempted to grab her and take her back upstairs. He'd already started to reach for her when he caught himself. He couldn't miss the gala tonight. He was the host. He took a deep breath and forced himself to pretend he was civilized.

"I have something for you, *cara*. The perfect addition to your dress."

Reaching into his tuxedo jacket pocket, he pulled out a flat black velvet box. Inside it was a sparkling diamond necklace. As she gasped, he put it gently around her neck, attaching the clasp at the back.

Hallie looked down at the glittering stones. "They're beautiful."

"Nothing compared to you, my beautiful wife," he whispered, kissing her. Feeling her lips against his was pure heaven, making him tremble with the power of her unconscious sensuality. When he finally drew back, he was more determined than ever to make her submit to his will, to keep their perfect marriage exactly as it was.

He held out his arm. "Shall we go?"

She hesitated, then took his arm, wrapping her hands around the sleeve of his black tuxedo jacket.

After helping her into his red sports car, he drove the short distance to the new Campania Hotel Cavello, clinging to a rocky cliff overlooking the village across the bay. A uniformed valet took their car, and they walked into the hotel on a red carpet. She clung to his arm as photographers flashed pictures of them. "Look over here!"

"Signora!"

"Mrs. Moretti!"

Hallie didn't exhale until they were inside. Then her eyes widened as she breathed, "Wow."

She looked around the lobby of his new hotel. The Campania Cavello made up for its boutique size by the lavishness of its furnishings and incredible view. Seeing the awe on Hallie's face, Cristiano felt his heart swell with pride.

"And this is just the lobby," he said, putting his hand over hers. "Wait until you see the ballroom."

Joining the other illustrious, glamorous guests, he led her into the gilded ballroom. She stared up at the high ceilings, the bright mirrors, the chandeliers. Multiple French doors opened straight onto an expansive terrace, decked with bright pink flowers, and, beyond that, the moonlit sea.

Whirling back to face him, she breathed, "This place is amazing." Her head suddenly craned. "Is that Nadia Cruz?"

Cristiano shrugged as the famous Spanish actress, now married to a duke, walked by in a tight dress. He had eyes for only one woman. He wanted her in his arms. Against his body. In his bed.

But the object of the evening was to celebrate the grand opening of the hotel with the celebrities who would be his future guests. Any hotel, no matter how exquisite, depended upon publicity from a certain type of clientele to make the property popular amongst the glitterati.

So for the next hour, he forced himself to greet power-ful guests with all the force of his charm. He gave them his complete attention, until the new hotel's manager pri-vately informed him they were already booked up through Christmas, and the red-carpet arrivals had drawn attention from the press worldwide.

The Campania Cavello was a smashing success.

As soon as the music began, Cristiano took Hallie's hand. "Dance with me."

She looked around nervously at all the famous people in the ballroom. "We should let someone else go first."

"No one," he said arrogantly, "would dare."

Holding her hand tightly, he led her to the center of the ballroom floor. He felt the eyes of all the guests on him, heard their whispered comments, and he knew that every man here envied him tonight. Not for his money or power—for the beautiful woman in his arms.

He'd been envied before, as a well-known playboy, a free-spirited billionaire who traveled the world, never set-tling down in any place or with any person.

This was different. Successful beyond imagination, he was now also married to a beautiful woman who'd been untouched by any other man. She'd not only given him the best sex of his life, she'd given him a son, an heir to carry on his line. Cristiano's future was secure.

He deserved to be envied.

As they danced, Cristiano looked around the gilded ball-room of the lavish Amalfi Coast hotel. This was his. Cris-tiano's hands tightened on Hallie. And so was she.

He'd come a long way from hardscrabble poverty in Na-ples, when he'd been unwanted, unloved and often hungry and dirty. His parents hadn't wanted him. His mother had resented him; his father had abandoned him.

Now he had a new family.

From the beginning, when he'd first charmed that rich

widow in Rome into selling her *palazzo* for a song, Cristiano's charm had been his second-greatest asset.

The first, of course, was his ruthlessness.

I've conquered the past completely, he thought. *I've won.*

Dancing with Hallie, he couldn't take his eyes off her.

"You are so beautiful," he said huskily, swaying her in his arms. "Every man here wishes he could be in my place."

"To own this hotel."

"To be in your bed."

She glanced around shyly. "Don't be silly."

"You have no idea how desirable you are," he whispered against her cheek, leaning forward. "Later tonight, you can apologize for that foolishness with Bennato," he murmured lazily, running his hand down her back. "And I will forgive you. Because I can deny you nothing."

"I'm not sorry," she said.

With an intake of breath, Cristiano looked down at her.

"Because I did it for a good reason." Her caramel-brown eyes were feverishly bright.

"What is that?" he said coldly.

Her red, luscious lips curved in a tremulous smile.

"Because I love you," she whispered.

For a few seconds, frozen on the dance floor, he stared at her as couples continued to whirl around them.

"You love me," he said slowly.

"Yes." Hallie's face was deliriously happy. "I know it wasn't supposed to happen. But it has. I love you, Cristiano. For the boy you were. The man you are. The man you'll be."

The boy you were.

Hallie's words felt like ice in his heart. She saw past his defenses? Past all his wealth and power, to see the helpless boy he'd once been?

His hands tightened on her.

"I love you," she choked out, searching his gaze desperately. "I'm not your enemy. And I'm not your servant. I'm your wife. I'm fighting for our family. For our home. I'm fighting for you…because I love you."

Music swelled around them in the ballroom. A warm sea breeze blew in from doors opened wide to the moonlit terrace.

Hallie *loved* him.

How could she?

Then he got it.

A low, fierce laugh bubbled up from inside him as he realized what she was doing. He relaxed instantly.

"What's so funny?"

"Nothing," he said, still laughing. He shook his head admiringly. "I just respect you."

"You *respect* me?"

"Yes." He sometimes thought that women didn't realize how valuable it was, respect. Most men he knew could tolerate a lack of love far better than any lack of respect. But the women he'd known in his life, starting with his mother, seemed to feel the opposite, willing to put up with a total lack of respect from their lovers, finding it acceptable to be taken for granted and talked down to, as long as they were loved. He'd never understood that.

Hallie clearly didn't see his perspective, either. Her deep brown eyes looked hurt. "That's all you have to say?"

"I don't blame you for trying. You thought that angle might work. But it will take more than that to manipulate me."

Her beautiful face was pale. "You think that's what I was trying to do? Manipulate you?"

"Of course it is." Leaning down, he confided, "You're wasting your time. That emotional stuff doesn't work on me, but—" reaching down, he twisted a tendril of her hair "—you're welcome to try to convince me in bed. Not that it will work, but we'll both enjoy it."

Angrily she pulled her head away. "I'm telling you the truth!"

"Fine." He rolled his eyes. She seemed determined to stick with her story. "But there will be no more complaining. We will never stop traveling. We will never settle in just one place. And if you ever speak to Bennato again—" he looked at her evenly "—I will divorce you."

Her brown eyes were cold. "You would divorce me? Just for talking to someone?"

Cristiano would have thought it obvious. "For talking to my enemy."

Men in tuxedos and women in bright, sparkling gowns continued to dance around them, in a ballroom lit by gilded chandeliers and flooded with silvery moonlight.

"That's how the world is to you, isn't it?" Hallie said slowly. "Either a person is your enemy or your slave." Her eyes were huge as she whispered, "You're never going to change, are you?"

His expression hardened. "Hallie—"

"No!"

She ripped her arm away, leaving him alone on the ballroom floor. His illustrious guests were now staring at him with big eyes and rising glee. Of course. The only thing people liked better than heroes with enviable lives was seeing those lives fall apart spectacularly.

Turning, he followed his wife out of the hotel.

She was already halfway up the twisting street, climbing the hill. She meant to walk the mile back to the villa, he realized. Even in that impractical red ball gown and high heels. Most of the paparazzi had gone, but a scruffy-looking photographer was following a few feet behind her, peppering her with questions.

Cristiano's whole body felt tight as he turned to the valet. "My Ferrari."

The young valet got his car back in thirty seconds. Jumping into the sports car, Cristiano roared along the street and quickly caught up with her. He rolled down the window.

"Get in the car," he barked. "Now."

Hallie didn't even look in his direction. She just kept climbing up the steep road in her high heels and red ball gown.

By now, the photographer had backed off and was simply taking pictures of them both. Cristiano ground his teeth. He had no doubt that the celebrity gossip sites would be full of stories about "Trouble in Paradise" tomorrow.

"Now," he ordered.

She tripped on a rock, nearly twisting her ankle. Muttering under his breath, he pulled over, blocking her path with his car. Still not looking at him, she climbed in, slamming the door behind her. Without a word, he pressed on the gas, and the powerful engine leaped forward with a roar.

Everything seemed to have changed between them. She remained silent, seeming fragile, brittle. A side of her he'd never seen before.

The pleasurable night, which had seemed so bright and delicious, was suddenly lost. Entering the security code at the gate, he drove up the sweeping drive. The villa was frosted by the opalescent moon in the dark, velvety sky.

After pulling the car into the separate six-car garage, he turned off the engine. They both sat for a moment in silence. Then Hallie turned to him with sudden desperation.

"Could you ever love me? Could you?"

It was a serious question. He looked at her across the car. She hadn't been trying to manipulate him, after all. She actually believed she loved him.

The thought chilled him to the bone. He had the sudden memory of himself as a boy, hungry and cold and pathetically desperate for love. Crying for it.

He'd never feel that way again.

"No," he said quietly. "I will never love you. Or anyone."

Her face became a sickly green. She turned to open her door. Stumbling out of the car, she rushed from the garage and onto the driveway, red skirts flying behind her.

"Hallie, wait," he said tersely, slamming the car door behind him.

She didn't slow down. She fled toward the villa's gardens overlooking the sea, the skirt of her red dress flying behind her, a slash of scarlet in the moonlight.

He followed, reaching her at the hedge maze, with the eight-foot-tall, sharply cut hedges towering above them, luring them into the shadows of the green labyrinth.

"Hallie, damn you! Stop!"

Grasping her arm, he twisted her around, pressing her back against the hedge.

"Let me go," she panted, struggling. "You—are a *liar*!"

Her breath came in hot, quick gasps. His lips parted to argue, but as he looked from the fury in her eyes to the quick pant of her full breasts, pushing up against the strapless bodice of her dress, desire overwhelmed him. He tried to kiss her.

For the first time, Hallie turned her head away so he could not.

Cristiano stared down at her with narrowed eyes, his own heart suddenly pounding with anger at her rejection.

"I never asked for your love," he ground out. "I never wanted it."

She lifted her chin, and her eyes glittered in the moonlight. "No. You just want to possess me. You want my body. Not my heart."

Silence fell, with the only sound the angry pant of her breath. His gaze again fell to her sweetly seductive mouth. Her pink tongue licked the corners of her red lips.

"Love me if you want. I don't care." He looked down at her. "But you will obey me."

"*Obey* you?" She gave a harsh laugh. "This isn't the Middle Ages. I am not your property. And I never will be."

"Aren't you?" He breathed in the scent of her, like vanilla and summer flowers. Her skin beneath his grasp felt hot to the touch. Her dark eyes sucked him into fury and despair, all tangled up in wanton, desperate desire.

Gripping her wrists against the hedge, Cristiano lowered his head roughly to hers.

He did it to prove a point. To master her. But as he kissed her, as her struggles ended and he felt her surrender, when he felt her desire rise against him like a tide, he too was suddenly lost.

I love you, she'd said. *I am not your property.*

Kissing her, he was dizzy with need. He wanted to take her right here, right now, in the moonlight and shadows of the labyrinth.

Hallie wrenched away. "Don't touch me," she whispered harshly.

He stared down at her in shock. Without her in his arms, he felt suddenly bereft. Rejected. *Vulnerable.*

The one feeling he'd vowed he'd never feel again.

Rage exploded inside him. He let it build until it was all encompassing, blocking out any other emotion.

Looking down at his wife, he narrowed his eyes and spoke the words he knew would hurt her more than any others.

"You want me to tell you I love you, Hallie? Fine," Cristiano said coldly. "I love you."

Hallie stared up at him, her heart in her throat.

He loved her?

Trembling, she stumbled back a step into the shadows of the hedge maze. She whispered, "You do?"

"Want me to be more convincing?" Coming closer, he

kissed her cheek, her lips, her throat. "I love you, *cara mia*," he whispered. "I love you. *Ti amo*."

And she heard the mockery behind his words.

Tearfully she said, "I didn't know you had such cruelty in you!"

"Did you not?" he said, looking devastatingly handsome and cold as marble in his perfectly cut tuxedo. "Then you chose to be blind."

Hallie felt like crying. The way he'd looked at her at the gala had made her bold. It had made her brave. All her instincts had told her that if she took the risk, if she told him she loved him, she could rescue him from his dark past.

Her instincts had been wrong.

Now, standing in her red dress in the shadowy hedge maze, she felt like she was in a Gothic Victorian nightmare. Knowing he didn't love her back was heartbreaking, but she might have been able to endure it as long as she had hope that, someday, perhaps he could.

Cristiano had taken even that hope away from her, and then used her own words of love to mock her. He'd made it clear that their marriage would be on his terms alone.

She was to fill his bed and raise his child, and he would give her nothing in return. Not his heart. Not his love.

Not even a home.

She wiped her eyes. "You heartless bastard," she whispered. "What have you done to me?"

"Now it's my fault, because I cannot return the love I never asked you to feel?" He looked down at her icily. "I do not have the ability to produce feelings on command. What you want from me, I cannot give."

Pain ripped through her and, along with it, the humiliating realization that for all his coldness and cruelty, she loved him. Still.

"What will we do?" she whispered.

"Our marriage will continue as always."

Her eyes widened. "Are you serious?"

"Nothing has changed between us. We leave for Tokyo in the morning."

Hallie didn't realize her knees had buckled beneath her until he was beside her, supporting her arm.

"It's late, Hallie," he said quietly. "You're tired. Come inside."

She looked up at him wordlessly as he half carried her into the villa. Inside, it was dark and quiet. The rooms were elegant and empty. They seemed to go on forever.

On the second floor, they found Agata sitting outside the nursery, knitting. The older woman looked between them, then said only, "The baby had a good night. He just fell asleep."

In the darkened nursery, Hallie looked down at her sleeping baby. Jack's fat arms stretched back above his head. His chubby cheeks moved as his mouth pursed in his sleep.

Coming behind her, Cristiano put his hands heavily on her shoulders, his voice firm. "Let's put our quarrel behind us, Hallie. This is what's important." He looked down at the crib. "Our son. Our family."

A lump rose in Hallie's throat.

He was right. Family was the most important thing to her. For years, all she'd tried to do was recapture what she'd lost. To have a family again. A home.

How had it all gone so wrong? A lifetime in a loveless marriage stretched ahead of her. Instead of having a home, surrounded by friends, at her husband's command she would be forced to travel from hotel to hotel.

Her hands tightened at her sides. And her son would be raised to think this was *normal*. He'd see the cold relationship between his parents and think it was what marriage was. What *family* was. He'd never know what a family was meant to be—a rowdy, chaotic life of give and take, of arguing and joking and kisses, filled with love.

Her tiny baby's soul would be warped by this, just as Cristiano's had once been.

With an intake of breath, Hallie looked up.

Cristiano frowned when he saw her expression. "What is it?"

She'd thought commitment made a home. That was why she'd married him. She'd thought, if she took his name, if they lived under the same roof, under his protection, they'd be a family.

But there was a reason that, in spite of all his money and lavish gifts, Hallie hadn't felt as happy and secure as she had as a child. A reason, even in this amazing, luxurious villa, she'd never truly felt at home.

"Love makes a family," she breathed. "Love makes a home."

Certainty rushed through her, clanging like a bell. Her husband had said he would never love her. He would never take that risk. He would never give up anything he couldn't afford to lose. He would never give himself.

Hallie's heart tightened. Her back snapped straight.

Turning on her heel, she went to the enormous master bedroom. She took a suitcase from the shelf of the walk-in closet.

Cristiano's voice came from the doorway. "What do you think you're doing?"

There wasn't much to take. She didn't need all the expensive designer clothes, not anymore. And she'd left her family treasures back in New York. Along with her friends.

She looked at him.

"I'm going home."

"Home," he scoffed.

"New York." Saying the name aloud made her realize how desperate she was to return. "I'm going home to the people who love me."

She turned back to the closet, then stopped. He'd bought

her so much, but what did she actually need? Nothing. She didn't want anything he'd bought her. Because he hadn't been buying her clothes. He'd been buying her soul. Telling her how she had to behave and where she would live and who she would be.

Looking down at herself, she couldn't bear for the beautiful red ball gown to be touching her skin. It reminded her of how naive she'd been, to believe she could just tell him she loved him and magically change him, like some fairy tale!

Reaching back, she savagely yanked on the zipper, pulling off the dress and kicking it away from her body. She stood in front of him, wearing only a white lace bra and panties and the cold diamond necklace on her throat.

"Hallie, don't do anything foolish."

"You don't believe in love. You don't believe in home." Reaching up, she pulled off the glittering diamond necklace and held it out, a hard heap of metal and stone. "Take it back."

When he didn't move, she opened her hand, letting it drop heavily to the floor. Turning away, she dug through the closet until she found one of her old cotton sundresses. Pulling it over her body, she left the closet, carrying the empty suitcase.

"Go, then," he growled.

Stopping by the enormous bed where he'd once given her such joy, she whirled to face him. His eyes were black.

"Go off in search of this imaginary man who will feel whatever you want him to feel, whenever you want it, trained on your command like a barking dog."

She took a deep breath, her heart full of anguish. "That's not what I—"

"*You* can go," he interrupted. He paused. "My son stays."

Hallie's mouth went dry.

"What?" she croaked.

Her husband's dark eyes glittered as his cruel, sensual lips curved. "You heard me."

"You would take him from me?" she whispered. "From his own mother?"

"You are the one abandoning him, if you leave. And, as I warned you from the beginning, he is my priority. Not you."

His words stabbed her in the heart. "But—but you're hardly ever home! You spend all your time working. You'd rather see Jack raised by some paid nanny?" She lifted her chin. "I don't care what you say, no judge would agree to that!"

Cristiano tilted his head. "It seems you didn't read our prenuptial agreement carefully, *cara*. In the event of a divorce, unless I am in breach of our agreement, primary custody goes to me." He smiled. "You are, of course, welcome to visit Jack whenever you wish."

His voice was silky, as if he knew he'd just beaten her. And he had. She staggered back, unable to believe that the man she loved could be so cold and unforgiving.

"You bastard," she whispered.

"Me?" His eyes suddenly blazed. "I've done everything for you, Hallie," he ground out. "Everything. I've given you everything any woman could possibly desire. I bought you this house—"

"Because you wanted revenge against your father! Nothing to do with me!"

"This house was for you. Hurting Bennato was just a bonus. And yet you still decided to go behind my back and try to help him infiltrate our family."

"He never meant to abandon you! Why won't you even talk to him?"

"Because he would say anything to try to hurt me. And, at the moment, so would you."

That made Hallie gasp. "Do you really believe that?"

"You're either with me or against me."

Searching his gaze, she choked out, "Are you trying to make me hate you?"

"Perhaps. At least hate," Cristiano said softly, tucking back a tendril of her hair, "is an emotion I believe in."

They were so close, facing each other in the luxurious bedroom, next to the enormous four-poster bed. Beyond that, the French doors opened to the terrace on the edge of the sea.

Hallie looked up at her husband. The powerful, sexy billionaire that every other woman wanted. To the outside world, she knew it seemed as if she had everything any woman could ever want.

But he was so damaged inside, the truth was she had nothing at all.

She said, "I won't let you take my baby away."

"I won't have to." He gave her a hard smile. "Because you're not going anywhere. We will remain one big happy family. You will remain at my side. In my bed. Bearing my children."

"Children?" Her voice was strangled.

He lifted an eyebrow. "We will have other children," he said mildly. "Surely you would not want Jack to be alone?"

It was the final straw. Closing her eyes, Hallie took a deep breath.

She knew what she had to do. The thought turned her heart to ice. It wasn't what she wanted.

But he'd left her no choice.

"I'm done arguing about this," Cristiano said. "You will be happy, as you were before. You will appreciate what I can give you and ignore what I cannot." Reaching out, he cupped her cheek.

Opening her eyes, she spoke, her voice clear and un-flinching. "You missed dinner with us this week."

He frowned. "What?"

"Twice. You were gone from dawn till midnight. You

didn't share a single meal with us on those days, as Agata and other staff members can attest."

His shoulders were suddenly tense. He knew what she meant. Dropping his hand, he said defensively, "I was working at the hotel—"

"It doesn't matter. You failed to uphold my rules. So you're in breach of our agreement," she said, stepping back.

Her husband stared at her, his dark eyes wide. His lips parted to speak and closed again.

He looked vulnerable. Shaken.

Hallie forced herself not to care, to treat him exactly as he'd treated her.

"As you're in breach of the prenup, I will get primary custody. So I'm taking Jack with me to New York. Please feel free," she added lightly, in the same tone he'd used, "to visit whenever you want."

Cristiano stared at her in shock, not moving.

No. Hallie blocked the pain from her heart. She wasn't going to feel anything. She wasn't going to let him push her around ever again.

She turned away, dragging the suitcase behind her. Stopping at the door, she faced him one last time across the shadowy bedroom where they'd once set the world on fire.

"Thank you, Cristiano." Her voice echoed between them as she said flatly, "Thank you for teaching me how the world really is."

And she left.

CHAPTER NINE

"Signor." Looking up from where he'd been pacing the hotel's terrace just after dawn, Cristiano saw Luca Pizzati, the new manager. The young man gave him an apologetic smile. "Sir, you are acting crazy. The entire staff is threatening to quit."

Cristiano's mouth fell open. How could the man say such a thing?

The day after his wife and child left him, Cristiano had planned to leave for Tokyo. And after that, Seoul. And after that… Cristiano couldn't remember. But he'd been forced to stay in Cavello. Something wasn't right here, and until he could find the source of the problem, he couldn't leave. He could barely eat or sleep. All he could do was pace the halls of the hotel, checking every detail, trying to find the problem that haunted him, taunted him, just out of his reach.

"Look at this," Cristiano ground out. He yanked a purple flower from a bougainvillea bush that was a slightly different shade from the rest. "A disgrace! Do I have to fix everything?"

The young manager looked at the flower, then Cristiano.

"Signor Moretti," he said gently, "when was the last time you slept?"

He bit out furiously, "How can I sleep, until the hotel is perfect?"

"It will never be perfect," the manager said. "Because people are living in it."

Cristiano took a deep breath. Blinking hard, he looked up at the beautiful new hotel. It was already full of guests and getting nothing but praise. He looked down at the flower in his hand. He'd been about to scream at the gardening staff because the bougainvillea flowers were not all the exact same shade of purple.

Pizzati was right. He *was* acting crazy.

Crushing the bloom in his fingers, Cristiano tossed it to the ground.

"You're right," he said in a low voice. "Please give the staff my apologies. I… I will stop."

The manager came closer, a look of concern in his eyes. "Shall I send for your driver? Or would you like Esposito to take you home?"

The empty villa was the last place Cristiano wanted to be. There, he heard only the echoes of his baby son's laughter in the nursery, of his wife's sweet singing in the garden. And in the bedroom, the haunting echo of her soft moans from the times he'd made love to her.

Lost, all lost.

And he was tired. So tired. Thinking of his wife and child, a strange ice spread slowly through Cristiano's body, down his neck, to his spine, until his fingers and toes felt numb. At that point he felt nothing, absolutely nothing.

"Sir?"

He focused with effort. Then he nodded heavily. "Thank you, Mr. Pizzati. I leave the hotel in good hands. Please order my pilot to ready the plane for Tokyo."

"Of course, sir." The manager sounded relieved. Cristiano could only imagine how many problems he'd caused the man over the last ten days.

He tried to remember what his scheduled meetings in Asia were about. Marcia had left him multiple messages, as had various board members, all of which he'd ignored. He took a deep breath. He pictured the Campania Hotel Tokyo, ultramodern and gleaming in the Shinjuku district.

But when he tried to recall the details, all he could remember was the darkness in his wife's eyes the night she'd left him.

Thank you for teaching me how the world really is.

"Have a pleasant trip, sir," the manager said.

Turning, Cristiano left the terrace without a word. When he came out of the lobby into the bright Italian sunshine, Marco was waiting to take him back home.

Home. The word tasted bitter on his tongue. There was no such thing. It was a lie. A dream. Like love.

As the Rolls-Royce passed through the gate one last time, he looked up at the magnificent nineteenth-century villa. He wished he'd never come here. He'd done it to prove that he'd triumphed over his past.

Instead, it had triumphed over him.

When Hallie had told him she loved him, he should have said the words back to her and made her believe them. Why hadn't he tried? It would have been a lie, but at least their marriage would have endured. She would never have known the difference.

Why, instead, had he mocked her, then told her the truth—that he didn't have the ability to love her or anyone? Was it pride?

Or had he just wanted one person on earth to really, truly know who he was deep inside? A man so flawed that he didn't know what love was, or home?

But he did know one thing.

He looked at Luigi Bennato's spectacular villa, clinging to the cliffs above the bright blue sea.

He was done with this place. He would put it on the market at once.

An hour later, after the staff had packed his clothes, he was on the way to a private airport twenty minutes inland.

Cristiano stared out of the sedan's back seat window, not noticing the palm trees or tiny stone churches or lush groves of lemon trees.

He wondered how Hallie was enjoying New York. Was she happy? How was the baby?

Was Hallie already looking for a new home? A new love? His stomach twisted.

He'd heard she'd signed some kind of record deal with a top executive at an independent label in New York, the man who'd casually given her that card in Rome. Life could be like that. One chance meeting could change your life.

Like coming home early to find a beautiful maid singing in his penthouse while she changed the sheets of his bed.

Clarence Loggia, the manager of the Campania New York, had called Cristiano last night to tell him that Hallie's agent had arranged for her to make her big debut tonight at the Blue Hour, the hotel's jazz club.

"I assume you approve," Clarence had said delicately.

His wife? Appearing on stage, singing for strangers, while Cristiano was on the other side of the ocean? No way. He wanted her to sing only for him, like a songbird in a cage.

Closing her eyes, he'd thought of Hallie's sweet, haunting voice. Her songs of longing and heartbreak. Love. Home. Family.

"No..." Cristiano had started, but he forced himself to finish, "No problem. Tell the club's manager to give her everything she needs. The best time slot, good lighting, advertising. Everything."

"Of course, Signor Moretti." He'd paused. "You will be there, no?"

"No," Cristiano had replied, and he'd hung up.

He wondered how Hallie was feeling right before her New York debut. Was she scared? Would the audience appreciate her, as she deserved? Would they realize what a gift she was to them?

Staring out the window, he saw they were passing an old shack he knew, even though he'd never been there.

There was only one way to put the past behind him. Only

one way to truly triumph over it, once and for all. And it had nothing to do with money.

You'll never talk to him, will you? You hate him beyond all reason. You'll never be free.

"Stop," he said.

His driver looked confused but obligingly pulled over into a gravel drive on the side of the road.

"Wait here," he told Marco and Salvatore.

Outside, as he shut the sedan door behind him, he could hear the roar of the sea beneath the cliff, hear the soft sway of palm trees in the hot summer wind, scented with sea salt and spices from across the Mediterranean.

His heart was pounding as he slowly went to the front door. *I'm afraid of nothing*, he told himself. He pounded on the door with his fist. He heard footsteps. Then it opened.

And Cristiano saw Luigi Bennato for the first time in fifteen years.

The man looked bowed, gray. A shadow of the boisterous, vital man he remembered. Had time done this? he wondered. Or had it been his betrayal?

Seeing him, Luigi's dark eyes widened. Suddenly life and color came back into the old man's pale cheeks. "Cristiano?"

"I'm giving you back your villa," he said tersely. "It's yours. Keep it. Just never contact me or my family again."

Hands clenching at his sides, he turned away.

"No," the old man said.

Cristiano stopped, turning around in shock. "What?"

The gray-haired man looked at him. "I don't need a villa. What I need," he whispered, "is a son."

"You should have thought of that before you tried to force my mother to get rid of me when she was pregnant," he said, "then tossed her out on the street."

"All I did was keep her from drinking while she was pregnant. And she hated me for it."

"Why would you do that?"

"Because from the moment Violetta told me she was pregnant, I loved you."

The wind blew softly against Cristiano's face. From a distance, he could hear traffic on the road, the cry of seagulls.

"That's a lie," he said in a low voice.

"You know how she was. You know better than anyone," he said sadly. "Violetta was beautiful. Charming. But so broken. She accused me of keeping her prisoner. A few months before you were born, she disappeared without a trace."

Cristiano thought of his mother's fury if anyone tried to take her alcohol away. Once, when he was nine, he'd dared to pour out her bottles of whiskey while she was passed out. She'd slapped him so hard his ears rang for weeks.

"You made her a drunk."

"I did?" Luigi slowly shook his head. "We met in a bar, when she offered to buy me a drink. I'd never seen any woman hold her liquor so well. Stupidly, I was impressed."

That made sense to Cristiano, too. Agata had told him that when she worked for Bennato, the man had rarely touched alcohol. He took a deep breath.

"If you knew I existed, and you claim to care," he said slowly, "why didn't you keep trying to find me?"

"I did. For years," the old man choked out. He blinked fast, shaking his head. Tears streamed down his wrinkled cheeks. "But you're right," he whispered. "I should have looked harder. It wasn't until I saw her picture in the paper, a few days after she died, that I knew where you were. But before I could leave for Naples, you showed up at my hotel in Capri, asking for a job. I thought it was a miracle. I thought it was my chance."

"Why didn't you say anything?"

"I told myself I needed proof first. But the truth was... I

was afraid." He swallowed. "After the way Violetta raised you, why would you ever forgive me? I was a coward. And I waited too long. By the time I had proof you were my son, you'd already left. And I didn't want to cause you more pain."

"I betrayed you."

"I didn't see it as a betrayal."

"How did you see it?"

The elderly man whispered, "Justice."

A tear slid down his wrinkled cheek.

Cristiano stared down at him in shock. Everything was different than he'd imagined. Everything.

"Can you ever forgive me?" Luigi choked out. He reached his shaking hand to Cristiano's shoulder. "I loved you so much. But I could not protect you. I failed."

Cristiano stood frozen in front of the old wooden shack. The sun felt too bright on his face. Clenching his jaw, he looked out at the sea.

Hallie had tried to tell him. She'd tried to save him from his own darkness.

"So you just let me destroy you," Cristiano said slowly. "You let me take everything from you, and make it mine."

"Of course I did," Luigi said quietly. "You're my son. Your happiness means more to me than my own. I love you."

Cristiano heard the echo of Hallie's voice.

Love makes a family. Love makes a home.

"My mother said you abandoned us," he said. "After she died, I wanted to make you suffer."

"It's not your fault, my son," Luigi said hoarsely. "I should have taken you into my arms the day you walked into my hotel. I should have—"

With a sob, Luigi pulled him into his arms.

For a moment, Cristiano stiffened.

"So much time has been lost," Luigi whispered, hugging

him. "Because I was afraid. Because I was ashamed. Years we can never get back. Oh, my son. Can you forgive me?"

So much time has been lost.

Still held in his father's arms, Cristiano thought of the ten days he'd been separated from his wife and child. Ten days had felt like eternity, driving him half-mad.

What if they were separated for a lifetime? Until he, too, was apologizing for his cowardice and shame?

He gasped, and suddenly realized he was hugging his father back. Hearing Luigi's sobs of joy, Cristiano's heart cracked in his chest.

Emotions suddenly poured through him. Grief and anguish and every other feeling he'd blocked for years. Everything he hadn't let himself feel.

And love.

Love so big it seemed to be exploding out of his body with light brighter than the sun.

As he stood in a little village on the edge of the Amalfi Coast, hugged by his father for the very first time, Cristiano took a deep breath. Even the air seemed different in his lungs.

"Thank you for that," Luigi said, finally releasing him. He wiped his eyes. "You've made an old man so happy."

As Cristiano stared down at his father, everything became crystal clear.

Hallie.

Oh, God, how could he not have realized it before?

She was the one who'd tried to convince him to forgive his father. She'd loved Cristiano, even when he didn't deserve it. She'd seen the hurt and darkness inside him, and, instead of scorning him, she'd tried to heal it. She'd been brave enough to love him, flawed as he was.

He'd tossed it back in her face.

His spine snapped straight as he looked across the sea

and realized, for the first time, exactly what love meant. What *family* meant.

Love didn't consume, like fire.

It gave, like the sun.

Cristiano took a deep breath and felt his shoulders expand as he sucked all the world into his lungs. His eyes narrowed in a private vow.

If she forgave him, he would show her that her faith in him hadn't been wrong.

He would give his wife, every single day on earth, a reason to sing.

"Cristiano?"

Eyes wide, Cristiano stumbled back from his father.

"I have to go find Hallie," he said. "I have to tell her… tell her…"

"Go." His father smiled at him through his tears. "And when you see her, please tell her something more. Tell her *thank you*."

"I can't do this," Hallie whispered.

"You can," Lola told her firmly. "I didn't go to all the trouble of getting dressed and leaving the house with a newborn just for you to back out at the last minute. You can do it."

From behind the Blue Hour's curtain, Hallie glanced out at the audience. "There are so many people."

"They'll love you. Look," Tess said. "I've got your biggest fan right here!"

Hallie smiled down at Jack, who was in a stroller next to Esme's, trying to grab his own chubby feet.

Hallie bit her lip as she looked out again from the wings of the jazz club's small stage. She would have preferred some out-of-the-way coffeehouse, with only five or six people in the audience. But her agent was no fool. He'd argued for Hallie to make her debut at the Blue Hour. "Why would you go anywhere else? You're married to Cristiano Moretti!"

Even for someone with half a million hits, the number of people who'd watched the YouTube video of her singing in Rome, it wasn't easy to perform in such an exclusive venue. So she'd told her agent to ask the manager, confident that when Cristiano heard about it he'd tell them all to go to hell.

But, apparently, he'd agreed.

Why was Cristiano being supportive of her career, when he'd made it clear he didn't give a damn about her?

It was a mystery.

Even after ten days, Hallie still couldn't believe he'd let them go so easily. Cristiano wasn't the kind of man to let himself be defeated, certainly not by some legal technicality. Why hadn't he come after her? Why hadn't he fought?

The answer had to be that he was secretly relieved to be rid of them.

She took a deep breath, looking down at the short black dress the music label's stylist had found for her. Tomorrow she was supposed to start work on an album, followed by a publicity tour. Once, this would have felt like a dream come true.

Now, it just felt like a job. A way to support her child so she wouldn't have to depend on a man who didn't love her.

The truth was that she didn't want to sing for strangers. She wanted to sing for the people she loved. For Cristiano. And she would have given it all up in a second if he'd come for her, to fight for her. For their family.

But he hadn't.

A jagged pain filled her throat. *Bad for singing*, she thought, and tried to think of happier things. She'd used some of that hundred-thousand-dollar check, which she'd tucked away in her savings account, to lease a one-bedroom walk-up apartment in the Lower East Side. But she was trying not to spend that. She wanted to save it for Jack's future, so she never had to ask Cristiano for anything ever again. Not even the alimony required by the prenuptial agreement. She hadn't filed for divorce. The mere thought of divorce filled her with blinding pain.

At the moment it felt like she was barely putting one foot ahead of the other. She didn't know how she would have survived without her friends.

"Stop that," Tess said, as she caught Lola yawning behind Hallie.

"I can't help it," the blonde said. "I only got four hours of sleep last night. Thanks to you," she said to her tiny baby with mock severity.

"Four hours isn't so bad," Tess said encouragingly. Lola rolled her eyes.

"One hour. Four times."

"Oh," Tess said, because there wasn't much good to say about that. Then she brightened. "But before you know it, your baby will be as big as Esme." She looked down at her five-month-old daughter, a dark-haired baby with adorable fat rolls on her thighs and bright emerald-green eyes.

"It's time," the stage manager called, and Hallie sucked in her breath.

Lola squeezed Hallie's shoulder. "I know you'll be great."

Tess gave her a sideways hug. "We'll be cheering for you!"

Then they left with the babies, and Hallie was alone. She heard the club's host announce, "And let's have a big Blue Hour welcome for debut artist… Hallie Hatfield!"

She'd left the Moretti name behind. The glamorous bride celebrated in the fashion blogs, the woman who'd brought the famous Cristiano Moretti to his knees—that obviously wasn't her. She was just Hallie, plain and simple.

Trembling, she went out on stage, in front of the house band. Beneath the spotlight, she couldn't see anyone in the audience, not even Tess or Lola or the babies. She gulped. She wasn't sure she could do this.

Then...

Closing her eyes, she focused on the music. The songs her mother and father had once sung to her, and her grand-parents before.

Hallie's lips parted, and against her will she saw Cristiano's face. She sang directly to the man she loved. The man she'd lost.

Tears streamed down her cheeks as she sang of longing and heartbreak and regret. When she finally sang her last note, silence fell across the club.

Opening her eyes, Hallie looked out into the darkness beyond the spotlight. Had everyone left? Had they hated her songs and just gone home?

Then she heard it, sweeping across the club like a low roll of thunder.

A rush of applause built to shouts and cheers, lifting her sad heart. She smiled, overwhelmed with gratitude. She hadn't failed the audience who'd come to hear her, but still she felt sad.

"Thank you," she choked out. Wiping her tears, she stepped back from the microphone. As she turned away, she heard one man's voice above the rest.

"Hallie."

There was a collective intake of breath across the club. Turning back, she narrowed her eyes, trying to see who was calling to her. It sounded like...but it couldn't be...

The spotlight moved, and she saw him.

Her husband stood in the middle of the crowded jazz club, amid all the tables, his dark suit more rumpled than she'd ever seen it.

"Cristiano?" she breathed.

His dark eyes cut through her soul. Turning to the crowd, he held out his arm toward her. "Hallie is my wife."

He spread his arms wide. "Have you ever heard such a voice?"

The audience applauded and hooted, stomping their feet. But Hallie had eyes only for him.

"What are you doing here?"

Cristiano's voice carried across the room as he turned to face her. "I don't need you, Hallie."

She sucked in her breath.

"At least that's what I told myself." He started walking past the crowded tables, toward the stage. "The truth was, I was afraid to need you." He stopped in front of the stage, staring up at her. "Because I was dead inside."

The club was so quiet you could have heard a pin drop.

"But you brought me to life." Cristiano smiled at her, his dark eyes shining. "It was your voice that caused the first crack in the wall around my heart. The first time I heard you sing. Do you remember?"

She nodded, a lump in her throat. How could she forget?

"I saw you, so vibrant and sexy and alive, and I knew from that moment that I had to have you. But it wasn't just your incredible voice that drew me. Not even your beautiful face and body. It was your soul, Hallie," he whispered. "Your heart."

By now, camera phones had appeared at every table, lighting up the club like candle flames, recording the moment as the famous billionaire Cristiano Moretti went onstage to join his wife.

"No." She struggled to speak. "I can't believe it."

"I spoke with my father," he said humbly. "And you were right. Everything you said. You were right."

Her heart was in her throat as she looked up at him.

"I know what love means now," he whispered. Then, to her shock, he fell to his knees on the stage in front of her. There was a gasp across the club.

Cristiano looked up at her. His eyes were vulnerable and

raw. For the first time, the darkness was gone. For the first time, she truly saw his soul.

"Let me try to win back your heart. Let me show you I can be the man I was always meant to be." He took her hand in both of his. "I need you, Hallie," he whispered. "I love you."

Reaching down, she put her hand to his rough cheek in amazement. "You love me?"

He nodded, blinking back tears. "Tell me I'm not too late." His voice broke. "Tell me I still have the chance to be the man you deserve."

She pulled him to his feet. "The chance? No. You don't have a chance to win back my love." Hallie smiled at him through her tears. "Because I never stopped loving you, Cristiano."

His handsome face filled with joy. Cupping her face in both his hands, he kissed her, long and hard. Hallie felt the flame spark between them, as always.

But something was different. Something was new. They knew each other now, really and truly. The fire burned bright and clear between them, in a blaze she knew would last forever.

Ignoring the applause and hoots from the audience, Cristiano looked down at her. "And you were right about something else."

"What?"

He gave her an impish grin. "The house you loved on Bank Street. The one you told me about. It does have a garden. And it was for sale, just like you said. I told my broker to put in an offer."

"What!"

"If you still want it," he amended. He searched her gaze. "Do you, *cara*?"

"Oh, Cristiano." Happy tears filled Hallie's eyes at the

thought of having the home she'd dreamed of for all her life. "Do you really mean it? We can stay?"

"Forever, if you want." He cupped her cheek. "Because you're not just my wife. You're my love song," he whispered. "My happiness, my heartbreak and joy. You're my everything."

Looking down at her hand wrapped in his larger one, Hallie felt her heart in her throat.

"And you're mine." She looked up at him, blinking back tears. "From the moment you said you loved me, all my childhood dreams came true. We can live in New York, or anywhere in the world. Because now I know, for the rest of our lives," she breathed, her eyes shining with joy, "wherever we live, we're home."

* * * * *

MARRYING HIS
RUNAWAY HEIRESS

THERESE BEHARRIE

For Grant, because he's the reason I experienced Italy and its beauty and romance.

I think by law that means I have to dedicate this book to him.

Also, because he loves me unconditionally, which never fails to surprise and overwhelm me.

Thank you.

CHAPTER ONE

If ELENA JOHN hadn't known better, she'd have thought Micah Williams was simply being thoughtful. But she did know better. He wasn't being thoughtful; he was trying to charm her. Soften her up.

If they'd met before she would have told him not to bother.

Instead, she climbed into the limousine that had pulled up in front of her house with a resigned sigh. It was as luxurious on the inside as it was on the outside. In one corner a mini-bar packed with her favourite drinks—which couldn't be a coincidence since her favourite drinks were undeniably strange—and a basket of snacks in another corner. Music streamed through the speakers. Soft, unassuming, bland music no one could find offensive. Then there was the driver, who checked on her constantly, and the flight attendant, who took over from the driver once Elena reached the airport.

The longer she thought about it though, the more she liked the idea of Mr Williams trying to charm her. It wouldn't work, but the fact that he was trying reminded her of what she'd accomplished. Five years at her newspaper and finally, *finally* she'd got assigned an important story. A story about a powerful man. Now, the powerful man was trying to nudge her towards writing a good story.

She'd shadowed enough journalists, transcribed enough interviews, heard enough stories to know sometimes people did that.

She'd spent enough time with powerful men to know sometimes they did that, too.

Considering the situation she was leaving behind, the thought that Mr Williams was trying to manipulate her should have angered her. But this was for her job. She had prepared for this her entire career. And for once, she wasn't the one in the helpless position. So what if the limousines and private planes, the obedient and careful staff, and the access to her favourite things reminded her of the first sixteen years of her life?

It might be a precursor to the next years of your life, too.

The thought made her faintly nauseous.

'Ms John?' The flight attendant was staring at her, his spine so straight, his posture so poised, she wanted to know if he'd practised it. 'Through here.'

'Yes.'

She followed him through the blue velvet curtain into the plush luxury of Micah Williams's private plane. The design was different from her father's, which was mostly for efficiency and productivity. Here the open space was a balance of that and relaxation, with comfortable-looking chairs on either side of the aisle in front of a modern desk. The biggest difference though was the man standing in front of that desk.

Micah Williams.

He was handsome. She didn't bother tiptoeing around it. His skin was an awe-inspiring shade of brown, as if the heavens had opened and a stream of both light and dark shone on him. His body was clad in a suit that was made for his broad shoulders, his narrow waist, his long legs. His hair was dark and short, his stubble a length that told her it had been purposefully groomed that way. None of it was a surprise. Her research had prepared her.

What surprised her was the intensity of his gaze. The way he looked at her as if she had the answer to a question he'd had all his life. She wasn't prepared for how his mouth curved at the side when he realised she was staring. When she realised he was staring right back.

She resisted the urge to smooth down the red pants suit she wore. She still wore her black coat over it, but the red was visible. She'd purposefully chosen to wear the colour. It was *her* colour. That knowledge was one of the few things her mother had left her before she'd packed her bags to travel the world.

Having a colour made Elena feel good; being in her colour made her feel strong. Strength helped her accept that this man was staring at her so intensely.

'Ms John,' he said smoothly, stepping forward. 'Thank you for coming.'

'Did I have a choice?' she asked lightly. She gave herself a moment to enjoy his surprise. It flitted over the intensity, making it seem lighter. She knew it was an illusion. 'It's a free trip to Italy.'

Something twitched on his face. 'That's what you meant, is it?' His tone was dry. 'It has nothing to do with this being for your job?'

'No. It's all about a gondola ride.'

'You've been on a gondola before,' he said confidently.

'No.' She searched his face. 'Why does that surprise you?'

'For the same reason I don't believe you need a free trip to Italy.'

He knew who she was.

She schooled her face, trying hard not to give in to disappointment. It wasn't the end of the world. Her identity wasn't a secret. But—did this mean what she thought it meant? The only way to find out was to ask.

'Are you referring to the fact that my family owns the John Diamond Company?'

The intense look was back. Bemusement was there, too. 'I am.'

'Is that why I'm here, Mr Williams? Because of my family?'

The seconds ticked by. Eventually, he said, 'It is.'

She sighed. 'Wonderful.' Paused. 'Your attempts to butter me up were ridiculous, by the way.' It was an immature comment, and nowhere near an appropriate response to what he was admitting or the implications of it. But he didn't get a chance to answer her.

'We're about to take off,' the flight attendant said behind her. 'Can you please take your seats?'

She settled in a seat next to the window. Tried to steady herself by looking out at the city she loved. There was nothing on the tarmac besides a few other planes. Bright green grass was scattered beyond the tar, the dew of the brisk day settling on it. If she looked close enough, she'd swear she'd find ice sitting on the tips of the blades of grass. If nothing else, she was leaving a cold, wet South Africa for a sunny, warm Italy. If nothing else, she was leaving behind two men who thought they could control her life.

You're thinking about letting them though.

She exhaled slowly.

'I've upset you.'

They were in the air already, though barely, when Micah spoke.

'No.' She kept her gaze on the window. Outside it was all blue now, with white puffs of clouds around them. 'Why would you think that?'

'You insulted my attempts at cordiality.'

She almost laughed at the indignation in his voice. 'So try harder next time.'

A strangled sound came from the vicinity of his seat. She allowed herself to enjoy it, but didn't turn to look at him, or let him see her smile. It was a while longer before he said anything again.

'I didn't only ask for you to do this story because of your name, you know.'

So he had asked for her. Which meant that she likely hadn't earned this assignment as she initially believed. And she was more helpless than she initially believed. It smarted, and the sting of it coated her tongue, slipping into her words, her tone.

'I'm sure. It's those pop culture articles I wrote, isn't it? Speculating on who someone will end up with next truly does display the depth of my talent.'

'I did enjoy the article about the ex-rugby player bad boy who faked a relationship but fell in love for real.'

At that, Elena turned to look at him. He was sitting on the only other seat opposite her, lounging back in his chair, watching her as if he had nothing else to do. Elena knew that couldn't be true. The man ran an empire. His business had grown immensely in the ten years since he'd started it. His company sold luxury goods in Africa, primarily South Africa, and he'd recently partnered with two non-African brands worth millions to do that for. She suspected another brand would be added to that in Italy.

It was all part of why Elena's newspaper had selected him as their Businessperson of the Year. She was supposed to be writing an article about how amazingly busy he was. There was no way he had time to converse with her.

'You read that?'

'I did.'

He flicked a forearm out, rolled back his shirt sleeve. He did the same on the other side. She watched, stuck on the fact that he'd taken off his suit jacket. Also, on his forearms. His *forearms*. They were muscular, with lines of veins that looked as if they were pulsing. They made her want to trace them with her fingertips, then grip that swelling just before his elbow to feel the muscle there. She wanted to—

Nothing. She wanted to nothing.

What did Jameson's forearms look like? Did it matter? The marriage he and her father had proposed was purely business. Purely name. Which made what Micah had done sting sharper. She was there for her name, too. Not for his admittedly good-looking forearms.

Wait—Micah? When had she started calling him Micah?

'I have to admit, there was a lot of speculation, even in that.'

Okay, he was speaking again. Yes, right. She needed to reply. That was how conversations worked. If she remembered correctly, and honestly, she wasn't sure she did.

'Pop culture articles are speculative by nature. Unless you have a reliable source, but that changes things. The tone of the article. It shifts the attention. You have people focusing more on who the source could be as opposed to the content. Generally, I use sources for articles that are already more fact than opinion. Which, I guess, is the difference between having my piece in the entertainment section of the printed paper versus only the digital edition.'

The silence that followed her answer alerted her to how much she'd said. She'd surprised them both with it, but she refused to feel embarrassed. She knew what she was doing. Writing was not only her job, but her passion. She read articles and books on writing, did online courses, followed noted journalists on social media. All of this was over and above her responsibilities at the newspaper.

She was *capable*. It was part of why Micah Williams asking for her annoyed her. He shouldn't have had to ask; she should have been given this. She deserved it.

'This is exactly why I thought you'd do well on this article,' Micah said. 'There was something about your work that felt intentional. Even the fluff pieces, which I enjoyed immensely.'

'How could you not?' she countered. 'Everyone knows how much people enjoy fluff.'

He laughed. It was surprising and arousing. At that point, Elena should have known she was already in trouble. Then he said, 'Ms John, you'll quickly discover that my tastes aren't similar to most people's.' There was a slight pause. 'I'm going to enjoy showing you that.'

The fact that she *wanted* him to show her? That she thought she would *enjoy* it? Oh, yeah. Trouble.

Micah Williams hadn't expected the John heiress to be so…
Interesting.

The word seemed woefully inadequate to describe the woman sitting opposite him. As a result, he watched her more than was necessary. Her expressions were animated, her tone dry and sharp in equal measure, and she was surprisingly candid. Surprisingly attractive, too.

Not her appearance. He'd seen that in pictures. The wild, curly hair. The gloss of her brown skin and the dusting of freckles on only her left cheek, though that detail hadn't been clear in the pictures. He noted it now because it had a certain charm. As did the way her mouth was painted bright red. Her lips were full, plump, and he'd experienced plenty of people in his lifetime who would have

been embarrassed by that abundance. Ms John seemed to
have embraced it.

That peek into her personality was really the most attractive thing about her.

She embraced plenty of things, it seemed. The admittedly extra nature of how he'd brought her to his plane—
not that he'd expected her to point it out. The fact that he
knew who she was. That he'd requested her for the article.
Micah hadn't expected it to be easy to get Elena on his side,
but now he thought her honesty might aid him. Maybe that
was why he offered her such honesty in return.

Either that, or those red lips. And that luscious body,
tall and curved, clad in a red pants suit visible despite her
coat. The white T-shirt she wore beneath it clung to ample
breasts. And her heels, white as well, highlighted the most
beautiful set of ankles he'd seen in his life.

He blinked. Ankles? Since when had he noticed a
woman's ankles? Of all the things he'd been attracted to,
ankles had never appeared on the list. His eyes lowered
to her legs. She'd crossed them.

So maybe he simply hadn't seen the *right* pair of ankles.
Interesting. Irrelevant, but interesting.

'Do you know, if you'd started our conversation with
the fact that you've read my work, things would have been
a lot less contentious?'

'Contentious?' he repeated. 'I don't know what you
mean, Ms John.'

'Elena, please.' There was a slight pause. She hesitated.
Undid her seat belt and stood, offering him a hand. 'I'm
sorry. I didn't introduce myself properly. I am Elena.'

She didn't say her surname. He stored it into the vault
of information he had about her, undid his own seat belt,
and stood.

'Micah.'

'Good to meet you, Mr Williams.'

She took his hand. Shook in two quick pumps. It shouldn't have heated his blood. Shouldn't have had any effect on him whatsoever.

It did.

'If I call you Elena, you'll have to call me Micah,' he said, hoping to heaven his voice was normal and not tinted with the desire he suddenly felt.

'It feels…' she hesitated '…wrong to call you Micah.'

'Wrong?' Another interesting fact. 'How so?'

'Unprofessional,' she clarified.

'This is about the article.'

'Yes, of course.' She frowned. 'What else could it be about?'

This unexpected attraction between us?

'Nothing else. We're on the same page.'

He pressed the button that called the flight attendant, and when the man appeared ordered himself a drink. With alcohol. To shock his system into behaving. Elena ordered a water. There was that professionalism again. It obviously meant a lot to her. But why?

'I promise not to consider you unprofessional if you use my first name,' he said, accepting the glass from the flight attendant. 'I won't tell anyone at the newspaper either.'

'Thank you.' Her tone was somehow a mixture of dryness and gratitude. Fascinating creature, the John heiress. 'I'll call you Micah—' he ignored the thrill that beat in his heart '—for the duration of this week. Since we are spending it together, it might be strange to continue speaking to you so formally.' She didn't give him a chance to process before she was asking, 'Is the itinerary for this week finalised?'

She was putting distance between them, he realised. He kept his smile to himself. He wasn't sure what was amusing him more: the fact that she felt the need to put distance between them when they'd barely known one another for an hour; or how seamlessly she'd done so. He was being managed. Expertly. He hadn't thought much about how her being an heiress would affect this business trip. Well, other than his plan to endear himself to her. But now he was experiencing it.

A journalist had never put him in his place so skilfully before. Nor a woman. He barely felt that he'd been moved, let alone gently, if firmly, lowered to the ground. It was tied into the professionalism somehow. The attraction. He had no idea—and he wanted to know. Except that wasn't why she was here. He needed to remember that.

'It is. The one my assistant emailed to you is accurate, apart from two meetings that I have scheduled for our last day in Rome. It was the only time my client was available,' he added apologetically.

'You don't have to explain,' she said with a shake of her head. 'I know how it goes with business trips.'

'I imagine you do.'

Her brow lifted, but she didn't engage. 'Is there a reason Serena isn't joining us?'

'I wanted time to speak with you.'

'That's why you don't have your laptop open either?'

'I wouldn't have my laptop open when I have a guest.'

She laughed. It was a light, bubbly sound he found delightful. Again, not relevant.

'We both know guests don't get in the way of business, Micah.'

He lifted his glass to his lips thoughtfully. 'I'm beginning to think your experience of business and the way I conduct mine are different.'

She studied him for a moment, then reached into the huge white handbag she'd brought with her and pulled out her phone. She pressed a few buttons, and suddenly a large red dot was gleaming up at him.

'I'm beginning to think so, too,' she replied, despite the minutes that had passed. 'Why don't we start talking about those differences?' She touched her finger to her phone's screen. The device began recording. 'What inspired you to start this business, Mr Williams?'

An expert at managing, he thought again, and answered her.

CHAPTER TWO

MICAH WILLIAMS WAS too suave for his own good. Or for Elena's own good. She wanted to get beneath the business-person persona. That wasn't part of her job, obviously. She was only meant to portray the businessperson. She had enough of the basics to write a good introduction. She could already see it.

> *Micah Williams is charming, but ruthless—a fact he wouldn't want you to believe. The latter, that is. He enjoys his charm almost as much as he thinks his audience does. And perhaps his audience does.*
>
> *His eyes light up when he talks business, though there's always an intensity shadowed there, regardless of the business topic. He knows just what to say and he relishes saying it, knowing it's exactly what he should be saying.*
>
> *But it's in that very fact that his ruthlessness lies. Williams has no qualms about telling you what you want to hear even as he uses what you don't want to hear against you. He's a lion, circling his prey, if the lion was tall and handsome, and—*

Maybe she needed to work on that last line.
But the sentiment remained. Micah was giving her in-

formation she could have surmised from the handful of interviews he'd done before her.

She was good at reading people through what they didn't say as much as through what they did. It was what made her so good at writing pop culture pieces. She could deduce what people wanted the public to know and what they didn't. So she narrowed in on what they didn't; there was almost always a story there.

There was definitely more to Micah's success than 'hard work and good luck'. It had something to do with both his charm and his ruthlessness. If he so much as got a whiff of the fact that she thought him ruthless though, he'd protest. He was trying much too hard to get her to believe he was a harmless domestic animal.

He was definitely a lion. Nothing else.

She particularly knew it because of the way he was circling around her family.

She refused to indulge him.

'Can we take a break?' he asked after they'd been talking for an hour. 'I'm starving.'

Since they'd covered a lot more than she thought they would on the first day, travelling, she said, 'Sure. Will we be eating Chef Gardner or Ike today?'

He smiled. 'You've done your research.'

'I'm insulted you thought otherwise.'

'Wouldn't want that,' he purred. 'I apologise.'

She stared. 'You aren't as charming as you think you are, you know.'

His eyelashes fluttered. She mentally patted herself on the back for surprising him.

'I have no idea what I did to deserve that.'

'Of course you don't. You're on, all the time. It means you don't have time to reflect. Probably,' she added in the unlikely event that she was wrong.

His jaw tightened. 'Presumptuous.'

He wasn't trying to hide that he didn't like that comment. It was the first authentic reaction she'd seen from him—the first one that wasn't an acceptable reaction—and it made her heart thud.

'Journalists presume until they don't have to,' she said.

'Journalists?' There was a deliberate pause. 'Or heiresses?'

When threatened, a lion would attack. Micah had done just that to the elephant in the room.

An uncomfortable ripple went through her, but she was saved from replying when the flight attendant came in and took their orders for food. She was going to be eating steak on a plane, which was the kind of food she'd forgotten about eating on a plane since her parents had divorced. Her life had changed then.

If only it had changed enough for her to stop trying to please her unpleasant father.

'You're offended,' he commented after the flight attendant left. His expression was smooth again, as if he hadn't shown he was human minutes earlier.

'You implied my talents were a result of having a rich family.' She paused. 'You implied other journalists wouldn't have those talents unless they come from a rich family.'

'You're offended on behalf of other people?'

'It's called empathy. It's what makes me a damn good writer.'

And person.

She'd worked hard at that after her parents had all but abandoned her after the divorce. Granted, they hadn't been model parents before. Her mother had always been distant; her father an unyielding presence. That didn't stop her from trying to get their approval. Their love. A normal task for any child; a useless task for her. Her mother was travelling the world, living as though she had no child. Which was…fair. For all intents and purposes, Helen John *did* have no children. And Elena had no mother.

As for her father… Things were more complicated with him. The fact that he wanted her to marry someone for the sake of his business proved it. Especially when 'wanted' was a tame word to describe Cliff John's demands.

But indulging family issues wasn't professional.

'I…er… I shouldn't have said that,' she said.

Emotion flickered in his eyes. She had no idea what that emotion was, or why it felt dangerous. Alluring.

'I shouldn't have mentioned your family.'

'I'd appreciate it if you refrained from mentioning them again.'

The dangerous, alluring emotion flickered again. It gave her the distinct impression she was being toyed with. Everything inside her went on alert.

'Things aren't what they seem in the John family, then?'

She took a moment. Leaned forward. 'If you want to do this, Micah, you better be ready to do this. Because if my family isn't off-limits, neither is yours.'

A challenge.

Micah thought he'd learnt everything he needed to know about Elena during the interview portion of their conversation. She was sharp, insightful, compassionate. He wouldn't have thought her combative though. But how else could he interpret her challenge?

A fair response to you pushing the issue of her family?

That might have been it. Beyond wanting to know more about the John empire, he had no real reason to keep pushing. Did he *want* to provoke her, then? And if so, wasn't it fair for her to respond in kind? Except she wouldn't be able to if he didn't reveal how much of a sensitive topic his family was. He needed to pull back before he did.

This was part of why he never wanted to engage with people on more than simply a surface level. He didn't want to talk about his parents, or the distance they'd put into their relationship with him. He certainly didn't want to talk about his efforts to breach that distance. Efforts that had failed over and over again.

It made putting effort into any other relationship too exhausting to contemplate. So he didn't. Which wasn't entirely a problem since people who wanted relationships wanted to be engaged on more than a surface level. Even those who claimed they didn't want that. The women he dated always said they were fine with what he offered—at the beginning. As the months went by and he continued to dedicate himself to his business, to his relationship with his parents, they would express unhappiness. Eventually, they left. He no longer believed them when they said they wanted what he could give.

But he believed Elena. Believed that she would dig deeper into his family if he didn't stop her now. He couldn't afford to be intrigued by her. She might have been a puzzle of emotions he couldn't solve, but she was dangerous. He couldn't keep trying to put the pieces together, especially when he didn't have the full picture to work from. She wouldn't provide her picture, and he wouldn't provide his, and they would get along fine.

Why did that feel like a lie?

'I've already told you about my family,' he said, keeping his voice steady.

'You were "raised by a single mother, a lawyer with her own firm, and saw your father on occasion",' she recited. Tilted her head. 'Is that right?'

The side of his mouth tilted up. 'Yes.'

'That's what all the other articles about you said, too.' She pretended to examine her nails. 'It would be great to go into more detail. What was it like having a mother with her own law firm? Was it challenging? Inspiring? Did her success affect her relationship with your father? Did it affect yours?'

'Good,' he said after a beat. 'Great, in fact. Get all these questions out now, in the plane, so that when we get to Italy we don't have to waste time going through them.'

Her lips curved. 'Not fun, is it?'

It took him a moment. 'That was a trap.'

'It was and it wasn't,' she said easily. 'I would love to have that information for the article. But I also understand that you don't want it in the public realm. Because of my *empathy*.'

He studied her. Saw both triumph and sincerity on her face. She was slippery. Smart, too. He wasn't sure if he liked the combination. No—he wasn't sure what it meant that he *did* like the combination.

He didn't dwell on it. He needed to figure out what to do about her curiosity first. He didn't want to tell her the truth about his family. What would his parents say if they were included in an article about him? Would they even care?

His father had a brand-new family. Well, not new any more. His baby sister was twenty and his brother, seventeen. Regardless, his father had other things to worry about than what his thirty-two-year-old son said about him. Back when his father had had him, the idea of legitimacy still mattered. That was how his father had treated him. Like a mistake he didn't have to validate except on the rare occasion, when his guilt got the better of him.

And his mother? His mother would…not read the paper. She worked, hard, and that gave her little to no time for leisure. Elena had hit it on the head; his mother running her own law firm was both challenging and inspiring. But it was the inspiring part that mattered most. Perhaps, if he said something like that, Elena wouldn't speculate. And if his mother did ever see this, there would be no reason for her to be upset.

'Fine.' His tone was reluctant. Annoyed. He could see it in her smile. He cleared his throat. Hoped it cleared the emotion he didn't need her seeing. 'I'll answer one of your questions. We won't talk about family again after this.'

He didn't expect the agreement he got.

'Really?' he asked. 'It's that easy?'

'It's that easy,' she replied. There was nothing but sincerity in her tone now. 'I'm writing an article about you. I'm shadowing you for the next seven days to do so. None of that will work without a bit of give and take. From both of us.'

Those last words were heavy with implication. He barely refrained from rolling his eyes.

'We're in agreement, then. Family is off-limits?'

'Between me and you, yes,' she said brightly. 'I still want to offer my readers a good article.'

She'd told him he wasn't as charming as he thought; what would she think if he told her she was more charming than she could ever believe?

He stiffened at the thought. Told himself to get a grip. He was getting distracted from his plan. Elena herself— her personality, her looks, all of her—had already caused him to trip on some of the steps. But he would keep his goal in mind. That meant thinking clearly, strategically. No distractions.

'My mother is incredibly successful,' he said, keeping it concise. 'She worked hard, and was ready for the opportunities that came her way. That's what she taught me, too. To work hard and be ready. I did, and I was.'

'With Killian Leather and The Perfume Company?' she asked, naming the two clients he'd signed in the last year. Two of his biggest clients, who were part of the reason he'd been named Businessperson of the Year.

'Exactly.'

'She sounds like she inspired you.'

He tensed, but answered. 'She did.'

'Wonderful, thanks.' She switched off the phone he hadn't even realised she'd put on again. 'That was great.'

He nodded. Slowly let out the air that had been accumulating in his lungs. He'd survived it. He'd survived talking about his mother. Elena seemed content with his answer, which was great. She wouldn't ask any more. Or was he being naïve, believing her? He wasn't sure he would believe anyone else. But Elena was genuine in a way the other journalists he'd talked with hadn't been.

What if that was wishful thinking?

A sigh distracted him.

'What?' he asked.

'I can almost taste the steak.' She sank down in her chair, closing her eyes. Her hair pushed forward, framing her face with thousands of curly strands. 'I'm going out on a limb here, but I bet there'll be fries with it. Maybe a mushroom sauce.' She looked at him. 'Am I right?'

He lifted a finger of one hand and picked up his phone with the other. He relayed Elena's suggestions to the chef, who grumbled as neither had been on his menu. But he agreed. Micah did pay him a significant amount of money for that agreement.

'Yes, you're right,' he said when he was done.

'You didn't have to do that.'

'What's the point of having a private chef when you can't do that?'

'It's so…privileged, isn't it?'

She spoke thoughtfully, giving him a clue that he shouldn't give the startled laugh he wanted to.

'I'm sorry,' he said after a moment. 'I have no idea how to respond to that.'

'You aren't that out of touch that you don't know people don't live like this.' She gestured around them.

'Of course not. I used to be one of those people.'

Her pensive expression deepened. 'Not entirely though. I can't imagine the mother that owned a law firm left you struggling in your life.'

'A lot of my mother's money went back into the firm.'

'Are you saying you grew up poor?'

'No, I'm not,' he answered immediately. 'And since I seem to be speaking to a reporter, let me clarify: all of this is off the record.'

She lifted her hands in surrender.

'I didn't grow up poor,' he said. 'I had enough. My needs were more than fulfilled.'

'But?'

'But…my wants weren't.'

He wasn't talking financially, though it was true. He hadn't ever had the courage to ask his mother for something he wanted. He didn't want to be a nuisance or a burden. He made do with what she gave him, even when it meant he didn't have the things he wanted. He couldn't exactly complain about that when he had everything he needed, could he?

'Your wants involved a private plane? Private chefs?'

'Elena,' he interrupted when she opened her mouth to add something else to his list of faults. 'Is there a reason you're interrogating me like this? I try to use my money in a way that makes me as efficient as I can be. I also spend a significant portion of that money trying to help other people. I have no doubt we'll speak about that in depth in the coming week. So, why are you judging me?'

'I'm not judging you.' She shook her head. 'This is all just…familiar. But at the same time, it's not. It's like déjà vu, except in reverse. This has happened to me before, and I remember that it did, but I can't… I *don't*…feel like it's real.'

Faint lines appeared between her brows. It was adorable. It was concerning that he found it adorable.

'You don't live a life of luxury any more?' He didn't expect her expression to turn to stone. 'Wait—you don't live like an heiress?'

'No.' She straightened. It was as effective as her putting up a shield. 'I gave up the private planes and chefs a while ago. I even left behind the gold cutlery, diamond plates, designer cell-phone covers.' Her eyes sparkled with challenge. 'It's been a tough transition, but somehow, I manage.'

He couldn't help the smile, but he didn't know what to say. The research his assistant had dug up on Elena seemed woefully inadequate now. Or did it? He hadn't gone through all of it. He hadn't had the time. But he'd read her entire portfolio. Noted her earlier articles weren't as good as her current ones. Her personal information hadn't seemed important to him. He wanted a path to her father, not a relationship. It was foolishly naïve of him not to realise the personal information would have given him a clue to whether she was the right path to her father.

In fact, now it seemed embarrassingly clear that she might not be in her father's good graces. She was an heiress to billions, yet she was working as a journalist for a newspaper. As many other people had, he'd thought this was a flight of fancy; an indulgence. But now he saw she needed the job. It was her livelihood. She loved it, clearly, but it made her sharpness, her growth, the offence she'd taken at him attributing skill to wealth more nuanced.

He wanted to know how that would affect his plans. But he also wanted to know why. Why was Elena supporting herself when her father could do so without feeling it?

He needed to read the rest of what his assistant had dug up on Elena. For research purposes. For his plan. That it would maybe answer his other questions about her was irrelevant. No, those *questions* were irrelevant. There was only the plan.

There could only be the plan.

CHAPTER THREE

ELENA WAS BEGINNING to realise Micah's intensity came in different forms. Amusement. Concern. Hesitance. Annoyance. She wanted to know what other forms there were. Would he be that intense in a romantic relationship? In a physical one? The thought turned her skin into gooseflesh. It was probably best not to examine why. Not that she needed to examine why. That was pretty clear.

She blew out a breath.

Entertaining her attraction to Micah was a bad idea. She knew it. Yet she still thought those inappropriate things about his intensity. And when he offered her the bed at the back of the plane to rest, she wanted to invite him to share it with her.

Maybe she had altitude sickness because she was on a plane. That was what that meant, right? She'd lost her ability to think clearly because of a lack of oxygen or something. Except she was still thinking clearly. She knew Micah's intensity was dangerous. His power was dangerous. Her father had both, and he used them without a thought of the consequences. Even if those consequences were people's lives. His daughter's life.

Marrying Jameson will ensure your security for the rest of your life. Even if, say, you happen to lose your job.

What he was really saying was that if she didn't marry

Jameson, she would lose her job. Her security. After her
father had used his money to control her for the first sixteen years of her life, she'd fought for her independence.
Her job and security came because of *her* efforts. They
had nothing to do with him. But she had no doubts he'd be
able to strip away the fruits of those efforts. He was powerful enough that if he wanted, Elena would lose the job
she loved. She would lose everything else she loved—her
house, her car, herself—too.

She tried not to judge herself too harshly for considering her father's proposal then. She hated that she was, but
she hated what would happen if she didn't give in, too. The
entire situation turned her stomach. A work trip to Italy
gave her the perfect excuse to escape the constant loop of
thinking about it. Or so she'd thought. She hadn't anticipated her reaction to Micah. She hadn't anticipated that he
would use the same tactics her father had to get her here.
But they were cut from the same cloth. If she allowed it,
that cloth would wrap around her face and suffocate her.

She stood. She was feeling too restless to sleep. She'd let
Micah have the bed for the next couple of hours, and she'd
get a start on transcribing the interview she and Micah had
had before the conversation had veered onto steak.

She slid through the doorway that separated the bedroom from the rest of the plane. Then she stopped. Micah
was there, pacing the length of the space. His shirt was
open from his neck to midway down his chest, as if he'd
started to change but had forgotten. He had papers in his
hand, and he looked down at them at various moments
during the pacing, his lips moving. He was clearly practising something. Based on the shirt, the way he ran his
hand over his face, practice was not going as he wanted.

'Do you want some help?'

He whirled around, his eyes wide, and Elena thought it might be the only time she'd see Micah unprepared.

'Holy smokes, you almost gave me a heart attack.'

'Holy smokes? *Holy smokes?*' She couldn't help the laugh. 'I thought you were, like, thirty? Thirty-year-olds don't say *holy smokes.*'

'I thought you were in your twenties,' he grumbled back. 'People in their twenties shouldn't wear unicorns.'

She looked down. Well, crap. She'd forgotten to change. She'd pulled on her favourite nightshirt when she climbed into bed. It was raggedy, admittedly, stretched so it fitted over her shoulders loosely, skimming her thighs. It was perfectly modest otherwise, and the vest top she wore under pressed her breasts to her chest so hopefully, they wouldn't give him an eyeful. She absolutely didn't want that.

She cleared her throat. 'Unicorns are a magical species that appear when you open yourself up to the possibility.'

There was the briefest pause.

'Are you saying I don't believe in unicorns so they've chosen not to appear to me?'

'I think that's a question you have to answer for yourself.'

Don't suffocate, her brain reminded her. Yes. Yes, that was important. Why did it feel as if she wanted to forget it?

'So—do you want me to help you practise whatever it is you're practising?'

'It's Italian. You wouldn't understand.'

'Oh, we're jumping right to the patronisation then.' She straightened from where she'd been leaning against the doorway. 'In that case, I guess you don't want my help.'

'No, wait.'

She hadn't moved. The fact that he thought she had—and how much power that implied she had—shimmered through her.

'Can you speak Italian?'

'I can, actually.'

'Seriously?'

'Micah, stop this. You're embarrassing yourself every time you underestimate me.' She walked to sit at the seat he'd been sitting in earlier, and curled her legs under her. 'Okay, first give me context.'

He lowered to the seat she'd been in earlier, bracing his forearms on his knees. 'I'm supposed to speak at this banquet once we arrive in Rome. It's in honour of our partnership with Vittoria, which is—'

'The handbag company there were whispers about you signing with. Congratulations. But please, continue.'

'Thank you.' But he gave her a *How did you know?* look. 'I have to say a couple of words. But my Italian is…basic. I had a translator help me, but I think I'm screwing up.'

She held out a hand for the paper he had, scanned through it when she got it.

'There's nothing wrong with this. It's quick, to the point. Passionate, even.'

'I don't want my speech to be passionate.'

'Relax. The Italians will love it.' She handed the paper back to him. 'I'm listening.'

And she did, without comment as he went through the quick, to the point, passionate words. By the end of it, she thought she might deserve a medal. He was butchering the longer words, words clearly unfamiliar to him, though the easier ones he went through seamlessly. She took the page again when he was done, ignoring his questions, and tried to fix some of the words that had seemed too complicated for him. When she gave it back, he sighed.

'I have to learn this now?'

'Only if you want to sound better than you currently do.' She shifted forward, putting her hands in her lap.

'You don't sound bad. Your peers will appreciate the effort, I'm sure.'

He gave her a dark look. 'You like having this kind of power over me.'

'Not over you, over everyone. Must be the wealthy world I lived in as a child.'

Now he pulled a face. It was all very animated. Too animated for the smooth, charming millionaire. He was clearly frustrated.

'Fine, I get it. I overstepped. No need to rehash it.'

'Man, you cannot take being wrong.'

'I wasn't—' He stopped himself. Lifted the pages. 'Thank you for this.'

'You're welcome,' she said sweetly. Didn't move. When he stared at her, she shrugged. 'You don't want me to help you?'

'I'll call you in an hour.'

'Why? Just practise in front of me. I'll help you if you need it as you go along.'

He shook his head, giving her a forced chuckle as he did. 'I'm not doing that.'

'Why not?'

'You're going to make fun of me.'

'Me?' She put a hand to her chest. 'I would never.'

He didn't reply. She shook her head.

'You're serious? Okay, I promise not to make fun of you. I swear I don't deserve having to tell you that, but there you go. You have my reassurances nevertheless.'

'This is a very different side to you.'

'I can say the same about you.'

She'd already thought that. As for herself… He was right. She was relaxing into her personality, despite her own warnings to keep her guard up. She needed to stay professional. She needed to keep herself safe.

'I don't like it.'

'My side, or yours?'

His look was wry. 'Both.'

The way that made her smile told her staying safe was going to be hard work.

Micah had no idea how he could pay attention to what she said when he was still trying to get over the unicorn. But it wasn't *really* the unicorn. It was the body beneath the unicorn. Her legs, long and full, brown and possibly the best thing he'd seen in his life. Her shoulders, visible through the stretched material of her nightshirt. She wore a strappy top beneath the shirt, so he wasn't treated to the breasts he somehow knew would be free if she were home. Though the rest of the shirt was loose and gave him nothing else of her body, his own reacted.

Tightened, tingled, made him feel like a damn teenager with all the need. And now she was teasing him, helping him, seeing through him.

Seeing through him.

He didn't like it. Any of it.

'I'll practise. Let's practise.'

She gave a satisfied nod, her eyes displaying the same mood, and she took his breath away. The surprise of it didn't help either. He hadn't ever responded this way to anyone. The women he dated were always the same type. The women who moved in his circles. There was nothing wrong with those women; they simply weren't who interested him. It was easy to stay unattached from women who didn't interest him.

He'd learned from his father that attachments would put him in situations he didn't want to be in. Micah was his father's attachment, after all.

Whatever this was with Elena needed to stop.

'Are you going to start?' she asked.

'Yeah. Yes.'

He cleared his throat. Started saying what was on the page. It felt better now. More natural. He had no idea how she'd even known what would feel more natural coming out of his mouth. But he was grateful. He was grateful for her patience as he messed up, more times than he cared to admit. He liked the way she teased him as she corrected him, how there was no malice in anything she said. She wasn't making fun of him; he'd conflated the ease with which she talked to him with that. Maybe because he didn't know what banter looked like. What ease looked like. What friendship looked like.

He stopped at that thought. Erased the memory of it from his mind. There was no friendship. No attraction. *Nothing.* Hadn't he just told himself why there couldn't be?

'That sounds pretty good,' Elena said after what felt like the millionth time they ran through it. 'When do you have to do this?'

'Tomorrow evening.'

'Then you have about thirty or so hours to practise.' She sat back in the chair. 'Plenty of time to sound like a natural second-language speaker.'

'Second language? Not first language?'

She wrinkled her nose. 'I can't perform miracles in such a short space of time, sorry.'

He bit the inside of his lip to keep from smiling. 'If you had more time though, right?'

'Exactly.' She smiled. 'Seriously, you sound fine. Everyone there will love you.'

'You should be there.'

Immediately after he said it, he wished he could take it back. But then he saw her face. She...glowed was the best way he could describe it. It was like being in a dark room and having someone suddenly put on a light.

'I will be. Though I don't have this event on my itinerary.'

'That's strange.' Since he hadn't had Serena put it on her itinerary, he was lying now, too. 'It should have been there.'

'Hmm.' She took a second. 'Well, then, if it should have been there…'

'I didn't realise you could speak Italian,' he added. 'It gives me another reason to have you there.'

'Another reason?' she asked. 'What's the first?'

'Er… I… You're writing a piece on me. Of course.' He swallowed. 'You should see this.'

'I will. I was just going to explore Rome anyway. It's my first time in Italy.'

'You speak Italian fluently and it's your first time?'

Her expression closed, shutting in the light along with it. 'I took it at school with some other languages. I thought I would need it for…' She trailed off.

'But you didn't?' he asked, even though it was clear what the answer would be.

'No.'

There was something so troubling in her tone that he didn't push. He wanted to. The fact that he did told him he was getting invested in…in *her*, he supposed. It wouldn't benefit either of them to continue down that path.

'We're landing soon,' he said. Smoothly, because he didn't care about troubling emotions.

'Oh. Okay.'

She looked lost for a moment. Vulnerable. He shifted his weight between his legs. Reminded himself that he didn't care.

He didn't care. He didn't care. He didn't care.

'I'll…er… I'll get changed.' She stood and walked towards the back of the plane.

You don't care. You don't care. You don't care.

'Are you all right?' he blurted out. Because he did care. No matter how much he wanted to believe otherwise. No matter how confused he was by it.

She stopped, only looking over her shoulder.

'Of course. I'm always all right.'

With that, she disappeared into the bedroom. Again, he told himself that he didn't care. This time, it was because she'd lied to him.

CHAPTER FOUR

As a rule, Elena tried not to be miserable in the morning. When her parents divorced, her father sent her to boarding school immediately. She'd fast learnt the value of mornings then. They were the only time of day she had in silence.

Her first year, she'd spent thinking about what she'd done wrong. Her father wouldn't have sent her away because of the divorce. She'd had nothing to do with that. It had nothing to do with *her*. Besides, she didn't bother her parents when she was home. Her efforts before—the tea or coffee she'd brought them; the baking she'd done; the dinners she'd made—had received ambivalent reactions at best, annoyance at worst. She was doing what the staff did. Did she expect recognition for that?

No, she'd expected love.

But as she'd grown older she'd realised that wasn't the way to go. She'd shifted gears. Tried to excel at school, or in extracurricular activities, because those were things people noticed. If people noticed, her parents would be more likely to notice, too. Maybe they would finally be proud of her. They hadn't been. Though she'd come close, once, with her father. She'd 'bested' one of his business rivals' children by passing her school year at the top of her grade. She'd carried around the approval he'd shown in that brief moment when she'd told him for years.

She suspected recreating that moment motivated all her future efforts to please him. Like considering a marriage that would stifle her.

It was silly. She knew it. His approval had come shortly before he shipped her off to boarding school without any reasons. It meant nothing. His punishment, however, could irrevocably change her life. That was what could happen if she refused to get engaged. That was what *had* happened after the divorce, when she'd finally realised, courtesy of an innocent comment from a schoolmate, she was being sent away because she looked like her mother.

Her father wasn't punishing her; he was punishing her mother. Or maybe he was punishing her, too, because she reminded him of his failure. That was how people like her father thought. Relationships were either successful or they failed. For reasons completely outside the effort they put into the person they were in a relationship with or the relationship itself.

Micah probably thought that way, too. It was a good reminder. She couldn't let how adorably insecure he'd been with his speech ingratiate him with her heart.

Elena took a deep breath and tried to stay in the present. It was early, the sun just lighting the sky, and she was standing in front of St Peter's Square, staring. She didn't have any desire to do anything but stare. Or simply *be*.

The Vatican wasn't first on the list of what she wanted to see in Italy, but she had been walking and stopped because of the peace and quiet. The early hour meant she'd beat out most of the tourists. As she walked to the square, pigeons scurried around, searching for food. They did so in the square as well, more of them, and that was the most activity in the place.

Elena walked between the stone pillars on the outer boundary of the square, wondering why they called it that when it was technically a circle. She imagined what it would be like when the Pope celebrated Mass there. She wandered aimlessly from one side of the square to the other. She took pictures, thinking about who she'd show them to. There were people in her life. People at the newspaper, mostly. Proximity friends.

It had been the same at school. Real friendships were hard work. Harder for someone like her. She'd experienced, more than once, people wanting to be her friend because of who she was. Those who didn't know her background almost always changed once they realised it. Once they realised she had money. When she started to refuse her father's money—it came at too high a cost—they treated her differently because now she had none. Kind of like how Micah had treated her once he realised she didn't live with her father's money.

Was that what he did?

She refused to dwell on the answer to that. She was in Italy. For work, yes, but this *being* wasn't work. She had the morning free because, according to Micah's itinerary, he had a business meeting until lunch. Most of the itinerary she received were hours blocked out for business meetings, actually. Which was fine. She didn't expect them to hang out as if they were *friends*.

But she did wonder why he wanted her in Italy if he was only going to spend meals with her. They could have done that in South Africa. She knew why the newspaper had agreed to send her to Italy though. She could watch him take over the world first-hand and take readers on that journey, too. It would hopefully lead to a boost in sales for the edition, which would make up the expenses of sending her on a seven-day trip to Italy.

Micah must have got involved to get the higher-ups to agree to that length of time. Most profiles, if they involved some sort of shadowing, were two or three days long. Why Micah got involved at all had been a question to her. She had her answer now. He wanted her to write about him because she was a John.

It couldn't be as simple as that, she knew. Still, she was intrigued by him. From a purely professional perspective. It was part of why she had woken up early that morning. She'd hoped to have breakfast with him, to ask him questions about his charity work, so she could get started on her article if she was bored. She had missed him, which didn't seem like a loss now that she was exploring. She certainly wasn't bored. In fact, she wanted to see more. And as she thought it, she noticed a group of passengers getting on a sightseeing bus some distance away.

She hurried towards them, but the bus had left by the time she got there. A couple of conversations later though, she had her own ticket to a different sightseeing bus. It was leaving in thirty minutes, so she ducked into a café while waiting. It was busy, clearly a place both tourists and residents visited. When she asked for a recommendation on a café speciality, she was offered hot chocolate. Literal, melted hot chocolate. By the end of it, she was convinced she was meant to live near a place that served the drink.

After a leisurely morning of sightseeing, she got off at a stop closest to where she was supposed to meet Micah for lunch. Or so she thought. Apparently, Rome had two streets named the same about thirty minutes from one another, and so she was thirty minutes late. She stumbled into the restaurant hot and sweaty.

'Oh, my word, I am so sorry.'

She wiped a hand over her forehead as she slid into the chair opposite Micah. He was watching her over his glass of champagne, looking cool and calm. Of course he looked cool and calm. He'd been in this air-conditioned restaurant for at least half an hour. She, on the other hand, must have looked like a troll. Maybe the look would have worked, had she had bright hair. But her boring brown hair would make her look like a troll without the mitigating cuteness.

'You're mad, aren't you?' she asked when he didn't reply. 'I'm sorry. I was on a bus, and I got off at the wrong stop, then I had to take a taxi to get here, which was ridiculously expensive, by the way, and—'

'Why didn't you just take the car I sent for you?' he interrupted her, his eyebrow quirking in a way she wouldn't have thought sexy on anyone else.

'The car? What car?'

'I sent a car to the hotel.'

'Ah.' A waiter arrived and poured her a glass of water. He disappeared as mysteriously. Or maybe not. She was too busy drinking the water to notice. 'That would have entailed being at the hotel, and, as I said, I was on a bus.'

'A bus.'

'Yes. Sightseeing,' she added brightly. 'It was wonderful seeing the city. The Colosseum is as gorgeous in real life as it is in pictures. From the outside, at least. I didn't see the inside because I didn't want to be late to this although I am now and what would it have mattered?'

'Elena,' he asked after a pause. 'Are you…uncomfortable by any chance?'

'I…' She faltered. Pressed a hand to her chest when she realised there was, indeed, a flutter of nerves congregating there. 'How did you know?'

His lips twitched. 'A hunch.'

She thought back over the last few minutes. 'Oh. It's because I was talking so much. Hmm. You're perceptive.' She emptied her glass of water before continuing. She was already speaking when the waiter refilled it and disappeared again. 'I hate being late. I hate contravening anything considered to be polite. Politeness was drilled into me for eighteen years. From the moment I was born, I'm sure, until I left school.'

'It sounds exhausting.'

His eyes were kinder than she'd seen before. Maybe that was why she said, 'It was. But it was part of being a John.'

'What happened when you left school?'

She barked out a laugh. 'A lot. This isn't about me, though I know you prefer it that way.' She let that linger. 'How was your meeting?'

He smiled, but not in a friendly way. It was satisfactory or knowing. It was also possibly both or something else entirely. The effect it had on her was distracting her from being able to tell. There was a fluttering in her chest and her skin was clammy. But then, she'd been late, and it was hot. Why did it increase after Micah smiled? She had no idea. She was considering an engagement to someone else. She shouldn't be noticing other men's smiles.

But she was. The wrong man's smile, because Micah wasn't a good match. He was too powerful, too intense, too distractingly handsome for her. It didn't matter though. What she felt for him was more than she'd ever felt for Jameson. Even though their marriage would be purely in name, that didn't sit right with her. Nor did the thought that Jameson would likely sate his physical needs with women outside their marriage. Heaven knew she didn't want to sleep with him, but she doubted he would be discreet about his relationships. How would that affect her as his wife?

'It went well,' he said, interrupting her panic. 'It was with the executive board of Vittoria. Just to iron out some details about the way forward.'

She waited as he gestured to the waiter, gave an order for a wine she would die to taste, before she asked her question.

'What does it feel like to be so successful in your thirties?'

She'd taken out her phone, pressed record while she'd been waiting for him to finish with the waiter.

'It feels…like a challenge.' He shrugged when she looked at him. 'It wasn't easy to gain success. It took ten years of eighteen-hour days, seven days a week. Most of the time, I pushed to see if I could. Now, of course, there's the pressure to continue being successful. Otherwise, I'm a fluke. It's a challenge.'

She leaned forward. 'That light in your eyes tells me you're up for it.'

Now his smile was catlike. 'I wouldn't be who I am, where I am, if I weren't.' There was a short pause. 'When people say "Do what you love and you'll never work a day in your life", I laugh. *Anything* you spend a significant amount of time on is work. Be that in your professional or personal life. The key is that when you find something you love doing, you won't mind putting in the work.' He sat back. 'Is that a good enough soundbite?'

She switched off her phone and mirrored his position. 'It would be an excellent soundbite—if I needed one. I don't. I'm writing about you.'

He narrowed his eyes. 'You know what I mean.'

She smiled. 'I do. But it's nice to see someone so easily confident get annoyed.'

'I wasn't annoyed.'

'I know.' But she smiled. Just in case it would annoy him.

He tilted his head, then shook it and laughed. 'You're something else, Elena.'

And you like it.

She startled herself. Those words were on the tip of her tongue. It sounded like…like *flirting*. She wasn't a flirt though. She chose her words carefully to avoid being one. Except in Micah's presence, apparently. Then, she spoke freely, and damn if that freedom didn't make her feel good.

'I took the liberty of discussing a menu for us with the chef, by the way,' Micah said. 'I thought it might be nice for you to experience full Italian dining.'

'Chefs must *love* you,' she said with a small laugh. 'Honestly, you realise you're not the only patron in this…'

She trailed off when she realised they were, indeed, alone.

He kept his eyes on her face as she realised it was only the two of them in the room. When she met his gaze, her confusion had the butterflies in his stomach scattering as if a stone had been thrown at them.

'There's no one here,' she said.

'I'm aware.'

She looked around again. What did she see? Sophistication in the wooden floors and accents throughout the restaurant? Class in the white and brown lines of the wallpaper on one of the walls, the brown and white paint on the others? Did she see romance in the white tablecloths, the candles adorning them? Or was it homeliness in the green leaves spilling over pot plants at strategic places; the framed pictures of the Italian family who'd created this wonderful place?

He'd seen all of it when he'd walked in an hour ago. He could do nothing about the décor, but he'd contemplated the candles. It was a warm summer's day outside. Why else would she think they needed candles?

For light, a voice in his head told him. He hadn't asked for the candles; they illuminated the darkness inside the restaurant. It wasn't overwhelmingly dark, but enough so that the candles were needed. He was probably being overly sensitive. He didn't need a waiter to tell him that. So he said nothing. Except now, as she looked around, he thought he should have.

'Two things,' she asked, her gaze meeting his.

He agreed with a nod. He couldn't speak because he was afraid of what his voice would sound like. Spellbound by how he'd just noticed the brown of her eyes were lined with some magical make-up thing. It made her eyes sparkle. It turned him into an idiot who indulged fantastical thoughts.

'One: do you own this place?'

'No.'

'Okay, then, two: did you do this for me?'

'I did it for us.' He stood now, walking to the bar where the waiter was standing and trying to be inconspicuous as he readied their wine. 'This place is usually closed this time of day, especially in the summer. I pulled some strings so we could have…lunch.'

He almost said privacy. That would have sounded dodgy. Luckily, the waiter offered him the wine to try. He went through the motions of tasting it, though it was one of his favourites and he didn't need to. With a nod of his head, Micah moved to Elena and offered her the glass. She did the same thing he had, but her eyes didn't leave his. He had no idea how drinking from the same glass could be erotic, but it was. Especially when Elena brought the glass to her lips, parted them, and he got the quickest glimpse of her tongue.

His blood got heavy, his skin grew tight, and heat spread through his body as if a fire had been lit inside him. Elena didn't help one bit. She was still staring at him with her beautiful brown eyes, her hair wild around her face, her lips red again, the colour mixing with the wine. The glass she offered him now had the trace of her lipstick on it, and it was the sexiest damn thing.

'Do you like it?' he asked, accepting the glass. It still had the tiniest bit of liquid in it, and he gave in to temptation by drinking it.

He placed his mouth on the outline of her lips.

'Yes.' Her voice was throaty. It did strange things to his body. 'Very much.'

The left side of his mouth lifted, and he lingered for much longer than he should have. But she was a magnet, and he was attracted to her, and he wanted, no, needed, to be as close to her as possible. Slowly, he turned around and walked to the bar.

'We're happy with this,' he told the waiter softly. The man gave him a knowing look, but it was gone before Micah could say something about it. All that was left was cool professionalism. Micah needed to follow his lead.

'Shall I get the starters ready, sir?'

'Please.'

He took the two glasses of wine the waiter poured to the table, offering Elena hers before settling in his chair.

'How was the sightseeing today?'

'You're deflecting,' she replied.

'From what?' he asked, because he was deflecting, but he didn't think she'd be straightforward about the chemistry that had happened between them.

Did chemistry happen? Or was it something two people experienced? Either way, they had it, they experienced it, and Micah wasn't happy about it. He had a plan. She was part of those plans. Except…suddenly that didn't feel right any more.

Maybe he *was* deflecting. Maybe he was deflecting so much he couldn't even tell what he was deflecting from.

'The fact that we're alone. You don't have to impress me.'

'I know.' Relief made him say the words with a smile. 'If it makes you feel any better, I had the restaurant for the meeting before this lunch, too.' He hadn't. This had been entirely for her, but he couldn't admit it now. She was entirely too observant and after the chemistry? He couldn't admit the truth, even though he hated lying.

'Really?' Did she deflate? Was he projecting? 'No wonder it went well, then.'

'It's part of it, I'm sure. Now, would you tell me about your day?'

She narrowed her eyes, as if she couldn't trust his interest in her. He was offended. Partly because she was right to distrust him—his plan included getting her comfortable with him. But that wasn't the reason he asked. He wanted to know about her day.

It disturbed him, the intensity he felt in that desire. He couldn't remember ever being interested in knowing about someone's day. Days seemed so mundane. When he spoke, even during small talk when things were supposed to be mundane, he asked about events. Events had purposes. The same couldn't be said for days. Wanting to know about Elena's day, wanting to know with an intensity? It rightfully worried him.

It didn't stop him from being engrossed in her descriptions.

'I don't know, Micah. I guess it could be because I haven't travelled in such a long time. Or that I'm here, one of the places I always wanted to visit.' The small smile on her face was an intimate glimpse into her mind. He tried to memorise it. 'It's wonderful. Every single thing. Even the pigeon who tried to bite my finger off when I tried to pet it.'

'You tried to pet a pigeon?'

Her cheeks pinkened. 'I know, I know. I got caught up in the magic!' she exclaimed, lifting her hands in front of her. Then she laughed. 'When I was standing in front of the Trevi Fountain, I was the main character of a fairy tale. I would have sung, if I could. Instead, I tried to pet a bird.' She laughed again, but this time, buried her face into her hands. 'I am such a dork.'

'Yes, you are.' When she looked up long enough to stick her tongue out at him, he laughed. 'I like it, Elena. It's…refreshing.'

'Well, then, if it's refreshing.'

And she rolled her eyes. Damn if that wasn't refreshing, too.

CHAPTER FIVE

HAD SHE THOUGHT she was in a fairy tale before? She must have been confused. Standing in front of a beautiful fountain, seeing people throw coins into it and make wishes was magical, yes. But getting ready for a fancy event, a dress waiting for her in her room along with fairies who did hair and make-up? It was something from her past. So far in her past she found it surreal.

She caught her breath at the elegant black gown. The material was soft and glossy, simple and sophisticated. Micah intended on her wearing it as it was, she was sure, but she had the perfect necklace to go with it. It was bright and African, the yellow, black, red and green of it mixing in a pattern perfectly representing her home. Her make-up and hair were flawless, and when she looked at herself in the mirror, she barely recognised the woman looking back at her.

It had been over a decade since she'd felt so luxurious.

She took a deep breath, pushed back the memories that were still coated with pain. Looked in the mirror again. She wouldn't be the woman missing a life where she had never been enough. Contemplating a life where the things that fulfilled her were gone, regardless of what she decided to do about marrying Jameson. She would be the woman looking back at her. The African princess from some fairy tale she'd created in her mind. For one night, she could forget the rest and be that woman.

She felt like that woman when she walked into the passage of the hotel and found Micah waiting for her.

His eyes widened, and his lips parted to such an extent that she wondered if it counted as his jaw dropping. Colour flooded his skin. She didn't think he realised it, or knew that he was clenching and unclenching the hand that hung at his side. His other hand was in his pocket, and she would have bet everything she had that he was clenching his fist there, too.

He wasn't the only one stunned by the other's looks, though she hoped she was controlling her response more than he was. She would forgive herself if she wasn't. Every fairy-tale princess needed a dashing counterpart and damn if he didn't provide the perfect one.

He'd shaved since their lunch. Got his hair cut, too. It made his face look more angular, his cheekbones more visible, that jaw more defined. His tuxedo accentuated every line of his body—which was magnificent, the muscles and softness she thought he might be a combination of. She would never know without touching him, and suddenly she understood what Micah's fingers curling and uncurling meant. He was fighting against reaching out and touching her. Now, she was doing the same.

Her heart pumped a little harder, more erratically.

'You look…' He trailed off before looking at her. The intensity was there, and this time she knew it was admiration, and maybe desire. 'I don't even have the words for it, if I'm honest.'

'I'd accept nice,' she said, her fingers curling around the yellow clutch she'd stuffed her lipstick and phone into. The latter was for recording the evening's events. And ignoring the calls from her father's office. She hadn't made her decision yet. He would have to wait.

'You don't look nice though.'

She gave a surprised laugh. 'I think you're supposed to pretend, at the very least.'

'No. No,' he said again. 'I meant you look…more than nice.'

Her laugh was more genuine this time. 'Thank you.'

His smile was sheepish. 'I told you I didn't have the words.'

'But you have the smile. And the general look of a man who likes what he sees. It's enough.'

Their gazes locked, lingered. She felt something intimate crawl up her spine. Her skin turned to gooseflesh in response.

'I bought you a plain dress for a reason,' he said softly, taking a step closer. 'I should have known you would take something plain and turn it into something magnificent.'

'You should have,' she whispered. 'It's exactly what I intend on doing with the story I write about you.'

He grinned. It was free, unrestrained. *Sexy.* She'd never seen him smile that way before. She felt as if she were seeing her dress for the first time again—that admiration, that longing—but more intense. As if she'd seen a million of those dresses at the same time. She had no idea what was happening to her, but she didn't care. She only cared about this man. The way he looked at her. The way he made her feel.

It wasn't how Jameson and her father made her feel. Small, vulnerable. Coerced. She'd met Jameson the day her father had called her to his office, outlining his plans for her life as if she had no say in it. Jameson had simply sat there, giving her a smile that was self-satisfied, though she was sure he thought he offered comfort. Her lungs had

tightened. Her head had swirled. And she'd had to summon every ounce of strength to say she'd think about it. A
month later, she was still thinking about it. Her time was
running out, as her father's phone calls indicated.

But now, with Micah, everything felt different. Time
was endless. She didn't feel small, and the vulnerability
she was experiencing was *powerful*. She knew she had a
choice here, standing in front of him. And that she'd made
a mistake when she'd said he was just like her father.

He was more dangerous than her father. He made her
feel strong. Desirable. Like a woman who wouldn't allow
herself to be strong-armed into sacrificing her freedom
for someone who wouldn't do the same for her.

'Micah,' she whispered, stuck in his gaze.

She all but felt him touching her. Her imagination made
her shiver at the contact. She could only guess what would
happen if he really did touch her.

'I know.'

He moved closer to her. Then swiftly, suddenly, she
was pinned against the wall between his arms.

Micah was well aware that he was seducing Elena. He
was as aware that it was a mistake. He had asked Serena
to resend him Elena's personal information. In it had been
plenty of clues to the state of her relationship with her father. Where she lived, how she lived. None of it came as
a surprise after their conversations. What *did* come as
a surprise was that she was about to announce her engagement. In a lavish party the day after they returned
to South Africa.

As soon as he read it, he wanted to speak with her. Demand to know if it was the truth. But a cursory Internet
search told him it was. It was the talk of every gossip site
in South Africa. The elite of the elite had been invited. It

soured his mood. Clung to his body as he got ready for a banquet he didn't feel like going to. Got heavier when he realised he shouldn't feel this way at all. He hardly knew the woman.

Then he saw her in her dress, and all rational thought flew from his mind, leaving only emotion. A possessiveness he only now recognised as the cause of his dark mood demanded he make her see that there was something between them. He fought against it, had managed enough to give her some harmless compliments. To tease. But something changed in her gaze, in her body, and fighting was no longer working.

Now they were pressed together against a wall.

There had been space between their bodies when he'd moved her there; there was none now. She arched against him, aligning their bodies so that he could feel how her breath was leaving her lungs in short, quick puffs. So she could feel how having her delightful, curvaceous body against his made him feel.

He didn't give a single damn.

'Elena,' he whispered, tracing the lips that she had painted red again. It made her lipstick smudge, and he had to resist the urge to press his mouth against the shadows of red. 'What are you doing to me?'

'Nothing.' Her hand touched his hip tentatively. Then her fingers sank into his flesh. It didn't matter that there were two layers of clothing between his skin and her hand. He felt the contact. Worried that he'd always feel the contact. 'I can't do anything to you, Micah.'

He stiffened, but didn't move. Couldn't move. He would despise himself for it later—for seducing her, for touching her, when she was someone else's—but he was caught in a spell. A curse. A curse that made the first woman he'd ever felt this way about be unavailable.

'Do you love him?'

She frowned. 'Who?'

'The man you're getting engaged to. St Clair.'

Her lashes fluttered seconds before the vulnerability that had been in her eyes when he'd first touched her disappeared. The heiress was back. He was a hundred per cent certain that the heiress wasn't who she was any more, but she was there nevertheless. She was there when she'd first boarded that plane, and she was here now.

It wouldn't have bothered him so much if he didn't know she wasn't the heiress. If he didn't know the heiress only came out when she felt threatened. He made her feel *threatened*.

He took a step back.

'I'm sorry. I shouldn't have…' He shook his head.

'No, I'm sorry. I just…' Her voice faded. She lifted a hand to her forehead, obscuring her gaze. 'You caught me off guard.'

'Because you're getting engaged.'

'Yes. No. I… I haven't decided yet.'

'You haven't—' He broke off. 'What the hell does that mean?'

When she looked at him, her gaze was dangerously blank. 'It means your background check didn't tell you everything.'

'I didn't need a background check. It's all over the Internet.'

Colour seeped from her face. 'What?'

She fumbled with her clutch purse, took out her phone, typed in hard, quick movements. He hadn't thought it possible, but she went paler as she read. Having just experienced the shock himself—though heaven only knew why *she* was shocked—he took a step forward. Her head snapped up, and the fire there kept him from moving any closer.

'You didn't know?' he asked carefully.

'That I'm announcing an engagement I haven't decided on when I get back? No,' she said in a cold voice. 'I didn't.'

CHAPTER SIX

HE WAS ON EDGE. He shouldn't have drunk all that coffee before his big speech. Then he remembered that he hadn't drunk any coffee that day. It wasn't caffeine making him jittery, but the entire incident with Elena. Her reaction had been…disturbing. Or maybe it was just nerves about his upcoming speech.

Yes, nerves. Not Elena.

He ordered a bottle of water at the bar and, when it arrived, guzzled it down like a man dying of thirst. It would make him need the bathroom, and was likely not a good idea, but he had to do something. He hadn't been this nervous since he'd…

Since he'd pitched his business to his mother.

Oh, great. This was exactly what he needed. A reminder of the woman who never thought he was good enough for anything, let alone a speech. He blew out a breath. That was a tad melodramatic. His mother thought he was a perfectly okay human being. She treated him as she would anyone else.

That had been a big part of his problem as a kid. He was *her* kid; he didn't want her to treat him as she would anyone else. But he hadn't realised that until one day, when he'd been nine or so, and she'd dragged him along to some benefit. It had only happened once in his life—she had no one to babysit him and even she wouldn't leave a nine-year-old alone—probably because she'd learnt her lesson and had back-up babysitters for her back-up babysitters. In any case, he'd gone with her, sat quietly at her table because he was so damn glad to spend time with her that he wouldn't do anything else, and watched her.

She'd smiled. At so many of her clients. She'd chatted and laughed and had turned into a person he hadn't recognised. And he realised what was wrong with their relationship: he hadn't given her an incentive to care about him. He was just her kid. She didn't love his father, or want a kid, so no wonder she didn't want him. But if he made her care? If he was important enough to make her care? Yeah, that would change things.

It had taken him two and a half decades to do it, but he finally had. Tonight was merely the beginning. One part of his plan to get his mother to notice him. Though the memories were painful, he needed them, and he was glad to have them.

So why was it Elena's face he sought in the crowd? Why did he feel confident and at ease because he looked at her? His mother was supposed to be his inspiration. Hell, he'd even take his father. What did it mean that Elena had burrowed her way into that plan?

Why did he feel guilty about the plans that involved her? And torn by the emotions he felt about her?

He set it aside and focused on his speech, which garnered him a rousing applause. He worked the crowd as he'd learnt to do over the years, before he realised Elena had disappeared. He gestured to Serena, told her to find Elena and bring her to him, and minutes later, she was at his side.

'Have you met Elena John, Lucca?' he said to the man he was speaking to from the executive committee for Vittoria. 'She's the reason I could deliver that speech this evening.'

Lucca exclaimed in delight. There were a few seconds of rapid conversation in Italian that he could barely follow, and then they were both laughing.

'Lucca says I should have let you make a fool of yourself,' Elena told him with a smile that didn't quite touch her eyes. 'He says I took away an opportunity for you to learn humility.'

'And you think I need it?' Micah asked in Italian. The bark of laughter he got in return told him all he needed to know. 'Well, now you have it,' he said good-naturedly.

Another quick sprint of Italian.

'You've endeared yourself to him,' Elena said.

'And it only took humiliation.'

'Do not worry,' Lucca said, patting him on the back. 'It happens to all of us at some time.'

'I sincerely hope to find it happening to you some time soon.'

Their laughter attracted a few more people, and before he knew it he was socialising with the executive committee of the company he'd just partnered with.

He had, of course, expected to chat with everyone. He hadn't expected socialising, with wine and laughter and teasing. He'd never experienced any of it before, at any of the galas he'd been to. He could have said it was the Italians, who had a greater desire for joviality than his other business partners. It would have been a lie though. The real difference was Elena.

She switched between Italian and English effortlessly, charmed easily, and ensured she spoke with everyone at least once. This wasn't her party—it wasn't even his— and he knew she was still distracted by what happened earlier. But she'd claimed the role of hostess as if it had been designed solely for her. He wanted to speak with her, to thank her, to give her a chance to breathe, but he couldn't get a second alone with her, she was so popular. In the end, he gestured to her with his head, and left the group under the guise of getting another drink. She joined him in the foyer.

'Your business parties are exhausting.'

'They are for the life of the party.'

She shook her head. 'That's not a role I want, nor deserve.'

'You might not want it, but you deserve it.' He offered her his arm before she could reply. 'Can we go somewhere private to talk?'

Elena hesitated, her expression tightening. But she placed her hand on his. They walked over the soft blue carpet of the hotel's foyer to the elevator. Elena didn't say a word when he pressed the button for the roof. When they got up there, she gasped.

'Why didn't they have the banquet up here?'

He looked around. Glass gave them the perfect view of a night sky that was, in his opinion, showing off. Stars twinkled brightly above them, enticing people to stay outside, to pay attention to their beauty. Beneath them, Rome showed off as audaciously, lights sparkling, people moving, music thumping. It seemed that Rome's night life was more active than its day life, which he understood. It was summer, the night was slightly cooler, though by no means cool. It was the perfect weather for parties or dinners on a terrace.

It was the perfect weather for seduction, temptation. For making mistakes. Even the prospect had him shivering. He set the desire aside.

'Thank you. For what you did down there.'

'It was nothing.'

'No, it wasn't,' he said. 'You're the reason those executives are looking forward to working with me. I seem like a great guy.'

'You don't think you are?'

He opened his mouth, but discovered he had no answer.

When she realised it, she gave a small nod, then walked across the stone-coloured tiles that lined the pathways between the rooftop garden the hotel had created on one side of the room. The garden was mostly made of potted plants and flowers, though large trees full of green leaves peeked over those pots. The side of the room he was standing on had tables and chairs, and he wondered why they'd chosen not to integrate the two so it didn't feel so disjointed.

'I can't quite figure you out,' she said, facing him.

His breath did something odd—tightened, caught, gushed out of his lungs. He knew it was because she made a picture in her black dress, her necklace gleaming bright against her almost gold skin with the backdrop of greenery behind her.

'What do you want to know?' He would tell her anything.

'Is it always about business for you?'

The question was more serious than she let on, he knew.

'It has been for the last decade or so. Since I went to university.' He walked to the edge of the room, leaned his back against the glass. 'It's given me purpose.'

'I understand that.' She was quiet for a long time. 'My work's done the same for me.'

'For how long?'

Her eyebrow quirked. 'Since I turned sixteen.'

'You wanted to work since you were sixteen?'

'No. I found purpose in work when I was sixteen. That's when my parents got divorced.'

He didn't answer, only waited for more. She was walking before she spoke, her gait smooth, elegant, as if she walked runways instead of streets. Part of him wanted to blame it on her upbringing. Wealth made people believe the world was theirs to claim, much as models did the runway. But something deep inside him resisted. Her upbringing might have taught her that, but somewhere along the way she'd learned to earn the world, too. At least her part of it. Everything he knew about her from the last two days they'd spent together pointed to it.

'I'm not the kind of person who almost kisses another man when they're supposed to be engaged,' she said. 'I need you to know that.'

He studied her. 'Then what kind of person are you?'

Her mouth twisted. 'A pawn in a powerful man's game.'

'What do you mean?'

She wanted to close her eyes and sink to the floor. The evening had taken so much of her energy. As had discovering her father and Jameson had planned an engagement party and invited the entire world before she'd even given her answer.

Because they think they already know your answer.

And why wouldn't they? Her father was used to using his power over her as a bargaining tool in her life. His money, when she'd needed something at school and he'd tell her to attend some event in return. To pretend the divorce hadn't changed their perfect little family, even though her mother was halfway across the world. When she'd got a scholarship that paid for university and accommodation and she no longer needed his money, he began to use her need for his love. He'd promised a dinner, to accompany her to a social event, to put in a good word for her at a potential employer. She needed his approval so much she would accept anything from him, despite how terrible it made her feel after.

Because she was compromising to get it. Her values, her independence, herself. This latest request was the biggest, and her father was pulling out all the stops to get her to agree. Threatening her job, promising her security, implying his approval. It wasn't worth it, she knew, but it was tempting. She didn't want to lose the life she'd spent almost a decade building. She didn't want to lose her chance of her father ever truly loving her.

Now there was Micah, complicating it all with his power over her. Because he had some. Why else was she there, trying to explain herself to him? Why else did she still want to kiss him? To let him hold her and make *her* feel powerful again?

It was a trap. It couldn't be anything else. And it was bound to make her feel as terrible as giving in to her father did.

'You're a powerful man, Micah. You know you play games. Use people.'

Anything she could have read on his face was covered by a blank expression. 'I don't know what you're talking about.'

That wasn't the reaction she had expected. She'd expected denial, or confusion. Genuine confusion, not this practised nonsense he was going for.

An uncomfortable feeling slithered down her spine. It hissed in her ears, saying *I told you so.*

'What are you hiding?' she asked softly.

'I'm not hiding anything.'

'Yes, you are.' She took a step closer. 'And it has to do with me.'

He didn't reply, only watched her with a guarded expression. She blinked, and stumbled back. It *did* have something to do with her. And if she took the rest of the conversation into account, it meant he was using her, too. But for what?

It didn't matter. The only thing that did was knowing she couldn't trust him.

She hated that it sent a crack rippling through her heart.

CHAPTER SEVEN

ELENA'S SECOND FULL day in Rome wasn't as exciting as the first. She spent the majority of it tailing Micah to his meetings. She'd expected it—that was what had been on the itinerary, and Serena had invited her to join him—and she'd brought her observation A game. She was quiet, discreet, and only spoke when spoken to. She was doing exceedingly well, actually, which was why Micah's stony expression whenever he spoke to her annoyed the hell out of her.

Actually, no. The real reason she was annoyed was because he was treating her as if *she* were the one keeping secrets. And she was sure it wasn't only keeping secrets either. His reaction to her questions the night before told her there was more there. She had set it aside though. She was a professional, after all. Except him showing everyone his disapproval of her made them both look *unprofessional*. She would have told him that, too, if she'd had any time alone with him that day.

But his meetings were back to back. When they had to change venues, they went in different cars, something she was sure he'd arranged. All of it made her annoyance grow. She stewed in it. Plotted her revenge. It wouldn't be sophisticated, but it would be satisfying. Like throwing her tablet at Micah. She would love to see his expression after that. But logic told her tablets were expensive—and so was Micah—so she settled for fantasising about his defeat instead.

They were supposed to have dinner at the end of the day, but Elena ducked out of it. She didn't want to socialise with him. She'd got enough information on his business habits during that day to write her article. Serena had sent her information about his charity work, and with the personal information Elena had got on the plane and in the restaurant, she could write a decent article. A *good* article. She didn't have to spend any more time with him. She relished that.

Her phone rang. Her finger hovered over the denial button, but it was Jameson calling now, not her father's office. He was the lesser of the evils. Besides, she had some things to say to him now that she'd processed the news of the party a bit more.

'Where have you been?' he said as soon as she picked up. 'We've been trying to get a hold of you.'

'Hello, Jameson. How are you?'

'Busy. Work and…' There was a pause. 'Stuff.'

'Yes, *stuff*,' she said slowly. 'Like the party you and my father are planning to announce our engagement at?'

'Elena—'

'It's a little presumptuous, don't you think?' she continued, ignoring what would surely be some form of manipulation. 'Or is it strategic? I'm not in the country, so you can plan your party without my protests.'

'Elena.' Jameson's voice was sharp now. 'Your hysteria is helping no one. Calm down.'

She almost swore at him. Barely caught the words before they jumped from her lips.

'We were merely moving things forward.'

'Moving me forward, you mean.'

'Your father assured me your answer would be in the affirmative.'

'I'm sure he did,' she murmured, her anger changing from sharp heat to something…cold. 'Is that why he's been trying to get a hold of me, then?'

'Having confirmation from you would be helpful.'

Not to me.

So say no, another voice said in her head.

And she wanted to listen to it. She wanted to say those words. But they wouldn't leave her lips, no matter how hard she tried. Something entirely different came out instead.

'I'm working,' she said woodenly. 'So you'll have to wait a little longer for that confirmation.'

He cursed. 'You're prioritising that man over me? Your future husband?'

'It's not about a man.' *And you might not be my husband.* 'It's about my job, and the fact that anyone could have got this assignment, but they gave it to me.'

'They gave it to you because you're a John. You don't have to prove yourself, if that's why you're doing this. You already have.'

She didn't bother to reply. Jameson would think that her worth was solely in her surname. It made Micah's assumption of the same on the day they met worse. She didn't indulge her thoughts about why that was. Accepted that she was raw when it came to Micah and left it at that.

'It's not a huge leap to assume Williams asked for you,' Jameson continued, apparently not caring that she hadn't responded. Though the way he hit the nail on the head felt like a whip against her heart. 'He probably thinks you're his key to partnering with the John Diamond Company.' Jameson laughed. 'Our engagement will secure my and your family's partnership though, so he'll quickly realise having you there was for nothing.'

For one horrifying moment, she thought she would gasp. Her head swirled, and she stumbled back to the bed, lowering so she had support for the knees that had gone shaky.

'Elena? Are you there?'

Her training kicked in. The sixteen years before the life she knew had fallen apart consisted of her parents coaching her in the art of vulnerability. That was, to never be vulnerable. People would use it against her. Powerful people would use it against her.

Micah had used it against her.

'Well, this has been lovely,' she said, her voice sounding odd, even to herself. 'We're travelling to the country tomorrow, so I'll be out of cell-phone range. Goodbye.'

She put down the phone before he could reply. She was about to switch it off for good measure when she saw a message from Micah.

Are you okay?

No. She wasn't okay. But she sure as hell wasn't going to admit that to a man who was using her. Just like every other man in her life.

What had she done to deserve this? To deserve feeling this alone?

She gave herself a few minutes to wallow, then went to her laptop to write.

Elena was waiting for him at breakfast. She wore a pink headband, curls spiralling around her head behind it, along with a pants suit—black this time—and a top that matched the headband. Her lips were painted the same soft colour, but she wore no other make-up that he could see.

She looked up when he arrived, took her cell phone out, pressed some buttons, then put it away.

'I emailed you the story I plan on submitting to my editor. It's only due when I get back, so feel free to add your comments and email them to me before the end of the trip. I'll apply them if they're reasonable,' she added with a warning glance.

'You're done?'

'I was inspired last night.' Her tone was flat.

'Serena told me you had a headache. That's why you didn't come to dinner.'

'I lied. I didn't come to dinner because you acted like a jerk the entire day. I didn't want to experience that for any longer than I had to.' She stood. 'Thank you for the opportunity to—'

'Wait,' he said, standing out of surprise. 'You're leaving?'

'I am.' Her spine straightened, as if she was daring him to argue with her. 'I'm going to Venice.'

'Why?'

'A number of reasons. None of which,' she added as he was about to ask, 'I'd like to share with you.'

'Okay, wait. Just…give me a second to catch up.' He looked around desperately. 'Coffee? Let's have one coffee together.'

Her expression was emotionless. 'Your driver is standing in the doorway, Mr Williams. If I remember correctly, your meeting starts in thirty minutes.'

'Elena,' he said sternly now. He softened his tone when her eyebrow rose. 'I'm sorry. Just…please. Coffee?'

He didn't know how long he waited for her to give the nod that eventually came. All he knew was he was offering to get coffee for them, even though a server could have done it. But he needed time to process. To ask himself why he hadn't expected her to stand up for herself. Why he'd wasted a day that he could have spent with her.

His emotions. He didn't know how to work through them. They'd shared a tense almost kiss; he'd seen her fit seamlessly into his world; and he'd discovered she was about to be engaged. He hadn't been prepared for any of it. Then she'd come dangerously close to figuring out his plan and his instincts had told him to shut down. To protect himself. So he did. He'd spent an entire day trying to ignore her and being unable to because she was so damn vibrant and beautiful and he was pulled to her in a way he couldn't understand.

Damn his parents, he thought suddenly, unexpectedly, *furiously*. If they hadn't all but abandoned him, if they'd taught him how to engage with people, he wouldn't feel so lost now. He would know what to do with his feelings. He'd be able to deal with them in healthy ways. He wouldn't have sulked at Elena like a teenager because he liked her and didn't want to.

He liked her.

Coffee slopped over the cup onto his hand, burning his skin much as that realisation burnt his heart. He set the mug down, gritted his teeth, though a part of him wanted to brace over the counter. But he wasn't helpless; he could handle some feelings. With that thought, he refilled the liquid that'd spilled onto his hand, grabbed the other mug and went back to his table.

Elena didn't speak, only watched him as she accepted the coffee, bringing it to her lips immediately.

He swallowed. 'Elena—'

Her sigh cut him off. His eyebrows lifted before he could stop them.

'I'm sorry, did my voice annoy you?'

She didn't even pretend. 'I don't want an apology from you, Micah, which I can already see on your face is what you were planning on saying. I want to catch my train to

Venice. I want to watch the green fields through the windows and enjoy the peace of not arguing with you.'

He studied her. There was something more going on.

'This is why you didn't reply to my message yesterday, isn't it?' he asked quietly. 'You're not okay.'

She closed her eyes. When she opened them, he sat back. He needed the support of his chair to understand what he saw there.

'No, I'm not okay. But you're part of the reason I'm not, Micah, so I don't have any desire to talk to you about it.'

CHAPTER EIGHT

IT PROBABLY HADN'T been her best idea to accept Micah's offer of coffee. Not when she was obviously in a fragile state—why else hadn't she controlled her tongue?

Oh, right. That look of complete and utter anguish on his face.

'You won't let me apologise,' he said, his voice low.

'Do you know what you're apologising for?'

His brow knitted. 'Yesterday. For acting like an inconsiderate, stubborn—' He exhaled. 'I was wrong yesterday.'

'What about the day before?' she asked. 'When you claimed you weren't hiding anything?'

His lips parted, but he didn't say anything.

'That's why I didn't want your apologies,' she said, pushing her chair back so she could stand. 'They don't mean a thing.'

'Elena—'

'No!' She slammed a hand on the table. 'I don't want to hear your excuses. I just want the truth. Did you or did you not bring me here because you want a partnership with my father?'

When he stared at her, the little hope she had that Jameson had been incorrectly speculating fluttered away, disappearing in the wind.

'Micah,' she said on what sounded like a hiccup, but

couldn't be. That would involve having emotions about the situation. But she'd prepared herself for this, so, obviously, she had no emotions whatsoever.

'I was going to tell you,' he said softly.

'Were you?'

'I...' He paused. 'Not if I didn't have to, no.'

She pressed her lips together and tried to control the emotions she did, apparently, have. Control was better than feeling them. That swirl of disappointment and betrayal that made no sense when she'd known this man for days. When she was, essentially, working with him.

'I didn't think it would come to this,' he continued in that same soft voice. 'I didn't expect for us to...' He frowned. 'I only wanted you to introduce us.' The frown deepened. 'You shouldn't have been hurt by this.'

But I am.

She didn't say it.

'You could have found a million other ways to be introduced to my father,' she pointed out, proud of how steady her voice was. 'You could probably contact him now and he'd agree to meet with you.'

'I've tried that.' Despite his frown, the sternness he spoke with, he seemed vulnerable. Why did *he* seem vulnerable when he was the one with all the power? 'I wasn't as successful then. He wouldn't take a meeting with me.'

'He will now.'

'How do you know?'

She gave a mirthless laugh. 'If Jameson knows about you, my father knows about you.'

'Jameson... Your fiancé?'

The repressed emotion in his voice had her pressing the heels of her hands into her eyes. This was...a lot to deal with. At least she hadn't put on eye make-up that morning. She'd been too tired. All the effort she'd been able to

muster was to put something on her lips to distract from
the rings around her eyes. She was aware that wasn't how
make-up worked, but it was the best she could do.

She dropped her hands. 'He's not my fiancé. He's just
the man my father wants me to marry to strengthen his
company.'

'What? *What?*'

The outrage almost amused her.

'I'm a pawn to him,' she said simply. 'Not unlike how
you intended on using me for an introduction.'

'That's not… It's not the same.'

She only looked at him.

'Elena, my intentions weren't malicious. I promise. I
was just…' He took a deep breath. Then he met her eyes.
Fierceness had woven itself between vulnerability, the result so captivating she couldn't look away. 'You're right. I
should have tried to get in contact with your father through
other means. But I was afraid that…that my mother would
find out.'

'Your mother?'

'John Diamond Company is a client of hers.' He was
continuing before she had time to process that. 'Partnering
with your father has little to do with my business, and everything to do with her. We… We don't have a relationship.
I was hoping to change that.' The pause before he went on
this time was longer. 'But if she thinks I orchestrated this,
the chances of that happening…' He shook his head. 'She
wouldn't appreciate being manipulated.'

'I can understand that,' Elena said bluntly.

He nodded. 'That's fair. But… This is how I do business. I make plans. I follow them. I don't think about the
people involved.'

'That sounds callous.'

His jaw jutted out. 'It is.' He paused. 'I thought about you.'

She wanted to believe him, but… 'Did that change how you treated me?'

'It made things more complicated.' He sighed. Continued speaking as if releasing the breath had also expelled his resistance. 'I struggled with it. That's what happened yesterday. Among other things.' His fingers curled into a fist. 'It's easier to pretend not to know how my plans affect other people. For many reasons. Most of all because being callous makes me—'

'Like my father,' she cut in.

'I was going to say like my mother.' He heaved out another sigh. 'I don't entirely know how I feel about that. I'm working through some things.'

'Clearly.'

The side of his mouth lifted. 'You seem to be, too, with your father.' He paused. 'He really expects you to marry this guy? Say no.'

'Easier said than done.'

'Isn't there someone who can intervene?' he asked. 'Your mother?'

'I haven't spoken to my mother since my parents divorced when I was sixteen.'

Surprised fluttered over his face. 'I'm sorry.'

'Don't be. We didn't have much of a relationship before. I wasn't losing out.'

'But…she's your mother.'

'That doesn't mean much if she doesn't want to be my mother.'

'But—'

She interrupted him before he could ask more intrusive questions.

'If you'd just told me you wanted to meet my father, things would have been a lot easier. Instead, you were manipulative. And now I'm wondering things like if I'm good enough at my job to be here.' *Or if anything that happened between us was real.* 'I don't even know if I should trust anything you say. Are you telling me about your mother because you want me to understand your motivations? Or are you doing it for some calculating reason I'll only discover once I trust you again? I won't do that to myself.'

She stood. 'Send me your opinions on the article if you want. Otherwise, I'll see you on the flight home.' She didn't look back when she left.

It took him the rest of the day to clear his schedule. Micah did it without hesitation. There was a high likelihood the executive committee of his company would have something to say about that, but he could afford to ignore them this time. He'd brought in several high-profile clients over the last year. And if he got John Diamond Company—

He stopped. It was exactly that kind of thinking that got him into trouble. Admittedly, it was hard to shut down. He was used to methodical thinking. He'd been practising it for over a decade. Probably before that if he was truly examining things.

His mother was an excellent businessperson. Sharp, motivated, strategic. He witnessed these characteristics before he could describe what they were, especially when she used them on him. There weren't many traditionally maternal things about his mother. She spoke to him as if speaking to an employee. If the employee was an intern. Or someone she didn't want to deal with but had to.

The easiest way of processing it was if he responded in the way she treated him. She'd appreciated that, in that she hadn't looked too annoyed at him. In fact, the more he became like her, the less annoyed she was at him. But she also appreciated creativity, a fact he'd come to know after he'd written an essay at school about wha he wanted to be when he grew up. He'd got an A for the essay, had shown it to her proudly. After one look, she'd said, 'Micah, you don't have the skills to become a lawyer.' He'd never learnt what skills she thought that was. 'Show a little creativity.'

And so his trajectory had changed. When he was old enough to figure out where it was headed to, he did research. On the kinds of clients his mother represented, on the kind of business she appreciated. It led him to the affluent market, and soon he'd seen a path to getting what he wanted. He happened to be damn good at it, too.

He was less good at relationships. Turned out the characteristics his mother had inadvertently taught him—the ones that made him so successful—didn't work as well in his personal life. He should have known. His mother hadn't been there for him at all. Nor for his father, which was part of why things hadn't worked out between them. That was based on his father's point of view, which he'd been privy to before his father had married and started a family with someone else.

The one significant thing about his father's marriage was that it showed Micah there was hope relationships could work. He'd never cared about that before. He struggled with the fact that he cared about it now. But he did. He cared that he'd hurt Elena. That she thought he was like her father, who wanted to use her as though she weren't a person. That he was like the man who would accept her as his wife, but thought of her in the same way.

He didn't understand relationships, but he knew he wanted more for Elena. He wanted more *with* Elena. She was the first person in his life to make him feel…things. He would accept being her friend if that was the only relationship they could have. But he needed to prove that she could trust him first.

Which was why he was now walking the narrow paths of Venice to his hotel. Elena had told Serena where she would be staying and had given her all the relevant contact details. It had taken some convincing—unsurprisingly, Elena had inspired loyalty in the woman that had worked for him his entire career—but his assistant had got him a booking at the same hotel. He had no idea if Elena was out exploring, or if she was dining at the hotel's restaurant, or if she was simply sleeping. But he had to take a chance, and hope he hadn't crossed a line by coming to see her.

After he booked in, he called her cell. She didn't answer. He rolled his eyes. His annoyance was both because she hadn't answered and because he'd expected her not to. He sent her a message.

I need a moment of your time, please.

He got a reply within seconds.

You had a moment of my time this morning.

He could picture her saying it, her lips pressed against one another, her eyes daring him to contradict her. For some inexplicable reason, it made him smile.

We both know this morning didn't go well.

Whose fault is that?

His smile widened. He probably looked like a fool standing in the foyer, staring at his phone and smiling. He didn't care.

Mine. That's why I'd like to apologise.

I don't want apologies.

You deserve them.

There was some time before the next message came.

I'm not answering your calls.

You don't have to. Just tell me your room number and we can talk in person.

What?

No.

You're not here?

Those three messages came in quick succession.

Give me your room number and check for yourself.

His bottom lip curled beneath the top row of his teeth as he waited for her to reply. He knew it was impossible, but he wondered if she knew how hard his heart was beating and was punishing him. But that didn't seem like Elena's style. She seemed more like the physical torture kind, not the psychological one.

As if confirming it, her message came.

Room 542

He almost ran to the elevator before he realised he'd refused the porter so he could contact Elena. In hindsight, he should have only contacted her after he was settled.

But Elena was angry at him, and it felt as if a sword were waiting above his head. It made no sense. It didn't have to. He would explain himself to Elena soon and that feeling would go away.

Ten minutes later, he'd thrown his bags into his room and was knocking on the door of room 542. An elderly lady answered.

'Well,' she said, after scanning him up and down. 'I didn't expect this as room service, but I can hardly complain.'

'Oh.' It took him a beat to realise Elena had duped him. 'No, ma'am, I'm sorry. This isn't—'

'Did you just call me ma'am?' Her accent became more pronounced.

'Yes. I'm sorry. It's something we use out of respect for—' He cut himself off. They didn't need to go into detail about what older women were called in South Africa. 'I'm not from here. Customs aren't the same. Please accept my apology.'

'You do like to apologise, don't you?' came a drawl from opposite them.

He glanced back to see Elena leaning against a doorframe with folded arms. Her hair was piled at the top of her head, her skim gleaming with what he assumed was sunblock, though it was evening and he was probably wrong. His brain quickly noted the other things about her—she wore a sun dress, lilac and simple, and nothing on her feet—before he shifted.

'There you are, darling.' He kept his tone even. 'I forgot my key card and went to the wrong room.'

'It must be because of all the alcohol you drank at the parade,' she said easily.

'Getting locked out of my room quickly sobered me

up,' he replied dryly, then turned his attention to the older woman. 'I'm sorry for disturbing you, ma'am.'

She didn't reply, only shut the door in his face. What would it have been like if he'd gone into her room for what she'd wanted? He shuddered.

'If you're cold, you should probably go inside.'

He turned. Noted her expression. 'You mean of my own room.'

'I do.' She smiled at him. It wasn't friendly. 'I have to admit when I didn't see you through the peephole after five minutes I thought you were lying.'

'That's why you told me the wrong room number?'

'No. I told you the wrong room number because I thought it would be funny.'

'Hilarious.'

Her smile was full of amusement now. 'Oh, I know.' There was a short silence after she sobered. 'What are you doing here, Micah?'

'I prefer not talking about this in the passage. Where I'm sure we have some eyes. And ears,' he added, easily picturing the woman who'd slammed the door on him eavesdropping.

'I prefer not talking about this at all, yet here we are.'

She wasn't going to make this easy, then. Okay. He expected as much.

'Can I come in? Please? Please,' he said again, for good measure.

She gave him a wary look, but stepped back to let him in.

CHAPTER NINE

SHE WAS EITHER the biggest fool in the world, or a sucker for a man who was prepared to grovel. Perhaps both. Probably both, she thought, as she stepped aside for Micah. Both, she confirmed when he walked past her and politely waited for her to close the door before he did anything else.

Both for him, a voice whispered in her head.

She shouldn't have answered his messages, or told him where to find her, or let him into her room. He put her in danger. He *was* danger.

'Your room is nice.'

'It's generic and dark, but clean and comfortable. I don't know if that qualifies as nice.' She sat on the bed. 'You didn't come here to compliment my room though.'

'No.'

He shifted, revealing his nerves. She shouldn't have used the opportunity to check him out. He wore jeans despite the heat, though he was dressed the most casually she'd ever seen; he'd replaced his usual shirt with a T-shirt. It was tight over a body that looked muscular, but had the softness of someone who had been buff once, but didn't get to the gym as much any more. She had no idea whether that was true, or whether Micah's body simply looked like that.

What she did know was that she wanted to run her

hands over his broad shoulders, down the firm rounding of his torso, back up. She wanted to kiss the crook of his neck and make her way down to the firmness of his bicep. She wanted to—

She closed her eyes. She didn't need this attraction. It only reminded her that she couldn't afford to share it with Micah. She didn't trust him. But it also forced her to think about the decision she had to make. How could she marry Jameson when she felt this way about another man? Would she indulge in an extramarital relationship as he no doubt would? The very thought of it made her uncomfortable. And she doubted Micah would want a relationship with a married woman anyway.

She shook her head. She shouldn't be thinking about this.

'Sit down, Micah,' she said softly. 'You're making me nervous.'

'At least we'll be on equal ground, then,' he muttered, but sat. 'So… I'm…er… I'm sorry.' It was so sincere she didn't even feel tempted to interrupt the apology. 'For everything, but mostly because I made you feel used. That… sickens me.'

She looked at him for a long time. Saw that he was telling the truth. It shifted something in her brain. In her heart. 'Thank you,' she said.

Her acceptance drew a frown, but he nodded. Then blew out a breath. 'I'd like to tell you why I did all this. Please.'

'Okay.'

'I've just…never spoken to anyone about it before.'

She resisted taking his hand. Resisted comforting him. It took more strength than she would have liked. 'When you're ready.'

After another nod and a breath, he began.

'My parents never married. They were dating while at

university, found out they were having me, had me. They were about to graduate and they weren't meant to be serious. My mom already had a law firm she was going to do her articles at, and when they wanted to drop her because of her pregnancy, she threatened to sue them. They played nice, and she worked her butt off while my dad looked after me.'

He stood.

'They weren't happy together, but the arrangement worked for them, especially since my dad wasn't working and my mom was. But my mom was never home, and my dad realised he wanted more from life. When I was seven, they broke up for real. It was fine for my mom because she had a good job by then and she could send me to a school. My dad got a job of his own, and every semblance of family I had ended.' He walked to her fridge, took a bottle of water out. After he downed it, he said, 'I'll pay for it.'

She didn't care about that. She did care about the sad look in his eyes. It wasn't obvious. There was a resignation as he told the story, as if he were recounting something he'd told a million times before. Now she knew why he was so tight-lipped about his family. She also knew him telling her this was…significant.

'My point is,' he said suddenly, speaking fast, 'I don't know how to treat people.'

'You not having a family means you don't know how to treat people?'

'No.' He exhaled irritably. She preferred it to the sadness. 'It means I don't know… It means,' he said more deliberately, 'people are hard for me. Relationships are hard for me.'

'Who said anything about a relationship?'

'I didn't mean a *relationship*.'

'That's wh—'

'I know that's what I said,' he interrupted curtly. Exhaled. 'My mother raised me. But what she did wasn't really raising. I had food on the table, shelter, but I didn't have anything else. So, I followed my mother's example. I... I shut down the emotions. I was efficient and had single-minded focus.'

'That's why you're so successful,' she murmured.

'Yes.' He didn't blink an eye. 'But apparently, those characteristics don't do well when you're trying to befriend someone.'

Her lips curved. 'You're trying to befriend me?'

He heaved out a sigh and sat down next to her. 'Do you think I came here simply to torture myself?'

She thought for a moment. 'Thank you for coming here. For being honest.'

'I'm trying.'

'So I see.' Emotion swelled in her chest. She cleared her throat. 'I don't like being used.'

'I understand why.' He gave her another one of his intense looks. 'Does your father really expect you to marry for his business?'

She stood and walked to the window. 'Yes.'

'Will you?'

She didn't answer him for a long time. 'I don't know.'

Her considering marriage at her father's behest still sounded like a fantasy. It didn't belong in the real world. It didn't belong in *her* world. She was determined, independent, strong. Why would someone like that put themselves in that position?

'Why?' he asked eventually. He needed to know.

'It's a difficult decision.'

'You know that's not what I meant.'

She sighed, but didn't answer him. He stood and joined her at the window. It was night, and all they could see were shadows below them. Occasionally, the light from someone's cell phone would come along and given them glimpses of outlines of faces and walls and cobbled stones. But Micah wasn't paying attention to that. He was looking at Elena.

The light in her room was bright and clear, allowing him to see every nuance of her expression. Naked emotions stalked across her face leisurely, as if it were a hot summer's day and they were prancing around the pool. She didn't try to hide them, and he could see the battle between guardedness and a desire to tell him. She met his gaze, but didn't speak. The rawness in her eyes made him want to pull her into his arms and tell her it was okay. She would be okay.

'We don't speak much these days,' she started. 'Me and my father, I mean. Contact mostly came from me, anyway, and when I got old enough for self-preservation to win out over my desire to…' She trailed off. 'Anyway, he called me to his office. He never did that, and there was just this…hope inside me. Foolish,' she scoffed at herself. 'He wouldn't call me to his office to apologise for the years of neglect or for using me when he needed me. He only called to use me again.'

She leaned back against the window frame, her gaze now shifting to outside. 'When I got there, he told me about a mining accident that had killed two John employees. I already knew, of course. It was all over the news and it's my job to know the news.' She dropped his hand and folded her arms. 'He said stock was tanking and he needed something else for the media to focus on. And he'd found a way.'

'Marriage.'

She gave a curt nod. 'To the heir to a rival mining company. The company would be strengthened because of the combined power and the society wedding would be all anyone would talk about. Romeo and Juliet, minus the part where I kill myself.'

'But you'd kill a part of yourself.' He could see it in her eyes.

She tilted her head. 'It's meant to be a business arrangement. A publicity stunt. We pretend to be a couple, but we live as though we aren't married.'

'What does that mean?'

She shrugged. 'We would have to move to the same house, but other than that, everything would stay the same. I'd have my separate life. He'd have his.'

'He'd have mistresses.'

'So would I. Well, misters.' Her mouth lifted. 'Sounds great, doesn't it?'

'You're not married yet,' he reminded her. 'You're not even engaged. It's not too late.'

She didn't answer him for a long time. It made him wonder if he'd misinterpreted her 'great' as sarcasm. Maybe she *wanted* to marry this Jameson man. Why else would she agree to her father's suggestion?

Had it been a suggestion though? Perhaps it had been a command. But why would she obey it? What was the worst thing that could happen if she didn't?

'Elena,' he said softly. 'What are you not telling me?'

She looked at him, and what he saw there told him not to prod. So he waited. When the waiting spanned minutes, he reached out and took her hand. As the minutes ticked by, he shifted closer. By the time she spoke, they were standing a breath apart.

His heart was thumping, and he was afraid their proximity would mean she could hear it. Or worse, feel it. Either way, she would know how much this was affecting him. How much the fact that she'd taken the last two steps towards him meant to him. They were sharing an intimacy he hadn't shared with anyone else in their conversation. He was drawn to her physically unlike anyone else. He wanted to kiss her. To share *more* with her.

He didn't want her to marry that man.

'He threatened my job,' she said hoarsely. She was staring up at him with big brown eyes that told him as much as her words did. She was scared. 'He didn't say it outright, but he didn't have to. My father... He's powerful.'

Anger pulsed through his body. 'So am I. I'll get you another job.'

'I don't want another job.' She bit her lip. 'I want this job. *My* job that I worked for, for years. The job that brought me here.' Her voice caught. 'It's not fair.'

He slid an arm around her waist, taking great care to be gentle and not give in to the emotion that told him to throw her over his shoulder and run away with her.

'And now there's this stupid engagement party in four days. *Four days*, Micah. I didn't even agree, but my father's invited everyone to it and the media's latched onto the whispers exactly as my father intended.'

'He's trying to strong-arm you into doing this.'

'Yes.' She let out a shaky breath. 'Along with threatening the one thing he knows means the world to me, he's pulling out all the stops to get me to agree.'

'Has he done this before?'

'Not to this extent.'

'That's why you stopped using his money. Why you put distance in your relationship.' She nodded, though he was really confirming more than asking. 'Why did you go to his office that day? You said hope, but for what?'

She rested her hands on his chest. 'If your mother called

you and asked you to do something for her, without warning or context, would you do it?'

And finally, he saw. He understood. She'd hoped for a relationship, for the love of a parent. She worried that if she didn't do this, she would lose not only her job, but that chance of love. As someone who'd spent his entire life searching for that love, doing what he thought he had to in order to get that love, he couldn't judge her. It was an impossible situation for a child. His heart broke for her even as he hated her father for putting her in that situation in the first place.

She cracked the first real smile she'd given since they started talking. 'You understand now why I jumped at the chance to be here. To escape it.'

She gently pulled away from him and walked towards the bed.

'Besides, you know, it being a wonderful opportunity. Writing a cover story is career gold for me. Or it was,' she said, narrowing her eyes at him. 'Now that I know I wasn't asked because of my skill, the ask has been tainted.'

He winced. 'I'm sorry. But regardless of how the opportunity came about, you're here, right? You do a good job, it won't matter how you got here.'

She opened her mouth, but no sound came out for a while. 'That's a good point.'

'That hurt, didn't it?'

She smirked. 'Maybe.'

He studied her, but her expression was as closed a book as it had been open earlier. He thought about pushing, but it didn't feel right. So he simply said, 'They wouldn't have agreed for you to write the story if you hadn't earned it, Elena.'

'I believe you. What?' she said in response to his surprise. 'You have pull with a demographic we've been struggling with for some time. Millennials. A solid portion of who will find you attractive. They need this story to be good.'

His face burned. 'We weren't talking about me.'

'No, we weren't.' She smiled. 'It's cute that you're flustered by people finding you attractive.'

'Why couldn't you just take the compliment and leave it at that?' he grumbled.

Her smile widened. 'Thank you for your compliment.' She put a hand on her hip. 'You know, I came here to forget. Not to rehash all of this.' She shook her shoulders. 'I needed an Italian escape with a tycoon, not an Italian confession with one.'

'You're strange, you know that?' Her laugh warmed the parts inside him he hadn't realise had gone cold during her story. 'But you have a point. I can't do much about your decision, but I can distract you. Have you made any plans for Venice yet?'

'Some.' She closed the space between them. 'Nothing that can't be cancelled.'

'I'll work around them.'

Tentatively, he opened his arms. She immediately stepped into them. Rested her head on his chest. It was comfortable. Warm. It felt exactly right.

'We'll make these the best days of your life.'

'Thank you.'

He couldn't resist the kiss he pressed to her forehead in reply.

CHAPTER TEN

WHEN ELENA WOKE the next morning, she asked herself whether she'd dreamed the night before. Micah had apologised and opened up to her about his family. In turn, she had told him about the impossible situation with her father. Now, they were going to spend the remaining days in Italy exploring Venice.

It was wild. But her life had, over the last month, been wild. Unrecognisable. One day she'd been living the life she created for herself, the next day she was contemplating marriage to a stranger. She hadn't paid attention to how little she'd liked the disruption. She had simply been focused on getting through it.

Micah forced her to think about it though. Spending time with him, being attracted to him, talking to him. It made her think about how she didn't like what her father was doing. It made her realise the full capacity of what Cliff was asking her to sacrifice.

It wasn't so much marriage itself, since the institution was easily escapable, as her parents' marriage had shown. If the marriage was based on normal things, that was. Love or respect or mutual admiration. Things that might fade over time. But *her* marriage would be a business contract. Those were harder to get out of. Business contracts with her father would be impossible to get out of. Was a job, however much she loved it, worth sacrificing her freedom for? Was the chance—the *chance*—of her father's love and approval worth giving up her future?

It caused her chest to ache, that thought. The *knowledge*. She knew that her father wouldn't change simply because she'd done what he'd asked. She'd had years and years of experience that told her that wouldn't happen. He would go back to ignoring her—or, worse, using her again and again because she was more accessible to him. It would break her. But now the question was whether giving up the hope of a proper relationship with her father would break her more than that would.

The emptiness and hurt echoing in her body reminded her why she hadn't examined her feelings about the situation. She shut them down, took a shower, and prepared for her day with Micah. He would ensure that she'd forget her problems, at least for the next few days. Her eagerness for him had nothing to do with *him* though. Things might have shifted slightly between them the night before, but this? This was all about forgetting her situation. It had nothing to do with him.

Her heart begged to differ when she got to breakfast. It skipped a beat when Micah looked up from his tablet and smiled. His teeth were white against his brown skin, bouncing off the white of the linen shirt he wore. When he stood, she saw he'd paired the shirt with dark blue chinos and white sneakers that could have been brand new, they were so immaculate.

'You look pretty hip,' she said, taking a seat opposite him.

'I had to look decent since I was spending the day with you.'

She pinched her thigh under the table so she wouldn't swoon at those words. 'What did you look like before?'

'A businessperson.'

'Ah, yes, and we both know businesspeople don't look decent.'

He narrowed his eyes. 'I wanted to look appropriately tourist-like.'

'You absolutely succeed.' She gestured around them. 'As you can see, most of the tourists here look as if they've walked off the catwalk.'

'Elena,' he said, expression pained, 'would you like me to change?'

'I was teasing.' She shook her napkin out and set it on her lap. 'You should have known that, since I was clearly complimenting you. Are you nervous about how you look or something?'

'No.'

He said it too quickly. He *was* nervous, so much so that he didn't want to talk about it. She had questions: Was it because the clothes were new? Did he never dress casually? Had he never simply been a tourist before? Were all his experiences overseas business?

She asked none of it. Because he'd clearly tried, for her benefit, and that was sweeter than she knew how to articulate.

'I think there was a compliment in there for me, too,' she said instead. 'Clearly you're aspiring to my fashion sense and I appreciate that.'

She wondered if he knew how much relief was in his smile.

'You do look…er…decent today. I like the crown.'

She smiled and touched the arrangement of flowers on her head. 'I bought it in a shop nearby. It's ridiculously extra, but I like it. Plus, it makes me look like a silly tourist and I kind of like that.' She rolled her eyes. 'I know it's silly. Who wants to look like a tourist? It's like putting a target on my back. Or on my forehead. But I don't know, I guess...'

She trailed off at the way he was looking at her. 'What?'

'You're rambling.'

'Micah,' she said slowly, 'I know you're not an expert on social interactions, but pointing things like that out isn't polite.'

'I thought you wanted me to be honest?'

She had nothing to say to that. Because yeah, she wanted him to be honest. But how did she tell him there was a thing like being too honest?

His chuckle drew her out of her confusion.

'Oh, you think this is funny?'

'It is.' He grinned. 'Payback is always fun.'

'Payback... Oh, for your clothes?' At his nod, she laughed. 'Haven't you heard the phrase "Revenge is a dish best served cold"?'

'I've never been a big believer of that. Personally, I think revenge is best served as soon as possible so neither party forgets.'

'Your brain is a wonder,' she said, shaking her head.

'Thank you.'

She rolled her eyes at that response. 'So. What's on the agenda today?'

She stole his coffee as he went through their day, interrupting occasionally to ask a question or tease him. He made it so easy. He often said something that could be understood in several different ways, and she would purposely understand the wrong meanings. That frustrated him, or annoyed him, which made her laugh, then he would laugh, and it all made her breathe more easily than she had in a long time.

It was leaps and bounds away from how she'd perceived him before. He was still charming, but that charm came from him being himself. From his mistakes, his laughter. The way he wasn't performing a persona. She didn't think he'd appreciate if she announced it to the world, but he didn't mind being that way with her. She felt touched. And warm. That warmth was so precious that she held it close, like the only light in a room of darkness.

That metaphor was alarming, even to her.

'I know that I shouldn't be this excited to go on a boat since I've done it before, but this makes me so happy.'

Elena did a little stomp with her legs, before twirling in a circle. It made the skirt of her dress whirl around her. Micah tried to focus on the top half of her, but there was a delay in the shift of his gaze—he couldn't help it—and he got a glimpse of full brown flesh. It was as enticing as the rest of her. She wore a bright yellow dress, as if she'd realised how much sunlight she'd brought to his life. With her flower crown, she looked like a summer goddess.

It worried him how badly he wanted to worship her.

'It isn't a boat. It's a gondola.'

'My mistake,' she said blandly, and made him smile. She did that a lot. And he was smiling more than he ever had before. That worried him, too. But it didn't stop him from smiling at her. Or from thinking about how different she was now, when she wasn't thinking about the decision she had to make.

What if she didn't have to make it?

He couldn't pay attention to the thought when the gondolier called for them to get in. He did, using the man's help, then gently nudged him aside to help Elena. She smiled brightly, and it became obvious why he'd wanted to help her. Apparently, he would do anything to get that smile. To keep it there, too.

It stuck as they sat down and the gondola began to float

down the canal. It was a bright, sunny day, and the blue-green of the water around them sparkled as it stretched between buildings. A gentleman began to sing, rich and deep, and Elena sighed at his side. She snuggled closer, not intentionally, he didn't think, but it made him hold his breath.

That might not have been the right description of it. It was more like someone was squeezing his lungs, so he had less capacity to breathe. He'd felt that way the entire day. When they'd been exploring the stores around St Mark's Square. Or when Elena had insisted on feeding the pigeons, then got alarmed when more and more of them came.

'What is it with you and pigeons?' he'd asked. 'I told you this wouldn't end well.'

'I thought you were exaggerating. You exaggerate.'

'You live in Cape Town, Elena. You've been to the Waterfront. You know what pigeons are like.'

'I thought European pigeons would be different.'

He'd laughed, harder when she hid behind him. She'd ended up giving the bag of seeds to a kid before running away, causing the pigeons to scatter. They'd eaten pasta and chocolate crêpes and taken pictures. Once, Elena had photobombed another couple, then apologised profusely and taken about twenty pictures of them alone to make up for it. Now they were here, on the canal, having someone sing to them.

It was a lot to process. Not the experience, but the emotions that accompanied it. And the thoughts. Those insidious thoughts that had popped into his mind all day, then scurried away before he could put his finger on what they were suggesting. They all pooled together now though, growing into an idea that stole his breath.

It was based on never wanting to see Elena as tortured as she had been the night before. To keep her as happy as she was now, as she had been all day. It was built by the memories of how she'd elevated his business banquet that night in Rome because she fitted so perfectly into his world. She went head to head with him when he did something stupid, forced him to think about the way he treated people, and made him feel more like himself than he ever had. If he'd ever encountered his equal, she was it.

She was it.

'This is so nice,' Elena said at that moment, as if sensing his confusing thoughts. And his body, as if confused itself, responding by putting an arm around Elena's shoulders.

He froze. Until she rested her entire body against him. Then he melted.

It was like the hug from the night before. Warm and comfortable. Except there was more now. She was looking up at him, smiling, and he felt himself stumble. Whatever part of him had been standing steady in the face of the onslaught that Elena was unknowingly waging against him broke down. Whatever sanity he had left that told him not to indulge his ridiculous idea fled.

The proposal spilled out of his mouth.

'Marry me.'

CHAPTER ELEVEN

ELENA DIDN'T HAVE a moment to process before the clouds of celebration broke above her and it began to rain.

'A proposal!' the gondolier cried. He shouted in Italian to another gondolier close by. 'A proposal!' he said again.

'Oh, no,' Elena started to say, shaking her head, but the man had stopped steering.

He reached out to take Micah's hand, then grabbed both of Elena's and kissed them. When he saw she had no ring, he clapped, shouting about spontaneity and romance in Italian to his colleagues. There were two women who squealed happily, and another who wished them well quietly. All the while, Elena couldn't say a word. Micah replied to them weakly, accepting the congratulations as more gondolas drew near.

By the time they reached land again, Elena had regained her composure. She smiled her thanks and waved at the women who'd squealed earlier. She let Micah help her out of the boat and even managed a smile for him. Their gondolier was still looking at them with pride, and she allowed him to hug her.

When they were walking away from all the commotion, Elena felt herself deflate. She almost stumbled down a set of stairs, but a steady arm snaked around her waist. It seared through her clothing, and, despite the drama he'd caused in the last hour, reminded her they had something.

But that didn't mean she wanted to marry him. She was still working through the situation with her father and Jameson. How was she supposed to marry Micah with that going on? And what had provoked his proposal in the first place? They had spent a lovely day together, yes, but a day didn't make a marriage.

Or was it the *more* that could make their marriage? She'd felt connected to him from the moment they'd met, after all. She'd been comparing her relationship with Jameson to him ever since then. Oh, no. This…this *thing* he'd done was making her lose her mind. She didn't appreciate it. Not one bit.

Micah had the wisdom not to try to talk to her until they were back at the hotel. Wordlessly, he followed her to her room. She stepped back to allow him inside, then closed the door and leaned her back against it. Neither of them spoke for a long while.

'What just happened?' she asked eventually.

'I… I proposed.'

He looked as stunned as she felt.

'Yes, you did. I suppose that question was too vague, then. *Why* did you propose?'

'I don't know.' He looked at her. Ran a hand over his head. 'No—I do know.'

She waited for the rest.

He sighed. 'I wanted to save you from marrying someone you didn't know.'

He seemed genuine. And his motives were…she didn't want to say pure, because that had implications she didn't want to think about. He was well intentioned.

Still.

'You can't just propose to someone, Micah.'

'I know.'

'I mean, it's one thing if we were dating and this was a surprise. In which case, a proposal on a gondola would be appropriate.' Perfect, actually. Because if she removed the fact that he'd put her on the spot, and that they weren't dating, she would have been thrilled with the proposal. 'But obviously this isn't a romantic proposal. It's a business proposal.'

He didn't answer for a beat. 'It's another option. From a…' he hesitated '…a friend.'

Friends. That description didn't seem right to her. It seemed inadequate. But at the same time, she'd rather he call her a friend than try to figure out what other label fit.

'I don't know what to say, Micah. We've only known one another for days. We spent a solid portion of that time not speaking.'

'But when we spoke, it meant something, didn't it?' he asked quietly. 'And days might not be long, but it's longer than what you've spent with the man your father wants you to marry. Isn't it?' he prodded when she didn't reply.

She nodded. Not only to his question, but to the rest of what he said. She knew him better than she knew Jameson. She trusted him more than she trusted Jameson. Which wasn't saying much, considering how little she trusted Jameson. Relief rippled through her. She quickly realised it was because the notion of trusting Micah…was nerve-racking. Thinking that she didn't trust him *that much* felt safer than thinking that she did. After what he'd done to her, the games he'd played, she was right to be cautious.

But he'd also apologised for doing that. He'd had a sincere motive, which she, of all people, could understand. He'd tried to earn back her trust. Told her the truth about his parents and cancelled all his plans to spend the last few days in Italy with her. She felt comforted in his arms; she felt alive in his arms.

But did that mean he was a safer choice than marrying Jameson?

'Why marry you?' she asked, a little desperately. 'Shouldn't I just say no to my father?'

He walked over to her refrigerator and took another bottle of water. He downed it as quickly as he had the bottle the day before.

'According to my understanding, if you say no to your father, you'll be punished,' he said long after he finished drinking. 'You'll lose a job that's important to you. I assume that puts you in a difficult position with your financial responsibilities. And you obviously won't be offered help from your father. Not that you'd accept it.'

She angled her head, accepting all his presuppositions.

'I can keep you from losing your job.'

She blinked. 'How?'

He gave her a wry smile. 'The same way I got you to do this story on me.'

'You can…you can really do that?'

'I can.'

'No,' she said, shaking her head. 'My father is powerful. He has connections. Friends. He'll buy the paper if he has to.'

'I'll buy the company that owns the paper,' Micah said patiently. 'I can arrange for it before we go home.'

'Wh—why?'

'If you're my wife, I'll do anything I have to in order to protect you.'

And he had the power to, she realised. He could fight her father on his level. He could *beat* him. She would never have to do anything her father bid her to do again if she had Micah protecting her.

It removed the fear of her losing her job and security from the equation of the Jameson situation. But what about the rest? She paced the floor, silently thanking Micah for giving her a moment to think. The media would go wild for a marriage between her and Micah. She was an heiress; he was a self-made millionaire. And they got married after she was assigned to write a story about him? It was a romance novel in real life, and the press would portray it as such. The focus from the tragedy at the John diamond mine would shift, and the John image would be elevated.

Her father would love it.

As for the business… Her father would love that, too, if she was honest. He would love to hitch his wagon to Micah's star. Micah was a fresh, young businessperson who would invigorate John Diamond Company's image—and potentially the business itself—and make Cliff John look like a visionary.

Had Micah thought about that, too?

'What's in this for you?'

'Beyond helping a friend?' She narrowed her eyes. He smiled. 'Fine. I can't deny the business advantages our partnership will have.'

'You mean a partnership with my father.'

No, I mean *our* partnership. You were magnificent at the banquet, Elena. Your presence there is part of the reason Lucca and the rest of the Vittoria board are looking forward to working with me.'

'You could have achieved that without me.'

'I would have mangled my speech, annoyed people with my bluntness, and had them whispering about me learning humility if it wasn't for you.' The ends of his mouth tilted up. 'You make me look good. You make my business look good. Advantages.'

Stunned, she swallowed. 'This has…nothing to do with my father?'

'I've been planning to pitch to him for years,' he said, smile disappearing. 'That won't change if we marry. It can't.' His eyes pleaded with her to understand.

She did. Even if it stung a little.

'Of course.'

'I can make sure whatever business we do together doesn't affect you in any way.' He moved closer to her, but didn't touch her. 'I can protect you from him.'

'Can you stop me from wanting his love, too? No,' she said quickly. 'That was unfair. I'm sorry.' Her legs were shaking, so she sat down on the bed. 'This is a lot to think about.'

He came to sit next to her. 'I know. And I'll give you as long as you need. As long as is feasible, considering your father wants to announce your engagement to another man in a matter of days.'

She nodded, but didn't speak.

'I'll give you every assurance you need to feel safe,' he said softly. 'Not in the form of promises, but in a contract. We can stipulate everything legally. If I do anything to break that contract, you can take me to the cleaners.'

Her lips curved. 'I don't want your money.'

'I know. It's part of the reason I want to marry you.'

'Worried about gold-diggers?'

He gave a surprised laugh. 'No. I was thinking that your reasons for marrying me are nobler than money.' He paused. 'But come to think of it, it would be nice not to worry about gold-diggers.'

She snorted, but her mind was already wandering. Past all the business stuff, past her father, both of which they agreed on. It settled on the more dangerous things. The emotions that sat in a tight little ball in her chest marked with Micah's name. If that ball ever unfurled, it would cause untold damage. It was more likely to unfurl if they were married. As would the physical attraction she had for him. That ball sat *much* lower, felt like fire whenever he touched her, and begged her to touch him.

'You joke now,' she said, desperate to get away from the thoughts that made her heart pound, 'but what if you want a real relationship one day? What if you fall in love with someone and—what?' she asked at his smile.

'I barely managed to keep this friendship alive, Elena. I have no hopes that I'll be able to keep a flirtation alive, let alone a real relationship.'

'If you speak with them the way you've spoken with me—'

'Let me rephrase,' he interrupted. 'I don't want to flirt, or date, or marry. For real, I mean.' His smile was wry now. 'It's too much time and effort. I won't be missing out on anything by marrying you. But if you feel like you will be—'

'I don't.' She sighed. 'I just want to focus on work and—' She stopped herself. 'Children. What about children?'

He frowned. 'Never thought about them.'

'But do you want them?' she pressed.

'Do you?' he countered.

She shook her head vehemently. 'If I have my parents' genes in me, it would be better for both me and the non-existent child if we didn't cross paths.'

'You would be a great mother.'

'We'll never find out,' she told him.

'Agreed.'

'So easily?'

'I've never thought about them, and you don't want them. Seems pretty easy to me.'

She studied him. 'You're being pretty cool about this. Too cool, for someone who's about to be married.'

'You haven't said yes yet.'

She almost said it then, but thought better of it.

'I need time to think.'

To figure out if saving myself from this situation I'm in with Jameson is worth risking you hurting me some day.

'You have as long as you need.' He stood. 'Just remember this.'

She looked at him. 'What?'

'There could be worse things than being married to someone who respects you. Who you respect. Hopefully,' he added.

'I do,' she said softly. And knew he was right.

Micah called his lawyers immediately after he left Elena's room. He paid them a lot of money for the privilege of their advice, though he did feel bad about the hour. Not bad enough not to call them. He wanted to be ready if Elena agreed to his proposal. And he had a feeling she would. Which meant he might be married soon.

He should have been worried. Anxious. Something along those lines. He shouldn't be feeling…whatever he was feeling now. A hum, a buzz inside him. As if he'd consumed a swarm of bees and they were making their way through his body. He wouldn't call the feeling excitement. More anticipation.

He couldn't deny the advantages to marrying Elena. Everything he told her was true. She was the perfect business spouse; her linguistic skills were more helpful than he could have imagined; it would make a potential business partnership with her father easier. But he hadn't only been thinking about business when he proposed. He'd been caught by her. In the way the sun glinted off her hair. The smell of the salt of the canal and the perfume on her skin. When she was tucked into his side, he felt fortified. He felt whole. An illusion, he knew. No one could make him whole besides himself.

But that was it. Elena made him feel as though he *could* make himself whole. He hadn't even known the version of himself when he was with her existed, to be frank. He laughed, relaxed. His brain turned off, not constantly calculating or devising his next steps. It was different from how he'd been in the thirty-two years of his life and he liked it. He liked who he was with her.

And *that* should have worried him. That there was more than business involved in his decision to propose. That he was considering marriage at all when it hadn't appealed to him in the past. His parents hadn't married, so he didn't have anything to—or not to—emulate. And the people around him who were married treated the institution cavalierly. Adultery and disrespect were as much a part of marriage for his peers as their spouses were. Micah had no doubts, considering what his research revealed about the man, that Elena's would-be fiancé would follow that custom if they did marry.

It highlighted another alarming reason for his proposal: he wanted to protect her. From her father, who seemed callous and uncaring of the woman Elena was. From the man her father wanted her to marry, who would likely find ways to erase Elena's personality. He couldn't bear the thought of it. She was too vibrant, too vital.

Marriage might not have appealed to him, but being in Elena's presence did. Being in a partnership where they could treat one another as equals and respect each other for who they were? He could get on board with marriage for that.

Why did he just become aware of a slight trepidation kicking with every beat of his heart?

He went to the bar and took out a tiny bottle of brandy. He poured half of it into a glass and drank it, then poured the other half into it and added ice. He took the glass to the sliding doors, and opened them to Venice.

Laughter and music from some far-off place drifted up to him. He couldn't see much, but he could hear the water of the canal. It lapped against buildings, lightly, so that the sound was barely more than a whisper. The light breeze was likely the cause of it, but as it touched his face Micah couldn't fault it. The balcony he stood on was small, about five steps away from his hotel room, but it was enough to house two small chairs. He settled into one, and tried to figure out that trepidation.

Downsides. There had to be a downside to marrying Elena. *Everything* had downsides. There would be legal complications that came with being married, wouldn't there? But he had a team of competent lawyers and both he and Elena would stipulate the terms of the agreement. That didn't seem so much of a downside as it was admin. He could handle admin.

Children. He had never thought about them. To him, that said enough. Children deserved parents who wanted them. At the very least, parents who thought about wanting them. He had no desire to repeat the mistakes of his parents. Elena didn't want children either. That solved the problem easily, if making prospects for the physical part of their relationship less exciting.

Well. That posed a problem he didn't think could be easily solved. He couldn't see himself dating if he was married to Elena. Not only because the thought made him slightly nauseous for reasons he'd rather not examine, but because no woman had appealed to him the way Elena did. He had no interest in discovering if someone in the future could appeal to him in that way. It complicated sating his physical needs. But could the same be said for Elena?

If she wanted to go outside their marriage, he would have to respect it. He didn't own her; he didn't believe marriage or any relationship would change that. But he didn't want her to go outside their marriage. He wanted her to turn to him if she needed…that.

And *that* was a downside that made things a hell of a lot harder for the both of them.

CHAPTER TWELVE

'DO YOU UNPACK your belongings when you're staying at a hotel, or do you keep things in your luggage?'

Elena thought it was a strange morning greeting from a man who had just proposed to her, but she answered. 'I keep most things in my luggage. Generally my toiletries go in the bathroom and I have to pack those up. Good morning, by the way.' She slid into the booth opposite Micah. 'Did you sleep well?'

'I had a solid three hours, yeah.'

'Three hours?' She lifted her brows. 'Did you have something to think about?'

He smiled. It was teasing and a little sly, and it made her stomach jump. Or was that her hunger? In the whirlwind of the night before, she hadn't eaten. She'd drunk numerous cups of tea as she'd sat up and thought Micah's proposal through. She'd exhausted herself, but she thought she had an answer. That smile was making her doubt it though. Could she be his wife if his smile made her—?

Hungry, she interrupted her thoughts. She was *hungry. I bet.*

It was as if her thoughts were punishing her for interrupting them.

No, she told them firmly. *Stop misbehaving.*

'Yes, I did, which you know.' He eyed her. 'How much sleep did you get?'

She pretended to count. 'Oh, about three hours, too. They weren't solid though.'

'I'm sorry.'

She waved away the apology. 'You weren't in bed keeping me awake. Oh, you ordered me coffee?' she exclaimed when the waiter put a cup down in front of her. 'You're a lifesaver.'

He didn't reply, but his eyes had gone intense again. Not that it said much; that was his normal state. Although he had seemed lighter recently. Lighter compared to who he usually was, which was saying something, what with the proposal.

'What's wrong?' she asked when she'd taken a drink of her coffee and he was still staring at her.

'Nothing. You said… Never mind.' He picked up his menu. 'I'm thinking full breakfast this morning. It's going to be a long day.'

'Hold on. I'm still…'

She trailed off, replaying her words. When they caught up with her, she nearly dropped the cup she was bringing to her lips again. Not at what she'd said—that was perfectly harmless if Micah didn't have such a dirty mind—but at his reaction. It told her they needed to talk about that *thing* she'd thought about at several points of the night.

'Why…er…why is today going to be a long day?' she said, drinking her coffee as she intended to. It had nothing to do with the much needed caffeine and everything to do with hiding her blush. It also distracted her from having to talk about sex with her future husband and she was looking forward to that.

Not looking forward to that. *Not.*

In response to that correction, her mind offered her the

memory of Micah pinning her to the wall. Heat flooded her body and, instinctively, she pressed her legs together. Then she cursed both her body and her mind for betraying her, and tried not to think about how sensitive every part of her body had suddenly become.

She took another gulp of coffee.

'I…er… I thought we could go to Tuscany.' Micah took a sip from his coffee, too. Were his motives the same as hers? 'There's a small town there that would be perfect for today.'

'Oh, I don't want you to go out of your way to show me Italy. Venice is plenty.'

'But we've done Venice,' he said with a small smile. 'You've seen most of it. Of course, we can spend more time finding the jewels of the city. But wouldn't you rather go to the countryside? Sip wine in the vineyards? Eat homemade pasta?'

She stared at him for a long time. 'You're a hell of a businessperson. I'm pretty stubborn, but I swear you can talk me into almost anything.'

'Almost anything?' he enquired gently.

She opened her mouth to tell him what she'd decided, but the words wouldn't come out. She frowned. Was she being cautious? Or did she feel hesitant?

'It's okay, Elena.' His eyes were softer than usual. 'We don't have to talk about it now.'

'But we have to talk about it,' she insisted.

'We will. After the wine and pasta.' He smiled.

'You already know me so well,' she teased, though a part of her meant it. 'But yes, wine and pasta it is.'

That was how Elena found herself in the beautiful town of San Gimignano later that morning. It took them some time to get there by train, but the journey was beautiful. Green stretched out through the windows for kilometres as Micah told her about San Gimignano as if he were a tour guide. That was how she knew that the town was in the heart of Italy's wine country, and that it had narrow streets and old architecture much like Italy's cities.

But his descriptions couldn't prepare her for the feeling she got once they were there. It felt like history and peace, an uncommon combination, yet somehow it captured the atmosphere perfectly. The buildings were tall and old, as promised, but they felt rich with culture and were beautiful. They stretched up like stone trees to the sky, with ivy creeping up them as if wanting to see the sky, too.

They stopped at a rustic restaurant Micah had been to before, and were guided to a terrace that overlooked the vineyards. The terrace itself was beautiful. Flowers were planted in a large square in the middle of the space, and terracotta pots with flowers stood on the boundaries of it.

They were seated at the edge of the terrace and had the best view. Then the wine and the pasta came, and Elena thought it was the best day.

'Are you trying to persuade me to marry you, Micah?' she teased when their meal was done. She wouldn't have done it, but it was her third glass of the delicious wine, and she was in a teasing mood.

'You'll have to tell me if it's working before I admit that,' he said with a small smile. He was as tipsy as her, unless he could hold his wine better than she could. She doubted that.

'It might be.' She sighed contently. 'I've been more relaxed yesterday and today than I've ever been in my life.' She thought about it. 'In fact, this entire trip has done a world of good for my mental health. Despite those unexpectedly tense moments between us.'

'Tense moments?'

'Oops. Probably shouldn't have said that. But don't pretend like you don't know what I'm talking about.' She wagged a finger at him, then used the hand to count down the tense incidents. 'In the plane, when you looked at me in my unicorn shirt. At the banquet when you pinned me against the wall. After the banquet when we fought about—' she waved her hand '—something. Our conversation in my hotel room. The proposal.' She waved her hand at him. 'We need to stop it now or I'll run out of fingers to count on.'

'You have another hand.'

'Good point. Though that's not *my* point, so maybe it isn't.'

'Are you drunk, Elena?' he asked, this time with his annoyingly sexy smile on display.

'Of course I'm not drunk.' She said it a tad loud. She knew that because the people at the table next to her looked over in amusement. 'Hmm. Maybe I should switch to water.'

She studied her wine glass, drank the last drop then filled it with water and downed that.

'At least it has the same taste as the wine.'

'You're cute when you're drunk.'

She snorted. 'Please. We both know I'm cute when I'm sober, too.'

His smile went from his lips to his eyes. Somehow. He wasn't smiling at her, but she could tell he was still amused, and it had something to do with his eyes. Hmm. He could definitely hold his wine better than she could. She would have to remember that for their marriage.

Their marriage. She was marrying him. And she hadn't told him yet. She should probably tell him.

'We need to talk about sex,' she said instead.

And the shock of it sobered her right up.

* * *

'Do you want some dessert?' the server asked, oblivious to the tension between him and Elena.

'No,' he said quickly.

'But coffee, please,' Elena added.

'And for you, sir?'

'No. Yes. Yes,' he repeated. He could do with some coffee if they were going to be having this conversation.

The server disappeared, but Elena didn't say anything. She poured herself another glass of water and drank it, though slower than she had before. He suspected it was to delay the conversation, but he would wait as long as he had to. It was a skill he'd mastered in business negotiations, waiting. There was no way he would speak before she did. Let alone on this topic.

'I'm sorry,' she said, clearing her throat. 'I shouldn't have been so blunt about it.'

Micah drank from his water glass, too. He didn't want her to think he was panicked at her bringing this up. In fact, he was elated. It meant they were on the same page in terms of what they were trying to prepare for with their marriage. It meant she was probably thinking about saying yes to him. It meant he wouldn't have to bring it up.

'It's fine. You want to talk about it, we can talk about it.'

'Are we calling it "it" like we're two teenagers?' she asked lightly. '"Are we going to do 'it', Micah?"' She was shaking her head before she even finished. 'I am so sorry I did that. The fact that it went through my filter tells me I should have stopped after that second glass.'

'Elena, it's okay. You're just nervous.' He couldn't help his chuckle though.

She gave him an unimpressed look. 'If I was—and I'm not saying I am—the only thing I'd want from you is your laughter. So, thank you.'

He lifted up his hands, and shut his mouth. But she was so adorable. Her cheeks were red from the wine or the sun, he didn't know. Both, he decided. Her hair was an intricate web of curls at the top of her head, slightly off balance because of the hat she'd replaced the flower crown with. She'd brightened as soon as she'd put it on, and walked around with it all day until now, despite the bulk it created on her head.

She was wearing another charming summer dress, white and red this time, and had paired it with her signature red lipstick. It was faded from the food she'd eaten and wine she'd drunk, but he could still see. He wanted to kiss her lips.

'Okay, before I get there, I need to say that I'm… I'm going to say yes to marrying you.'

Her words didn't have the lyrical cadence they'd had earlier, and he thought the water was working fast. Then he realised she'd told him what he wanted and he wasn't processing it. The server arrived before he could and, after he thanked the man, Elena began to speak again.

'I need to talk to you about two things first though. One is sex, but we'll get to that. Not to the sex. To the topic.' She frowned and stared at the black coffee. 'I should have ordered an espresso.'

He didn't speak, half amused, half entranced by her words. By everything about her.

'Look, you've never had a personal…friendship, or whatever, like this before. I don't mean physically—' she blushed, but pressed on '—but emotionally. You've never had someone who wants to spend time with you. Not the business you, or millionaire you or whatever you, but *you*. I…um…care about you, and I guess you sense that, and I just wanted you to know that you don't have to marry me because I'm the first person to do that.'

She bit her lip at the end of it, as if keeping herself from adding to what she said. What more could she add? He almost asked her, but now he was thinking about whether she was right. Was he offering to marry her because he felt obligated to? Was this a response to someone who cared about him?

He had no means of comparison, so he struggled to answer that question. He didn't know what a personal friendship—or whatever, he thought wryly—was like. His relationship with his parents was non-existent, so he wasn't sure how he responded to love. Which sounded dramatic since he knew his parents loved him. In their way. So if he was responding to love, it was to his brand of love. The fact that someone loved him in a way that he could actually feel.

Wait—not love, care. Elena cared about him. He was responding to how she *cared* about him.

'How would I know if I'm doing that?'

Elena tilted her head. 'I'm not sure.'

'How do you know you're not accepting me because you don't know what any of that looks like either?'

Her lips parted, then formed an oh. She gave a little laugh. 'I guess I don't know that either.'

He brought his coffee to his lips. 'It's not exactly something I hoped you and I would have in common.'

'We have plenty of other things in common,' she said with a shake of her head. She continued, but he made a mental note to ask about those things later. 'And I came up with an answer. Kind of.' The knit in her brow deepened. 'We know how we felt when our parents treated us the way they did.' She paused. 'The not great stuff, and the way it made us feel. I don't feel that way now, with you.' She swallowed. 'But there was one time my father…almost acted proud of me.' She looked down, as if she were ashamed. He barely stopped himself from reaching out to her. 'And it made me feel...warm. Valued.' Now she met his eyes. 'Kind of how you make me feel.'

He had no idea what to do with the feelings that admission awoke in him. It felt as if a volcano had burst. He tried to focus on something else; *anything* other than the hot lava of emotion spreading inside him. Logic chose her relationship with her father. What she told him helped him understand why she was so eager to please the man. She wanted to feel warm and valued again. He couldn't blame her for that. Especially not when he wanted to feel that way just once with his parents.

Especially not when she made him feel that way, too.

Something skittish skipped through his chest.

'I'm sorry. I didn't mean to make things so sombre.'

'You didn't.'

Her eyes softened. 'I appreciate that lie.'

'Elena,' he said slowly, trying to get his thoughts in order. 'There are many reasons I asked you to marry me. Many logical reasons that have nothing to do with the fact that you...care about me.'

'Oh. Yes, of course.' She gave a quick shake of her head. 'I didn't mean to imply—'

'But,' he interrupted, 'the fact that you're concerned I might be doing this for less straightforward reasons, if you will, is also a part of why I asked. You're a rare breed of person,' he continued carefully. 'I would be honoured to be your husband.'

Their eyes met, held, and he was reminded of the lava again.

Which he promptly fell into when she said, 'Even at the cost of what you want to achieve with your mother?'

CHAPTER THIRTEEN

'WHAT DO YOU MEAN?' Micah asked once he resurfaced.

'What if my father chooses to punish me for going against his wishes by refusing to partner with you?' Her voice was low. 'You said that plan had something to do with your mother, didn't you?'

'Yes,' he murmured, realising he hadn't told her the details of it. 'She cares about her career more than anything else. I thought she would care about mine, too, if I partnered with your father. He's her biggest client.'

'And if she cared about your career, she might start to care more about you, too.'

He gave a curt nod. She studied him for a while.

'Is it worth it, Micah? Am I…? Is *this* worth the risk?'

It was a damn good question. And the fact that she was asking it meant more to him than he could comprehend. It told him it was worth the risk. Despite her deliberate rephrasing, he thought *she* was worth the risk. His gut agreed. It also told him she would care about him even if he didn't do anything to make her care about him.

She wasn't like his mother.

It was a confusing realisation in the context of everything that was happening. His mother was the reason he and Elena were even having this conversation. His desire to get her attention had put him on this path. Now he was considering throwing that away? Why? Because someone was offering him a relationship he didn't have to work so damn hard for?

Yes.

The lack of turmoil he felt at that was refreshing.

'I don't know what it means that I'm saying this.' He spoke slowly, in case something changed. It didn't. 'But I'd still like to marry you.'

'Micah,' Elena breathed. She reached out and covered his hand with hers. 'Are you sure?'

He turned his hand over and threaded his fingers through hers. 'Yes.'

Elena studied him. Seconds later, she shifted to the seat beside him, then grabbed his hand again.

'There's no shame in wanting a relationship with your mother. Even at the cost of this.'

'I know.' Because he couldn't resist it, he cupped her face. 'But I think my life will be fuller with you in it. My life will just be…different, with my mother in it.'

Emotion flooded her eyes. 'I'm sorry,' she whispered, clasping her hands around the wrist of the hand that held her face.

He could tell she meant it. She wasn't controlling her facial expressions. She was showing him her heart and, in it, he could see her sincerity. And more. So much more. More than he'd ever thought he could hope for when any-one looked at him.

'You don't have to be sorry for something outside your control,' he said.

'Not marrying you is *inside* my control.'

'It wouldn't make a difference to my relationship with my mother.' Somehow he knew that with certainty. 'I have no guarantee working with your father would either. I do know that marrying you would make a difference to my life.'

She bit her lip, her eyes not leaving his. 'Are you sure?'

He nodded. 'If you are.'

She nodded, too. 'I am.'

'Then let's get married.'

'We need to talk about something else first.'

He dropped his hand and groaned. 'I think we've talked enough.'

'You're right.' Her eyes sparkled. 'Maybe we should try a kiss, then?'

She didn't care that she was being forward. Micah's actual proposal had been clumsy—romantic, but clumsy—but this? This admission of what he thought his life would be with her in it? It was swoon-worthy. It was movie-worthy. It was romance-novel-worthy, kiss-you-until-you're-breathless-worthy. She wanted to be breathless.

'Are you sure?' he asked, though he'd already shifted forward, bringing their lips close together.

'I wouldn't have suggested it if I weren't.'

'Ah, yes. I forget you say what you mean.' He put his hand at the base of her neck. It sent a shiver through her. 'It's refreshing.'

'So you keep saying.'

Now she moved closer, running her index finger around the button at the top of his shirt. It was another white shirt, like the day before, except this one was short sleeved instead of rolled up. It revealed round biceps, and, before she'd fully thought it through, she was running her finger along the veins she could see there.

'You know what *would* be refreshing?' she said lazily. 'If you stopped talking and kissed me.'

She only had a flash of his smile before his lips met hers.

The sensation was other-worldly. A foolish description.

A fanciful description. It fit. Not once in her lifetime on earth had she felt so consumed by a kiss as she did now. The world around them ceased to exist. Only the heat that went from her lips down to her core, trailing a path that pulsed with desire, existed.

Then he slipped his tongue into her mouth, and she realised that existed, too.

It was probably a good idea to establish that both their bodies existed on this plane she was on. Her hands had somehow found both his biceps, and were holding on for dear life. His hands were resting on her thighs, squeezing her flesh as if anchoring his fingers there. Their mouths moved in union, giving and taking, enjoying and lusting.

There was more to the lusting than the physical. It felt deeper. It felt as if it touched her heart. It raced as Micah kissed her; a testament to his skill and his words. He kissed as intensely as she'd imagined he would, but with a hesitance that told her he was paying attention. To her responses, to her body. To what gave her pleasure so that he could continue to give it.

All of it told her he was a good man. And that, really, was what her heart was reacting to. He made sure she wanted to kiss him before acting on her suggestion. Even now, he was being careful. If his hands ever moved from her thighs, it would be after a question. Either verbally, or through a subtle touch that asked for permission. When she gave it, he would pay attention to her body as thoroughly as he was currently doing to her mouth. He would ask her for guidance, she knew, and would obey when she offered it to him.

He would torture her in all the right ways. His kiss—this simple kiss—told her so. Now, more than ever, she was glad she'd broached the topic of sex with Micah. The sooner they clarified their positions on it, the sooner they could act on those positions. She was certain of what he wanted. She knew what she wanted, too. She had never been as eager to sate her needs with anyone else.

'Micah,' she said, the shock of it forcing her to pull away.

Her breath took a long time to catch up to that shock. As it did, she lifted trembling hands to her mouth. It felt swollen. It felt used. Both felt like triumphs.

'It was too much too soon,' Micah said hoarsely. He reached for his water and emptied the glass in seconds. Then, seemingly having a handle on himself, he poured another glass and handed it to her.

'No, that's not it,' she said, accepting the water.

'Then what?'

Or maybe that *was* it. Not the kiss, but the realisations. The emotions. Too many too soon. But she couldn't tell him that.

'I was just thinking… I'm glad it's you. Not Jameson, I mean.' She tucked a stray curl behind her ear. 'We wouldn't share that.'

'Did you…er…?' He cleared his throat. 'Did you try?'

She gave him an amused look. 'Did I try to kiss a man who saw me as only a business arrangement? No.'

'Good.'

'Is it?' she asked casually. Colour touched his cheeks. It was the first time she'd ever seen him blush. He shifted, telling her he didn't like it as much as she did, and she took mercy on him. 'Honestly, I don't think Jameson would have ever been interested in me. I don't think I'm his type. Too mouthy.'

She'd been joking, but he didn't crack a smile. He didn't even reply. It wouldn't have been a conversation if he didn't shift, avoiding her gaze.

'What?'

'Nothing,' he said quickly. Too quickly.

'Then why are you acting so weird?'

'No reason.'

'Micah.'

'It's not relevant any more.'

'So you should have no problem telling me then.'

He narrowed his eyes. 'You're just as formidable as you say I am, you know that?'

'Thank you,' she said. 'Now spill.'

After a long pause, he answered. 'I had Serena send me over some information about the man you were going to marry.'

'Did you?' she asked lightly. 'Any particular reason?'

'I was…interested.'

'Hmm.'

'In any case,' he said quickly, 'there was a story from this week that… Well, I'm sure you've seen it. You're a journalist.'

'I don't see *every* story.'

'No, I suppose not.' He cleared his throat. 'You probably have an alert for the man you're thinking about marrying though.'

'Surprisingly, no. But,' she said conversationally, 'if you keep stalling, I might reconsider marrying you. Or spill this glass of water on your pants and tell everyone you've had an accident. Probably the latter. Less dramatic.'

Micah frowned. 'Those are both dramatic options.'

'Micah.'

'Fine.' He cleared his throat for the millionth time. 'There was a photo on a gossip site. It was purely speculation, in light of, I think, the news of your impending engagement. They claimed the man was Jameson St Clair.' He paused. 'With another woman.'

Elena took a second. 'Do you have the link to the story?'

He studied her, but took his phone out, typed on it for

a moment, then handed it to her. The headline was sala-
cious, which she expected, but she focused on the picture. It showed a man walking into a hotel with a woman.
She was dressed in a sophisticated black dress that was
tight and ended above her knee. The man wore a distinctive suit—bright blue, with white pinstripes. It was what
Jameson had worn the day her father had suggested their
marriage. The shock of the suggestion had every detail
embedded in her mind.

Jameson had been with another woman the same day
he said he would marry her.

'Well. I guess mouthy has nothing to do with it. It's
because I'm brunette,' she said, handing the phone back
to Micah.

'It's him?'

'It is. And that's the same day he and my father said
they wanted us to marry. The suit,' she answered when his
brows rose. 'It stuck in my mind.'

'I'm sorry.'

'Don't be.' She shrugged. 'This would have been the
reality of my life. You've given me another option.' She
reached for the coffee they'd both forgotten, finding it
lukewarm. Still, she drank it. She needed the kick for the
question she was about to ask him. 'Unless there'll be pictures of you coming out like this?'

His gaze didn't waver. 'Heavens no. I prefer brunettes.
Mouthy brunettes, to be specific.'

She sat back in her chair and grinned. Couldn't help
it. 'We should probably start planning our wedding, then,
huh?'

CHAPTER FOURTEEN

THEY LEFT SAN GIMIGNANO that night. They'd spent the afternoon discussing their plan, and they'd both decided going back to South Africa a day early would only benefit them. They could go to Micah's lawyer's offices, sign a prenuptial agreement, and tell her father.

At least, that had been Micah's suggestion. Elena's was more radical.

'We should get married before we tell my father,' she said matter-of-factly. 'There's no point rushing on the prenup unless we're getting married soon. And getting married soon will put us in a better position when we see my father.' She glanced at him. 'If you need to buy the parent company of my paper, you can do it for your wife, not your fiancée.'

'I trust you,' he said once he could form a coherent reply. 'I'll do it for my fiancée, too.'

'Yeah. Yeah, it's too fast,' she said, shaking her head. 'Sorry.'

The expression in her eyes had him saying, 'There's more to this, isn't there?' She bit her lip. It tugged at his heart. 'Elena, you can tell me.'

It was a while before she did. 'I'd feel safer—more protected—if we were married when we speak to him.'

It did him in, her vulnerability. He nodded. 'So let's get married before we see him.'

The first half of the plane ride, they spoke about every possible condition they wanted in their pre-nup. Elena's professional independence was assured—at Micah's insistence—as was Micah's wealth—at Elena's insistence. They added clauses about business commitments and personal functions, birthdays and special occasions. They stipulated that neither of them wanted children, and if they did it, both parties would have to agree on it and put it in writing. There would be a probationary period where both of them would have to display the behaviour they wanted to see in a parent. Essentially assuring the other they could do work/home balance.

'Just in case,' Elena said.

'Just in case,' he agreed, but he was sure it wouldn't be necessary.

After they repeated all that and more to their lawyers, who recorded it with their permission, they ended the call and sat staring at one another.

'That was interesting,' he said.

'It was.' There was a beat of silence. 'We didn't talk about sex.'

He paused as he reached for his drink, but continued when he realised he couldn't delay any longer. 'No, we didn't.'

'We'll need to tell them if they need to put an infidelity clause in the contract,' she said nonchalantly. 'I know what you said after the Jameson thing, but if you've changed your mind, we should be prepared for that.'

The way she was picking at her trousers told her she wasn't as relaxed as she was pretending to be.

'I haven't changed my mind,' he said, watching her. 'But I've already had the clause inserted.'

'Yeah?' Her fingers stopped moving. 'What did you say?'

'If I cheat, you can leave.'

She frowned. 'What about me?'

He cleared his throat. 'I told them I would confirm later.'

There was a long pause. She reached over and took the drink from his hands. Unlike him, though, she drank it. He watched her swallow. Only she could make it seem like an action that belonged in a seduction. She pressed the glass to her lips before handing it back to him, as if she'd realised it wasn't hers.

'You know, it's not cheating if we both agree we can go outside the marriage for sex,' she said, watching him closely.

'No, it's not.'

He drank the remaining liquid in one quick gulp.

'We haven't made any decisions about that. Why would you involve the lawyers?'

'I went into this knowing that I didn't want to—' He broke off to clear his throat. Actually, he was giving himself time to figure out what he wanted to say. It wasn't working, so he stopped trying. 'I don't want to go outside our marriage. I know it's not strictly a real marriage, but it feels disrespectful. What if someone saw me and this other woman? The speculation in the media would be as bad as with Jameson.' He shook his head. 'I'm not him.'

'Yet you're telling me *I* can choose that?' She stood and came to sit down next to him. His seat wasn't meant for two, so he ended up half sliding off it. It didn't help; Elena still ended up sitting on him. 'What about the speculation if the media sees me with another man?'

He tried to ignore how wonderful she smelled. How his skin was getting hot and every cell was becoming more aware of her proximity.

'There wouldn't be as much attention on you if you wanted to do that.'

She studied him. 'Stop being so careful, Micah. Tell me what you feel.'

What would it be like to trail a finger over the skin near her collarbone? It looked so smooth, so silky. When they'd been kissing, he hadn't had the benefit of touching her the way he wanted to. He wanted another chance, but in the same breath, he wanted—

'Micah.'

Oh, yes. She was talking to him. 'What?'

She snorted. 'You're being so careful. It's working on my nerves. I'm sure my questions are doing the same for you.' She didn't wait for an answer. 'I'm going to tell you what I think. Honestly. You might not want to hear it.'

She waited for an answer now, as if he would have one. Should he have one? He tried to ignore the allure of her skin, her collarbone, the memories of that kiss with her, and thought about what she said. She wanted to tell him what she thought about fidelity in marriage. Right. And she wanted to do so honestly because she thought he was being cautious.

He frowned. 'I'm not being careful.'

'You're not saying what you want to say either,' she countered easily, unsurprised by his delayed response.

'I… Elena, I don't know how to say what I want to say.'

'Because you're trying to think like a businessperson. Don't. Think like *you*. A man, a husband, or whatever the hell role will help you to be honest.'

'You really want that?'

'*Yes.*'

'Fine.' He didn't let himself think. 'I don't want to go outside our marriage for sex for a number of reasons. I've given you a lot of them. The most important is that I find you incredibly attractive, Elena.' His voice dropped. 'I feel…something for you that I have no interest in feeling with anyone else. I doubt I could.' He couldn't help the caress he gave her, starting at that pulse in her neck, tracing the soft skin to her shoulder. 'I don't want to cheat because I don't think I'd want anyone as much as I want you.'

Elena's lips parted, but he didn't think it was only surprise. He had been terribly candid. But the quick breath that pushed through her lips when he skimmed her collarbone told him it was lust, too. She cleared her throat.

'Why would you want me to find someone else then?' Her voice was barely above a whisper.

He put an arm around her waist. When she leaned into him, he pulled her onto his lap. She immediately locked her arms around his neck.

'Did I give you the impression I wanted that?' With her closer now, he could let his lips do the work his fingers had done. He brushed them over that spot at her collarbone. She arched her neck. He kissed the exposed skin. 'Elena, what I want is for you to come to me for your physical needs. But I believe in your independence and your ability to choose what's right for you. If you don't believe in what I believe, I can't fault you for that.'

'Hmm.'

It was all she said. He didn't blame her for the lack of response when he was the reason she wasn't responding. He assumed. His hands were skimming the sides of her breasts now, his thumbs brushing over the light padding of her bra. He didn't linger there—he would lose his mind if he did—but there was no lack of places to touch. She wore a wraparound shirt with her trousers, perfectly respectable as it ended right where her pants started. It was less respectable if someone pushed the end of the shirt up to expose her skin.

He was up for the task.

Her skin was glorious. Soft beneath his touch, the faint

strip of brown he'd revealed. She shivered as he touched her, all around her waist, and when he looked at her again, she was watching him with hooded eyes.

'You know,' she said lazily, 'I was going to tell you pretty much the same thing. Not the things about finding you attractive—' she paused to give him a saucy smile '—but that I don't think going outside our marriage for something we could get inside it would be productive for either of us. Of course,' she continued, shifting so that she was straddling him, 'there's an argument that could be made for sex making things murky between us.'

Plump flesh peeked out at him from the V at her chest. He dragged his eyes up.

'Will you be making that argument?'

'I can keep a clear head when it counts,' she told him.

'So, no?'

Her lips curved. 'No. How about you?'

'Please,' he said with a snort.

'Wonderful. Personally, I don't think we should include lawyers in this.' She opened the buttons at the top of his shirt. 'They already know too much about our relationship as is.'

'If you're sure.'

Quite frankly, he didn't care. Not when she was kissing the skin she'd exposed in some sensual tit for tat that he was looking forward to exploring. She sat back at his answer though.

'The way you've handled this whole thing…makes me sure,' she repeated. 'I believe what you say. And I promise I won't cheat on you. I won't break your trust.' She shimmied off his lap, giving him a mild look when he made a noise of protest. 'We should keep things respectable between us until we're married.'

He smiled despite the lust travelling through his veins. 'Should we?'

'Yes.' She sniffed. 'I'm a respectable woman.' She straightened her top and then her shoulders. 'A respectable woman who knows the value of delayed gratification.'

He rested his forearms on his legs, watching her as amusement and dark desire tangled inside him. 'You should tell me more about that.'

With a reflection of his amusement and desire sparkling on her face, she did.

The ethics of marrying a man when she was supposed to announce her engagement to another confused Elena if she thought about it too much. But she was sure it was the right thing to do. If she and Micah didn't get married before they went to speak with her father, she was afraid they never would. She couldn't risk that. This marriage had become a shiny light in a darkness she hadn't realised she'd entered into. It made her feel strong again. She had no idea when she'd lost that feeling, but she had, and to have it back was heady. Especially when she didn't know if it was permanent.

It might be, Elena comforted herself. She might hold on to her strength, her power when they saw her father and told him the news. But the fact that she wasn't sure was enough to make her feel unsteady. Looking at herself in the outfit she was going to get married in didn't make her feel that way though. Nor did the fact that she was about to get married.

Elena stared at herself in the mirror of the hotel suite. They'd arrived in Cape Town hours before, had gone straight to Micah's lawyers and signed their papers. Something had come up for Micah's attention while they were there, and they'd parted, agreeing to meet at the hotel they'd booked a suite in until things were finalised.

She had no idea what that meant, or how it would look, but for illogical reasons it felt like the right thing to do. A part of her expected paparazzi to be at her home, taking pictures of her before she could speak with her father. Or worse, Jameson would be there. Or her *father*. None of that was likely, but she didn't want to worry about that, too. So she accepted Micah's offer of the suite, went to a store and bought herself something to get married in. Then she got ready to get married.

Her outfit of choice was a white suit and lace vest. It was pretty much like the other suits she wore, but fancier. The material was softer, more expensive because it was her wedding day. It was also much sexier than any suit she wore. The lace vest was to thank for that. It covered everything it had to, but it clung, and, with the material like a spider's web, seemed created for temptation.

She felt more comfortable in it than she would a wedding dress, she was sure. And it meant something to her that she wasn't giving up a part of herself to marry someone for her father. Although strictly speaking, she *was* marrying someone for her father. She wouldn't be marrying at all if it weren't for him.

But at least this way he can't weaponise the fact that you aren't married against you. At least now you're safe.

She hadn't realised how much she'd needed that security until now. She hadn't realised how powerful the threat of her father's presence—the threat of his demands—was in her life. Her heart pained that this was her reality, but it was time she faced it. Just as she had to face that she would rather have the peace of no longer being threatened by her father than the hope of being loved by him. Facing it made her smart. Accepting it would make her happy. At this point, she could only manage the first.

A knock on the door brought her out of her head. Thank goodness. She went to open it.

Micah stared at her dumbly. Shook his head. 'Wow.'

'Hello to you, too,' she said with a smile. It lightened the darkness inside her. Reminded her why she'd agreed to marry him. The light grew when his eyes kept dipping to her outfit. 'You know I have a face, right?'

'Right,' he said, his head snapping up. His eyes widened then, too, and if she didn't think he'd tease her for it, she'd thank him for the reaction. It soothed any remaining shakiness thinking about her father had brought.

'I thought you looked beautiful that night at the banquet. No—I thought you couldn't look *more* beautiful than you did that night at the banquet.' He blinked. 'I was wrong.'

Good heavens, this man was a charmer. She wanted to be annoyed by it, but she couldn't be. The gooeyness slid into her bloodstream, carried to her heart before she could even try.

'Thank you. I'm glad this non-wedding wedding has some wedding wedding elements.'

His eyes grew concerned. 'You know we don't have to do this today.'

She stepped back so he could walk into the room. 'You know we *have* to do this today.'

He brushed a hand against hers as he walked past her. 'Fine. We can have another wedding. A *wedding* wedding.'

'I appreciate the offer, Micah, but I don't want a wedding wedding. The elements of a wedding I want, I have. A man I respect is marrying me. Also someone so completely enthralled by my good looks that he's aware of how lucky he is.'

Micah smiled. 'I guess you do have it, then. But we can talk about it later. The business thing took longer than expected. We have about twenty minutes before we have to leave for Home Affairs.'

'It's unlikely a government-run department is going to require us to be there on time,' she replied, rolling her eyes.

'Only if you don't have connections.' He winked. 'I'm going to have a shower.'

On his way to the bedroom with its en-suite bathroom, he pressed a kiss to her forehead. Elena spent much too long thinking about the casual gesture. It was just so… *easy*. She didn't completely trust it. Not because she didn't want to; precisely because she wanted to. Whenever things seemed too good to be true, they usually were. At least when it came to Elena and relationships.

She was trying not to think about it when Micah walked into the living room of the suite wearing only a towel. It was like an advertisement, but it was anyone's guess for what. Cotton, for the towel? He was clean-shaven, so it could have been anything to do with shaving. The scent trailing after him was powerful, but not overwhelming, so perhaps he was selling some perfect combination of men's cologne. Or perhaps he was selling nothing. Perhaps his intention had always been to make her salivate.

When they met, she remembered admiring the muscle that was clear in his frame. Now, she could do it first-hand. She'd been right to think there was a layer of softness insulating that muscle. It made Elena wonder why only perfectly sculpted men were used as models. Micah's build made it clear that he was strong and human; he had a life beyond the gym.

As it turned out, that build was *exactly* her type.

And Micah knew it, too.

'Should I worry about the way you're looking at me?' he asked casually.

'Why did you come out of the bedroom if you didn't want me to look at you like this?'

'I'm looking for the suit bag with my clothes in.'

'The one you took into the bedroom?'

He smirked. 'Did I? I must have missed it.' He paused. It felt as though he was giving the electricity between them time to spark. 'I'm not mad about it.'

'I don't imagine you are,' she said in the same mild tone he used. 'Now, get ready so we can go.'

He was smiling when he went back into the bedroom, and when he emerged again minutes later, he looked exactly like the models she wanted to see in fashion campaigns. His suit was tailored to fit his broad shoulders and lean hips, and the navy colour was perfect against his brown skin.

'You look nice,' Elena said when he reached her.

His eyes danced with amusement. 'If that's what your face looks like when I look nice, I might have to call an ambulance to check your heart on days I look gorgeous.'

She rolled her eyes. 'The ego on you.'

'It's not ego when it's the truth.'

'I can't believe I'm marrying someone who said that.'

He offered her an arm. 'Let's make it official anyway.'

She took the arm with a firm grip and a nod that was just as firm. 'Yes. Let's.'

CHAPTER FIFTEEN

MICAH'S CONTACTS ENSURED they were in and out of the Home Affairs office in exactly forty minutes. Married.

They were now married.

Elena refused his offer to get dinner to celebrate. She was worried someone might recognise them and take photos. Those photos would almost certainly reach her father, and they wouldn't have the opportunity to surprise him with the truth.

'It'll be easier if we surprise him, trust me.'

That was all she said until they reached the suite.

He hadn't thought to book two separate rooms for them. Not based on the way they had responded to one another when they'd kissed, or on the plane. Their kiss after they made their vows to one another hadn't been as hot as either of those occasions, but it had lingered, and he'd felt a promise in it. Perhaps that had been presumptuous, but Micah thought he could be on the night of his wedding. Now, he doubted it. Elena had all but curled into herself, and nothing he said lured her out of it.

'Do you want something to eat?' he asked, loosening his tie.

She kicked off her shoes and shook her head. 'No, thank you.'

He didn't think she'd eaten anything since that morning, so he knew she wasn't denying it because she wasn't hungry. He was about to ask when she grabbed her phone and disappeared onto the balcony.

He didn't follow immediately. She needed time and space, clearly. Otherwise, she wouldn't have taken it. But he wanted to follow her. He wanted to demand she talk to him. They were married now, for heaven's sake. He didn't want their marriage to start off on this foot, where they didn't speak with one another.

He had enough of that growing up.

He swore at the reminder.

He'd been avoiding thoughts about his parents since he'd had that revelation about his relationship with his mother. It had been easy to do with everything that had happened in the last few days. But it was still there, as it always was. Lurking around the distractions he offered himself, waiting for an in. Apparently, he'd given it one now.

He threw off his suit jacket and tossed the tie on the bed. He undid his cufflinks and set them on the bedside table. He rolled up his shirt's sleeves, kicked off his shoes, then headed for the minibar in the living room. It was fully stocked, and he grabbed a brandy as he had the night he'd proposed to Elena. Now though, it wasn't to celebrate his actions; it was to clear his thoughts.

His mother would never know about his plan to gain her attention by partnering with Elena's father. That simple fact anchored him. If she knew, he would feel more pathetic than he already did. He was a grown man, and he thought he could get his mother to pay more attention to him through a business transaction. If he had his mother's attention, he wouldn't feel so bad about not having his father's. It would still smart, there was no doubt, but at least he wouldn't feel as abandoned as he did now. Because at least his father had left him for a reason—another family. The kind his father had always wanted, no doubt.

His mother though? She'd left him for a business. For work. Something that had no value in the grand scheme of things.

That very thought told him how much things had shifted in his brain. He'd felt the same way about work as she had for the longest time. Up until this trip to Italy, in fact. In Italy, he'd learnt he could be himself. Have his interests, and still be cared about. He didn't have to twist into impossible shapes for that to happen either. It had just happened, naturally, and it had put a lot of things into perspective.

He was still processing all of it, but he knew this: Elena was his family now. Their marriage might be a business agreement, but their relationship had more emotion in it than anything he'd experienced with his real family. He trusted her, and she wouldn't hurt him the way his mother did. He knew it.

The thought had him stalking to the balcony and opening the sliding doors. He found Elena sitting with her feet against the railing, her phone in her lap.

'It's beautiful, isn't it?' she said before he could talk. 'I will never forget Italy and everything we saw there, but this? This is…' She trailed off with a head shake. 'This is home.'

Slowly, he took a seat next to her. The hotel was in Cape Town's centre, and looked out on the buildings and streets of the business hub of the city. They were up high enough that they could see the ocean during the day. Table Mountain loomed above it, dark and steady at night. It didn't have the quietness or the quaintness that Italy had, but the sounds were familiar, the stars were brighter and, as Elena said, it was home.

'I sent Jameson a message telling him I'm not marrying him.' She wasn't looking at him, so she didn't see his head whip towards her. 'Then I messaged my father to tell him there wouldn't be an engagement party tomorrow, and that I'd see him at eleven a.m. to explain why. Figured I'd give us some time to have breakfast, at least.'

No wonder she'd gone quiet.

Even as his instincts congratulated themselves on knowing something wasn't right with her, his heart chastised him. He'd forgotten about the party. He should have known saying no to it, to the engagement, would be hard on her. She was worried about disappointing her father, about sacrificing what she wanted from him. Their wedding hadn't only been about them, not for her, and he should have known that.

'How do you feel?'

There was a long silence.

'Good.' She laughed, but it didn't sound free or unburdened. It sounded as if it was wrenched from somewhere deep inside her. 'I feel good. I'm so relieved I made the decision—the right one—and I don't feel like I'm betraying him.'

Her voice changed as she spoke, getting higher and less steady, and he stood and gently pulled her into his arms so she could lean on him.

'No, no, I'm fine,' Elena assured him, but her face was pressed into his chest and he could barely hear her. He was also fairly certain his shirt was wet. 'I'm glad it's you,' she said with a hiccup. She leaned back. She was crying, but she didn't seem to know it was happening. Perhaps she was refusing to acknowledge it.

'I'm *so* glad it's you.' She pressed her lips together. 'This feeling in my chest that used to be there isn't there any more. It feels weird. Empty. Which I know makes no sense because it also feels right.' She curled her hands into his shirt. 'We feel right.'

Now she lifted to her toes and kissed him lightly on the lips.

'I'm so glad it's you,' she whispered again, before wrapping her arms around him and hugging him more tightly than he'd ever been hugged before.

Maybe that was why it felt as if something clicked inside him.

She'd just fixed something broken.

Elena was sure there were rules about not blubbering all over a spouse on the night of a wedding. Too bad. She hadn't paid attention to the rules before when it came to Micah. Though it might have been more accurate to say their relationship hadn't followed the rules since she hadn't actively willed it that way.

She wasn't supposed to feel as though a man she'd met a week ago was the only person she could trust in the world. Trust. It terrified her that she even thought it. There were still parts of her that worried Micah would turn out like her father. Or like any of the powerful men she'd come to know in her life. But she also knew that was unfair. He had proved to her that he was different. Ever since he came to Venice to find her, he'd offered her honesty. He was protecting her. He'd held her when she cried. And when he touched her, he made her head spin and her heart fill.

It was that filling heart that was the *really* scary part about trusting him.

She tried to talk herself out of the fear. Things weren't too good to be true. It was okay to feel safe with him. She didn't have to worry about her father or Jameson or losing her job any more. She would be okay.

'I'm sorry for messing up your shirt,' she said as she

pulled back and saw the damage. Smeared make-up and wetness didn't do anything for what she was sure was an expensive piece of clothing. 'I'll pay to have it cleaned.'

'I'll take care of it,' he said. He didn't move closer to her, but it felt as if he wanted to. She had no idea how she knew it. 'Just tell me you're okay.'

'I'm fine.' She walked back into the room. 'It was residual stress from the last few days. Or the last month. I'm fine,' she said again.

'If you're sure.' He was watching her intently. 'Tea?'

'Please.' She watched him go through the motions for a second, then said, 'Who told you to give someone tea when they're feeling shaky?'

He glanced over his shoulder. 'That's a thing?' He smiled when she gave him a look. 'It's part of pop culture. I'm not completely oblivious.'

'Thank goodness for that,' she murmured. She went to the bathroom, washed her face and tied her curls up. She was still wearing her wedding suit, but she had her Italy suitcase with her. She could change into a sleepshirt.

When she left the bathroom, her tea was steaming on the table in the little lounge of their suite. The sleepshirt could wait, she thought, but took off the jacket of her suit and draped it over the back of a chair.

'Thank you,' she said to Micah, who was sitting in the seat opposite the one she'd taken.

'It's a relatively simple way to make you feel better.'

His eyes pierced hers as she took a sip from her tea. She sighed as the warmth soothed the remaining unsteadiness. Then she sighed when she found Micah still looking at her.

'I feel a lot better, I promise. It was really just tension. And all the stuff with my father and Jameson.'

'I understand.' His drink was brown liquor. He sipped it slowly. 'I also understand that you don't always deal with your feelings when they come up, which means something like this happens, I'm betting, quite frequently.'

'No,' she said defensively. 'It's never happened before.'

'Guess I'm wrong then.'

'Not entirely. I mean, I could be better about…' She trailed off. 'This is not a therapy session.'

'It's a hell of a lot cheaper than a therapy session,' he said with a small smile.

'Yeah, I only had to sell my singledom to you. Ooh,' she said when he opened his mouth, 'was that too far? Did I make you feel uncomfortable?'

'No.' He narrowed his eyes. 'I *am* wondering about your sense of humour. That was…dark.'

She laughed. 'Best you know that now before we really get stuck into this marriage thing.'

He smiled, but didn't reply, and they sat drinking their beverages in companionable silence.

'I'm sorry I worried you,' she said softly. 'I wasn't thinking about you… It'll take some time, but I'll get there, I'm sure.

'If it makes you feel any better,' he said in the same tone of voice, 'I wasn't thinking about you either. I should have known marrying me when you had telling your father hanging over your head would be hard.'

'It wasn't—'

'You didn't want to sit on my lap yesterday because of it.' His eyebrows rose. 'Wasn't the respectability about that?'

'Well,' she said, frowning. 'I was doing a little more than sitting on your lap, Micah.'

'I don't remember that.'

There was a challenge in his voice that switched the atmosphere in the room from comfortable to…something else. She couldn't describe what it was, exactly, but it felt dangerous. Not in a *you might get hurt* way, but in an *adrenaline makes you see life differently* way. Suddenly she was aware of the breeze fluttering through the sliding door he hadn't closed. It was a warm night, uncommonly so for the season, so the wind only felt seductive.

She could have been projecting since she also just noticed Micah had unbuttoned the first few buttons of his shirt and rolled up his sleeves. It exposed delicious skin that she wanted to touch. And if she touched, she was certain she would end up wanting more...

'Well,' she said again, setting the empty teacup on the table, 'I can't blame you. I hardly remember it myself. Not the way you touched or kissed me here—' she traced the skin at her neck as he'd done with a finger '—or here.' She touched her midriff, and felt the lace material beneath it.

She wanted to take it off, to offer Micah this piece of her she'd kept guarded for as long as she could remember. But that felt too rash, too brazen. Especially after she'd exposed her emotions to him.

Except that made her feel *more* connected to him. It made her *want* to be rash, brazen. In the end, she settled for loosening her hair and fluffing the curls. His eyes followed the movement, and his fingers twitched. He wanted to touch them. She wanted him to touch them.

'I don't remember that at all,' he said, setting his own glass down. He stood. Began unbuttoning his shirt. 'I should probably get ready for bed. It'll be a long day tomorrow.'

He pulled the shirt off, revealing the body she'd drooled over earlier that day.

Damn him. He was winning.

'We both should.' She stood and unbuttoned her trousers. Heaven only knew where the modesty she'd felt seconds ago had gone to. Her competitiveness had consumed it.

Her lust had devoured it.

Rash and brazen indeed.

'Is there just this one bed?' she asked, walking past him as she shimmied the trousers over her hips. She'd worn the appropriate underwear for white trousers. She hadn't realised how appropriate it would be for her wedding night. Was that by sheer force of will or ignorance?

'I…er… I didn't think I needed to…'

His words were slow, stammering. She turned around.

'Is something wrong?'

'No.'

But his eyes were sweeping up and down her body. When they rested on her face, the hunger there threatened to steal her breath. The only reason it didn't was because she felt the echo of it inside her. She was playing a game with him, but the truth of it was that she wanted him. Not because of the way he looked without a shirt on, or because of how he wore a suit, or because he looked like the models she'd never had the common sense to conjure.

She wanted him because she wanted to be close to him. She wanted to feel that trust they'd built in a new way. He thought about her as no one had before. He was considerate and cautious, and he wanted her to be independent, to keep her own mind and make her own choices. Despite what he wanted.

It was hugely different from the conditions they'd met under. Or was it? Micah hadn't known her then. He'd been on his own for the longest time, and he didn't know how to think about other people. He hadn't learnt that from his mother since she hadn't shown that to *him*. So he'd emulated what he saw and did what he had been taught. Then Elena had come along, and communicated that honesty, that respect, were important. He'd immediately adhered to that. Though no one had taught him how to consider someone else, he'd done it for her.

That was the man she wanted to make love with. And suddenly her hesitancy, and perhaps even her shame at wanting it, melted away.

'Elena,' he whispered. 'You're so beautiful.'

She bit her lip. 'I don't think you're supposed to say that. Not if you want to win.'

He closed the space between them, his arms resting on her hips. When she didn't shift, the grip of his hands tightened. 'I don't know what competition we were in, but I'm pretty sure I'm winning doing exactly this.'

She circled her arms around his neck. 'I used to think your charm was annoying.'

His head reared back slightly. 'What?'

She chuckled. 'You always knew the right thing to say.'

'And that was annoying?'

'Yes. Because it didn't seem genuine. It seemed…practised.'

'I do *not* practise my charm.'

Again, she laughed at his indignation. 'Of course not. I just meant… It felt like something you had to do. It didn't sound like something you wanted to do.' Her eyes dropped to his lips. 'Now, I know that everything you say comes from you.' She brushed her thumb over his bottom lip. 'The real you, not the person you think you have to be.'

'Elena,' he whispered. 'Let me kiss you.'

She lifted her head to his in response.

CHAPTER SIXTEEN

HE WOKE UP as the sun hit the curtains, the thin material barely keeping the rays of light out. But he didn't mind. He was waking up to a new life, a new world, it felt like. The reason for it lay with her head on his chest, her curls tickling his chin.

Micah ran his finger up and down her spine, his body responding to the touch as much as it did the memories of the night before. He couldn't help but to think about it. To think of her, beneath him, as they made love for the first time. The complete trust on her face, flushed with pleasure. He liked to think he'd earned that flush with the attention he'd lavished on her. The worship of her body—her breasts, her thighs, what lay in between.

When she stirred beside him, he was ready to make new memories.

'Hmm,' she said as he shifted to face her. 'Morning.'

He pressed a kiss to her neck. 'Good morning.'

Her head fell back. 'I think I read an article about this once.'

His kisses made the trail back up until he was kissing behind her ear, a spot he'd discovered she enjoyed quite a bit.

'About this specifically?' he whispered.

'No,' she said with a hoarse laugh. 'It was about marriage. About being careful about what you start your marriage with because your spouse might come to expect it. I think the article was directed at traditionally female roles in the household—don't iron shirts if you don't want to keep doing it, those kinds of things—but it definitely applies now.' Her fingers slipped under his chin. 'Unless you plan on waking me up with seduction every morning, don't do it now.'

'In that case, I should probably give you more realistic expectations.'

He didn't give her a chance to reply before he kissed her. She immediately opened up to him, pressing her body close to him. He gave himself a moment to process the onslaught of sensation. The feeling of her breasts pressed against his chest. Of her skin heating against his. Of the heat of more of her—of *all* of her.

Then he focused on kissing her. He wasn't ever going to tire of it. Good thing, too, because the more he kissed her, the more responsive she became. The hand that wasn't caught beneath her trailed down his back, lingering, caressing. When it moved to his front, reaching between them, he heard the groan as if it came from outside himself.

The touches, the kisses, the intense intimacy. The emotion, the connection, the feeling of only *them*. All of it made him feel as if he were floating above his body. Then she welcomed him into hers, and he dropped back to earth, overwhelmed by pleasure and gratitude for his wife. His partner. His...equal.

After, Elena told him to shower first so she could call down for breakfast. As the water beat down on him, he pondered his thoughts during their lovemaking. Explored how they made him feel. It was strange, but there was no alarm. Only an odd kind of acceptance. This was his life now. Elena was his wife, his partner, his equal. It was a life he'd never contemplated, and now, he couldn't imagine it being any different.

He left the bathroom with a bemused smile—which immediately faded when he saw Elena. She was standing in a hotel robe, phone in her hand, a tight expression on her face.

'I put it on to check if my father called.' Her voice was disturbingly detached. 'He did. I didn't listen to the voicemails, but I have a message that says I'd better have an explanation.'

He walked over and pulled her into his arms. 'We knew this was going to happen, Elena. Your father was never going to accept the embarrassment of cancelling an engagement party without an explanation.'

'Even *with* an explanation he might not.' She was chewing her thumbnail even as her head rested on his chest. 'I know we expected this. I just...'

She didn't finish her sentence, only pulling away from him to look out through the sliding door.

'Elena?'

She took a deep breath. 'This is going to be hard.'

He shoved his hands into his pockets. She'd moved away from his physical offer of comfort, and he didn't know if he should keep trying. He didn't know if he had the right to. It was a confusing thought to have after what they'd shared the night before, that morning. After his thoughts in the shower. But he didn't know if a spouse or partner or equal meant... Well, this. Emotional comfort, he supposed, though that didn't feel like an adequate explanation.

It was all clouded, muddled, so he focused on what was clear.

'It is going to be hard.'

She gave him a shrewd look. 'I'm pretty sure you're supposed to say something more supportive than that.'

He curved his lips, but it wasn't a smile. 'I *am* being

supportive. If I tell you it'll be easy, you'll know it's a lie. At least this way, we can prepare for hard.'

'We?'

He shrugged, though her question felt as if it clouded things even more. 'We're partners, aren't we?' He didn't wait for an answer. 'I'm expecting this to be like a business meeting. A particularly difficult one, but a business meeting nevertheless. We're offering him the reality of our situation. The way he engages with that is his problem.'

She kept biting her nail. He took a step forward. Stopped.

'Elena, look at me.' Her eyes lifted. 'You don't have to be afraid of him.'

'Don't I?' she asked in a small voice.

'You're married to a man who's just as powerful as your father is. Maybe more. Externally,' he clarified. 'But *you're* the person who's dealt with him your entire life, despite being afraid of him, and come out on the other side.' He couldn't resist walking to her now, or tipping up her chin. 'That takes courage. You've built a successful career outside him. That takes strength. You're kind and sharp and annoyingly quick-witted—' he smiled when her eyes narrowed a fraction '—and that makes you just as powerful as he is. More.'

Her eyes filled, and she bit the bottom of her lip when it started to tremble. Then, in movements quicker than he could anticipate, she rose to her toes and gave him a passionate kiss. She pressed her body into his, wrapping her arms around him and tightening them so much he thought she was trying to become a part of him.

But she already has.

The thought had him breaking off the kiss, pulling away. He was panting, but he didn't know if it was from her or from the shock of that thought.

She gave him a little nod, acknowledging his response

in some knowing way, before disappearing into the bathroom. Micah stared after her for a long time.

What did she think she knew? And why did he feel as if that would change things more than any realisation he had about their relationship?

It was hard to imagine that once upon a time, she'd lived in this house with her parents. She'd thought she had a good life. A normal life. But she hadn't known then that mothers didn't tend to be as cool with their children as her mother had been with her. She hadn't known that most children didn't feel as though they needed to earn their parents' love and approval. That fathers didn't treat their children as objects.

Her parents' divorce had changed many things, but most of all, it had opened her eyes. And when she'd started seeing, something had cracked open inside her. Nothing had been able to fill that crack. Not friendships, though she didn't have enough of those to judge. Not her job, though she'd tried her hardest for it to. But this morning, when Micah had been tenderly outlining all the things that meant she could take on her father, Elena had felt the crack fill.

She was forced to face it then. Forced to face what she'd been running from since Italy.

She was in love with him.

It was concerning in many ways. They'd known one another for just over a week. A *week*. She scoffed at people who claimed to fall in love so quickly. Now, she wanted to talk to them all and ask them how it was possible. Did they fall for the other person's sincerity? Their willingness to change? Did they fall for the efforts their person made *to* change?

Or was it the quiet determination their partner vowed

to protect them with? Or the passionate tenderness they made love with?

Was it just that Micah was this way? That he was the person she was meant to be with? That falling in love with him was simply inevitable?

She couldn't deny they'd had a connection from the moment they met. Getting married had sealed that bond. Sleeping together had solidified it. Deepened it. In between the pleasure and sighs, Elena's world had changed and she didn't know what to do about it.

Especially when she was sure Micah's world had stayed the same.

Micah squeezed her hand. She looked over, realised he'd been watching her. He thought the turmoil on her face was because they were about to see her father. Tension skittered through her body. Yes, this meeting was more pressing than her feelings. She'd have to put off dealing with falling in love with her husband until *after* she'd dealt with the first man whose love she wanted, but would never receive.

She stilled. Then nausea welled inside her and she had to exert every ounce of control to ignore it.

They walked to the large house that had been painted from white to grey since she'd moved out. She hadn't been here since. Then her father summoned her to his office and now here she was. She should never have answered the call.

The area in front of the house had been designed around a circle. Trees and bushes formed the inner and outer circle, with gravel filling the spaces in between. There was already a car parked on the gravel when they arrived, and it took her all of two seconds to recognise it as Jameson's. Her father's cars would be parked in the garage at the back of the house. Something rebellious inside her had almost guided Micah there as well, but she resisted. She didn't understand why she felt disappointed that she had.

'You okay?' Micah asked as they rang the doorbell. He spoke under his breath, as if he was worried someone would hear. Clever. She wouldn't put it past her father to put a camera at the door so he could watch unsuspecting guests.

'Good.' Her voice cracked.

'Do you want me to do this alone?'

At that, she turned. Gave him a faint smile. 'I have to do this. I have to.' She spoke as much to herself as she did to him.

He opened his mouth, but the door opened before he could.

'Elena,' the woman at the door said when she saw them, her eyes going wide.

'Rosie,' Elena said, not quite believing it. 'You're still here.'

She walked into the open arms of the John housekeeper, feeling a warmth she'd missed since they'd started preparing for the meeting. Rosie had always been kind to her, though professional—her parents wouldn't accept anything else—and Elena hadn't seen her since she'd left either.

'Of course I'm still here.' Rosie's voice still held the traces of her native country. 'You would have known that if you'd come to visit.'

'You know why I haven't,' Elena said, the warmth dimming. 'It wouldn't have gone well for either of us.'

'I see,' Rosie said, her eyes tight. 'Well, child, you've grown up well. I am happy about that, if nothing else.'

'And I'm happy you *are* still here. I thought your sharp mouth would have got you into trouble.'

Elena was teasing, but it was a legitimate concern. Rosie meant well, but she was too honest. She spoke her mind even when she wasn't asked, though that had been reserved for Elena's ears. But with no one else listening, Elena had wondered if her father had been a recipient of

Rosie's comments. If he had been, there would not have been the same indulgence.

'My mouth is not so sharp these days.' Her eyes were, though, and they told Elena Rosie had learnt that lesson the hard way. Her heart beat painfully, but she managed a smile.

'I hope it'll still be with me.'

'Child, you are supposed to announce an engagement today. Your husband will have a sharp mouth to put you in your place.'

'There it is.' A relieved laugh tickled Elena's throat, but despite the reprieve from her tension, she wasn't in the mood to laugh. 'Actually, that's why I'm here. To introduce my father to my husband.'

She gestured to Micah. He held out his hand, smiling as charmingly as he'd been taught. But before he could speak, a voice thundered from the top of the stairs.

'What the hell did I just hear?' A tall, stately man descended, but stopped after three steps. 'Did you say this man is your husband?'

Elena's breath left her for a second. Somehow, despite it, she managed a small, 'Yes, Dad. This is my husband.'

Micah wanted to throttle the man who made Elena's voice change like that. From warm to cool; from strong to almost broken. He'd hated everything about the last hours they spent together. She'd barely spoken to him, the fire that was essential to her nowhere to be found.

If he thought it was only because of her father, he would have understood. But something about the way he caught her looking at him—the way she quickly looked away when he did—made him think this had to do with *him*. It was easier to blame her father. Easier than examining everything he'd done, trying to figure out what had made her respond this way.

He forced himself into the present. Elena's father was coming down the stairs, followed by a man Micah recognised as her would-be fiancé. The man's gaze was on him: a sharp, accusatory stare that didn't bother Micah a single bit. If looks had any effect on him, he wouldn't have been the man he was, nor the businessperson.

'Please explain to me why you're saying you're already married when we're supposed to announce your engagement tonight?' Cliff John asked stonily.

Elena's shoulders hunched slightly. Rosie inched forward, as if to comfort Elena, but Elena shot her a look and the woman left the room, shaking her head. Micah shifted closer to Elena, just a fraction, so she could feel him by her side. No matter what was going on between them, he would show his support. That was what their marriage was about.

She cleared her throat. 'Dad, this is Micah Williams. He's the man I was doing the story on for the newspaper.' Elena turned to him. 'Micah, this is my father. Cliff John. And this is…' She faded, then shook her head, her shoulders straightening again. A fierce pride shot up inside him. 'This is Jameson St Clair.'

He waited until both men were level with them before moving over the gleaming white tiles to offer his hand.

'Mr John. I've heard a lot about you.'

He left it at that. Cliff John stared at him for a moment, but took his hand. Micah turned to Jameson. He didn't offer a hand, but gave the man a slight nod.

'Mr St Clair.'

He moved back to Elena's side immediately.

'Elena, is it true?' Jameson asked before Micah got there. 'You're married to him?'

'Yes.'

Elena stared at him in a mixture of defiance and

strength. Micah resisted his smile, but welcomed the enjoyment. *This* was his Elena. This was his wife.

'Explain yourself, Elena,' Cliff said. 'I won't ask again.'

Micah ground down on his teeth to keep from responding. He waited for Elena—they all did. She was quiet for a long time, though her defiance and strength didn't falter. She didn't need his protection, he realised. Perhaps externally, as he said, but not where it mattered.

'I didn't want to marry Jameson,' she said eventually. Simply. 'You didn't give me much of a choice, so I had to create one for myself.'

'So you married *him*?' Jameson snapped. 'The man I told you was using you to get to your father?'

Micah did his best not to look at Elena, but he understood why her anger had been so fierce now. She had every right to be angry, regardless of how she had found out, but finding out from Jameson? From another man using her? It must have stung. Micah would have done anything to go back and change his motives. He didn't want to be on the list of men who'd tried to use her.

'It isn't so different from how you wanted to use me, is it? At least Micah had the decency to care about me.'

'I can't imagine why you thought you didn't have a choice, Elena.' Her father's voice was disinterested, as were his eyes, but Micah wasn't fooled. His lips were thinned under his white moustache, the skin between his eyebrows furrowed. Micah was good at reading people, and Cliff John was upset.

No, not upset. Livid.

He could feel Elena tremble at his side, but her chin lifted. 'You threatened my job.'

'Did I?' Cliff asked, edging forward. Elena moved back, without realising it, he was sure. Micah shifted, too, but he wished with all his strength he'd stood behind her so she would have backed into him and realised what she was doing.

'I thought I was merely offering you something you've always wanted: to make me happy,' Cliff continued.

Micah felt the change in Elena's body at that statement. The trembling stopped; *everything* stopped. She didn't move, didn't blink, didn't breathe. Just when he thought he would have to intervene, she exhaled sharply. Her inhalation was just as sharp. She looked at Micah, and the emotion there, along with everything else he'd witnessed over the last few minutes, handed the baton over to him.

'And she still is, Mr John,' Micah said smoothly. 'Elena conveyed your intentions regarding the marriage you proposed.' Disgust coated his tongue at that line, but he continued. 'We believe we can still reach those ends with different means.'

Micah didn't spare a glance at Jameson when the man snorted. He had Cliff's attention. And if he had it, Elena didn't. She could process whatever was happening in her brain.

He angled his head. 'You've probably already heard of me, Mr John, but I'll assume you haven't and tell you who I am.' He didn't pause at the slight rise of Cliff's eyebrows. 'I sell a lifestyle to all of Africa. Recently, I've expanded to Europe. I don't have to tell you what a partnership between my business and yours could mean for both of us.' He let it linger. 'But mostly for you.'

'You're arrogant.'

'Confident,' Micah corrected. Then smiled. 'Perhaps arrogant suits, too. It's semantics, honestly. Would you like to discuss semantics, Mr John, or would you like to discuss how I can make John Diamond Company the talk of the diamond industry? Not only in Africa, but the world?'

'You can't do that,' Jameson said, speaking for the first

time since Micah started his pitch. 'John Diamond Company existed long before you and your business. What can a partnership with you do for their profile that they couldn't do themselves?'

'I imagine it's the same thing a partnership with your family could do for them.' He still didn't look at Jameson directly, because he knew it would annoy the man and impress Cliff. 'Except on a much larger scale. I just signed a contract with the second biggest jewellery store chain in Italy. The contract was based on me providing them with diamonds from Africa that are reliable, well known and ethically sourced. I was hoping you'd be my supplier, but, if not, I'd be happy to offer the opportunity to someone else.'

Micah experienced the stunned silence with the same satisfaction he did every successful business deal. He was certain he'd won Cliff John over. He wouldn't need to secure Elena's job—although he'd already put out feelers to do that, if necessary—because Cliff had come over to their side. His daughter's disobedience had brought damn near world domination for his company right to his doorstep. He wouldn't dare do anything to make her unhappy now.

It wasn't the emotional support Micah wanted to offer her that morning, but it was the best he could do.

'Mr Williams—may I call you Micah?' Cliff's tone had eased into a charm he was willing to bet was Cliff's 'closer' voice.

'Of course. We are family.'

'Micah.' Cliff's smile was all teeth. 'Why don't you come up to my office and we can discuss this in more detail?'

Micah turned to Elena. Her expression was closed, but that wasn't unsurprising if she was still processing. 'Would you like to come with?'

'No,' she said softly. She smiled at him, but it didn't reach her eyes. Alarm fluttered through him. 'No, thank

you. I don't have anything to add to that conversation.'
Elena waved a hand. 'I'll see you at home.'

'You're leaving?'

'Only because it's business.' She leaned forward and
brushed a kiss on his cheek. Then she turned to her father.
'I assume this is fine with you?'

Her voice was cool and, again, pride filled him. She
was fighting back. He knew it cost her, but they would
deal with that together.

'Perfectly fine.'

'You asked me to be here, Cliff,' Jameson said, all rage.
'You told me we'd get to the bottom of this misunderstanding. How am I supposed to explain this to everyone? What
am I supposed to do with everything we've bought and
planned for today?'

'I'll cover any financial costs you've incurred,' Micah
said, looking away from Elena to Jameson. 'It's the least
I can do.'

'You son—'

'Jameson,' Cliff interrupted. His voice was a mirror of
the coldness of Elena's, and stopped Jameson in his tracks.
'I think it's clear there hasn't been a misunderstanding.
I'll make sure people believe the engagement was only
rumours. When they announce the marriage to the world,
all will be forgiven.'

'Wh—what about me?' Jameson asked, eyes wide.
'What about my family's company?'

'This is business,' Cliff said, his smile shark-like. 'Deals
fall through every day.'

Jameson stared at them, stunned. Elena broke the silence.

'I think I'll get Rosie to call me a car.'

She left all three men with that. Micah stared after her,
willing her to look back, to acknowledge their win. She
didn't.

CHAPTER SEVENTEEN

ELENA SPENT THE ride to the hotel wondering what she was going to do next.

The suite was booked for another night, but she couldn't bear to stay there again. She cherished the memories that had been created there. She'd got ready for her wedding there. She'd talked and laughed and made love to her husband there. She had never felt closer to another person than she had in that room.

It would be a constant reminder that she was in love with Micah and he would never be in love with her.

She might have been overreacting. But as she'd watched him go to bat for her she'd realised two things. One, she loved him even more deeply than she first thought she did. He protected her exactly as he said he would. More importantly, he supported her. His steady presence, his proximity... All of it had given her the courage to finally stand up to her father. To finally see, *truly* see, the extent of how her father was using her.

Cliff knew that she wanted his love and approval and he'd used that against her. A man like that didn't deserve Elena's love and attention. It hurt more than she could possibly express, but she had been clinging to her father for too long. To the hope that he would love her because if he didn't, who else would? Not her mother, who had forgotten Elena existed years ago. Elena didn't have friends, or other family members. She had a husband, but her second realisation told her he wouldn't love her either. Because as she watched him handle the situation with her father, she knew he was perfectly happy with the arrangement they'd made.

Their *business* arrangement. Not a marriage, but a partnership. She couldn't live with him, sleep with him, love him knowing that he would only ever see it that way.

She'd spent her entire life trying to get one man to love her. She couldn't spend the rest of it trying to do the same with another.

She pressed her lips together as she packed her belongings into her bag and called a car. She was about to grab her wedding outfit in the garment bag in the closet, but stopped. It would only hurt her to see it. For it to remind her that she loved her husband and needed him to love her back, but he didn't. Without a backward glance, she left the room and went to her home.

When she was there, she opened her laptop to check her emails. She'd been avoiding work and the implications of her marriage for much too long. Micah hadn't replied to the email about her story, so she assumed he had no notes. Not that it mattered. There was no way she could write the story as his wife.

Her heart broke as she outlined the information for her boss, attaching what she had written so whoever got assigned to the story would benefit from her trip to Italy. She'd come back the day before, yet it felt like a dream. The exploration, the privacy, the newness. Now she was back home, feeling more exposed than she ever had, by a situation she shouldn't have put herself in.

The response from her editor—that was somehow a rebuke, congratulations, and request in one—told her to focus on work. It was reliable. And with Micah as her husband, her job was safe. She closed her eyes. Shook her head. Focused. She might have messed up her old assignment, but she wouldn't mess up this new one. She would write about her whirlwind courtship with Micah for the newspaper. It would be more fiction than fact, but the readers would never know. And they would love it. If they did, this could still be a way forward for her.

She wrote back, then got up to make herself a cup of tea. She was nursing it on her couch when the knock on the door came.

She'd been expecting it. With one last sip of her tea, she set it on the coffee table and opened the door.

'Elena?' Micah walked in, moving in for a kiss. She assumed. She stepped back before he could touch her. She wouldn't torture herself with more memories. 'Are you okay? Your things weren't in our room when I got back.'

'You found me,' she said easily, closing the door behind him. 'Do you want tea? Coffee? I don't keep alcohol in the house. I'm sorry about that.'

'No.' His brow was creased so deeply she was sure there would be indentations once it smoothed. 'I want to know if you're okay.'

'No.' She went to sit on the couch again, bringing her tea with her and crossing her legs. 'But I will be.'

He didn't move a muscle, just kept standing there. She could almost see inside his brain. He was trying to work out what to say. Going through everything that had happened to check whether something had gone wrong.

He wouldn't be able to see it. He hadn't done anything wrong; *she'd* been the one to change. She was no longer happy with their arrangement. She needed him to love her. She needed the person she was in love with to love her. The fact that he didn't would torment her every day.

She'd do everything in her power to try and change his mind. She knew she would because that was what she'd done with her parents. With her father. And look where that had brought her.

Micah didn't deserve that. He didn't deserve her trying so hard to please him she lost herself. He'd made his arrangement with her; not the version of her that she thought he wanted.

Beyond that, Elena finally saw that *she* didn't deserve it. She deserved to be fulfilled and happy. She deserved to be herself.

'What's going on in your head, Elena?' Micah asked eventually.

'We made a mistake,' she said softly.

'What do you mean?' He moved now, sitting on the chair opposite her. His body was stiff.

'Last night,' she forced herself to say. 'Sleeping together. We shouldn't have done that.'

'Why not?'

She fortified her heart at the curt words.

You expected this. But if you don't do it now it'll be worse.

'I was right. It made things murky.'

'Is that supposed to make sense to me?' He stood. She merely lifted her chin. She wouldn't get up. Her knees wouldn't hold her. 'What are you saying? What are you *really* saying?'

She didn't know how to respond to his anger. She was already feeling vulnerable, and every word he said battered against her defences. She wanted to tell him that she loved him, that she wanted him to love her, but she couldn't stand to be rejected. Not after hearing her father use her love for him against her. Not after figuring out her feelings for Micah. It was all too much.

But she could do this. She could get through this. She had with her father, and she would now. After a few more breaths, she said, 'We have a business arrangement, and it works. We both got what we wanted from my father today. We'll likely continue to be successful working together in the future. But sleeping together adds a dimension to this relationship that…that won't work.' She took another breath. 'Business, Micah. Let's keep it that way.'

It was clawing at him, the familiarity of this situation. But the claws came from a dark place. He couldn't afford to shine a light on it when he needed all his attention to understand Elena. Her posture was stiff and cold, worse than it had been when they'd been at her father's. Her face was beautiful in its aloofness, he could admit, but he didn't like it. He preferred the beauty of her smiles, the animation in her eyes. When she was teasing him, or gazing at him with lazy pleasure. He wanted *his* Elena back, not the one who brought the claws and destroyed the light. The one he didn't understand.

'Why?'

'I told you—'

'You gave me some rubbish diplomatic answer,' he hissed. 'I want to know *why*? What changed between last night—this morning—and now?'

He realised he sounded desperate, but he couldn't help it. Panic had joined his complicated emotions, spurring the words.

Slowly, she set her tea down on the table in front of her. It was a round glass table held up by metal spirals painted gold. What a strange thing for him to note. Especially when his eyes shifted to her hands and he could see them shaking.

'I'm doing this to…to protect us.'

'From what?'

'From me.'

She blinked rapidly, showing emotion she hadn't given him since he'd come to find her. He thanked the universe for it. Emotion was what made *his* Elena, and if she was showing it, even in this form, it meant that she was coming back. If she came back, maybe this wasn't some warped repetition of his childhood.

He didn't have a chance to process that thought.

'I spent my life trying to get my father to love me because he's the only person I thought would.' A tear ran down her cheek, but her gaze was steady on him. Strong. 'A mistake. He showed me a fraction of approval once and I mistook it for love. I based all my hope on it.' She shook her head. Cleared her throat. 'I… I can't do the same thing with you, Micah.'

Her words paralysed him.

His thoughts kept running though. The panic kept fluttering. But now he saw it was for a completely different reason. Before, it had been because he was worried she would reject him—them. Now, he was worried she was about to change them. For ever.

'You're happy with the way things are between us.'

'I… Yes. It's *us*,' he said, his voice cracking towards the end.

'I'm not,' she replied softly. 'I want more from you. I *need* more. Can you give me more?'

He opened his mouth, but the claws were back, threatening to shred his tongue if he replied.

'It's okay,' she said, voice hoarse. 'It wasn't a fair question. I shouldn't have asked it.'

'Elena.' He shook his head. 'What are you saying?'

'You know what I'm saying.' She stood now, squaring off with him in a raw way that broke his heart. 'I can't say it. I won't say it, and complicate the arrangement we have.' She continued without letting him speak. Which was good. He had nothing to say. 'I'll keep to the agreement. I'll attend social functions, or business functions. Have Serena sync our social diaries and send me information and I'll be the perfect spouse.'

'I don't…expect you to do something you don't want to do.' He spoke slowly. Heard the emptiness of it. 'I won't use you like they did.'

'You won't be using me,' she said, shoulders straightening. 'We have a contract.'

'I won't keep to the contract.'

She stiffened. 'I'm a woman of my word.'

'If you were a woman of your word, you wouldn't be changing the terms of this relationship on me,' he spat. He knew he'd regret it later. Didn't care.

'Do you think I want this?' she demanded, ice melting into fire. 'I want to focus on healing after this whole thing happened with my father. I want to stay your friend, or whatever the hell we are, Micah. That's what I *want*. But the one thing isn't possible with the other. I can't be your friend if I want to heal.'

'I'm not your father.'

'No, you're my husband. But you can't love me in the same way he can't love me, so what does it matter? I can't live the rest of my life like that.' Her tears reappeared, but she ignored them. 'How can I live the rest of my life wanting someone to love me *again*? How does that help me heal?'

He took a breath, wanting to say words that would make them both feel better. But he couldn't. He was afraid, and the fear pulsed so loudly, he couldn't hear what words they were. He could only hear the warnings, could only feel the alarm. He said nothing.

'See?' she said softly. 'I was trying to protect us by giving you an easy way out. Now we're just in pieces.'

Slowly, so slowly, he walked to her door. 'Elena,' he said, turning around. 'I'm sorry. I want to—'

'Don't,' she interrupted. 'I understand. You can't love me because if you do, it makes you as vulnerable to me as you are to your parents. They've caused you enough pain. At least this way, you don't have to worry that I'll do to you what your parents did to you.'

His world stopped for a second. As it did, the darkness overtook his senses and he saw she was right. But it didn't matter because, now, *he* wanted to protect himself. To fight back the darkness, the fear, and crush the claws. He couldn't do that with her. She would remind him that he wasn't as strong as she was. She would remind him of a light he could never possess.

With one last look, he walked away from his wife.

CHAPTER EIGHTEEN

ELENA MIGHT HAVE got married, but her life was as normal as it had been before her wedding. Apart from the fact that she had to pretend to be living a blissful, married life, of course. Her editor had read her piece on her and Micah's marriage, had decided it would be a great companion piece to the profile Elena had done on Micah, and printed both. One on the front page of the business section; the other on the front page of the entertainment section.

Separation from her husband had no part in that. So Elena lived the lie.

No one would know it wasn't the truth. Micah's profile was high enough that no one expected him to carpool with her to work or pop in for lunch. Micah certainly wouldn't tell anyone. Things would become more complicated if there was an event Micah was at and Elena wasn't at his side. But it had been six weeks and that hadn't come up yet. She would worry about it if it did. In the meantime, she would enjoy the boost those articles had given her career.

After some adjustments, apparently. Her new workload had been a welcome distraction from her emotions, but it had left her feeling run-down. She was tired all the time, even when she woke up, and she had no appetite. It was more or less the same way her body had responded to the adjustment of boarding school, and then the school nurse had done some tests and prescribed some vitamins. She'd felt so much better afterwards though, so she forced herself to go to the doctor even though she had no time for it. She wasn't as understanding when they called to discuss the results.

'Doctor, I'm sure you have a lot of things to do today other than tell me my iron is low.' Elena offered the woman a winning smile. 'We can make this quick.'

'I appreciate the offer,' Dr Jack said dryly, 'but it's a little more complicated than an iron problem.'

'Oh?' She sat up straighter. 'No anaemia? Some other vitamin deficiency, then?'

'None of the above.' Her expression was kind. 'You're pregnant.'

'I'm—' Elena broke off with a laugh. 'Please. There's no way I'm...'

She trailed off when she realised there was a way. A very logical way, really, since she wasn't on anything and condoms were...

'Are you sure? I haven't had unprotected sex.'

'I am sure. This indicates you're about seven weeks pregnant?' Dr Jack showed her some page with levels of hormones, which she honest to goodness couldn't take in. 'If you tell me when your last period was, I'll be able to tell you more accurately. I also have an ultrasound machine in my examination room. If you'd like more certainty, we can do that?'

Elena nodded numbly. She did everything numbly after that. Except when the doctor smoothed gel over her belly, pressed the wand against her stomach, adjusted some things on the machine, and a heartbeat sounded in the small room.

A heartbeat. That was coming from inside her.

'That sounds good,' Dr Jack said, examining the machine. She tilted it towards Elena. 'This is your baby. They're still a small little thing at this point, which is normal based on how far along you are. Seven and a half weeks now that I have that information about your period.'

'But…the sex was…'

She couldn't finish that with the heartbeat still pumping. It was so fast. Was that normal?

'Well, we count based on the first day of your last period, though conception might take place later. Don't tell anyone I said so, but it's hard to say accurately.' There was a pause, and then the sound disappeared. Dr Jack set the wand back at the machine and sat down beside her. 'I can tell by your reaction that this is a surprise. I can talk to you about your options. I can also give you a copy of this so you can listen to it later when you're deciding about your options.'

'That seems a bit harsh, Doctor,' Elena managed to say. 'Am I supposed to make a decision while listening to…to that?'

Dr Jack smiled. 'You don't have to listen to it. I just want you to have the option of listening to it. Now, let's get you cleaned up here and have a conversation about what's going to happen next, shall we?'

'Mrs Williams? Mrs Williams, please.'

For a moment Micah wondered what Serena was doing calling his mother. But Elena was already in front of him before his brain could figure out the calling was happening inside his office.

'I'm sorry, Micah. She wouldn't listen to me.'

'I have to talk to you,' Elena said, looking a little wild.

He took her in—greedily, though he would never admit it—and made sure she was okay. Then he gave a little nod to his PA and waited until the door was shut.

'Wait, why did Serena call me Mrs Williams? She calls me Elena.'

'You've let the world know we're married, haven't you?' He clung to the coolness, though everything inside him yearned to hold her. 'Why have you barged into my office in the middle of a workday?'

She frowned. Shimmied her shoulders. 'I have to talk to you.'

He merely lifted his eyebrows.

'It's important.'

He tried not to let his concern show. It was tough, particularly since he'd spent most of the last six weeks wondering how she was. Even when he managed to bury it by burying himself with work, it popped into his thoughts. When he was in a meeting, or walking to one. When he got home and headed to bed and wondered what it would have been like to come home to her. To have her waiting in his bed.

Those thoughts flooded his mind more and more as the days passed. It would have forced him to face what was keeping them from being together even if his parents hadn't suddenly contacted him. His mother had reached out when she'd heard about his partnership with Cliff John. It had been less than he'd hoped for, but more than he'd expected. She'd arrived at his office, primly asked him out to dinner. When he'd accepted, she'd spent the evening talking about work. They had nothing else in common, he supposed, and still he'd longed for more. He hadn't heard from her since, and he had no desire to reach out from his side either.

It took a while to accept it, but he realised it had been in motion from the moment he'd proposed to Elena. He knew then already that the reunion with his mother would underwhelm him. It had tempered his expectations, hence the surprise at her offer of dinner. He'd been even more surprised when his father had congratulated him on his marriage. Micah hadn't read the profile Elena's newspaper had done on him, uninterested in reliving Italy when his memories of her feistiness, her laugh, her kiss there kept him awake at night.

Apparently, the article had been combined with an article on their whirlwind courtship and marriage. His father had relayed that fact; Micah hadn't read that article either. When his father asked if Micah and Elena wanted to join him and his wife for dinner some time, Micah told him he would get back to him. He never had. One, he and Elena weren't doing anything together any more. Two, if his father only wanted him to join his family for supper when he was a married man... Yeah, he could stuff that invitation.

His dream about reconciling with his parents had come true in the last weeks, and he was unhappy. Because he saw how damaging that dream was—how damaging *they* were. They'd taught him that opening his heart would only hurt him. Even when he wanted to open his heart, fear of disappointment kept him from doing so.

Screw them.

'Are you going to tell me this important thing?'

'It's better if I show you.'

Elena didn't seem deterred by his sharpness. He was annoyed that he wanted her to be. That he wanted to affect her in the same way she affected him.

She wanted a real relationship with you. What more do you want?

Anger and frustration—at himself—kept him from answering that question. It didn't stop his inhalation when he came to his side of the desk, putting a flash drive into his computer. He was a masochist, probably, but he wanted to see if he'd remembered her smell correctly. He had. It was still as soft and tempting as it had been that week in Italy.

That night in their hotel room.

'I have no idea what this is, but—'

A rhythmic sound stopped his words in their track. It was fast, loud—a *da-da,da-da,da-da* that went on and on and on. His eyes lifted to the screen of his computer. It was black and grey, but the grey was in a strange shape that—

Oh. His brain put the sound and the screen together and... Oh. *Oh.*

'What are we going to do about this?' Elena croaked at him. He looked at her. She was watching the screen, looking as helpless as he felt. 'It's a...a...'

'A baby.'

Now she looked at him. 'Yeah. A baby. That we made.' She laughed in a way that clearly indicated she didn't find it funny. 'Micah, we made a *baby.*'

A string of questions ran through his mind.

Are you sure? How sure? How did you find out? Are you okay? Is the baby okay? How are we going to be parents?

He got stuck on the last one, mainly because he thought Elena was, too. The other questions were kind of already answered by her appearance there. Of course she was sure—she wouldn't have been there otherwise. She'd found out from a doctor; he was looking at the evidence of that. And he was sure she would have told him by now if they weren't okay. She wouldn't have asked what they were going to do about it if they weren't...would she?

'Are you both okay?'

'Yeah, we're fine.' She exited the window on the computer, as if she was done watching the grey and black and hearing the *da-da,da-da,da-da.* 'I'm tired, and eating' a problem, which is why I went to the doctor in the firs place, but I'm fine otherwise. And things seem normal with the…you know.' She shrugged. 'It's early.'

He got stuck on one piece of information. 'You're nauseous?'

'No. I just…don't want to eat. I doubt that has anything to do with the pregnancy. I forgot to ask, actually. I guess I'll have to read up on it.'

'What else could it have to do with?'

She quirked a brow. 'Really? That's what you want to talk about?'

'I'm still processing the other thing.'

Her expression softened. 'Stress. I've been working a lot. The…um…the articles about you helped.'

Are you working a lot because of me? Because you're trying to forget me the same way I'm trying to forget you?

It was presumptuous, but he was sure that was why.

It wasn't only presumptuous though. It was unfair. She was the one who'd taken a risk. She had put her feelings out there, hoping for something more. He couldn't give her more.

Except apparently, he had. If she was keeping the baby, they'd be as linked by their child as they were by their marriage contract. More. They could ignore their marriage contract. They'd been doing that for six weeks now. They couldn't ignore their child.

They were going to have a child.

'Can I help?' he asked, a little woodenly. 'The stress probably isn't great for the baby. So. Can I help in some way?'

'Oh. No. Not unless you can write my stories for me.'

'I can get you an assistant to—'

'It's okay, Micah. I can manage.'

'With the baby?' he asked. 'Are we keeping it?'

'We?'

He looked at her. She didn't show any emotion, and he realised she was protecting herself. 'You don't need me, I know. But this is *our* responsibility.'

'When did I ever say I didn't need you?' she asked, a flicker of angst crossing her face before it was gone. 'I'd like to keep it. I… I don't know anything beyond that, but I'd like to.'

'Me, too,' he said softly. Unexpectedly. He had never thought he would be in this situation, so any answer he gave would have been unexpected. But wanting this child? He needed a moment to process because he did. He wanted this child.

'Look, I know things are…weird between us, but this child is going to need us. Both of us. We need to give them the best that we can, and we'll need to work together.' She moved away from him, clutching her handbag closer to herself. 'I can put my feelings aside so our child can have the kind of parents and family we didn't.'

He should have thought about that. About being a parent, about his parents, about himself. He didn't want his child to have the same life he had. He wanted better for them.

'You're right.'

'I know.' Her lips curved into a small smile. 'Why don't we take the day to…process? We can meet tomorrow morning to talk about things.'

He nodded again.

'I'll send you a message with the details,' she said. Then she was gone. As if she'd never been there at all.

But she had been there. Today, and almost seven weeks ago now when she'd come with him to Italy. She'd changed his life. She'd shown him what it was like when someone cared about him. She'd helped him grow. She'd offered him love and understood even when he couldn't offer it to her in return. At least not in the way she needed it. Now, she was giving him a family.

With one glance at the door, he opened the file with the video of his baby. Watched it for a long time. Knew he'd hear the sound of the child's heart beating in his dreams that night. And the next. Maybe for ever. It wouldn't be such a bad thing.

The longer he listened to it, the more grounded he felt. The more courageous he felt. This child gave him hope. He'd have an opportunity to do things the way they were supposed to be done. He would give his child the things he didn't have. Love, support, a family. His child would give him the same, if he allowed it.

Elena would have given him the same, if he'd allowed it.

He sat back, the truth of it hitting him over the head. Of course, he already knew on some level that he was in love with her. Why else would he be so terrified of letting her in? He compared her to his parents even though she didn't deserve it. He compared her to his parents even though, in Italy, he'd already known she wasn't like them. She'd offered herself to him unconditionally, and he'd been too cowardly to accept. Or to offer himself to her in return.

It didn't mean that he didn't feel the same way about her. He loved her, but telling her would mean risking rejection. He was tired of rejection. He was tired of working so hard not to face it, but having to face it anyway. It was a fine thing to worry about after he'd rejected his own parents. After he'd rejected her.

Now they were having a kid, and he felt so stupid it had taken that for him to be brave. But that little heartbeat asked him to be brave. Even if it was too late, he needed to try. If there was a chance his child wouldn't have to witness a broken relationship as he'd had to with his parents, he had to take it. If there was a chance he could be with the woman he loved enough to have a family with, he had to try. Elena had every right to reject him now, but he wouldn't let that stop him. This was the final step to freeing himself from his past with his parents. And freeing himself would mean fullness. Happiness. Love.

He'd known about Elena's pregnancy for all of thirty minutes, but it had already changed him. And *that* was what love from a parent to a child should look like. Courage. Growth. Trying. His child would never know what conditional love would feel like. There would be no hoops for them to jump through; there would only be love.

He hoped he had the opportunity to treat Elena the same way.

CHAPTER NINETEEN

ELENA KNEW HAVING a child was a life-changing experience. She hadn't expected finding out she was pregnant would be as dramatic.

After leaving Micah's office the day before, she'd gone home and cried. Not because she was pregnant—though heaven knew there was some of that in there, too—but because she missed him. She wanted him back in her life. She wanted them to raise their baby together and be a family.

It took her a while to realise she would have all of those things now that she was having their baby. Not in the package she wanted, but she would have them, nevertheless. For it to work, she would need to set her feelings aside. Her desire to not be around Micah so he didn't remind her of what she didn't have no longer mattered. Her biggest responsibility now was her child. And since she'd told Micah it was possible for her to ignore her feelings, she wiped up her tears and faced her reality.

Still, she didn't sleep much that night, her mind too busy processing. The one good thing was that it helped her realise her child deserved the love Elena didn't have in her life. All things considered, it would be nice to explore that with a child. Special, too, because she'd made that child with someone she cared about. It wasn't a perfect situation, but that was okay. She would focus on her baby and let that heal her.

The doorbell rang promptly at eight the next morning. She expected nothing less from the man she'd married.

'Hey,' she said when she opened the door. 'I thought it would be easier to meet here. More private, too. There's been some interest in our relationship since the article.'

'I heard,' Micah said. 'Can I come in? This is heavy.'

She nodded, letting him pass. He was carrying a box, which he set on her kitchen counter. It was strange seeing him in her space. It obviously wasn't the first time he'd been there, but she hadn't been paying attention then. But seeing him between her brown couches and cream walls and her various gold accents caused something in her chest to swell.

'You heard? I'm sorry,' she said with a wince. 'You've probably been teased about it.'

'No.' His expression told her that was the most ridiculous thing he'd heard. She resisted her smile. 'My father told me.'

'Your father?'

'He seemed to think marriage solicited a dinner invitation.'

She waited a beat. 'Your tone tells me little else solicited dinner invitations.'

'Nothing else,' he corrected.

'Well. I guess it's good that he's trying.' Again, his expression told her it wasn't good. 'How did the dinner go?'

'I didn't accept.'

'Why not?'

He shrugged. 'I'm done jumping through hoops for people who should love me unconditionally.'

'Oh. Wow.'

They stared at one another for a few seconds, then both started laughing softly.

'It's a good realisation,' she offered.

'It could have come a bit earlier,' he replied with a small smile.

'We all learn things at our own pace.'

'Yeah, we do.'

The amusement faded, but their eye contact remained. They were communicating on some level. Since she didn't know what level that was, and he wasn't offering anything more, she gestured to the box.

'What, er…what's in the box?'

He turned and looked at the box as if he hadn't brought it. She went to his side while she waited for an answer.

'It's for you,' he said after a long pause.

'It is?' She frowned when he pushed it towards her slightly. 'What's inside?'

'A care package.'

'A…'

She stopped speaking when she opened the box and saw what he meant. The box was filled to the brim with items. Herbal teas, crackers, ginger biscuits, books about pregnancy, movies about pregnancy, chocolate, chips, cocoa butter and stretch mark cream, a framed photo of their baby that he must have got from the video she'd shown him the day before. There was much more, but her hands faltered as she felt a strange tightness in her throat.

'You put this together?'

He ran a hand over his head. 'I looked up things that would be helpful to you. I didn't know about the creams and stuff, but a woman at the nature store helped me. She also said a cup of peppermint or chamomile tea would help with stress. That could help with your appetite thing.'

'I thought I said that wasn't a part of my pregnancy.'

'It can't make it any easier, can it?'

'No. It can't.'

She sat down on the kitchen stool in front of her counter and rested her hands in her head. The tightness in her throat had progressed to a burning at her eyes. She didn't think she'd cry, but she was pretty close to it. She spied a glass bottle of lemonade in the box—lemonade? Why?—and she reached in and took a sip. The sourness distracted her from the way her body was reacting. It helped her get her emotions under control.

Or not.

'You can't keep doing this.'

'What?'

'Reminding me that you're a great guy.'

'Oh.'

He looked as if he wanted to say more, but he didn't. So she said, 'I'm sorry. I shouldn't have said that. We should talk about the baby, right? Okay. I think—'

'Elena.'

'No, Micah. I can't… We can't do this.'

'Elena.'

She felt the tears falling down her cheeks. 'I'm sorry. I just… I need more time. I'll be okay with how things are between us soon. I promise. So let's just—'

'Damn it, Elena, look at me.' His voice was edged with desperation. It was reflected in his eyes when she met his gaze. 'I was a fool for pushing you away. That has nothing to do with the baby, and everything to do with me.' He hissed out a breath. 'I guess what I'm trying to say is that I love you. I love you, and I want to try again.'

In his dream the night before, Elena had fallen into his arms and told him she wanted to try again, too. But he was wide awake now. He knew that because now she was simply sitting, staring at him. He deserved it, he told himself, his heart thudding. He deserved the torture of waiting for her to say something.

'I think I misheard you,' she said slowly.

'You didn't.'

He reached over and took her hand. Prayed she wouldn't pull away. Then got distracted by the way she felt. Even in his dreams, he hadn't been able to capture what it was like when Elena touched him. The heat, the need, but, most importantly, the rightness that settled inside him.

'You're right, I pushed you away. I was scared. Scared you would be like my parents and reject me.' His grip tightened on her hand. Still, she didn't pull away. 'I don't know what it's like to love someone and have them love me back. I *do* know what it's like to love someone, and have them not love me the way I need to be loved.'

'Yeah, it sucks,' she said sullenly.

His lips curved. 'I know. And I'm sorry I made you feel that way because I didn't want to trust that first part. The part where I love you and you love me back.'

'You hurt me,' she said in a small voice. 'In the same way my parents hurt me. In the same way your parents hurt you.'

'I know. I know,' he said for the third time in as many minutes. 'I'm so sorry, Elena. If you'll let me, I'll spend the rest of my life making it up to you.'

She didn't speak for a long time. At first, he struggled against his instincts. He wanted to pull her into his arms, tell her they could be a family, kiss her, then take her to her bedroom and make love to her. But none of what he wanted mattered. It was only her, and her choice, and whatever that was, he would respect it.

But she was still holding his hand. That had to mean something.

'Do you really love me?' she asked. 'Not the baby—*me*. Would you have come here and told me this if it wasn't for the baby?

He took a breath. 'Yes. But probably not for a long time.' At her frown, he explained. 'I was already on my way to realising how stupid I'd been. I didn't only speak with my father, but my mother, too—later—' he said when she opened her mouth '—and I realised that they weren't worth the effort I was putting into them. They'd taught me to fear love, but they weren't worth what I was sacrificing with you.'

He pushed her hair back.

'But realising it didn't mean I had the courage to come here and tell you that. I would have needed time to, and maybe a knock over the head. Or a pregnancy surprise.' He gave her a small smile. 'But I would have told you regardless, I promise. Because I love you, and I have, probably since I saw you in that unicorn nightshirt and you told me I didn't see them because I didn't believe.'

'I'm not sure that's what I said.'

'We can argue about it later,' he teased, but sobered quickly. 'If you still want me here later.'

'I'll always want you here,' she said softly. 'My love for you isn't conditional. Even when you're being dumb, I still love you.'

'You know exactly what to say, don't you?' he asked, but before he was even done talking, she was hugging him so tightly he could barely breathe.

'I'm scared, too, you know. But I love you. I love you.'

His arms folded around her. 'I know you're scared. But you're braver than me. You're stronger than me. Our baby is going to have a wonderful mother.' He lifted her chin. 'You don't have to be scared any more. Your love is safe with me. Believe me.'

Her lips curved. 'I do. And yours is safe with me. You're safe with me.'

Her expression told him she would make sure he knew it for the rest of their lives.

And he would do the same for her. That understanding, their love, meant more to him than he could express. So he leaned forward and kissed her instead.

EPILOGUE

Four years later

'WHO THOUGHT BRINGING two children to Italy was a good idea?'

'I believe that was you,' Elena said easily, lifting her son's ice-cream cone when he tilted it to the side to lick his fingers. 'You said something about bringing them to where our love was established, or something equally corny.'

'You used to think that was charming.'

'Now I think you carrying a baby girl in a carrier at the front of your body is charming.' She brushed the hand she didn't hold her son with over the head of the baby gurgling against Micah's chest. 'It's also very sexy.'

She leaned forward and kissed him, lingering even though she probably shouldn't have.

'Hmm,' Micah murmured when she pulled away. 'How long until naptime?'

As if answering, Kai shouted, 'Bird!' at her feet. It startled his sister, and Ellie immediately gave a loud cry.

Elena laughed. 'Two children in Italy is not as romantic as two adults in Italy.'

'That's for sure,' Micah said, comforting Ellie.

Elena followed Kai to the pigeons, warning him against

feeding them his ice cream. She'd learnt that lesson the hard way her first time in Italy.

She'd learnt a lot since her first time in Italy. To be fair, it had been almost four years ago. She'd got married and had two children since then. Her job was still important to her, though a little less than her family was, and her recent promotion seemed to prove it. The newspaper was undeterred by her family planning, which she knew made her lucky. She also knew she had a unique angle on many of the stories their readers were interested in. The wife of a South African businessperson who wasn't afraid of telling the truth.

Fortunately, she had a husband who supported her.

They'd taken their time to build the foundation of their marriage. It was a strange approach considering they were married within a week of knowing one another and pregnant after their wedding night. But they'd both been hurt by their families. They'd made progress, even before they'd decided to try a relationship, but it still took work. And they put in the work. In between pregnancy and caring for an infant. In between caring for a toddler and finding out they were pregnant again.

Relationships took constant work, and neither of them was afraid of it. In fact, they welcomed it. Because working meant they still wanted to be there. They still wanted one another. It was a damn good feeling to be wanted.

'I don't suppose we could take them on a gondola ride,' Elena remarked later that day. 'No—what am I saying? Kai would be in the water within minutes.'

Micah laughed. They'd swapped children, both of whom were asleep, exhausted by the excitement of the day. She and Micah were walking back to the hotel, but lazily, the summer's day not dictating haste.

'Last time I was in a gondola I spontaneously proposed. Perhaps this family is not made for gondola rides.'

Now Elena laughed. 'Ah, we were such babies then. Could you imagine being where we are now, then? You, dominating the luxury goods industry. Me, dominating childbirth.' She shook her head. 'What powerful parents we are.'

'One more powerful than the other.' Micah made sure Kai was secure, then put an arm around Elena. 'I watched you give birth. It was…wild.'

'A euphemistic way to put that.' She leaned into him. 'I think this is the happiest I've ever been.'

'You say that all the time.'

'I mean it every time. More so today.' She stopped walking and turned to him. 'Our first family trip is to Italy. I wasn't this lucky. You weren't either. But we're doing it for our kids. There's a lot to be grateful for.'

'They won't remember this, you know,' Micah said, but his expression was soft. 'It didn't matter where we took them on vacation.'

'That's obviously not my point.'

'I know.' He lowered and kissed her gently. 'You're what these kids will be most grateful for some day. I know that because that's how I feel.'

'Right back at you, Daddy.'

'I thought we agreed you wouldn't ever call me that in public.'

'I thought you would keep a sentimental moment sacred, but you didn't. You used logic. So I guess we'll both just be disappointed then, won't we?'

Micah laughed and they resumed walking. It was companionable and quiet. It was perfect.

'Remind me to ask Kai about the pigeons when he wakes up,' Micah said suddenly.

'What about the pigeons?'

'I want to know if he thinks the ones in Europe are different from those in Africa, like his mother.'

She slapped him lightly on the shoulder, and his laughter echoed in the dusk.

* * * * *

MILLS & BOON

THE HEART OF ROMANCE

A ROMANCE FOR EVERY READER

MODERN

Prepare to be swept off your feet by sophisticated, sexy and seductive heroes, in some of the world's most glamourous and romantic locations, where power and passion collide.

HISTORICAL

Escape with historical heroes from time gone by. Whether your passion is for wicked Regency Rakes, muscled Vikings or rugged Highlanders, awaits the romance of the past.

MEDICAL

Set your pulse racing with dedicated, delectable doctors in the high-pressure world of medicine, where emotions run high and passion, comfort love are the best medicine.

True Love

Celebrate true love with tender stories of heartfelt romance, from the rush of falling in love to the joy a new baby can bring, and a focus on the emotional heart of a relationship.

Desire

Indulge in secrets and scandal, intense drama and plenty of sizzling hot action with powerful and passionate heroes who have it all: wealth, status good looks…everything but the right woman.

HEROES

Experience all the excitement of a gripping thriller, with an intense romance at its heart. Resourceful, true-to-life women and strong, fearless face danger and desire - a killer combination!

To see which titles are coming soon, please visit

millsandboon.co.uk/nextmonth

LET'S TALK
Romance

For exclusive extracts, competitions
and special offers, find us online:

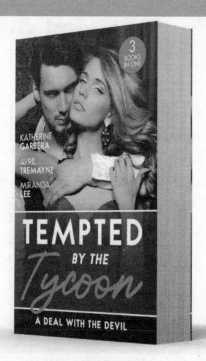